M000202713

THE BEAST OF BETHULIA PARK

S. P. CALDWELL

GRACEWING

We actually have before our eyes ... a fierce and lawless principle everywhere at work—a spirit of rebellion against God and man

St John Henry Newman, *The Times of Antichrist*

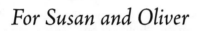

For Susan and Oliver

First published in England in 2022
by
Gracewing
2 Southern Avenue
Leominster
Herefordshire HR6 0QF
United Kingdom
www.gracewing.co.uk

No part of this publication may be reproduced, stored in a
retrieval system, or transmitted in any form or by any means,
electronic, mechanical, photocopying, recording or otherwise,
without the written permission of the publisher.

The right of S. P. Caldwell to be identified as the author of this
work has been asserted in accordance with the Copyright,
Designs and Patents Act 1988.

© 2022 S. P. Caldwell

ISBN 978 085244 700 0

Typeset by Gracewing

Cover design by Bernardita Peña Hurtado

This publication is entirely a work of fiction. All characters and
their names, excluding historical or public figures, are fictitious
and are wholly the product of the imagination of the author.
Any resemblance to actual persons is purely coincidental.
Bethulia Park Hospital NHS Trust is completely fictitious and
any resemblance to any existing trust is also entirely coincidental.

CONTENTS

Acknowledgements ix
Prologue: Too Hot for Bloodlust 1

Part I

1 The Parker Inquest 15
2 The Records Office 29
3 Unbearable Me...43
4 Madness and Mediocrity 53
5 Cold Mushy Peas 63
6 Pig Rooting 71
7 Judith Calls..81
8 Killer Queen...91
9 The Decline of Betty May...99
10 The Fifth Beatle 105

Part II

11 Breaking the Story..123
12 Good Friday 133
13 The Naughty Step...147

14 Find the Killers 155

15 Calvin's Problem 167

16 Wild Bob's Burglar 181

17 Nothing to See Here..197

18 The Steam Room 205

19 Swallowed Up 213

20 St Winefride's Well 225

21 A Winning Streak..243

Part III

22 Gagging for a Drink..255

23 Klein Shows His Hand.......................................261

24 Red Riding Hood...273

25 A New Housekeeper..289

26 The Cincinnati Kid 299

27 Baby Rats 311

28 Hacking Out 323

29 Judith's Prayer 339

30 Dressed to Kill 355

31 Kiss Me Like This 371

32 On the Run 379

33 Halo Goodbye..387

34 Hey Judith...401

Epilogue: Wolf in the Sheepfold 413

ACKNOWLEDGEMENTS

T he Beast of Bethulia Park began as a personal challenge in late 2020, a year in which I spent much of the long days of lockdown reading and turning to fiction for the first time in years.

At the time, my main ambition was to get the book finished and at times I didn't take it very seriously. The first draft was therefore a bit of a rookie effort, flawed but containing passages and pace with which I was pleased and which ignited the hope of eventual publication.

I showed this draft to Susan, my wife; Eileen, my mother, and Fr Ian O'Shea, the parish priest of St William's in Wigan, Lancashire, and I remain extremely grateful for feedback and sound advice which inspired me to improve the book. I am additionally grateful to Susan and to our son Oliver for their patience as The Beast of Bethulia Park developed into a preoccupation for me. Thank you so much for putting up with me when it seemed I was losing my marbles.

Following a second draft I shelved the project for six months. I took it up again in December 2021 after I returned to the Catholic Herald as associate editor with responsibility for news. William Cash, the editor and an author himself, showed an immediate interest in The Beast of Bethulia Park and he asked to read the third draft. He offered advice which helped me to bring up the narrative to a standard worthy of publication. I am very grateful to William for his generosity of spirit as well as for his wisdom, his enthusiasm and his consistent support.

At about the same time as William was reading the book, I had the good fortune to be reacquainted with Margaret Ashworth, a former colleague from *The Daily Mail*, where she served as splash sub-editor during a Fleet Street career spanning some 40 years. Margaret advised me on the penultimate draft and she knows personally how immeasurably grateful I am for her sterling contribution to this work.

I must also thank the Rev. Dr Paul Haffner, the editorial director of Gracewing, for taking a chance on an unknown, for the great belief he has shown in this project and for his determination to publish *The Beast of Bethulia Park* not just in the UK but in several countries around the world and in possibly three languages besides English. It has been an honour to be accompanied by so distinguished a champion on this journey.

There are many others who have offered advice and hope during the writing or revisions of *The Beast of Bethulia Park*, or whose writings, teachings and ideas have inspired parts of it, and I thank all of you for your contributions. I would also like to express my gratitude to my late father, Paul, who always encouraged me to write.

All the characters, scenes and events (except those which are matters of record) in *The Beast of Bethulia Park* are fictitious. But there are many families and individuals who in recent decades have suffered from medical malpractice and who have campaigned relentlessly for truth and for justice. In my work as a journalist I have met such people. Their stories and their examples have been always a source of inspiration to me, not least in the writing of this book. So have the doctors who have blown the whistle on the sort of abuses described in *The Beast of Bethulia Park*, often at substantial risk to their reputations and careers. I thank all of you for your inspiration and I salute your courage, your dedication, your perseverance and your witness. Keep fighting.

Finally, I would like to thank Almighty God, without whom I can do nothing of any value.

Simon Paul Caldwell, July 2022

PROLOGUE

TOO HOT FOR BLOODLUST

Wednesday July 19, 1679

The severed head was raised so high upon a pike by a cavalryman that the troop was forced from the shade of the trees into the sunshine. The riders feared the bloodied lump might become ensnared in lower branches, then dislodged and brought thumping down upon them.

The troopers' horses hated the open lane. Away from the line of trees, the scorching heat left them on the brink of exhaustion while the hard ground concussed their knees. They sought the sanctuary of soft grass at the wayside only to be pushed out time and again into the full blaze of day by the spurs of their riders.

Clouds of insatiable horseflies made their misery worse. They bit and harassed the animals no matter how much they shook their heads and swished their tails. Nor did the insects make any distinction between man and beast, and tormented the soldiers equally. Their choice was to soak in sweat under their scarlet woollen coats or to loosen their buttons and serve up more skin to relentless, stabbing bites.

As the troop arrived at the water meadows along the eastern bank of the River Dee, Captain Wild constantly swatted flies

1

away from himself and his mount, his hands whirling like windmills. He looked down from his saddle to watch the horse's grinding shoulders extend and retract and he felt a pang of sympathy for the beast labouring patiently beneath him. He scratched its withers affectionately and bent forward to speak reassuring words into its rotating and flickering ears, telling the animal that its work would soon be over. Then he returned to the task of slapping the flies dead with his open palms. It was all he could do to ease his horse's ordeal.

It was true. Soon their work would be over for both of them. It was a morning Wild wished to forget but he knew it would not be easy. The sight of an execution was far harder to brush off than any nasty living thing the troop would encounter in their long sweaty march to Puddington Hall– and to die in such a way was as horrible as anything the captain could ever see on the battlefield. He knew this because he had killed men by his own hand, running them through with his sword. He had hanged the worst kinds of criminals where he and his men had captured them, especially in the days he had pursued highwaymen under the command of Captain Talbott. It had been a sport to him then, and occasionally he had revelled in it. Nothing could have prepared him for the spectacle of the slow torture of an unarmed man, a most unlikely criminal in his opinion, who went to his death protesting his innocence amid the bloodlust of a crowd roaring and cheering at the sight of his humiliation and agony and who taunted him to his last breath.

Already Wild was craving whisky—or anything to blunt the shock and horror that he did well to disguise from his troopers. The moment would come, he told himself, when he could learn to obliterate such awful images. But it could start only when his work was done.

The ground was flat and even close to the river and Wild pulled up his horse to wait for the other troopers to catch up. There were eight men in total. Wild was at the front and the trooper with the pike rode in second file. Then came two soldiers riding in tandem followed by an open cart driven by another two soldiers. Behind them was a rearguard of two.

In the cart was a large basket, a frenzy of bluebottles above it. When the troop reassembled more tightly, they pressed forward again and soon reached a junction where they peeled away from the lane into the driveway that led down to a timber-framed hall. As the house came into view they could see that the great gates to the quadrangle courtyard were open and that on the forecourt between the moat and the brick-clad lower walls a crowd had assembled.

At least a hundred and fifty murmuring, restless people of all ages, classes and distinctions—men, women, children and the elderly, the ragged poor alongside the wealthy and the well-dressed, all awaiting the arrival of the remains of a man who just hours earlier had been their priest.

It was obvious to Captain Wild this was a different mob from the rabble who, half or fully drunk, had swarmed to watch the execution that morning, when the condemned man emerged into the public gaze, strapped to a hurdle and drawn from Chester Castle, his face fixed beneath the horse's tail to catch its defecation as he thumped over the ruts and cobbles of Castle Street, and along Bridge Street and Eastgate Street up to Gallows Hill at Boughton.

There the priest was offered his life if he would admit his complicity in the Popish Plot to kill King Charles II and replace him with James, his Catholic brother. Instead, the man maintained his innocence, willing to accept death as a testimony to the truth. His words echoed in Wild's ears. 'I protest in the sight of God and the Court of Heaven that I am absolutely innocent of the Plot so much discoursed of, and abhor such bloody and damnable designs.'

And what a terrible death it was. Positioned beside the sheriff, the captain had watched from horseback as the man was partially hanged, then roused to consciousness by the ripping of the knife as he was castrated and disembowelled and his organs burned before his eyes. Nauseated, the captain had turned away and focused on his duty to control the crowd that pressed forward to gain a better view, anticipating the triumphant moment when the gluey hands of the executioner held up the priest's palpitating heart. Rather than watch too keenly, the captain had chosen to trot his horse up and down the line of baying faces, his basket-hilted sword drawn and brandished, as the executioner brought the quasi-religious ritual to an awful climax by decapitating the priest with an axe and declaring: 'Behold the head of the traitor!'

Some laughed raucously when they saw the pike pushed through the severed neck to emerge from the crown, glistening red and wet with brains. The corpse was subsequently quartered with a heavy axe and a saw and the mob cheered their approval, while gorging themselves upon cherries sold from baskets on the wayside and swigging ale from tankards.

Yet others were in the midst of them, generally standing in scattered small groups, mostly at the rear. At times they shielded their eyes with their hands from the butchery, or simply looked away. Wild had seen some of them fainting, weeping and comforting each other with squeezes of their hands and tight little hugs.

It was the same kind of people who met him when his heavy boots landed on the stones as he dropped from his horse.

Ignoring them, he waited for a soldier to trot to the front, dismount and take the reins of both their horses while he approached the manor house. Few in the crowd watched them as they moved, their attention transfixed by the familiar but bloodied face that looked down on them from a pike.

'Open up!' Captain Wild called out, banging three times on the double oak doors. After a few seconds, they swung apart to reveal a tall and bearded man of about twenty, in breeches, stockings and a white shirt with long collars and sleeves. Tangled auburn hair tumbled across a face pallid from a loss of sleep and eyes puffed from mourning.

'I'm looking for the squire, William Massey,' announced the captain.

'You are speaking to him.'

'You know why I'm here,' said Wild, dabbing his dripping face with a handkerchief, not bothering with the courtesy of removing his broad-rimmed black hat.

'I've brought you the body of the traitor and I will see that the sentence of the court is carried out. You understand what that means?'

Shouts of 'murderers!' and 'butchers!' rose from the crowd.

'Yes, I know what the sentence is. You want me to display the quarters of my friend from the four corners of my house, so that I, my family and my good name are despoiled, humiliated and slandered by the false charge of treason, while his corpse is debased into a feast for the crows and the kites. Isn't that what Lord Scroggs is demanding? Isn't that you've come to enforce, for the good of the realm?'

'Egregious papist!' snarled the captain. 'I'll cut out your tongue if you mean to speak to me like this. You whelp! You mark my words! We'd all be gibbetted if you had your way. Where is your loyalty? You traitors! Your false religion would bathe us all in our own blood. But today you will do the bidding of the King unless you wish to follow your blackguard to the tree. Is that clear?'

'What? You'd hang us all? Even Captain Talbott? But you loved him, and he is a papist too,' answered Massey, unruffled. 'You pleaded for him when the mayor made him surrender his sword because of his religion. How can you forget that? Must you hang us all today? Don't you ever, somewhere in your heart, ever wonder when this madness will end? Do you even believe this so-called plot of Titus Oates to be true?'

Massey bent forward and whispered into Wild's ear. 'Isn't this a performance, Captain?'

He gagged when Wild's hand shot up to clutch his throat and squeeze hard, wrenching their faces close. The soldier released his grip with a strong and contemptuous push, flinging Massey stumbling on his heels back into the hall.

'Do as I tell you!' he shouted after him. 'I won't tell you again. Don't make me prove myself serious.'

The captain turned abruptly and, raising his voice above the clamour of the crowd, he called for the grim cargo to be unloaded.

As the quarters of the executed man were dumped on the forecourt by a soldier from the basket on the cart, another trooper held the pike of the second rider as he dismounted, then took his horse to allow him to use both hands to pull the head free.

Finding it stuck fast, the soldier rotated the pike and placed the instep of his boot on to the severed neck. Conscious that the crowd was viewing his ineptitude with a mixture of disgust and mockery, he tried to pull out the shaft while the head was wedged beneath his foot. It refused to budge so he placed his sole over the inverted lower jaw of the head and yanked hard, freeing the pike but dislocating the jaw and scattering human tissue across the cobbles, to a nauseated groan from the assembly. This became a roar as he bent to pick up the head.

There was a rush from the crowd. People darted in to dab cloth into the gore to save as relics but one tearful, heavy-boned woman went straight for the soldier, pummelling him with a succession of blows to his back and head as she screamed in uninhibited rage.

The trooper reared backwards with the dexterity and balance of a boxer and, twisting sharply to face his attacker, he delivered an open-handed slap across her face with the force of a punch, sending her flailing backwards. She hit the ground hard, her head smashing into the stones of the forecourt. A second surge from the crowd followed with seven or eight men scrambling over each other to attack the soldier, who was reaching for his sword, as two or three others went to help the dazed and stricken woman.

'Stop there!' roared the captain as he pulled a musket from his belt and waved it at the line of furious faces. 'I will kill the next man or woman to raise their hands against any of my men!'

The crowd eased back some five or six paces, but as he looked around him the captain saw the mob had increased in number, and now formed a crescent around the hall and his men.

A rock sailed through the air. None of the soldiers could see who threw it, and within seconds it was followed by others. Then the flurry turned into a cascade.

The captain felt an overpowering urge to retaliate, to visit his just, imminent and lethal wrath upon those who dared to challenge his authority. He and his men would kill some of them on the spot and would hang others soon after. He raised his musket as he searched the crowd for the assailants.

A rock hit a horse and it began to rear. Its rider, standing beside it, reached frantically for the bridle in an attempt to bring it under control, narrowly evading the punching front hooves of the terrified creature.

The panic spread to the other horses as rocks rained down on them from both sides.

Two broke into canter before the troopers were fully back into their saddles, speeding into gallop as they tore up the lane with the soldiers bouncing and hanging around their necks, struggling for their lives.

Captain Wild leapt on to his own mount, threatening the crowd with the musket in one hand as he gathered up his reins with the other, brushing his spur into the side of the horse to spin it around. He took off after his men.

After nearly a mile, the troop pulled the horses to a halt and looked back down the gentle slope towards the hall. They could see its purple slated roof among the elms and could pick out its twisted chimneys and the heavy painted beams of its frame.

Beyond the hall thatched cottages ran down to the Dee and the landing stage at Burton Head, where small moored boats swayed like toys on shimmering silvery waters. Directly opposite, across the river, rose the hills of North Wales and further west the soldiers looked over the estuary to a vast expanse of the sea.

'They're everywhere,' a trooper grumbled to the captain. 'Why must these traitors cling to their old religion, even now?'

'I doubt this slaughter will serve His Majesty's cause,' the captain said. 'They weren't all papists—I'm sure of that. Many people are turning against the hangings, and if they don't end soon I fear they will make papists of many good Protestants. No good will come of this, I tell you.'

He pointed to three figures on horseback who had appeared on the horizon.

'Who are they?' wondered a trooper.

'I think they're watching us to see if we return to see the sentence of the court through to the letter,' replied the captain.

'Are we going back to the hall?' asked the soldier. 'They must have planned that attack. They had those rocks ready before we arrived. Shouldn't we make them pay for that?'

'I don't think so,' answered the captain, counting five horseflies fall from the flat of his hand, vanquished by a single swat. 'We've killed their priest, I think we can leave them alone to bury him.'

Sated by suffering and death, the captain had no appetite for a fight. All he wanted was to give his men and his horses rest and to check for injuries. He craved a drink and he was sure his men felt the same way. They would happily overlook their duty to punish civilians in return for an afternoon in the nearest tavern. It was too hot for bloodlust. He considered their work to be done.

Moreover, Captain Wild privately harboured grave doubts about the claims of the renegade papist Titus Oates, which seemed to grow more sensational by the week. First came his allegations of a popish plot to shoot the King in St James's Park, which were followed by disclosures of similar plots to murder Charles at Windsor or Newmarket in the event of failure. This would be followed by a huge insurrection led by Jesuit priests.

The allegations were received unquestioningly, and the nation was pitched into a state of panic which bordered on national neurosis. Everywhere there were reports of secret activity. Heavily armed nightriders were said to thunder through towns and villages, waking the godly from their sleep, while reports of suspicious naval vessels poured in from ports all around the kingdom. Yet Wild, who was charged with helping to guarantee the peace and security of the realm, had seen nothing to substantiate any of the claims that came his way. He suspected Oates of peddling little more than a lethal fantasy. He had come dangerously close to confessing his misgivings to his men. He would have to be more careful.

It was also true, as Massey said, that he indeed loved Captain Talbott as a brother, and that he had never recognised in him a popish monster.

Massey's knowledge made Wild fearful. Who could have told him? Any of a number of people. There were many who, like him, were discovering something deeply sinister and contrived about the hysteria created by the plot, the panic and the abnegation of reason it produced in otherwise sober and sensible men and women, the transformation of reasonable and honest Protestants into fools more superstitious than the papists they despised, gripped by fevered delusions of imminent invasions from France and Ireland foretold by providential comets, springs running with blood, and apparitions.

That was the worst thing. The hysteria was a discredit, in his mind, to the religion he loved. He had never held any doubts about the truth of the reformed Protestant creed that he professed. It was the true faith and it deserved a better witness than this.

Because of his convictions he had imagined that he would be dispassionate about the execution of the popish priest. But the sincerity of Father Plessington's speech from the scaffold had affected his sense of purpose, perhaps more than the sight of the heartbroken papists who grieved for him. He was a soldier and he was not squeamish about death but he did not, as a conscientious Christian, wish to see the innocent suffer. The possibility that the priest had been wrongly convicted was a strong one.

He was surprised that the Sheriff refused to let Plessington hang until he was dead before dismemberment and chose instead to subject him to the full rigour of the law. The priest at least deserved to die quickly. It was a small mercy, but that was how mercy was demonstrated in cases of such dubious certainty. If this case did not merit mercy, surely none did.

Mercy. It was a sentiment which appealed to Captain Wild more than anything at that moment, and he smiled grimly at the realisation. I must be getting old, he thought as he dismounted.

'Everyone off except for you two with the cart,' he called to the troop. 'Our horses have worked hard enough for one day. We're going to show them kindness and we're going to walk. But we stop at the next tavern.'

The captain gathered the reins into his fist and held them close to his horse's mouth. He pointed its nose toward Chester as it tried to nuzzle him, perhaps in gratitude. His men followed with equal devotion.

As the troop were re-joining the main highway, the butchered corpse of Father Plessington was being reverently carried by Massey's servants into the hall. On a large oak table the remains were reassembled into the shape of the man who had lived only hours earlier.

Massey wept bitterly as he caressed one bloodied hand. He gripped its cold and bloody fingers, conscious that it was a hand which had once baptised babies, brought lovers together in marriage, consoled and anointed the sick and the dying, and turned bread and wine into the body and blood of Jesus Christ himself during the secret Masses at the hall. He felt a deep grief equal to losing his own father, but it was sharper and all the more painful

to have lost a man he loved to the malice of the evil and the preju-
dices of the ignorant.

'Dear, dear John,' he whispered as he wept and kissed each
finger. 'Pray for me now that you are in heaven, a saint in the
great company of all the saints.'

Massey rested the hand on the table and knelt for a moment
in prayer while the noise of the crowd throbbed through the
walls.

There was one thing he must do before he sent them home.
He rose and took hold of the battered head by the sides of the
face, averting his eyes from the hole in the skull. He shouted to
a servant to open a window and leaned out.

'Behold the head of a martyr!' he proclaimed, lifting it up for
the crowd to see.

The people fell silent, and some dropped to their knees.

When they were gone, Massey stood beside the remains of
his friend, deep in thought, when he was interrupted by a rap at
the door.

A man of about his own age entered with two others. 'The
soldiers have retired to Chester, William,' he told the squire, 'so
you might have no need to dishonour the body of the priest as
they intended.'

'I would never have allowed it,' said Massey.

The friend cast an eye over the corpse. 'Would you like us to
fetch you the coffin that was measured for him?' he asked.

'Thank you, that would be very kind,' said Massey. 'We will
be needing the coffin, but not just yet—and perhaps not for him
in any case.'

The other man smiled.

'Any news of Captain Talbott?' asked Massey, reading his
expression.

'He has just arrived,' came the reply, 'and he has company.'

Part I

'For You my soul is thirsting.
My body pines for You
Like a dry, weary land without water.'

Psalm 62

1

THE PARKER INQUEST

Thursday February 28, 2019

The first time I saw Dr Reinhard Klein was at the inquest into the death of Ray Parker, a man whose family claimed had died prematurely because of medical negligence. As soon as he entered the courtroom I knew he was a big guy. I don't mean that he was tall—he wasn't. He was probably less than six feet. But I recognised instantly that here was a 'big man' in a metaphysical sense. He strolled in and owned the room. What makes some people like that? Magnetism, charisma, confidence—Klein had these qualities by the bucketload. He was good-looking too, and he knew it. His lush brown hair was slicked tidily back. His navy suit was immaculately tailored, following the contours of his gym-toned physique as perfectly as a coat of paint. You know, if I could have touched Dr Klein on any part of his body I think I'd have felt silk—one hundred per cent mulberry Grade6A 22-momme silk.

I could certainly see why the nurses wanted to get close to him. Some seemed to have forgotten they were in a courtroom. I'd barely scratched the sleep from my eyes and there they were, the little coquettes, joking and laughing with him as he settled into their midst, batting their eyelashes and giggling playfully as he held court, those closest to him leaning into him with their breasts. For goodness sake, it was not even ten in the morning and they were throwing everything at him. They might have been seated on the velvet cushions of a booth in some nightclub, competing for his attention while getting lashed on prosecco cocktails. A big guy indeed.

Klein glanced up to see me staring at him from the Press bench and I realised my curiosity must have been obvious. I looked away, pretending my gaze was accidental, and switching my attention as artfully as I could to the rear of the room where a long bench reserved for members of the public was filling up.

What was a priest doing there? How odd. It was not just his presence that was incongruous. His youth and appearance seemed just as out of place. He was blond, tall and slender, more the sort of guy you might imagine on a surf board than sitting at the back of a court in a stuffy soutane. This was the first time I set eyes on Father Calvin Baines.

Right at the front of the room were some of Parker's immediate family—his elderly wife and two middle-aged sons. Angela Parker had come in a purple coat which looked ancient and weather-beaten and the men were ill at ease in their attire—a bit scruffy, if I'm honest. They looked as if they'd had to dig out old suits from the wardrobes where they were gathering dust since the last wedding or funeral. The older of the two men was wearing a pair of battered trainers too, probably, I guessed, because they were the only things he could find that were black.

The words 'all rise' broke the murmuring clamour. The room was like a church when the coroner entered and took his seat.

After inviting everyone to sit, Philip Roberts, a distinguished-looking grey-haired man in his early 60s, adjusted his glasses as he arranged the papers on the table in front of him. I turned to a clean page of my reporter's notepad as he went through the formalities, identifying the Parker family individually as 'interested persons', along with the Bethulia Park Hospital National Health Service Trust.

The point of such legal status for an institution, he explained, was to avail a lawyer of the opportunity to defend the Trust against any allegations of misconduct arising from a death by unnatural causes. Likewise, a solicitor appointed by the family could make representations on behalf of Mr Parker's relatives.

The Parker family had no one to represent them. I presumed they could not afford a lawyer. So it fell mostly to Ralph Parker, a delivery driver and son of the deceased, to put their case.

In hindsight, the entire thing was outrageously loaded against the family from the start, a David versus Goliath contest but without stones for the sling. That said, the 'interested person' of Ralph, the elder son, didn't do too badly against the 'interested person' of the Trust, its doctors and nurses, its publicly-funded lawyers and the police officers arrayed against him. The 'little guy' with his comparative lack of education and expertise, command over language, and limited knowledge of the law and medicine gave a good account of himself, I'd say. But he was never going to get what he wanted.

Ralph was the first witness. I grimaced as he stuttered like an outboard motor when he attempted to address the hearing. Roberts told him to take his time and he calmed down and eventually found his voice. He confirmed that he was Ray's next of kin and that his 73-year-old father was a retired brewery worker. Then he meticulously recounted his father's final weeks, telling the coroner how Ray was referred to hospital for ulcers on his legs. He told how Ray had swiftly responded to antibiotics, and how the family hoped he would soon be sent home. Meanwhile his father had CT and MRI scans.

Ralph told the coroner that after his father had been in hospital for about two weeks, Dr Klein, a consultant physician, invited the family to meet him to discuss Ray's condition and treatment. This was on September 11, 2018. Ralph said the date stuck in his mind because of the 9/11 terrorist attacks on the United States in 2001.

'What were you told about the investigation into your father's health?' asked the coroner.

'We were told my dad had cancer in his lungs and his throat, it were spreading, advanced and it were inoperable,' said Ralph.

'Who told you that?'

'Dr Klein,' he answered, nodding towards the medics. 'There was a Macmillan cancer nurse who told us that my dad had less than three months to live, and there were another nurse, I remember her because she had a scar on her neck. Dr Klein told my dad all that bad news about him while he was sat there in front of them, and Dad understood him. The doctor and the cancer nurse said they were going to make arrangements for him to die in a care home or a hospice. Dr Klein told us nothing could be done for Dad and said as well that if he suddenly became worse, he shouldn't be resuscitated.

'We agreed, you know, like you do when a doctor gives it to you like this, bad news, and my dad went along with it too. He was even joking about it. But while we were waiting for them to make arrangements for the hospice, the hospital stopped his anti-biotics. They said they would increase his suffering as the cancer spread. They started to give him diazepam and we think it made him drowsy, along with the morphine they were giving him as a painkiller because the ulcers on his legs made him uncomfortable.

'The medication really knocked the stuffing out of him and he couldn't feed himself, and we were worried that no one else was feeding him either. We raised this with the nurses—politely, like—but before they did anything he was moved into a side room because he had diarrhoea and they wanted to isolate him until it cleared up. At first they put up a drip and then they took it down. I asked them why they were doing that and told them my dad needed it, and they told me it wasn't doing him any good because the cancer was spreading so quickly. After that, he wasn't fed or given much water, as far as we were able to see. They just dabbed his lips with wet cotton wool. He died about two weeks later. We all thought the cancer had got him but they lied to us, didn't they? He never had cancer.'

'So your father was admitted on August 30th of 2018 and you say you were told on September 11th that he had cancer and that about three weeks after that he was started on end-of-life care?'

'Yes, that's correct,' said Ralph. 'First week in October, it was.'

'But your father died some time later—Tuesday October 16th, is that correct?'

'That's correct, yes—it seemed a long time after they told us his death were imminent, if you don't mind me adding, sir.'

After Ralph's evidence, a series of written statements from other members of the family were read out by the coroner, with a statement from Ray's GP about the medical history of his former patient, describing a gradual and irreversible decline of his mental and physical health with the onset of dementia.

The next witness was Dr David Harrington, the consultant pathologist who had performed the post-mortem. He told the inquest that Ray did not die from cancer but from an infection of Clostridium difficile, adding that pressure sores and the generally debilitated state of the patient were secondary factors.

Ralph called out that his father was debilitated because his food and fluids had been withdrawn along with his antibiotics. 'He was debilitated all right, he was a bag of bones. They did all that,' he said, gesticulating at the seated medics: 'They stopped his treatment when they decided he had cancer.'

'There was no cancer,' repeated the pathologist.

'We know that,' said Ralph. 'But what's all this about C. diff? No one told us about any C. diff. He didn't die of C. diff, he died of thirst. He was starved and dehydrated to death.'

Harrington took time to consider his response. 'I can understand your exasperation, Mr Parker,' he said finally. 'Please let me try to explain. Sometimes illnesses are misdiagnosed. Officially—by which I mean according to the Royal College of Pathologists—this happens in about five per cent of cases but some recent studies have shown that it's often much higher, perhaps a quarter or even in as much as a third of all cases are not properly explained. Doctors do their best, but I'm afraid they don't always get it right.'

Frowning, Ralph gathered himself and said: 'Can I ask you, doctor: how much did my father weigh when he died?'

'We don't have sufficient weighing equipment at our disposal to calculate the body mass indices of deceased patients, I'm afraid,' the pathologist answered.

The coroner interrupted: 'Mr Parker, why do you consider this information relevant to the proceedings?'

'Because my dad was a fairly big man and the last time I saw him he looked like a skeleton. If the RSPCA found a horse or a dog looking like that, I bet they'd have photographed it and weighed it as evidence. I beg your pardon, sir, but it seems a bit too convenient for the Trust that no one checked my father's weight after he died.'

'Continue,' said the coroner.

'Doctor Harrington, you say you didn't weigh my father but can I ask you how he looked to you when you saw his body?' asked Ralph. 'How did he appear physically? Can you remember?'

'Slim, perhaps slightly built, I recall, but I wouldn't necessarily conclude from that that he was somehow underweight.'

'Thank you, doctor,' said Ralph. He turned to the coroner. 'I haven't heard anyone describe my father as 'slim' since I was boy. Big, chunky, well-built, thick-set, even fat—that's what I've been hearing most of my life. If you knew him I think you'd be agreeing with me that he lost a vast amount of his body weight in hospital—when they starved him.'

'Your father died from C. diff,' interrupted the pathologist.

'He didn't, he was starved and dehydrated to death,' said Ralph, turning crimson. 'Why are you lying to the coroner? Why don't you tell the truth?'

'Mr Parker!'

'But sir, he's lying to you. Don't you see that? My father wasn't 'slim' when he died. He was emaciated. He looked like one of them victims of the sodding Nazis!'

'Restrain yourself, Mr Parker,' the coroner warned him. 'I can understand you are upset but I will not tolerate outbursts of this kind, or bad language, and I will not have you accusing witnesses of lying. Is that clear?'

Muttering an insincere apology, Ralph sat down.

The coroner called Dr Klein. He stood with an air of urbane sophistication before setting out, coolly and eloquently, the sequence of events leading to Ray Parker's death, an account very different from the family's version.

He described how cancer was initially suspected but rejected as a diagnosis during a meeting of a multi-disciplinary team toward the end of September. It was never acted upon, he said.

The coroner noted that Klein had not mentioned the meeting with the family which Ralph said took place on September 11.

'The family have told me today that there was a discussion with yourself in which you told them Mr Parker was terminally ill. You have heard Mr Ralph Parker say today that you told the family that the patient was suffering from inoperable, multiple and terminal cancers. What did you tell them at that meeting of September 11th?'

'What meeting?' said Dr Klein, his face elongating in an expression of surprise. 'I really have no idea what meeting the family could be referring to. There is nothing in the notes to show I had a meeting with them on that day. Meetings of this kind are always documented but there is nothing in our records to show that one took place.'

'Do you recall any conversations of this kind?'

'I cannot recall any such conversations,' Klein answered indignantly. 'We never once confirmed there was cancer. We were only investigating the possibility. Someone might have mentioned it to certain members of the family along the way, I suppose, but I don't recollect any formal meeting. Certainly, I was not party to any such conversations.'

He cleared his throat. 'It follows that if we didn't ever tell the family that cancer was confirmed there would have been little point in telling them that we knew, after thorough investigations, that we had reached the conclusion that he was not a cancer patient. Mr Parker was a patient with C. diff who was not responding to antibiotics. We withdrew them at first because we wanted to eliminate antibiotics as a possible cause of the diarrhoea. The treatment was also proving futile.

'The family was made aware of what we were doing, and of the limitations of what we were able to do for Mr Parker, a dying man. With the consent of family members we decided to manage the patient's medication conservatively and to concentrate on alleviating the symptoms of his condition, and they understood and accepted that, or at least seemed to at the time.

'Our nurses would certainly have offered food and drink to Mr Parker when he was capable of taking it from them, but any decisions to deliver nutrition and hydration intravenously would have been a matter for the dieticians and the speech therapists, not for me. I was not the only physician caring for Mr Parker, far from it, and on this particular point not the best qualified to speak.

'Nevertheless, I must say that I find the assertion that Mr Parker was deliberately dehydrated to death very unlikely and of course it is unsupported by any available evidence. We are trained to heal and care for patients. That's all we do. I fear there has been some sort of dreadful misunderstanding.'

The coroner asked why antibiotics were not reinstated after tests revealed they did not cause the diarrhoea, and why a Do Not Attempt Cardiopulmonary Resuscitation order was issued.

'The patient was extremely poorly by then,' said the doctor. 'We didn't believe we could cure him so we wanted to make him as comfortable as possible and treated him in that way. The treatment was tailored to his symptoms.'

'So when was the decision taken to put the patient on end-of-life care?'

'About a week or so before he died—about October 3rd, I think it was—when he was rapidly declining. Let me check my notes.'

Dr Klein fiddled through some files at his fingertips.

'That's about two weeks before he died, doctor,' said the coroner stonily, looking over the frame of his glasses. 'In your opinion was there anything more that could have been done at all for Mr Parker?'

'Sadly, sometimes patients are so weak that they die and there is not a lot we can do about it. It's tragic in every case but we always do our best for the patient. I'm certain we did everything we could to save Mr Parker's life but we couldn't do any more for him, I regret to say.'

A rumble of dissatisfaction erupted among the Parker family.

'That's not how we remember it,' shouted Ray's second son Michael, getting to his feet. 'You told us our dad had cancer and you told us on September 11th that he was going on end-of-life care, the same day you also said he would not be resuscitated. He was treated negligently from that moment. You've changed the dates around!'

Michael looked appealingly to the coroner. 'Surely the records show we're telling the truth. Please, sir, we're not making this up!'

The coroner gestured to him to sit down and instructed him to put his questions through Ralph when it was his turn to speak. He turned to Dr Klein. 'Is there anything in the records to substantiate this claim of the family?' he demanded. 'Is there anything in the records, even tangentially, to show that you had a meeting with the family on September 11th?'

'Nothing at all,' the doctor said.

Ralph folded his arms and stared at the surface of the desk in front of him, shaking his sinking head, as Dr Klein returned to his seat among his adoring coterie. Michael placed a consoling arm across his mother's shoulders, muttering in disbelief to himself as she dabbed the corners of her eyes with a handkerchief.

They sat still and silent as tombstones while several other hospital staff involved in Ray's treatment in the final weeks of his life were called. Over the next hour and a half the witnesses testified that the patient had received only the highest standards of care in keeping with the ethos of the hospital.

Finally, the coroner called Detective Inspector George Tarleton, a dark-haired man with a face charred by stubble. He smiled at his plain-clothed colleagues and two uniformed officers as he walked purposefully toward the front of the courtroom. Immediately he brushed aside the family's request for a criminal investigation.

'Our examination of the records of Mr Parker's final days suggests to us that he was indeed dying and that he was being treated correctly according to established protocols on the care of a dying patient,' he told the coroner. 'We found no breach of the duty of care by a single individual which would warrant a criminal investigation and a prosecution for gross negligence or manslaughter.'

Ralph steepled his fingers, then placed his sweating palms on the cool veneer of the desk and pushed himself to his feet. He put one question to the officer. 'How did you know he was dying?' he said.

'How did we know he was dying?' replied DI Tarleton, slightly startled. 'Believe me, we know what death looks like. In my career as a police officer I have seen things that no member of the public should ever see. We know what death looks like, natural and unnatural.'

Apparently becoming aware of the hardness of his tone and the inadequacy of his answer, he continued: 'What mattered to us is whether there was sufficient evidence to prosecute one or more individuals for gross negligence, manslaughter or murder. We didn't find it, sir. We did not find the evidence to meet the standards required for a criminal inquiry to proceed.'

A look of anxiety crossed his face as he contemplated the Parkers, his eyes sliding from left to right.

'I can see that this isn't what you wanted,' he said. 'You came here today expecting justice, and believing you have a right to it. I believe that too. If I could help you I would. If a criminal case existed I assure you I would pursue it.

'But the fact of the matter is that we, the police, are bound by legislation and case law when it comes to negligent criminality. We have studied the evidence thoroughly and, like I said, we can only conclude that it does not meet a criminal threshold. I'm genuinely sorry for you. I can't begin to imagine what you are all going through.'

When the coroner gave the 'interested persons' the right to address him for the last time, the Trust's lawyer Austin Watts enjoyed the easy ride, certain that the contest was well and truly over. Thanking the coroner for his 'assiduous pursuit of the truth' he addressed the family and cordially invited them to work out their grievances in private meetings offered by the hospital management.

The Parkers were not interested. 'We were told our dad had cancer, that he was dying from it and there was nothing anyone could do to help him,' said Ralph when it was his turn to speak.

'Isn't it all a bit convenient that there are no records of the meeting that we all remember so well and would prove the truth of what I've told you? Why can't the doctor find that information in his files? We believe Dr Klein is not being honest with you.

'Why would they assign a Macmillan nurse to my father if they weren't treating him as a cancer patient?'

His voice faltered as he said: 'My father must have been sixteen stone or more when he went in, and he weren't that when he came out, I can tell you. Why wasn't he weighed when he died? Our dad was unlawfully killed. It's what they did to him in there that brought his life to an end, not cancer, not C. diff, nothing else. He didn't die of any illness. It was not a natural death.'

By the impatient look on the coroner's face I could see he must have made up his mind long before Ralph finished.

'It is troubling that we have heard conflicting accounts in the evidence presented today,' Mr Roberts said. 'While I appreciate the sincerity with which the family make their case, it is regrettable that there is a paucity of documentary proof that might help to ascertain their version of events. It is an omission I cannot overlook.

'On the other hand, I have today heard ample evidence to show that Mr Parker was extremely poorly because of an infection of C. diff, which the pathologist said was ultimately fatal. I have no reason to doubt him.

'It leads me to conclude that there appears to have been a miscommunication, or even a breakdown in communication, between the family of Mr Parker and the treating doctors about the nature of the patient's illness. Because it is my duty to establish the cause of death I would not consider judging such failures of communication in my capacity here today other than to say that I am convinced they were not relevant to either the treatment or the death of the patient.

'Perhaps the matter of communication is one that the family might wish to pursue with the hospital at a later date, but this inquest is not the appropriate forum.'

The coroner wasted no time in returning a sugar-coated verdict of death by natural causes, expressing his 'deeply heartfelt condolences' to the family.

If his show of sympathy was meant to pacify the Parkers, it didn't work. They left the courtroom noisily and defiantly. Ralph stopped abruptly as he levelled with Dr Klein. He looked him in the eyes and hissed the word 'murderer' into his unblinking face. Klein smiled faintly as he watched the Parkers ushered out of the room by staff.

At the same time, Dennis Clarence, a reporter from the *Lancashire Sentinel* who was sitting on my right, turned to me, smirking. Then he began to laugh. Well, it was more like a honk, actually. 'Brilliant!' he said.

I couldn't be bothered to answer him. Let me be upfront about Clarence: I can't stand him. I was even less in the mood for him that day than normal. I brushed past him to hurry along the corridor, hoping to grab a few comments from one of the Parkers. But the family jumped straight into a taxi and I dashed from the courthouse into the street to see it pull away. As I made my way to the railway station I was disturbed by what I judged to be a cruel legal farce.

The case failed to make the evening television news bulletins, as I'd hoped, nor did it evoke the level of excitement among the busy news editors of the national newspapers that freelancers like me depended on.

There was, perhaps, a prevailing perception that the death of Ray Parker had been thoroughly investigated by the authorities, and that justice had been served, even if the health service had cocked things up, which it sometimes did. It was tough for the family, yes, and of course it would be better if such mistakes were never made, but since what was done could not be undone it was time to move on. They weren't going to get angry about this case. The general public loved and trusted their doctors. They wanted to love them. News editors wanted to love them too.

It was worth the effort, nevertheless. I had two sales, though not the column inches I would have liked. My piece was given eight paragraphs in the *Daily Telegraph*, with my byline—'By Jenny Bradshaigh'—always good to see. The story was cut down to a heavily-qualified article at the foot of page 32 of the *Daily Mail*. It also had my name on it, with a headline which read:

FAMILY FURY AT DAD'S 'FAKE' CANCER DEATH

Hardly Watergate, I know, and if I hadn't attended the inquest it might have failed to pique my interest too.

Of course, I had absolutely no idea a year ago how those reports would set in motion the chain of events which, for me, ended in a hospital bed with a broken neck.

2

THE RECORDS OFFICE

Father Calvin Baines watched from the canteen window as a group of nurses huddled outside the hospital to gossip over cigarettes.

He yawned, clutching his coffee, the third he had ordered that morning in the hope the caffeine might offset the fatigue that crept up on him in the stinging of his eyes, the light-headedness and the perceptible decline in the tact and patience that were so critical in his ministry to the gravely ill and their families.

He hadn't imagined hospital chaplaincy would be so tough. Conferring last rites was as serious a business as could be imagined for so principled a priest. He was conscious that this was a sort of make-or-break time, a chance for the souls of the sinful to turn to Jesus or be lost for all eternity.

The words 'Pray for us now and at the hour of our death', a central entreaty of the Hail Mary, hovered at the forefront of his mind as he went from bedside to bedside. He prayed almost constantly with the sick, diminished and dying, with their families and also alone, offering up petitions silently in his mind for them as he wandered the wards with a profound sense of meaning and purpose between the pager bleeps from nursing staff. What he found most emotionally draining was the 'pastoral' support he tried to offer to bereaved and panicking families, the times when he had to be like a figure of Christ at the scenes of emergencies or to see Christ in the faces of the wretched.

On his first day at the hospital, he was asked to help to pacify the hysterical mother of a fifteen-year-old boy who was comatose after he and his friends dropped tranquillising drugs into their eyes with a pipette. The sight of the boy as he blessed him shocked Calvin: the dilated pupils and a jaw drooping, as if halted in mid-sentence, frozen in time. The boy was a creature of the no man's land between life and death—a cadaver, yet alive.

On another morning Calvin ordered tea for the sobbing sister of a middle-aged man who had attempted suicide following the collapse of his marriage. He listened, consoled and reassured her, shared in her pain, and afterwards prayed for all of them. But his most emotionally demanding encounter so far was with a young couple in the maternity unit whose daughter had been stillborn. There was no training in the world that could have properly prepared him for such an extraordinary situation. 'Be a Jesus, be a Jesus,' he told himself repeatedly as he placed his arms gently across the heaving shoulders of the distraught couple before cradling and blessing their tiny, motionless baby, mesmerised by the awful perfection of beauty spoiling in cold and clammy skin. He could not help but weep with the parents too.

So immersed in his ministry was Calvin that often he lost all sense of self, and the time he spent grabbing a coffee, or even walking from patient to patient, was like emerging from deep water with lungs bursting and gulping in air.

His brief experiences at Bethulia Park Hospital had engendered a deep respect for the medical staff he saw serving patients and their families day after day, week after week. Clearly, they had found a certain vocation, just as he had discovered his. He felt a flush of sentimentality, of a noble solidarity, as he indulged in the notion that they were somehow all partners involved in the care of body, mind and spirit.

He came crashing down to earth the first time he bumped into Dr Klein. The priest entered a corridor from an eight-bed ward where he had just anointed a confused and debilitated man in his seventies who was in the advanced stages of Parkinson's disease. Klein, followed by a group of younger people, who Calvin thought were possibly students, stopped to look at him rather than turn straight into the ward, asking with his expression where he might have seen him before.

The doctor dropped his gaze to the lanyard around the priest's neck then sounded out 'Father—Calvin—Baines' slowly before fixing him with a look of amused disdain, putting him on edge with subtle menace.

'Oh, if you and I were ever to get married, you'd be Calvin Klein,' said the doctor. 'Would you like that?'

'It's not really my cup of tea,' said Calvin. 'But thanks for the offer.'

One of two of the doctor's entourage giggled.

'There's nobody up there, you know,' said the doctor.

'Well, I beg to differ,' answered the priest, smiling sheepishly as he attempted to interpret the comment as little more than a joke.

Klein refused to reciprocate. He glared icily at Calvin, deadpan, not wishing him to labour under any illusion of good-will. 'No, really, I couldn't be more serious,' he said. 'I'm sure you and some of the patients and their families all think what you do is really jolly good and I'm sure if it helps them, well, it might not be such a bad thing. What you imagine might be an 'emergency service'. But if I had it my way I don't think I'd have you here at all. This isn't a religious playground, it's a hospital.'

'Thanks for that, doctor,' said the priest.

'You're welcome,' replied Dr Klein as he departed into the ward with his small retinue, some of them still grinning.

Wounded and distracted, the priest's concentration shifted from the consuming exercise of his ministry to the other reason why he had volunteered for the chaplaincy rota a few weeks earlier—to look for a nurse with a scar on her throat. It was a promise he had made to Mrs Parker.

She was ashen when he saw her at Mass the Sunday after the inquest. She did not stick around to speak to him afterwards so, worrying about her, Calvin took the initiative of ringing her at home later.

She told him that some other aggrieved families had been in touch following the publicity over the inquest. They were planning to meet at her house on Ash Wednesday to share their experiences and to talk about a campaign, and possibly forming a Facebook group to reach out to other people like them. She invited him to come along.

Calvin arrived to find the living room of Mrs Parker's small terrace transformed into some kind of ante-room to hell, a dim cave crammed with misery, anguish, despair, anger, betrayal, loneliness, heartbreak and regret. Forlorn faces looked up at him as he came in, barely able to raise a polite smile of welcome. It was a gathering of people united by irreversible misfortune, like a leper colony or convicts in a prison yard. They were shamed and stigmatised by the unjust exposure of their vulnerability and their powerlessness, by their failure to protect those most dear to them.

Besides Mrs Parker and son Ralph, there were eight others representing five families. A jumble of chairs had been assembled from around the house but all were taken so Calvin, the last to arrive, propped himself against a wall next to the journalists Jenny Bradshaigh and Dennis Clarence, who were also standing.

A representative of each of family told their stories in turn and by the time they had finished, Calvin felt like he needed a seat. He was thankful he had eaten only the very light meal permitted on a day of obligatory fasting, or he would have retched. He wondered if his nausea resulted from the lack of food or from listening to some of the most harrowing accounts of human suffering he had ever heard.

Calvin's head spun as he tried to make sense of the ordeals of the patients and their relatives. He struggled to reconcile his own trust in the goodness of the health system with the sincerity with which the speakers expressed themselves. His understanding was hampered by their talk of such drugs as diamorphine, nozinan, cyclizine, haloperidol and midazolam, and of drips and syringe drivers. Yet the grief of those who spoke was so palpable to him, so real that he could practically taste it.

Ralph spoke repeatedly about how he wished to contact the nurse with the scar on her throat. She was at the meeting which he said Dr Klein lied about. He said she was always kind to his father and he was inclined to trust her. Afterwards, as the guests were leaving the house, Calvin took Mrs Parker aside.

'I'm glad you've taken the time out to come tonight, Father,' he remembered her saying to him. 'It's lovely that you care enough to be here.'

'It's the least I could do,' replied Calvin. 'I wish I could be more helpful. In fact, I have been thinking, I might be able to help you.'

'How?' asked Mrs Parker.

'Well, now that I've settled into the parish, I'm going to see the dean and ask to be added to the chaplaincy rota for the hospital. I might, if I'm lucky, be able to find that nurse for you.'

Stunned, Mrs Parker blinked repeatedly behind the thick lenses of her glasses. Overhearing the conversation, Jenny plunged into her handbag for a business card which she pressed forcefully into the palm of the priest.

'Ring me straight away if you make contact,' Jenny told him before Mrs Parker could speak. 'Oh, and by the way, I wouldn't bother with the other journalist, if I were you. Tax collectors and prostitutes, they're all right. But Dennis Clarence ...'

Finding and making contact with the nurse, or 'sounding her out' for the Parkers, was the little bit the priest believed he could do to help.

As the days passed, he had thought hard about what he would say to her if and when they met, probably on one of the wards, how he would introduce himself, what words he might choose to elicit her co-operation. The more he had reflected on such a possible encounter, however, the more he had come to realise the folly of his designs.

How could he turn to a nurse and start inquiring about the death of a patient at the hospital all those months ago? How would she react?

Even if they somehow became friends—which might not be proper for a priest—how much work and time would he have to invest before he could ask her to search the records department for a document which could incriminate a very senior colleague, to expose him as a manipulative liar, as criminally negligent? Surely this was madness.

He sensed that he had foolishly embarked on an impossible task, that he had made a promise which was both inappropriate and impossible to keep. He had read some of G K Chesterton's Father Brown stories but he had no ambition to be a priest-detective. Ashamed, it was a promise he was happy to forget as he threw himself into the salvific work of a hospital chaplain. That at least made sense to him.

But clearly not to Klein. As the hours passed, the doctor's contemptuous remarks bit deeper into the priest's pride, stoking anger. Calvin knew that his human weakness was getting the better of him, and he made a conscious effort to pardon the doctor and 'offer up' the insults in atonement for the times he himself had failed.

Yet something more visceral was at work, something rooted in his own masculine nature, in his youth. Yes, he would forgive, but not without resolving to do whatever he could to help the Parkers and their friends. He tried to persuade himself that he was motivated solely by charity on their account, but had to admit, deep down, that it would be good to see Klein sweat.

In the days that followed, he would not pass a ward without glancing in to see if a nurse like the woman who had been described to him was there, he would never fail to look across the car park to the smokers with every cup of coffee he sat down with in the canteen, just in case. He dropped references to her in conversation with one or two of the nurses he had come to trust, but none took the bait. Perhaps she has gone to work elsewhere, thought Calvin, but he didn't, nor wouldn't, stop searching for her.

Even so, by the end of his second week his hope was beginning to wane amid the more pressing obligations of his ministry. He might have given up completely and told Mrs Parker on the steps of St Winefride's after Sunday Mass that, sorry, but he couldn't find the nurse with the scar, but at least he'd tried. Then he ran into Tanya Torridge, and it changed everything.

Tanya was visiting her mother as Calvin arrived on the ward to administer last rites to a patient who was dead by the time he arrived.

A tall woman in her late 30s with knotted and unkempt honey-gold hair falling on to the shoulders of a long and expensive fur coat, she stood out not only because of her looks but because she was worn and angry. Calvin noticed her instantly.

Simultaneously, she locked on to him, her eyes tracking him like prey as he walked towards the ward exit. He stopped, almost in fear, when he could no longer ignore the intensity of her gaze, unyielding in its demanding for his attention. He was at the foot of her mother's bed, and Tanya was moving toward him. He felt he had to say something.

'Are you okay?' he asked. 'Is there anything I can do to help you?'

'Can you get her out of here?' snarled Tanya, flicking her head toward her mother. 'I don't want her here a second longer.'

'I'm sorry, I'm not a doctor …'

'I can see that. You're a vicar or a priest. But you're a man too, aren't you? What's the matter? Can't you do anything around here?' she said, halting a foot from him.

'That old lady who you came in to see …' she said. 'Christ, why has it taken you so long? Couldn't you have helped her? All of last week she's been crying out in the night. "Give me a drink, give me a drink, I need something to drink". Why didn't you come to see her then? None of the other women here could sleep. She'd be at it till dawn, till she tired herself out.

'Oh, they'd give her a drink all right, but they wouldn't help her to drink it. Left it at her bedside, on the table. But she's shaking all over the place and couldn't lift it to her lips on her own, could she? I went over myself sometimes, though it was none of my business. No other bugger around here was doing anything though, were they? And where were you? You've just come here right at the end, when the deed's done, to say a few prayers after they've packed her off? And then you sod off when you've done your bit, just like everyone else.

'They were never going to make her better, or give her a chance. That's what I think. Sedatives—that's what they give her in the end. Not to make her better, just to make her sleep so she wouldn't upset everyone else. I've seen it with my own eyes. It's an outrage. Why hasn't anyone done anything?

'What's the matter with you people? Why don't you do something that will make a difference? Are you too scared?'

'I don't know what you mean,' Calvin muttered.

Tanya raised a slender manicured hand and jabbed a sharp fingernail into his chest. 'You're a man, aren't you?' she repeated slowly and bitterly, prodding him again. 'Why didn't you do something?'

Her nostrils flared and Calvin thought she might strike him next. 'My mother,' she began again, 'came in here with a urinary tract infection which should have cleared up with the right course of antibiotics.

'A week ago they tell me she's got sepsis and that she's probably going to die soon. Well, you would with sepsis, wouldn't you? Progresses pretty quickly, doesn't it? She's sedated and they start taking down her tubes, saying she don't need 'em no more. So I say, "hey, what do you think you're doing? Get 'em back up". I wouldn't let them do that, take 'em down. And guess what? She doesn't die within twelve hours or a day, or whatever you'd expect from multiple organ failure, you know, when you've got sepsis. She just lies there, practically the same, day after day.

'She isn't bloody well dying and she never had sepsis. I'm getting her out of here, you just watch.'

Calvin nodded. 'Why don't you complain, or go to the police if it's that bad?' he said.

Tanya snorted and grinned at him for the first time, her eyes shining. 'My Bob don't go to the police,' she said. 'But he'll get her out of here. He reckons it's a bad place and he should know—he buries people for a living and he says a lot of people are dying here.'

Calvin smiled nervously and began to pull away. Tanya stopped him. 'What's your name, lad?' she asked, looking at his lanyard. 'Father Baines. I'm Tanya Torridge, and my mother, there, is Pamela Worthington. Listen, Father Baines. You must be here all the time. You need to open your eyes and take in what's happening around you. And then you need to do something. Don't you forget it. Do something, Father Baines.'

———

The next day was a Friday in the middle of Lent and Calvin was fasting solely on water, a sacrifice way beyond the requirements of the Church.

Calvin knew he was young and strong enough to fast hard, and he also felt the need for self-mortification, noticing too hungrily the curves of young women in the street, or quick to anger at some trivial annoyance. He needed to tame his flesh, to control his passions, to make them subservient to the will of God so that he could live his life as a man for other people, not for himself.

That evening he sat alone in the front room of the presbytery with the television off, faint with fatigue and nursing a deep, throbbing headache. Because it was Lent he had tried to read spiritual works instead of the histories or biographies he usually favoured. But he found himself labouring over the paragraphs, thoroughly disengaged, and he gave up after reading the same words over and again, unable to absorb their meaning.

He quite liked the silence because it usually gave him the time to think, and sometimes to discern what he believed was the quiet, still voice of God in his heart. Loneliness, on the other hand, was always a real struggle, a tremendous test of his faith and a constant, lingering question over his vocation, especially when it descended into sadness and a melancholy that bordered on depression.

Lent, for the most part, was an ordeal to him. It was not possible to have an enjoyable or even a good Lent, but only a successful or bad one.

Calvin had resigned himself to an early night when a message came from the hospital, urgently asking him to attend a dying patient on the cancer ward. It was something of a relief. Better to spend an evening helping a soul to paradise than in self-imposed solitude, hunger and pain.

Calvin put on his overcoat and picked up a small case containing prayer books, oils and the Viaticum, the Eucharist given to people at the point of death. It was visiting time when he arrived at the hospital and the car park was full, so he had to leave his Peugeot 208 a few streets away.

As he strode through the corridors he recalled—not for the first time—an anecdote imparted to him by an elderly priest about a mental patient who spoke no word in some thirty-five years but began to shriek about being tormented by Jesus, whom he called 'the Nazarene', when a chaplain, incognito, came on to his ward with the Blessed Sacrament under his coat. Was it true? The old boy insisted it was, though Calvin for a while was sceptical. Now a priest himself, the story abided with him. It especially played on his mind whenever he carried a consecrated Host through the hospital, a part of him always braced for an encounter with the supernatural. Arriving at the ward, he was met with a disturbance of a different kind.

A gaunt man in his late sixties or early seventies, his skin sallow behind a bushy grey moustache, was wrenching tubes out of his arm while fighting to climb from his bed. 'Git your 'ands off me!' he screamed in a thick Scouse accent at two nurses, one of whom was holding his free arm while the other was pushing on his shoulders to try to make him lie down.

'Git OFF me!' he yelled. 'I'm dischargin' meeself, and you carn stop me! I'm not goin' to die here! Yooz are not puddin me on one of yer bloody death pathways like yer did wit' me sister. I'm goin' 'ome. Now gerroff! GIT YOUR 'ANDS OFF ME! You're nuttin' but 'ired killers, the bloomin' lorra yer.'

His elderly wife shuffled to his aid, helping him down from the bed as she shot stares of angry indignation to the nurses who now stood away from them, her husband continuing his tirade.

'I'm goin' 'ome, an' I'll die there, thanks!' he said.

Noticing the audience he had won among the other patients, he shouted: 'Don't trust this lot, they'll kill yer!'

He hobbled towards the exit in his pyjamas, his wife's arm tight around his back, his own thrust over her shoulder. 'They'll kill yer! They killed me sister, and they were gunna kill me,' he shouted, adding in a final blast: 'Well, you're NOT!'

Stunned, Calvin wondered what sequence of events might have led to such a scene. He felt a twinge of sympathy for the nurses, who stood lost for words, shocked and humiliated. Seeing him, one of them took him to the dying pensioner.

After administering the final sacraments, Calvin left the woman sleeping, her son at the bedside.

He should have turned towards the ward exit at that point and gone home. But the fracas he had witnessed earlier had left him perturbed and a little guilty at the possibility that he had not done enough for the families whose grief he had briefly come to know at Ray Parker's inquest and later at Mrs Parker's house. Weren't they complaining of precisely the same thing? Yet he had failed to find the nurse who might be able to help them locate the missing records. They had trusted him to help to find the papers that just might prove the lethal negligence that had led to Ray's death. He had let them down.

'Do something!' The words of Tanya Torridge boomed through his mind, and he saw again the intensity of her noble and angry face, her eyes challenging him provocatively to act, to prove that he had a right to call himself a man.

Calvin reached a junction in the corridor. If he went straight on he would arrive at the car park, but if he turned left he would get to an administration block, a labyrinthine annexe. A sign set out the various departments at the end of that dark tunnel and it included the records office. It was late, the hospital was quiet, and there was barely a soul around. What if he could find Ray Parker's records? Was it worth a punt?

Aware that he could be making a dreadful mistake, Calvin headed towards the annexe, propelled by a heady mix of right-eousness and recklessness, a yearning to 'do something'. As he walked, automatic lights came on one after the other, rolling out an electronic carpet of light in an eerie welcome.

After ascending a flight of stairs, he was at the records office door. He looked both ways. There was no sign of CCTV cameras. He turned the handle. Damn! The door was locked. He noticed a keypad to one side—there was no way he was going get in without the code.

He banged the door handle, hoping somehow that it would yield to brute pressure. He thumped the edges of the jamb for a weakness that could somehow be exploited, and finally he kicked his right foot into the base of the door, all in the vain hope that it might miraculously swing open through sheer force of will.

'What do you think you're doing?'

Calvin turned sharply, feeling his rage recede with the blood from his face as he met the displeasure of a young nurse in navy blue scrubs and clutching a stack of files to her left breast. Another nurse following her looked equally exasperated.

The priest gulped as panic surged through him. He stared at the one who spoke to him. Then he saw it. The scar on her neck, the lightning bolt of raised and jagged pink tissue that flashed along the left side of her throat. It must be her. At last. He'd often wondered what she would look like. No one had mentioned to him that she was a beauty.

He looked from face to face, frantic for something plausible to say. 'Sorry, I'm looking for the way out. I thought this was the door to the stairwell.' With a hapless smile: 'It's been a long day.'

The two nurses stood to one side as he barged past and retreated down the stairs. The cool night air brought him more fully to his senses. What an idiot to try to force his way into the records office—and to get caught.

At the same time he was jubilant. He had probably found the nurse he sought.

As he walked back to his car, early revellers were laughing and chatting outside the pubs. The last of the shoppers and office workers were going home.

'Spare any change, sir?'

Calvin rounded to see the skeletal features of a man on his haunches, tattoos darkening his face and neck, hand outstretched. The priest reached into a trouser pocket and pressed a handful of loose change into the dirty palm.

'Thank you, sir,' said the man. 'She will be pleased with you for that! You like her, don't you? Oh, I know what you want to do to her! Disgusting!'

The beggar was grinning hideously at him. 'She'll have you, all right! She'll cut your head off, that's what she'll do! Ha ha ha ha! Ooh, you'll like her, all right! She's coming for you. She's coming after you. She's going to cut your head off, chop it right off your shoulders.'

The man simulated a sawing movement with his fingers across his throat. 'Ugh, ugh, ugghhhh! You're going to get it!' Then the swearing started, a torrent of filth and blasphemy. Calvin walked away, refusing to look back.

'Poor chap's probably got Tourette's,' he thought, promising himself that he would pray for him.

He began to shiver, long uncontrollable spasms, not because of the cold March wind but because he was penetrated by icy shards of fear.

'Who's going to cut my head off?' he wondered. It was an implicit acknowledgement that he had two women on his mind—and he liked them both.

3

UNBEARABLE ME

'So, what do you think of Kai's blue hair?' asked the nurse as she exhaled a plume of smoke into the cool morning air.

The other woman gazed, arms folded, at the lanky figure striding towards them, lost in his own thoughts or the music on his phone.

'Yeah, suppose it suits him, in a way,' she answered. 'He'll look good in the clubs. That's what matters to him, hey? The dance floor. But we can't call him Beaker any more, not until he goes back to orange, and that's a pity.'

The male nurse arrived at the double doors guarding a side entrance to Bethulia Park Hospital. As he drew level with the pair he raised an arm in a languid greeting.

'Mornin' Shaz,' he muttered. He glanced at Emerald but looked straight through her even though she smiled coyly.

As the doors swung shut, Sharyn stared after him, astonished by the naked animosity. Emerald giggled in embarrassment.

'I've just been blanked by a walking toothbrush,' she said. 'A human pineapple won't say hello to me. It's so sad.'

'Yeah, what's got into him? What've you done to deserve that?'

'We had a little row over bed pans.'

'Bed pans?' sniggered Sharyn.

'Well, you know what Kai's like. Don't get me wrong. He's all right and everythin' and until now I've always got on with him. But when it comes to rules he is one massive fat pain in the backside, that man. He wants to grow up.

'What all this is about is because I came on the ward the other day and there was that old dear who's had the hip op, you know who I mean, Mrs Saunders, and she was crying and screaming at him—like, she was really upset, you know.

'I thought it was something serious, but she was only dying for the loo. She was screaming at him for a bed pan and he was stood at the end of her bed tellin' her that he wouldn't help her because he wasn't her named nurse. It was Daisy but she was on her lunch, an' the rules said that she was her named nurse so he wasn't going to help her.

'So I says to him, in front her, "Are you just gunna let her pee herself, then, or what?" and he looked at me as if he hadn't even thought about it and he says to me again, "I'm not her named nurse".

'So I started to get mad at this point, my blood's boiling, and I squared up to him and told him that if a patient needs a bedpan, you get them a bedpan, named nurse or not. I could have cracked him one. Honestly, I was furious.

'But it didn't make any difference. I wasn't getting anywhere—he just ignored me—so I did it myself in the end, dead stroppy like, stamping my feet and all that, and I made sure he could see me. All the patients on the ward were watching too, all dead quiet, while he was pretending nothing was happening. Really, he was mad as hell. But now it's if, like, I've done something awful to him. He's taken it all so personally.

'But, you know, I ain't bothered. What he was doing to that old lady was wrong. Poor care was what that was. Does my head in. He's got the hump with me and he won't speak to me, but that's up to him, the soft git.'

Sharyn tapped her cigarette and smiled wryly. 'You're a proper little Florence Nightingale, aren't you?'

Emerald went quiet, her lips drawn tightly into a straight line, and she looked away as Sharyn took a long pull on her cigarette.

'Don't take it too seriously, love,' she told Emerald, detecting her awkwardness and discomfort. 'We don't give them bad care here, you know that, despite what they say in the papers. Some of them deserve it, though, especially those malingering bastards I come across.

'We had another one in the acute ward the other day—pretending to fit uncontrollably, she was. And of course she was telling us, in between, that only some whacking great doses of benzodiazepines could help her out.

'Off she goes again and we're all scrambling about while she starts thrashing, kicking and squirming and flinging her arms, whacking into things, knocking everything over. She has us all jumping all over the place, trying to get a grip on her.

'Then the next thing, her phone rings and she stops fitting to answer it. "Hullo!" she says, in this sweet little voice, almost posh it was. I swear I'm not kidding. I think she was worried that she might have missed an important call from her bank—or from her dealer or her boyfriend, or whatever. Honestly, me and Jackie, we just stared at each other, then we started laughin'. It was so outrageous. We could hardly stop. Could a done with a bedpan myself.'

Emerald cackled. 'So she didn't get her drugs then?'

'Did she bloody hell. We weren't having that and neither was the doctor. He sent her packing. She'll have to Google something else to fall suddenly ill with if she wants her drugs next time, unless she rocks up with the same stunt somewhere new. You never know with these types, do you?'

Emerald suddenly stopped laughing, her face transformed by deeper thoughts. 'I've never come across a genuine malingerer,' she said after a short pause. 'But I'd like to see one. There've been a few who've gone into these attacks of hysteria because of repressed trauma—child abuse, that kind of thing—but no-one yet who I could think of as a malingerer.'

Her colleague tapped her cigarette ash into the flower bed, and forced out a horizontal funnel of smoke as she contemplated the nurse's words.

'You'll meet one,' Sharyn said. 'There's so many dodgy people about these days, ain't there? I mean, what do you make of that chaplain last week? That was dodgy. What the hell was he playing at? Have you told Dr Klein about him yet?'

'No,' said Emerald. 'I've been meaning to, but Reinhard's been charging around like a rhinoceros since the Parker inquest, you know what I mean? Reiny the rhino. He's hard work at the moment. He's moodier than bloody Kai. I'm going to have to choose my moment, but I will tell him—deffo.'

Sharyn took a final pull from her cigarette and flicked the smouldering butt into a row of laurel bushes.

'You on with Doctor Dashing today?' she asked Emerald.

'Who, Klein? Yep, later on.'

'Now that's why you don't need to worry about poor care. I've never known a doctor like him. He could bring 'em back from the dead, that man. But I know what you mean about his mood since the inquest. Why's he so upset? He won, didn't he?'

Emerald hitched her bag on to her shoulder before moving toward the double doors.

'Suppose it made him look bad and he didn't like it,' she said.

Sharyn pulled open the door and the pair of them entered the building.

'That's understandable,' she said. 'It's outrageous to even think that about him. Those Parkers simply got the wrong end of the stick, like some of these families do. And the Press just lapped it up. You know we've cancelled those newspapers from the wards now. We're not having them in here after that.

'But, anyway, you know Jackie was sayin' that chaplain was kind of asking about you. What is it with him, do you reckon he fancies you or what?'

'Shouldn't think so, never seen him before in my life.'

'So why was he asking about you?'

'Was he? I don't know if it's true that he was.'

'Just think—if you were still going out with Dr Klein you could ask him to sort him out for you. He's a tough fella, isn't he? I bet he would. You could tell him he's a sex pest.'

'Me and Dr K are history,' said Emerald. 'I spend more time with my mum than anyone these days. I could do with a man. But look—it ain't going to be him again, and it ain't going to be no priest.'

Dr Klein wore a broad grin as Emerald approached him later that afternoon, but he noticed instantly that she struggled to reciprocate the warmth of his greeting, her expression solemn.

'What is it?' he said.

'It's Sheila Ramsbotham, the lady in the room off the Jordan Ward. Her son's in to visit her and he urgently wants to talk to one of the treating doctors before he goes back to London. They've told me that you might be available. Would you see him? He's rather upset about the prognosis about his mother and he's insistent that he speaks to someone before he goes.'

At Mrs Ramsbotham's bedside they found a man in his fifties, conspicuous by the smartness of his three-quarter length rain-coat and the gleam of his shoes.

Emerald busied herself with tidying up as Dr Klein discussed the treatment and condition of the patient. Her son was struggling to understand why staff at Bethulia Park Hospital thought his mother was approaching death when she had been admitted with a minor condition.

'Mr Ramsbotham, we've done an awful lot for your mother and much of it has been very successful,' explained Dr Klein. 'The infection has gone and we've stabilised almost all of her functions which were causing a little worry but, as you can see, she is still not very well. Please, sit down.'

The doctor pulled two chairs from the wall and opened a palm toward one them. The visitor sat down and the doctor placed the other chair directly opposite and lowered himself into it, leaning forward so their faces were just inches apart.

'She's a wonderful woman, your mother, I believe,' said Dr Klein warmly. 'Tell me some more about her.'

He smiled sympathetically as Ramsbotham spoke affectionately about his mother, her family and her achievements, and nodded in solidarity when the man spoke of his fears.

He patted the back of the man's hand. 'Eddie,' he said. 'Can I call you Eddie, or do you prefer Edward?

'Eddie, your mum isn't well but here she is going to receive the best care anyone could possibly wish for.

'Certainly, she hasn't responded well to all the treatments we have tried but that doesn't mean that we think the worst is going to happen or that she can't go home in a few days or perhaps a week.

'It just means we have to look after her a little bit longer. If we can, I promise you we will have her back on her feet sooner rather than later.

'It is always difficult when those we love fall ill, but sometimes they do. All I can say is that your mother is in good hands here. We will look after her and we will do our best to make her better.'

Ramsbotham was visibly consoled by the doctor's words.

'I don't think the prognosis that one of my good colleagues has imparted to you is intended to mean that we think she is approaching death,' Dr Klein said. 'What we should have said is that it could be an eventuality, but that could be said about any manner of things in a hospital setting.

'What you need to be conscious of, perhaps, is that your mother's age may not work in her favour. She's eighty now. Age is a major factor in every kind of illness. It can make patients weak and unresponsive in some cases, and our job here, with your mother, is to make sure she gets past all those complications so she can go home. Like you, that's what we want for her—more than anything.

'So we're by no means saying for certain that the worst will happen. But you must prepare yourself for death as a possible outcome if, in spite of our best efforts, your mother simply doesn't respond to treatment. But we will do everything we possibly can for her, I can assure you of that. We want her to get better, and I want to send her home.'

The man blinked hard and repeatedly as he surveyed his mother's sleeping face. She looked peaceful and comfortable, oblivious as a newborn to the fact that her only son was at her side, discussing her tenuous grasp on life with those who might have the power to save it.

He rose and stood at her bedside. He reached down and slipped his fingers into her hand. He was struck by the softness of her flesh, how tender and thin it was, and how with just the slightest of squeezes he could feel her bones. She had cared for him all of his childhood and he desired with all of his being to return that love now that she was the vulnerable one, her pearly eyelids flickering in unknowable dreams. A depth of sadness and pity he'd never imagined possible hit him as he raised her hand to observe the catheter pushed into a vein. He gently let her hand drop, acutely conscious of its flimsy unfeeling delicacy.

'Please do your best for her, doctor,' the man said. 'She's everything to me. She's still very fit and independent, you know. She's got to have a chance. It's a shock for me to see her like this, it really is.'

'Absolutely, we will do our best. I can promise you that,' replied Dr Klein. 'I have a mother myself, I understand only too well what you're going through. We boys love our mothers, don't we?'

The man returned Dr Klein's smile, heartened by the assurances that his mother was in safe and caring hands and wishing them to be true.

'I live and work in London, doctor, so unfortunately I can't get up quite as often as I'd like, but I'm going to try to take some time off work so I can be with her,' he said. 'Until I can sort that out my cousin has agreed to look in on her if he can find the time. He's a very busy man too, but he says he'll try.'

Dr Klein said: 'Really, don't worry yourself too much about your mother's care. If she responds to the treatment she will be going home soon. It is as simple as that. If not, she may have to stay here just a little while longer. Perhaps that's the best way to look at it. We have your details and we will be touch straight away if there are any dramatic changes to her condition. She will receive wonderful care. I give you my word.'

'Thank you, doctor,' said Ramsbotham. 'You don't know how much I appreciate it.'

He buttoned his coat and picked up a sports bag from the corner of the room. He shook the doctor's hand, smiled at Emerald, and planted a kiss on his mother's forehead. He whispered his love into her ear as he ran the outside of his finger along her cheek, listening to the fragile flutter of her breath. He left with his head bowed in a valiant attempt to conceal the weight of his worry and grief.

Emerald faced Dr Klein across the bed, waiting for him to speak now that they were alone together with the sleeping woman.

The doctor shrugged his shoulders in reply. He mulled over the figure of the woman, her head thrown back, exposing her throat. His eyes followed a tube running from the catheter up to a fluid bag dangling from the drip stand beside the bed.

'Emerald,' he said abruptly, 'I want you to take this down.'

'The IV lines?' she asked.

'She'll come around soon and she will be able to feed herself. She's on the mend, can't you see? I want you to do it, Emerald. I want you to do it now. Now do as I tell you. Come along now—it isn't like you haven't done it before.'

Dr Klein took a couple of steps back as Emerald, flint-faced, walked to his side of the bed, pulling on a pair of disposable gloves. He watched as she turned off the intravenous pump, disconnected the lines, hung the fluid bag on the drip stand and carefully removed the catheter from Mrs Ramsbotham's hand. The nurse emptied the fluids from the bag into the sink and dropped the empty container into a bin with the gloves, tubing and the catheter.

The nurse let the water splash in a torrent over her hands, taking her time to rub her fingers hard and vigorously, over and over again, as if trying to shift something horribly infectious.

'We won't be needing that drip stand either for the time being,' she heard the doctor say. 'Take that with you when you leave.'

She pulled herself together, and looked him in the eyes as she wiped her hands on a paper towel, faking a smile. 'Of course, doctor, I'll remove it now,' she said coolly.

Emerald walked toward the door and Dr Klein looked satisfied. If Mrs Ramsbotham were to open her eyes at that instant she might have seen Dr Klein also look lecherously at the arch of the nurse's back as she departed pushing the drip stand ahead of her. She might have noticed his eyes drop to the contours of the nurse's rump and follow her legs as she walked, and she might have wondered about his innermost thoughts.

4

MADNESS AND MEDIOCRITY

The woman, barefoot and in pyjama bottoms and a camisole, was sitting against a wall of her darkened bedroom, close to a wardrobe, her knees drawn up slightly. A boy of about two lay across her middle with his head on her shoulder, emitting repeated quick, sniffling sobs punctuated by longer heaving sighs. He was exhausted by crying.

The mother had shifted the toddler on to her right side since pain was racking the entire left of her body. Her scalp was sore where her ex-boyfriend had hauled her back into the terrace house by her hair when she attempted to escape. An eye was half closed from one of the three heavy punches he smashed into her face after he slammed the door shut behind them, and her cheek, neck and arm throbbed.

Each time she breathed, sharp pains shot through one side of her rib cage where the man had kicked her and stamped on her, furious that she had helped his seven-year-old daughter get out of the house to alert the neighbours.

The woman needed desperately to use the toilet but she was too frightened to ask, let alone to move. Her attacker was sitting across the room on a chair by the bed, a nine-inch kitchen knife beside him on the dressing table next to a near-empty bottle of whisky.

Drunk and stinking, the man did not share the woman's anxiety about personal hygiene in the hours that had passed since he dragged her to the bedroom. He simply stood and urinated in the corner and sometimes over the bed—her bed, and her pillow.

Sure, he wanted to insult her, to defile the place where they had transported each other into mutual ecstasy in happier days, but he also wished to avoid passing the bedroom window, now that police marksmen had taken up their positions.

Yawning, his eyes closed momentarily and his head jerked forward as if he was about to sink into sleep. He suddenly came to life again, seemingly thrilled by the whirring of the helicopter blades overhead and watching, as if hypnotised, the faint flicker of lights from the police cars illuminating the walls with a kaleidoscopic merry-go-round of colour.

'Please,' the woman squealed, 'I really need to go, and Jayden needs a drink. He hasn't had anything for hours, he's got a headache and he's really upset. Come on, let me get him something from the bathroom. None of this is his fault, he's done nothing to you.'

The man pushed greasy dark hair back from his forehead. He hated the woman so much that at times he wanted to murder her—just like the night before when he'd turned up and forced his way in. Yet he couldn't bring himself to ignore her entreaties. 'Okay, but I'm coming with you, and if you try anything this time, you're both dead—I'll kill the both of you. I mean it!'

He picked up the knife and, crouching, crossed quickly to the woman. When he reached the far wall he stood and pulled her on to her feet with a violent wrench of her right arm. 'Move!' he growled, pushing her toward the landing.

The man peered down the stairwell into the shadows while his former girlfriend sat on the lavatory, the bathroom door open so he could keep an eye on her. Unable to listen for noises downstairs because of the tinkling in the toilet bowl, he became angrier. 'Don't you dare flush!' he snarled. Grimacing, she turned her back on him and tried to persuade the terrified toddler to drink out of a plastic toothbrush mug.

She was trying to give the man the impression that she was ignoring him, but she was constantly watching and analysing his every move. She noticed he was yawning and blinking his eyes with greater frequency, that he was tired as well as drunk.

As he shoved her in front him, the child in her arms, back to the bedroom, she hoped he would soon fall asleep, and imagined she might then dare to creep out of the house. At once she dismissed the idea as too dangerous. She would never make it to the door in her debilitated state with a frightened and wailing child. Perhaps the police would make a move, she thought, and do whatever it was they had trained for in 'siege situations'. What would it be? Smoke grenades? How would they know when the man was asleep, and could they rescue her and her son in time? It would take just seconds for the man to wake up and plunge his blade into one or both of them.

Perhaps she could take the knife from him when he dropped off and cast it out of the open window. But how long would it take the brute to kill them with his bare hands?

A fourth option came into her mind. If the man fell asleep, and she could quieten her son, just for a few moments, then perhaps she could cross the room, seize the knife and finish it herself. Could she do that? She pictured herself thrusting the blade up into his heart through the soft flesh of his belly, scowling at him as his eyes opened and he screamed in pain, defeated and dying. It afforded her a brief moment of gratification and it gave her passion and strength. She knew exactly what she would say to him if ever she saw him breathe his last.

But for now, the only reality was the standoff. She returned to her place on the floor, where he commanded her to go, arms around her son, waiting in fear but more in hope that their captor would surrender to the police, that he would see the sense of handing himself in rather than killing them and turning the knife on himself as he was threatening.

The woman understood that, like her, the man had weighed up his options. The siege must end one way or another, and sooner rather than later. He must have been aware of it too.

Outside, police negotiators used loudhailers to call to the man at intervals, urging him to give up. Less obvious were the armed officers at the rear of the building, in the adjacent houses and the facing properties of a street which stood evacuated, its access road blocked by a striped tape.

Behind it were three TV camera crews and reporters from press agencies and local and national newspapers. Dog-walkers and other passers-by paused beside them while kids tore up and down behind the pack on skateboards, waiting for a chance to pull faces in the background when TV anchors were live on air.

Behind the media scrum were the open twin doors of *The Bird I'th Hand*, a pub whose billboards were promoting a karaoke night. The steady stream of people entering suggested that the evening was going ahead irrespective of the police operation.

One of a trio of smart casual men in their forties, hair still wet from showering and soaked in aftershave, interrupted Jenny as she scrolled through her emails on her phone.

'What's happening here, luv?' he inquired.

'There's a woman and a baby who've been taken hostage in the house halfway down on the right by an ex-boyfriend who's believed to be holding them at knifepoint,' she said, matter-of-fact. 'It started last night and it's been going on all day. We're all hoping it will be over soon. It's been a long shift, and it will be a bit of a bore if it drags into Saturday.'

'Is it on the telly?' said one of the others as they went up the pub steps.

Jenny didn't answer. She was well aware that the drama simply served as an opportunity for the older men to approach and chat her up. She was an attractive brunette in her late 20s,

56

with the flat stomach and toned thighs of a committed equestrian. She was quite used to being approached by admiring men when she was working, hired by newspapers for jobs like this. She didn't mind, as long as they cleared off reasonably quickly. She wouldn't stand for harassment.

Other small groups filed past without bothering her. People chatted and pointed, sometimes asking questions of each other as they stared up the street, but they were much keener to escape the chill of the wind for the warmth of the pub. Music began to pulse out into the street. The acts had begun.

Jenny rolled her eyes as she heard a man crowing out a tortured version of *Please Release Me (Let Me Go)* by Engelbert Humperdinck to a crescendo of laughter from inside.

She smiled faintly when the performance was followed by *Rescue Me* by Fontella Bass. She pictured the three men who had spoken to her earlier conspiring like mischievous teenagers over their pints about which song they would belt out next. She was in for a night of it.

How she yearned to be back in London working for the *Sunday News*, the newspaper that had taken her straight from Cambridge University to train her as a journalist. She was one of four who had qualified for the apprenticeship scheme and she flourished there, thriving on the excitement of reporting every day a story of national interest.

Proving highly capable and dependable, she was soon trusted with foreign and investigative assignments and was among the few journalists asked to bring her passport to work in case she was sent out of the country at a moment's notice. It helped that she could speak four languages and was proficient in others.

Had she stayed at the *News*, Jenny might have been soon promoted to a specialist, or to the rank of chief reporter. She would probably then have become news editor and, with a bit of luck, the day might have arrived when she was a senior editor of one kind or another.

Instead, she was back in the regions, reporting grubby crimes in one-horse towns. It just wasn't the same class of job.

'The things you do for love,' she thought to herself, sighing, as she stood bored in the street.

Then she saw Dennis Clarence coming toward her.

'At least they see the funny side of it, hey Jen?' he said through the corner of his mouth, tilting his head toward the pub.

She pretended she didn't understand him.

'Been here long?' he asked.

'All day,' she answered. 'The *Sun* asked me to cover the siege once it looked like it could turn into something. You replacing Michelle?'

He nodded. 'I bet you're gagging for a pint.'

It was true. She was cold, damp and her legs ached. But she would have endured another six hours under the elements rather sit down with Dennis Clarence.

'I'll wait till I get home,' she said. 'This can't go on much longer, surely.'

'So you haven't anything planned tonight, then?' inquired Clarence.

Jenny shot him a sideways glance, caught off guard by his curiosity about her private life.

'Well, no—I mean, I never do too much on a Friday. I'm usually knackered, and I always like to be a bit fresh for my ride. So I tend to take it easy, at least until Saturday. What's up, Dennis? Is this wrecking all your plans? Were you supposed to be out on the razz tonight?'

'I'm on the late shift, so no. But I'll make up for it, I promise you that. While you're doing pirouettes on your little pony, I'll probably just be turning in. It would help if this was over soon. What do you reckon?'

Jenny shrugged.

'Hey Jen,' Clarence began again after an awkward pause, 'have you got much on next week? Is there anything bubbling that you might like to share with an old mate, anything you could chuck my way?'

'An old mate? I wouldn't go that far, Dennis,' she answered coldly. 'And why would I give my exclusives to a reporter on a local weekly? You should be giving me the tips, Den, not the other way around. So go on, what can you tell me that's new?'

'My cupboard's bare, I'm sorry to say. That's why I'm asking you.'

'I don't suppose you do much in the way of off-diary stories,' Jenny said. 'You know, something your news editor doesn't serve to you on a plate. If you were working for me, Dennis, I'd want you to be like my cat, bringing me mice and dropping them at my feet. If you didn't do that, you wouldn't get any rewards.'

'What are you saying?' Clarence fired back. 'That I'm rubbish at my job? Course I do off-diary stories, you cheeky sod!'

'No, no. I wouldn't go that far. But I'd love the *Sentinel* to come up with the odd lead every now and then that I could follow up and turn into a national news story. They must be out there. You know, why haven't you done any stories on those families who met at Angela Parker's house after her husband's inquest? You were next to me in that living room the whole time and, like me, you heard story after story—yeah, and they were vile—and I've seen nothing in your paper about any of them since. Perhaps that could be a campaign for the *Sentinel* which could run for weeks. Don't you think?'

Dennis Clarence stared at Jenny. 'Get off my case,' he said. 'My problem with that lot is that I didn't believe them. It wasn't just exaggerated, it was so over the top that it stank. Some of those people sounded like they didn't understand what doctors do— you know, confused, out of their depth—and the other half seemed to have it in for the NHS, like they had an agenda. We ain't going to publish rubbish like that, not unless they can prove it. It's offensive.'

'Rubbish? So did you check any of their stories?'

'I did, actually, yes.'

'Who with?'

'With Dr Klein—and he knows what happened better than anyone else. He's highly respected. Ask anyone. And d'you know what? He doesn't believe those families either. He's got a lot of sound medical reasons for doubting them which he'll explain to you if you bother to give him a ring. Why don't you check their stories with him?'

Clarence was talking loudly now.

'Personally, I'm sure he's right. If their grievances are as strong as they make out, why haven't these people complained formally, or gone to the ombudsman, or gone to the police? Why are they kicking off about their so-called experiences only now? It all looks like bellyaching to me, a bunch of mischief-makers jumping on the bandwagon of the furore whipped up by your over-the-top coverage of the inquest. Probably looking for compo. That's why we're not touching it.'

'I beg your pardon?!'

'You heard me. Over the top—that's what they were. Dr Klein's mad with you, by the way. You better be ready for the regulator because that's where he's going with the stuff you've written.'

'Dennis, you were at the inquest. Now you tell me what was inaccurate or over the top about anything I wrote,' Jenny demanded. 'Go on, tell me.'

Clarence didn't answer.

'I thought not,' she snapped. 'For the record, about five or six of the families are going to the police over what happened to their relatives in that hospital. They want justice, not money. Now that's a story. There you go, Dennis, an exclusive for you.'

'Good luck with that,' he sniggered. 'You saw the police at the inquest. They aren't having a bar of it either, and if you think they didn't investigate the Parkers' complaints thoroughly then you're off your head. You're barking up the wrong tree, luv.'

'We'll see about that,' she said. 'Oh, and when the time comes, I'll be thorough. I'll give Dr Klein the chance to explain himself, don't you worry.'

A collective gasp went up from the media pack and the two reporters looked up the street to see police officers, some armed, issuing from parked cars and buildings surrounding the house as its front door swung open.

A pallid, bedraggled man in his thirties in dirty grey jogging pants, a black T-shirt and white trainers, stepped out. He had his hands in the air, holding the blade in his left.

'Drop the weapon!' yelled one of three marksmen pointing SIG Sauer P320 automatic pistols at his head at close range.

Another marksman, wearing a peaked cap and aiming a Remington 870 shotgun, came out of the opposite house.

The man stood motionless. After an agonising pause he opened his hand. The knife hit the pavement with a clang and at once two police officers were on top of him, slamming him to the floor, handcuffing him and pressing his face hard into the stone gutter.

Others ran into the house. Five minutes later several emerged supporting a woman who was struggling to walk. A uniformed female police officer came out behind them, cradling a child.

'Thank goodness for that,' muttered Jenny to herself as she observed the conclusion to the siege. 'Some good news at last.'

5

COLD MUSHY PEAS

Calvin surveyed the mountain of food set before him by Hannah Hoskins, his housekeeper, and sighed. How did she expect him to eat this lot—in Lent? A pan-size fillet of plaice was embanked with enough chips to feed two or three and on the far edge of the plate was a portion of mushy peas so large she had crafted it into a tower to fit it on.

To Mrs Hoskins it was as good as haute cuisine, her 'signature dish', but to Calvin it was an ordeal which called for a stratagem to strike a balance between eating himself to death and causing offence.

He muttered grace and got started. A plan was taking shape in his mind. He would leave at least a third and make the excuse that he needed to save some room for the cake she would inevitably offer. Then he would decline the cake.

From the kitchen, he could hear the housekeeper singing.

'I hear the voice of the mystic mountains callin' me back home,' she trilled, her voice coming closer. Now the priest could hear the thump of her heavy feet on the floorboards, and her singing became a blast as she entered the dining room.

'So take me back to the black hills, the black hills of Dakota, to the beautiful Indian country that I laaav!'

Calvin put down his knife and fork and clapped. 'Bravo, Mrs Hoskins. A splendid performance,' he said. 'What's that one again?'

'Do you not know it?' she said with genuine surprise. 'Well, I suppose you're only thirty. A baby. You young 'uns don't know what you're missing. Black Hills of Dakota. Doris Day sang it with Howard Keel in Calamity Jane. It's a classic.'

'I'll have to watch it some time,' said Calvin.

'You should,' said Mrs Hoskins. 'That Doris Day, she was a picture—sat on that horse with her guns and her 'at. And that Howard Keel. Ee was a gud 'un too. They don't make 'em like that any more. I must have watched it fifty times, Calamity Jane. It's always on TCM, you know. You can watch it whenever you want! You know, my old fella used to tell me I looked like Doris Day. That's what he used to tell his mates in the pub—that he was marrying Doris Day.'

Calvin looked at the 72-year-old woman. She was heavy and with sagging jowls, and he stretched his imagination to picture her in the vigour and beauty of youth, as her gigantic bosoms heaved with each laboured breath. He gave up, deciding to take her word for it.

He loved Mrs Hoskins. He recognised that without her he would have struggled to settle into the rural parish. In many ways, she was like a mother to him and he was like a son to her. She had never been able to have children with her late husband, Jack, and was only too willing to fuss over the young priest in her care. In spite of the gap in their ages they quickly bonded and became great friends. Industrious and cheerful, she ran around after him and took care of running the presbytery and the church while he applied himself to the more urgent business of his ministry. She also took on a lot of his secretarial and administrative work. It was more than she was paid to do, but she worked without complaint. They were a team. But the real value to Calvin was her company, her advice and her good humour. He would be lost without her. The solitude would be unbearable.

Mrs Hoskins was undoubtedly overweight, and she was tall too, a big woman who panted as she walked. Father Calvin occasionally, and with great tact, would raise his concerns about her workload and tell her to take good care of her health. But she would brush off his anxieties with a laugh. She had absolutely no intentions of relaxing. Since Jack's death a decade earlier she had become a dedicated daughter of the Church. To her, serving the parish priest was an honour which gave meaning and purpose to her life. Moreover, the churchgoing women were not only her friends but the totality of her social network since she had no surviving family except a brother in Australia whom she had not seen for twenty years. St Winefride's was all she had, and all that she needed.

'I'll sing you another one from the movie, if you like,' she offered, as she stood over the priest.

'I'm all right for now, thanks,' said Calvin hastily. 'You've cooked me a lovely meal.'

'Righto,' she answered. 'I'll leave you to it. The only reason I come back in was because I forgot to tell yer that there's a message for you on the machine. Jenny Bradshaigh, that journalist you said you met t'other week, wants to talk to you about marriage preparation. She said not to worry about calling her tonight because she's out on a job but she wants you to call her back tomorrow afternoon.'

Calvin thanked the housekeeper as she turned and lumbered away. He continued with his meal, thinking about the reporter who had approached him at the end of the meeting at Mrs Parker's house. He had seen her looking at him during the inquest too and wondered then what was going through her mind. Now he guessed it was because she was planning to marry soon and wanted to ask if he might officiate at her wedding. Calvin felt Jenny was open and direct, a person of uncomplicated honesty. He looked forward to talking to her the next day.

Not waiting for Mrs Hoskins to clear the table, he began to take the dishes and cutlery through to the kitchen, where he found the housekeeper washing up and whistling some other old tune.

'Thanks for supper, Mrs Hoskins,' he said as he handed back the plate arrayed with half-eaten food. 'It was lovely, I really enjoyed it. But it was a little bit too much for me, especially if I'm going to have some of your delicious cake as well.'

'Oh, don't worry. Just leave it there,' she said. 'I won't waste any of that.'

She picked up a tea towel to dry her hands.

'So, Father,' she began. 'Did your blessing of Angela Parker's home help her?'

'How did you know about that?'

'Oh, I've known Angela for years. She hasn't told many people about the sense she sez she has of Ray still being around. She's only told a few of her friends. It was an awful business that, wasn't it? Tellin' 'em all he had cancer when he didn't and then puttin' 'im on a death pathway, or whatever they call it. Angela reckons that's what did him in. Do you know about that?'

'Yes, I was at the inquest. She asked me to go. Her son Ralph told me it would be a good idea if I did. He said he thought it would support his mum, me being there. He's very worried about her.'

'So did your blessing work then?'

Calvin took a deep breath

'I saw her at Mass the Sunday after the inquest and she looked ill, really down in the dumps, so I rang her afterwards, late that afternoon, to check if she was all right.'

'And what did she say?'

'She said she still feels he's there.'

'I'm not sure I believe in ghosts,' said Mrs Hoskins. 'But where do they come from, just supposing they're real?'

'Heaven, hell or purgatory, I suppose. It's the only other places Scripture says exist outside the material world.'

'Heaven or hell?' repeated Mrs Hoskins timidly.

'We'll all end up in one of those two places in the end,' said Calvin. 'People tend to lose sight of that and it can be quite dangerous for them when they do.'

Mrs Hoskins looked a little fearful and, wishing to change the subject, she offered the priest the expected slice of cake. He politely declined, saying if she left a piece he might eat it later, knowing that he wouldn't. But he accepted her offer of a cup of tea and she finished off his fish and chips, shovelling in cold mushy peas while she waited for the kettle to boil. The pair of them sat down at the kitchen table.

Calvin produced a deck of cards from his jacket pocket.

'Let me show you what I mean about heaven and hell,' he said. 'Do you want to see a trick? I've been brushing up on a few. I show them to the kids when I go into the schools. It makes their RE lessons a little bit more interesting, gets their attention. They love 'em.'

Mrs Hoskins paused, open-mouthed, hesitating to answer as Calvin emptied the cards on to the table and began to shuffle them. He halved the pack and riffled the cards in a blur. Then he united the deck and tried to cut it again using only one hand.

He encouraged her to take the deck and shuffle the cards but she pushed them back to him. He picked up the deck and put it into his pocket.

'Don't you want to see the trick?'

'Yes—I do, I do,' protested Mrs Hoskins. 'I'm not much good at shuffling, that's all.'

Calvin took out the deck and put it on the table between them.

'Do you remember that passage in the Bible when Jesus comes back to judge the living and the dead, to separate people one from another as the shepherd separates sheep from goats? The good people are those who fed the hungry, gave drink to the thirsty, sheltered the homeless, clothed the naked, and visited the sick and those in prison. Jesus says, "In so far as you did this to the least of these, you did it to me".

'Then the bad people are identified as those who did the opposite, or didn't do anything at all, and Jesus sends them away "accursed" to the eternal fire prepared for the Devil and his angels.

'Now, let's pretend these cards are real people.'

The priest cut the pack and revealed the queen of hearts. 'Some people will be good,' he said.

He replaced the cards and cut the pack again, saying as he revealed the jack of spades: 'And some people will be bad.'

Mrs Hoskins was entranced.

'But you know it's not up to us to judge anyone. We can't look into the heart of any person and know for sure if they're good or bad and, anyhow, people might change. So it isn't for us to decide who is saved and who is lost. God alone can do that—only He can read our hearts.

'It means that in the end it will be Jesus who will judge what side we are on.'

Calvin cut the pack into halves. He offered one to the housekeeper and placed the other in front of himself. He instructed her to turn them face up at the same time as he was doing it himself.

She let out a loud gasp as she saw that all the cards in front of her belonged to the two red suits while those Calvin spread before him were the blacks of the spades and clubs.

'Like I said, God knows what side we're on and at the end of time this is what he will do,' he said with a touch of smugness. 'He will judge all people and separate the good from the bad— the good will go to heaven and the bad will go to hell.'

There was a long pause. 'I expect he'll be better than you at it,' said Mrs Hoskins. 'I've got a six of clubs in here.'

She laughed. Calvin kept a straight face. It was one of the rules of magic: never let them see you flustered when it goes wrong.

A few hours later, Calvin was finishing a four-mile run along darkening country lanes.

Within a few hundred yards of the presbytery he halted beside a bank of brambles. Wrapping his hand in the bottom of his t-shirt, he yanked out a long vine.

Inside the house, his legs flecked with the mud from a thousand puddles, he undressed and wrapped the bramble around his thigh, tightening the thorns into his flesh until he felt sharp pulses of pain and beads of blood sprang out. After a few moments he unwound it and washed away the dirt and the blood in a cold shower. It seemed to do the trick. The nurse was finally off his mind.

Calvin retired to bed in muted triumph at having pacified another assault on his senses, but reeling a little from the extent of the self-mortification he had just practised, marvelling that he had gone further than ever. Perhaps one day he might roll naked in a patch of nettles, like St Francis when he was tempted. Very soon he fell asleep.

But he did not have a good night. He was beleaguered by strange, exotic and disturbing dreams. One remained with him after the bleep of his alarm jolted him into consciousness. He opened his eyes in the darkness and lay for a moment, startled by the images played in the secret tunnels of his mind.

In his dream, he had toothache but instead of going to the dentist he was waiting in a sterile white corridor of a hospital.

'The doctor will see you now,' said a nurse in heavy make-up, a short skirt and high heels, beckoning to him from an open door. As he crossed the threshold the room transformed hazily from a surgery to the inside of a tent. It was filled with the ancient instruments of war and conquest—lances, swords, slings, bows and arrows, shields and armour, and lit with silver torches and decorated with animal furs, fleeces and tapestries. On one side, flies bounced up and down over a long table laid with fresh fruit, bread, sliced meats and poultry. On the other was a low, squat circular table at which bearded soldiers in glinting chain mail poured red wine from silver ewers into ornate goblets.

Waiting for one of the cups was a tall and bearded figure perched on the scarlet sheets of a bed elevated on a dais, soldiers of his guard languishing at his feet like greyhounds. The man was shrouded in semi-darkness beneath a canopy of purple and gold, a net studded with precious stones pulled half open around him. The sheen of the enormous muscles of his oiled arms and shoulders caught the red and orange flames in the half-light and gleamed. His eyes were ethereal, their whites glowing like lamps lit by their own power. They locked as cruelly as a cat's on to the stationary figure of the priest, and the man's lips ignited into a knowing smile.

Calvin saw the fingers of the man's right hand were caressing the elaborately engraved grip of a great scimitar. The thumb and the forefinger of the other pinched the flat of the curved blade, holding the weapon steady and levelling the razor edge in the direction of the priest.

Perhaps that was the impression that left such a powerful imprint on Calvin's memory and which caused the dream to endure. He had glimpsed a warrior of unprincipled and absolute power, a man of merciless violence. The priest carried a vague sensation of horror with him for the rest of his day, the threat and the menace as vivid as if he had not woken at all.

6

PIG ROOTING

I've always loved horses. Some girls grow up thinking about their dream husband. I dreamed of the horses I would own. Daphne was a dream come true. I bought her using some of the money I'd saved for a deposit for a flat in London when I was a staff reporter on the *Sunday News*. Then along came Seb Bennett, a carpet fitter I met one weekend in a Lancashire pub when I came home to see my parents. One thing led to another—well, it was quickly physical and we fell in love pretty much straight away, actually—and I eventually moved back to the North to be with him. We chucked in for a property at a fraction of a price we'd have paid in London, leaving me with a bit of change out.

I told myself I could have a career as a freelance but to leave the environment of a newspaper office so early in my career was a huge gamble, a massive sacrifice to make. Seb understood that. It was the prospect of owning a horse again which sweetened the pill, and Seb encouraged me to buy her. I could never have dreamed of it in London. But here, in the North, if all went well I could have my man, my career and the horse I've craved since I've been able to walk. It helped me to see that Seb wanted us to be very happy.

I've owned horses nearly all my life, but none quite like Daphne. An eight-year-old Irish sports horse, she was sleek, alert and usually eager to please. She stood just over sixteen hands and was chestnut all over, except for a single white sock on a hind leg. She had big hare-like ears which invariably pointed up and forwards during her work, giving me the assurance that she was revelling in the partnership just as much as I was.

I was glad that Daphne also had a long neck, given that one of the greatest upsets of my short equestrian career was to be thrown as a teenager from a pony at the second fence of a double jump and finding nothing to hang on to as I somersaulted over its head. It was as if the pony had slammed on the brakes as it reached the fence, going from a canter to a dead stop in an instant. Anticipating a jump, I'd made the mistake of sitting forward too soon and dived headlong towards the floor like a gannet into a school of mackerel. Luckily, the fence broke the worst of my fall, but my arm was broken. I had never endured pain like it.

The fall shook me up, dampening any ambitions I might have harboured to compete at high-level events. I considered quitting altogether and it took some mental persuasion before I felt at ease in the saddle again. But I could not stay away for ever. I simply love horses too much.

Like I said, Seb understands my passion for all things equestrian and he's often worked it to his own advantage, choosing my return from the stables as a moment to break any bad news in the knowledge I'd handle it better after a good ride, or to add to my joy with a gift or a surprise. It was one such moment, shortly before the Christmas of 2018, when I crossed the threshold of our home reeking of manure, my hair matted with sweat and my face spotted with mud that he went on one knee and asked me to marry him.

'Of course I will,' I said, rushing to hug him. It was true, I was happy. Seb told me later all he could smell was ordure, sweat and scurf, but that he didn't mind a bit. He'd been a semi-professional rugby league player and, as a sporty type himself, he likes it that I ride. He also likes me in boots and jodhpurs.

I like it that he is an athlete too. He has a lovely physique, a big strong man with big arms, muscles everywhere. But he isn't handsome. Too much rugby has left his face bumped and flattened like it's been squeezed, though he's still cute with his copper hair and his light golden beard. Yeah, he's a hunk but it's the devilry in him which I like the most. He's a bit edgy, a bit dangerous.

He can be funny but I wish he'd make me laugh more. I hate his long silences, and the amount of hours he spends gaming online with his mates—when he's not at the gym. Worst of all is the total lack of interest he sometimes shows in my work. It sends me around the twist. The sacrifices I have made in my career for that man still hurt—horse or no horse.

It was a relief to find Seb watching Warrington Wolves thrashing Hull FC on Sky Sports when I arrived home from the siege. I could talk to him instead of compete for his attention while he laughed and sniggered to people I couldn't see beneath a set of headphones and a microphone. I'd also half expected him to be in the pub but instead of going out with his mates while I worked he'd waited in for me. That was nice.

I bashed out a short piece for the *Sun* on my laptop while Seb watched the rest of the game. Then we spent a couple of hours drinking bottles of Australian merlot and fooling around. This was Seb at his best, when I liked him the most. We had fun that night, and perhaps it was the excitement of planning a wedding that kept us up so late.

'Why do we need to get married when it's already this good?' I remember whispering to him as I lay across his chest, listening to his heart beat in the early hours of Saturday morning. 'We don't have to change anything.'

'Change is going to come whatever we do,' he replied, pulling me closer with a huge tattooed right arm. 'Marriage gives us the best chance of making things even better, especially if you want to have kids.'

'You're such a traditionalist,' I said, lifting my head to look at him. 'But I know what you mean, and yes I do want a family.'

The price of our late night, for me, was a hangover next morning. My head thumped with every pulse and my mouth was like the bottom of a dirty sink. Uncharacteristically, I wasn't really in the mood for bouncing around on Daphne. I wasn't at my sharpest when I arrived at the stables where I kept her in livery.

But I'd arranged with Sarah, my best friend, to meet early for some pole work in the arena with the intention of improving the fitness of our horses. An unusually hectic workload in the previous weeks meant I hadn't spent as much time with Daphne as perhaps I should have, and my mare was growing lazy, forming a habit of collapsing too easily into a walk from both trot and canter. Horses are like that. They are smart and they have character. They understand the fine points of rules like lawyers and, if permitted, will often do just enough to evade sanction, but no more.

Daphne had an air of mischief that morning. It was as if she was attempting to assert mastery over our partnership and dictate to me, in my moment of weakness and negativity, how things were going to be done.

On the inside track of one length of the arena, about three feet from the perimeter fence, Sarah and I laid out three fence poles flat on the sand, roughly five feet apart at right angles to the barrier. Working in walk, trot and canter, the overall object of the exercises that day was to improve balance, rhythm and impulsion in the horses' gaits, to regulate their strides and to prepare both ourselves and our mounts for jumping.

As usual, Daphne was pleased to see me. I'd kiss her and I'd swear she'd try to kiss me too. She had this great personality. She would stand ever so politely while I groomed her, only moving to signal the location of an itch to me, as if she wanted me to work that little bit harder with the brush on that particular spot.

I always did what she wanted and she nuzzled me gently with her lips as if to say 'thank you'.

I did not feel the same warmth and enthusiasm from her when we were in the arena that morning, however, with little energy in the trot and vexed, defiant kicks from her hind legs in response to the tiny encouraging flicks of the dressage whip I felt compelled to use when she ignored the instructions from my legs to pick up pace.

After some scolding, Daphne relented and we were soon trotting briskly over the poles. Sarah and I decided we would step up the exercises by asking for canter, maintaining the faster gait for a half circle at the end of the arena before we transitioned down to a rising trot. After a few goes we would repeat the exercise in the other direction.

At the first attempt, I found myself again arguing with my horse when she struck into canter on the incorrect foreleg, leaving both of us unbalanced. I slowed her to a trot and shifted my outside leg behind the girth to ask once more for canter while time and space remained, but she refused to respond.

On my second attempt, the horse declined to offer even a smooth upwards transition into canter, suddenly dropping her head and arching her back as she bounced along, 'pig-rooting' with her nose into a succession of small bucks which scared the life out of me. I pulled her to an abrupt halt.

'She hasn't done that in ages,' I called to Sarah, trotting up behind me on Stella. 'I wonder if she is in some kind of pain or if she's just trying it on.'

I checked the position of her saddle but all seemed in order. Suspecting that the horse was indeed attempting to gain the upper hand in a battle of wills, I persisted in the exercise until she completed it to my satisfaction. I had to show her I was in charge. But I was dispirited by the bucking, and although I was ready to counter it by leaning slightly backwards as she went into canter to help to prevent her from raising her hindquarters, and lifting my hands to stop her from dropping her head, there was little I could do to restore my wilting self-belief, and the horse could sense it.

Inadvertently, I tightened the reins, pulling on her mouth, seeking security, perhaps, in the closer contact.

Again, I struggled to impose my will but once we completed the exercise we walked the horses across the diagonal of the arena to change direction of travel from the right to the left rein, and from clockwise to anti-clockwise as we looked from the gate.

This time, we planned to approach the far end of the arena in trot, then as soon as our horses bent to the left, we would ask for canter and maintain the pace as they swept over the poles before easing them down to a rising trot.

Sarah and Stella went first and completed the exercise effort-lessly, surging forward on a triple rhythm of hoof beats. Trotting on the far side of the arena, I was aware that Daphne was watching the other horse and it made me hopeful that she might have caught some of its enthusiasm for the task.

As we trotted into the bend, marked in the arena by the letter 'M', I asked for canter and was delighted by a perfect transition and by Daphne's forward energy. I relaxed and extended my hands as I straightened her with my seat and legs on the approach to the poles. I fully expected Daphne to float over them as she had done on so many occasions.

Then, from nowhere, she began to buck once more. Her spine came up in a sudden spike, bouncing me from the centre of the saddle. At the same time she plunged her head down repeatedly and I fought to haul it back up but did not have the strength. I was suddenly and seriously unbalanced, gripping with my knees and straining even to see her neck. Daphne yanked me forwards by the reins, resenting the uncomfortable pull on the bit in her mouth as she strained to move forward.

It was in the tiniest fraction of a moment when I realised that, for the first time in five years, I was going to come off.

Perhaps I could have thrown my arms in the direction of the horse's vanishing mane in the hope that I might have been able to swing my feet to the floor and land upright, maybe running. Something instinctively warned me against it. I was already plunging headlong over Daphne's shoulder. I had to raise my head out of the dive if I was not going to suffer some serious injury.

As I rolled fully extended in mid-air, I glimpsed the horse's saddle and hindquarters pass me. I smashed into the sand with a thump, landing flat on my right side, my head protected by my outstretched right arm.

I remember swearing loudly as pain convulsed my lower back.

Time stood still. Conscious of Daphne's hooves treading lightly around me and feeling her nose nudging me solicitously, I did not move but focused on what felt like a minor earthquake in the small of my back and my pelvis. I tried to analyse what it was telling me. 'No broken bones, thank God,' I thought, 'but my back!'

The horror of a spinal injury filled my mind, and I switched my attention to my legs, relieved that I still had sensation. Tentatively I began to move them, first my feet and then, wincing, I brought one knee up.

'What is the pain all about, what does it mean?' I asked myself insistently, still largely motionless on my back. Daphne's head hung over me and I could have sworn she looked sad, as if she wanted to say sorry.

As I breathed deeply, I felt the agony begin to ebb away in ever weakening waves, and for the first time I wondered if it was not as bad as I initially suspected.

Sarah dismounted and crossed the arena with Stella by the reins. She shouted for help as she took hold of Daphne, and she instructed me to stay where I was.

Soon a stable girl was at my side, asking where it hurt and telling me there was blood on my mouth where I had bitten my lip.

After a short while we concluded it was safe for me to attempt to stand up. I limped out of the arena, my arm over my lower back, my head still banging from the fall and the hangover, while the girl took Daphne back to her stable to untack her.

Before I could go home, I had to wait for the girl to return with an accident report form. As I filled it in, still in some pain, the girl was peppering me with questions. How many times had I fallen? What was the worst? Did it ever put me off riding?

Finally, she said: 'There's a doctor due here with his two daughters for the first lesson. They've just signed up. Perhaps we could ask him to look you over?'

'Who's that, then?'

'He's there.'

Dr Klein stared at me as he walked toward the arena. He had a winter tan which spoke of an expensive holiday, his long brown hair was gelled back and perfectly styled, and his aftershave so strong that it overpowered the stench of the steaming horse urine blowing in from the yard.

At his heels were two small girls in jodhpurs, boots and riding helmets adorned by silks spangled with stars and comedy bobbles.

'You're joking!' I gasped, slamming down the pen.

All I wanted to do was go home, and as I hobbled out of the paddock I was asking myself if it would be a good idea to move my horse elsewhere, perhaps to my parents' farm. I didn't want to be seeing Dr Klein at these stables every week.

'Just one moment!'

I stopped and looked up to face him, hoping he wouldn't recognise me as the author of the reports Dennis Clarence had said infuriated him. I was soon quite certain he knew who I was but he was pleasant to me. He could see I was hurt. He asked me about the pain and offered to make a cursory examination. His hand was warm, his touch gentle as he moved slowly along the curve of my spine to the small of my back.

'You seem okay but I can't be certain you haven't herniated any discs,' he told me. 'The best thing to do is to go home and have a long soak in a hot bath, and use any salts you might have. It will help take the pressure off your spine and it might help you to understand the extent to which you have hurt yourself. It's likely that you'll simply get over it, a woman of your age and health. If you have any lingering doubts my advice is to go to your GP or take yourself to Accident and Emergency.'

My hostility was melting.

'It's awful coming off a horse, I know that only too well,' Dr Klein said. 'I hunt, you see. We all take a dive every now and again. Most of the time it's nothing to worry about.'

I felt reassured. A man who likes horses, and he wanted to help me. I smiled and said thank you.

'You're very welcome,' he said. 'I wish I could be more helpful but the problem I have here is that your jodhpurs fasten very high and I can't examine you properly. You'd have to undress.'

'And you'd have to at least take me for lunch first,' I answered without thinking.

I don't know why I said that. Perhaps it was partly shock from the fall, perhaps I was still a bit drunk from the night before, or perhaps he had this way with women which made them want to flirt with him. I just don't know. But let me be clear: I didn't mean it, I was only joking.

Dr Klein offered no verbal interpretation of how he understood my remark, but I could see from the smile on his face and the fun in his eyes that he liked it very much.

7

JUDITH CALLS

Sitting in the confessional on Sunday afternoon hearing about sin and dispensing God's mercy, Calvin caught himself sometimes wishing it was him on the other side, discharging the weight of his own guilty conscience.

His regret at attempting to smash his way into the hospital records office, and being seen, for the past week had been a ready source of worry. He would have felt some remorse even had not been caught in flagrante. Now, he was additionally haunted by the sense of betraying the ministry entrusted to him.

The priest was also disappointed about his rush of reckless-ness because it came on a day in Lent when he was fasting, the very act of which he knew was supposed to give him greater self-control as he subordinated his own will to God's. It left him won-dering how he had managed to allow his passion to overcome his reason, why his conscience hadn't told him more forcefully to stop, and why God did not intervene. It led him to meditate about what, indeed, might be the will of God in his particular case.

The confessional was a small room built into the side of the church and was partitioned in two. One side was accessed by the priest through a door that led to the sacristy, the other by a door used by the faithful which opened from the main body of the church. Priest and penitent spoke to one another through a wire grille, over which a curtain could be drawn to guarantee perfect anonymity.

Giving absolution to another regular elderly penitent, Calvin glanced at his watch as he listened to the door on the other side of the curtain swing shut. It was 3.57pm and confessions ended at four. They would have finished perhaps half an hour earlier at any other time of the year but Lent, along with the early weeks of Advent, is a penitential season, one of the most fervent and busiest periods in the Christian calendar.

The priest leaned back, knowing that he would soon be out. After a minute he stood and was beginning to collect his books when he heard the door open and footsteps coming softly in. He sat down again, waiting for the person to speak. After what seemed an unnaturally long pause, he coughed gently and took the initiative to lead the penitent in prayer.

A woman's voice joined in as he made the sign of the cross. Then silence again.

'When was your last confession?' began the priest.

'Oh, about fifteen years ago,' the woman replied and from the mere five words Calvin, a Londoner, knew she too was in her twenties or thirties and either came from, or had spent, a substantial period of her life in the south-east of England.

'And what have you done since then?'

'Phew! Where do I begin? I've taken quite a lot of Class A drugs, and I've been drunk more times than I can count. I've had a long affair with a married man, which I regret, as well as few one-night stands, including a bit of an, er … heavy flirtation with a woman, but only once. I've lied, nicked stuff, cheated people out of money—lots of it sometimes—driven dangerously, you name it—all kinds. I could go on all afternoon if I put my mind to it. Yeah, I've missed Mass too. I don't think I've been since I was a kid when my dad used to make us all go. Is that bad?'

'It's a sin, yes,' said the priest. 'If you think that God has brought you here so that you can start afresh, if you want to make a new start in your life, for whatever reason, you could just say that you were sorry for all the sins of your past life. You wouldn't have to name them all if you can't remember them. What's most important is that you want to live a good life, a life of the Spirit, and that you find the grace to persevere in virtue, and to avoid sin. That you've returned to Jesus after so long is a grace in itself.'

'Thank you, Father, that's very reassuring,' the woman said assertively. 'But if I'm truly honest with you—which I really wish to be—a new start is not exactly the reason I'm here, though it's true that there are some things that have been really giving me grief, and I could do with getting them off my chest.

'I mean, how guilty am I when I know, for example, that someone has done something to someone else to end their life a little bit sooner? How much of the guilt do I share when they make me do that kind of thing and I go along with it—follow orders—out of the fear of losing my job?'

Calvin felt a cold sweat starting.

'Am I complicit in that person's death if I don't do something, or anything, about the things I know are happening?' she said. 'And what if I see it happen again and again and again and still don't do anything about it—because I don't know what to do about it? I mean, just how much of the blame do I share in this kind of thing, in bringing about these deaths when they might well have been avoidable?'

She paused. 'Do you know what I'm talking about or is this too cryptic for you?'

'I think so,' Calvin said tentatively.

'No—I really, really do think that you do know what I'm talking about,' said the woman. 'So which is worse? Adultery, drug abuse, or keeping quiet when you see others kill? You'd think being an accessory to murder is the easiest thing to avoid. But not in my job it ain't. Does it make me a coward if I just carry on regardless? Is cowardice a sin? Just how bad am I?'

She sounded angry and stopped for a moment, waiting for him to speak. When he didn't she began again, more slowly and in control.

'And what if I find a priest creeping around my place of work at night, trying to bust his way into a restricted area where confidential medical records and files on our patients are kept? Would it be a sin to report him? Or to protect him? You tell me, Father.'

From her side of the curtain, she heard the priest stir uncomfortably. She could taste the tension in the dark enclosed space in which the secrets of two strangers were being exposed. The woman guessed that if only she could see him, she would have witnessed almost a comical reversal of their roles, in which he, soaked in sweat, his face a shade of bright pink, his eyes glazed and a vein bouncing in his forehead, took the aspect of the repentant sinner begging forgiveness and she the wise counsellor.

As if he had read her mind, the priest spoke up. 'May I see you, please? I mean, this is something you want to talk about really, isn't it, rather than a confession?'

'I'd like to be able to see you too,' she answered.

Slowly, the priest pulled the curtain to one side and through the wire grille Calvin came face to face with Emerald for the second time.

He knew he would hate himself for it, but he couldn't help but be mesmerised by her beauty—the gleam of her skin and the fullness of her lips, the clear blue eyes and long hair glinting with the many hues of autumn. Calvin had once read that physical beauty lay not in perfection, but in imperfection—eyes that appeared too large, a pinched nose perhaps—but in the face that looked back at him he saw no imperfection at all. It was the most perfect face he thought he had ever seen. It was only her throat that wasn't perfect, the horribly scarred left side of her neck. The priest also realised that he had yet to see her smile. He knew she would be all the more irresistible when she did.

This was not the first time he had been inadvertently struck by female beauty. It had happened to him many times and as he progressed towards priesthood Calvin found himself sometimes having to rationalise his feelings, making the conscious distinction between the recognition of that which his senses found pleasing, and over which he had little control, and active, deliberate lust, which he trained himself to avoid. Still, at a time when he was already feeling bruised about his inadequacies as a priest, the reminder that he was always a man with the nature and instincts of a man left him feeling humbled and a little ashamed.

Emerald remained unsmiling. Unlike him, she was not flustered.

Calvin bowed slightly as he wiped his forehead with the back of his hand, and pulled at the top of his collar to release some of his body heat from his chest and neck. He felt he was being strangled.

'Okay, look, this is still a confession, as far as I am concerned,' he told her as he recovered from the initial shock of her questions. 'So it has the seal of the confessional, which means that everything we say goes no further—to anyone. It's absolutely confidential. In fact, it's inviolable. That's what it means to me. But what I'd like to know is what does it really mean to you? Are you recording this?'

'No, I'm not recording it!' snapped Emerald, slamming down her phone beside an 'act of contrition' prayer taped to the elbow rest. 'You can check that, if you want. It's off. The seal of the confessional suits me too. Now, Father, are you going to tell me what you were looking for?'

Calvin's first instinct was to lie, to stick to his original story, to pretend that he didn't know what she was talking about, and to deny that he was looking for anything. But he remembered where he was and what he was, checking himself swiftly in the sudden recognition of what a lie in the confessional would say about him. He would have to take a different route.

'No, I'm not going to say anything,' he told Emerald. 'You can draw whatever conclusions you like from what you saw, which in truth only amounts to me trying a locked door and not being able to open it. Is that really why you're here? To ask me why I was trying to open a door which was locked and which stayed locked?'

'C'mon, it was more than that,' she replied calmly. 'I saw you kicking that door. It was obvious you were desperate to get in. What were you looking for?'

'Okay, let's do this differently,' he said. 'What do you think I was looking for?'

'What I think you were looking for, I think I could find for you.'

'Is that an offer?' whispered Calvin. 'Why would you do that?'

'I've just told you,' she said. 'I'm sick of watching people die when they are not dying, if you know what I mean. I'm a bad girl, Father, but I want to do something good. I will never have self-respect if I don't do anything about the things I'm seeing. It sounds selfish, but in some ways this—coming here—is something I have to do for myself.'

Her words rang with urgency and in the silence that followed, as each held the other's gaze, the priest sensed she was not faking her candour.

'You,' Emerald began again, 'what you want are the missing notes from Ray Parker's file. Am I right?'

'Yes, you're right,' admitted Calvin.

'Good. I thought so. In fact, I knew it. Do you want to know why?'

'Go on.'

'Because you were at the inquest, you were at the meeting with those families at Angela Parker's house, because you've been looking for me and because you were trying to break into the records office.'

Calvin blanched. 'If I hadn't seen you in the hospital on Friday, dressed in your nurse's uniform, I'd have sworn you're a copper today,' he said. 'Are you sure you not taping this?'

'No, definitely not recording it. I'm on your side. I want to help the people you want to help. But we've got to be careful. Now listen to me. The reason I know about you attending the inquest and that meeting of the families at Angela Parker's house is because Dr Reinhard Klein has been talking about it. He's on to you—he doesn't trust you one bit, so you'd better watch your back.

'The nurses have been talking about you looking for me, that's how I know about that. They were trying to work out if you were gay—they think most priests are gay—but now they think you've got a crush on me. They gossip like hell so it might not be too long before Klein hears about it.'

She shook her head slightly.

'You know, you're so indiscreet I must be off my head taking the risk to come to talk to you now. But it's because I care, you see.

'One final point, what you need to remember is that I wasn't the only nurse to see you boot that door. Sharyn's a good girl and might not tell but you'd better have your answers ready if she does. It also means that we need to move quickly.'

Calvin was in no mood for moving an inch. On the contrary, he was now rueing the moment he ever took an interest in Ray Parker's death. The sensation of sinking deeply and irreparably into trouble left him devoid of motivation. He was frightened and Emerald could sense it.

'Don't lose your bottle, Father,' she said. 'You're part of it now. We simply have to make sure we tread very carefully. I'm not going to back down from this, I've been doing too much of that for too long. Believe me, it's not good for the soul. Are you in, or not?'

Calvin nodded, expressionless.

'Okay, this is what we will do,' said Emerald. 'I will get the copies of that documentation for you. I know where it is. Then you pass it on to that journalist.'

'Which journalist? There were two at the meeting.'

'The woman, Jenny. For Christ's sake, don't have anything to do with the guy from the *Sentinel*. He's batting for Klein, speaks to him regularly, that's who Klein's getting his information from. He knows about everyone who was at that meeting thanks to that reporter. He thinks he's well in, getting stories from his big contact on the inside, but Klein's just using him.'

'Doesn't Dr Klein suspect you? You came up at the meeting. Doesn't Dr Klein know the families want to contact you?'

'It stands to reason that the Parkers would want me to go public so I doubt Klein would be surprised by their interest,' she answered. 'But me and Klein, we're old friends and I've good reason to think he trusts me in a bizarre sort of way. Let's just say that he's put me through a lot and I've never let him down. As I was saying—I'll get you the documentation, if it's still there, and all you have to do is pass it on without being found out. I don't know Jenny, but you do. You'll be a link in the chain, that's all. I'll get you copies this week, if I can.'

She made it sound simple.

'Fine,' said Calvin. 'If I give you my number you can give me a call when you've got them and we can arrange to meet.'

'No, too risky. Forget about calling each other, texting, WhatsApp or Facebook messages, or about anything that leaves a trail, anything like that. This is serious stuff. Where do you do your shopping, Father?'

'Asda down the road, usually—every Monday, on my day off.'

'Could you do it in Tesco near the Bolton Wanderers' stadium next week instead? I'll be browsing the wine aisle at 10.40 in the morning, precisely. You can help me to lift down a case from a top shelf and I'll tell you if I've got hold of the documents. If I have, we'll meet out of town on another day for the handover.

Give it some thought about possible venues. Oh, when you do your shopping, zip up your jacket so no one can see you're a priest. That okay?'

'Yes.'

'Father, I don't want to sound rude, but I won't be coming here again. If you see me at the hospital you've got to act as if we never met. Never try to contact me. I will contact you if I need to, probably by ringing you at the presbytery.'

'I'm out a lot. What would you do if I'm not in?'

'I'm not going to leave a recorded message. Do you have a housekeeper?'

'Yes, Mrs Hoskins. You could leave a message with her. Do you know what, I don't even know your name. What is it?'

'I don't think I'm ready to tell you just yet,' she said. 'Probably better that way for now. Look, I really need to get going. See you down the aisle.'

'Wait,' said the priest. 'I meant it when I said this was really a confession. Was it really a confession for you? Do you want me to grant you absolution before you go?'

'I do actually, yes, for everything I said, but especially for the affair—I haven't felt clean since—and the things that man makes me do.'

The priest muttered the prayers of absolution and asked Emerald to make a determined effort to attend Mass at her local church each Sunday as a penance, treating her once more as a lost sheep returning to the fold, but still unsure of the extent to which she meant it.

As the nurse rose to leave after praying the act of contrition, Calvin called her back a second time. 'I'm sorry, but I should have asked. If you left a message with my housekeeper, who would you say had called?'

Emerald thought for a few seconds. 'You can call me Judith,' she answered. 'Yeah, I'll say that Judith called.'

KILLER QUEEN

D r Klein spent that afternoon with Octavia, like him a doctor, whom he had known some years previously. They were reintroduced to each other one evening at his country club, the haunt of so many aspirant professionals that its car park could be mistaken for the forecourt of a Mercedes dealership.

The club was always a great place to pick up women, with so many divorcees, bored wives and single women having nights out there, not a few in the hope of catching men with a bit more substance and zest than their extant or ex-husbands and boyfriends and perhaps with a few more fivers in their back pockets.

'Where are you supposed to be today?' he called to Octavia from the kitchen as he uncorked a bottle of chilled sauvignon blanc. He poured her a glass and put the kettle on for himself.

'Manchester, shopping,' she shouted back from the bedroom. 'And it's true. I've got all the bags in the car to prove it.'

Klein returned with her drink to find her sitting on top of the sheets, still naked, caressing the mahogany stock of a chunky .22 air rifle.

She positioned the barrel on her left knee and looked down the sights at him as she moved her right hand to the trigger.

'Bang, bang!' she said as she pretended to release a volley of lead into his heart.

He smiled slightly.

'When can we go shooting again, babe?' she asked in a plaintive little-girl voice, parting her legs and lifting her pelvis to make sure he saw what she wished to display.

Klein pushed away the barrel and passed her the glass of wine.

He smirked, visibly turned on. 'Sure you haven't got time to stay longer today?'

'I don't know. Hubby's expecting me. He's due to finish work soon. Maybe if you're quick.'

Five minutes later, Klein lay on his back staring at the white ceiling, panting and coated in a veneer of light sweat.

He had forgotten about his cup of tea. 'You really liked it on the moors, didn't you?' he asked.

Octavia took a swig of wine.

'You haven't taken me on many other dates, have you?' she said, patting his bare thigh. 'Don't worry, honey, I understand.'

That was the downside of affairs, thought Klein, they had to be secret all the time. Taking Octavia on a grouse shoot on the moors in the north east of the county was one of his calculated risks. He would have been damned unlucky if he was spotted with 'the other woman' there. He guessed she would love it too; she was the least sentimental person he had ever met.

This affair, like his others, had been for the most part conducted indoors—sometimes in a hotel, occasionally at Octavia's if her husband was working nights or weekends, but most of the time in the cottage where they now lay together.

It had been Klein's bachelor pad, and when he married Jane he decided to keep it as a country retreat rather than sell it. He loved the absence of any overlooking neighbours. In recent years, he had rented it out most of the time, but at that moment it stood conveniently empty.

This meant that he could see Octavia more frequently than previously, but still only sporadically. Like him, it very much depended if she was in the mood to meet. Sometimes it would be just once in a month.

'Can I ask you,' he started again, 'what you enjoyed so much about being up on the moors? Was it the killing?'

Octavia thought for a moment. 'That and the fresh air,' she said with a wide grin. 'What about you? You must like it too, surely?'

'Yes, I admit it. I enjoy blood sports—the finest manifestation of mankind's dominance over all living things, over all nature.'

'But do you like killing?' she said again, emphasising the last word.

'Birds and animals, yes. Humans, that's another matter. I don't derive pleasure from pulling the plug on some of those wretched creatures clinging on to life and I don't do it for profit. I don't go around forging wills, that kind of thing. My motives are pure, I'm providing a service. Old people are a drain on the system. Not all people see it that way, but perhaps one day most of them will. Times are changing. I might even get a knighthood for it. But you asked how it makes me feel personally, providing this kind of service. Well, I have to admit I do feel powerful, in control and, yep, merciful.'

Octavia raised an eyebrow. 'I worry about you, Hardy,' she said. 'You'll be telling me you're joining the Sally Army next.'

'Yes, I'm all for mercy,' sniggered Klein. 'It's an interesting concept. But it needs, like so much else, to be redefined into something you can actually believe in. It needs to be purified for our century.'

'I am surprised,' scoffed Octavia, mimicking dismay. 'Are you sure you're all right? I never had you down as someone hooked on purity—on moral purity. Are you redefining that too? That will be a laugh.'

She raised her glass to take another sip. 'So how many lives do you think you've ended prematurely then, in your years of sterling service?'

'Hundreds, I reckon, possibly more,' replied Klein. 'I helped four or five shuffle off their perches over the last few weeks or so, but you know how it is, many of them are on their way out anyway. It's a matter of giving them a gentle push. It's usually just the *coup de grâce*, so whether I'm the killer or not is an open question. Most of the time I'm just part of the process.'

He rolled to face her.

'So what's your tally? Are you still racking them up like you used to?'

'I'm very efficient, what would you expect? I'm not quite sure how many I've done but I think four figures would be realistic. I'm not a lightweight like you. I'm a tigress, not a pussy cat.'

She paused. 'Do you think that makes us serial killers, though?'

'No, I still don't see myself as a murderer,' responded Klein without hesitation. 'I mean, if one of us was ever tried and convicted, that's what we'd be called by the media, without a doubt. Bloody journalists, I can't stand them—they're like lawyers but worse, always looking to cash in on someone's misfortune. Parasites, leeches, the lot of them. How can you get any lower?

'But, as I explained, I don't really view what we do strictly as killing, and certainly not as murder. I think it's rather vocational in fact, fulfilling in a strange kind of way. And it's addictive. It always leaves you wanting more. Do you find that, sweetheart? It calls to me like you do, Octavia, darling, and it gives me moral purpose. It's more kind of restoring the role of nature in the process of dying, setting the balance right. Most of these people, if they'd been born in any other generation, would be dead rather than grey and shrivelled and lying there hooked up to antibiotics in a hospital bed. Now that's immoral, allowing them to carry on like that. I mean, what's the point? It's not right to keep them going like that. Same with many of the disabled. I mean, why would you bother?

'I mean it when I say that I think I'm providing a service. I really think you and I are ahead of our time and I'm certain that the rest of society, and the world, will catch up with people like us. It's already happening and when our history comes to be written it will be people like us who will be the leading lights of our times. Children will be taught that for many centuries it was cruel to preserve spent human lives pointlessly and people like us will be praised for bravely putting an end to this torture. You'll see. And Octavia, darling, I have you to thank for helping to broaden my mind.'

Octavia drained her glass and began to dress hastily. 'You know, I think you're right about it already starting to happen, attitudes changing, I mean, especially at the top. The Government actually paid me to help to increase the numbers of patients dying on end-of-life pathways. You can't tell me that they don't know precisely what that involves … you know, hurrying things along, or stopping things, however pre-maturely—if you dared to do it—and it's been like that for twenty years.'

She buttoned up her blouse tight over her breasts.

'I've faithfully implemented the policies that the Whitehall bean-counters have devised, that's all I've done in my time, and what's it achieved? Empty beds and less misery, that's what. Everyone's a winner. It's a service, all right. But would I expect them to back me up if the tide turns, you know, if there was some kind of a backlash? Forget it. I've already had a taste of that.

'They'd still do you for it, you know, if you got caught. We'd be serial killers, mark my words, though I think we'd have to be really, really unlucky or incredibly stupid to get nicked. After all, real murders start with a body, or more than one, and then the police go hunting for the killer. It won't ever be like that for us.

No one is looking for a body because no one thinks that anyone has been killed.

'It means that if we stay in the closet, at least for now, we'll be okay. It's only going to go wrong if we were to make mistakes. That's what happened with Harold Shipman, my husband tells me. He let himself be caught—and I think he wanted to be caught so he could show off—and then they worked out just how many lives he'd taken. Officially, it was nearly three hundred but some old lag claimed Shipman told him he'd killed more than five hundred altogether.

'All the same, if you don't make mistakes, if you're careful, you can practise medicine with a degree of flexibility, shall we say, and no one will ever know—and once they change the law, we'll have little to worry about. It will be a complete doddle. But you should definitely be more careful.'

She fired a gargoyle stare at him. 'You got yourself into a mess with Ray Parker. That's not like you, Reinhard. And by the way,' she added, slipping on her shoes, 'I love my job. I couldn't scratch that old itch without it.'

Octavia left the room and Klein listened to her pace hurriedly along the corridor to the bathroom.

At that moment, his mobile phone rang and, too lazy to sit up, he bounced his hand about the bedside table until he located it.

'Oh, hello George, how you doing?' he said. 'Yes, I'm fine. To what do I owe the pleasure of a call from you on a Sunday?'

Fixing her curly long blonde hair and reapplying her make-up in the bathroom mirror, Octavia could tell that Klein had received some bad news. She heard him say 'you're kidding me' with exasperation in his voice followed by 'you've got to be joking' and then by such repeated denials as 'no, that can't be right' and 'I'm sure that's not true' before he went on the offensive, challenging the credulity of the caller.

'You don't really believe any of this, do you?' she heard him say, as she quietly re-entered the bedroom.

'I'm quite sure, Detective Inspector, that this is organised mischief and the Parker family are probably behind it,' he said. 'What, you've really got to do that? That's your job, is it? Sure it's not a waste of police time? Fair enough, George, give me a call later in the week, and I'll arrange a time when you can come in and meet for a chat. Of course, we need to clear this thing up. Thanks for the call, for the heads up, and no, don't worry, you haven't inconvenienced me in the slightest. Have a good evening.'

Dr Klein put down his phone and faced Octavia with a troubled expression.

'Was that who I think it was?' she asked cautiously.

'Yep, your blasted husband,' said the doctor angrily. 'He says a group of families have made formal complaints of homicide and criminal negligence, unlawful killing, all sorts of allegations against the hospital directly to the Chief Constable and his officers have no option but to investigate them. He wants to meet next week. He doesn't think it's going to go anywhere. But it's not good, is it?'

'No, it's not,' she snapped back. 'He was in a low mood after that inquest. You have no idea, Hardy, just how much I'm doing for you, so bear that in mind next time you raise your voice around me.'

Octavia left the room without another word, picked up her coat and bag and walked towards the front door. Klein followed her, pulling on his dressing gown.

'Tavy,' he said in an apologetic tone. 'Sorry about that. Let's not worry about it. It was great today. We've got to meet up again soon, and we should definitely try to fix up another date for the moors. It's a good idea. Let's stay in touch.'

Mollified, she offered him her cheek and he kissed her gently. 'You're right, you'd better be getting back. He'll be wondering where you are.' He opened the door.

Octavia returned his smile and stepped on to the garden path. She whirled towards him, lifting her arms as if brandishing a firearm in his direction. 'Kaboom!' she said, firing off an imaginary bullet into his forehead. 'See you soon. Be careful now.'

'Weirdo,' muttered Klein, shaking his head with a dismissive sigh as he closed the door behind her.

9

THE DECLINE OF BETTY MAY

The missing notes from Ray Parker's file were exactly where Emerald had left them, to her relief. Infuriated by the ruling of the coroner, she had rooted about for them in the week following the inquest and found them in the correct filing cabinet but at the rear of the compartment, tucked among a growing sheaf of loose and unrelated documents for which no one seemed to want to take responsibility.

Many times she was tempted to hand them to Detective Inspector Tarleton herself, or to call him anonymously and tell them where they were, or photocopy them and send them in. But she had lost some of her confidence in the will of the police to act resolutely in the Parker case after she concluded, both from her own knowledge of Parker's death and from the press reports, that Tarleton had already failed to investigate diligently the full circumstances.

So she bided her time, while she ruminated over what the detective would do with the records, if anything. She suspected he might even simply hand them back to Dr Klein. It was a prospect she found painful to contemplate, but a mental image of the doctor and another self-regarding man in his mid to late thirties exchanging appreciative quips about an 'inside job' as the brown envelope changed hands formed readily, with the realisation that Klein would soon come looking for the leak.

Yet she was not willing to let the opportunity pass. Emerald reasoned that if the police were not wholly corrupt, or otherwise compromised, surely their intervention could be obtained by persuading—or compelling—them to do their job properly and by holding them to account if they didn't.

That was the point at which she decided that the Parker records would be most fruitful in the hands of a sympathetic journalist, since she doubted that police officers would be quite so slack under the gaze of the public.

It had been about three weeks since Emerald had returned the records to their correct file, checking occasionally to see if they had been moved again. She waited late into her evening shift on the orthopaedic ward before she ventured to the records office, choosing the quietest time of the night to stroll across with an assortment of files in one arm.

She tapped in the passcode and let herself in, glancing around to make sure that no one else was there. She went straight to Parker's file, finding no sign that it had been tampered with since her last inspection. She drew out the disputed documents and laid them on a table to her left. There they were—each of them opening with the printed name of Dr Reinhard Klein.

The first of the forms was dated September 10 and recorded a review of Parker's condition based on his tests, including a CT scan and an MRI scan, to demonstrate he was afflicted by advanced cancer of the lungs and throat among other ailments. Klein had circled an option to say he was the treating consultant.

The second document was dated September 11 and recorded in detail the meeting between the Parkers and Dr Klein at which Emerald was present.

'Informed family of advanced inoperable lung cancer and discussed end-of-life-care options,' the note said in the doctor's unmistakeable baroque hand-writing above his signature.

Emerald switched on the photocopier, and while it clicked and whirred into action she put away the files she had brought with her. Then she pulled out an old mobile phone—not her usual device—and photographed the Parker documents, before running them through the photocopier. She folded the copies and tucked them in a pocket of her trousers. She turned off the copier, put the original documents back in the file and returned it to the cabinet. Then, without a sound, she left the office, hearing the door click behind her as she went back down the corridor.

Klein must have chosen neither to destroy nor totally remove the documents, Emerald reckoned. Perhaps he wished to leave them where he could argue they had been placed accidentally. Was that, she wondered, because he was afraid she might break her silence about his meeting with the Parkers?

Better to argue that he had forgotten about the meeting in the midst of the manifold daily duties of a leading doctor in a busy hospital and in the absence of unfortunately misplaced supporting documents than to be suspected of shredding or hiding such evidence. But did that suggest he had factored in a possible betrayal—that he didn't trust her, that he saw her as a risk, a liability? Would that lack of trust place her in danger?

With such thoughts somersaulting through her mind, she returned to the orthopaedic ward, now relatively tranquil since the last of the visitors had departed.

In the first bed lay Betty May, a woman in her late seventies admitted to Bethulia Park after cracking her pelvis in a fall that morning. She lay in a stupor, just as still as when her anxious daughter had gently shaken her by the shoulder when she visited some hours previously.

The daughter was accompanied by her two boys, who were hoping to cheer up their grandmother with crayon drawings—including one scene from *Strictly Come Dancing*, her favourite TV programme—which they had made for her. The children were upset to see her as unresponsive and inert as a waxwork. They were disappointed that she did not wake to fuss over them or praise them and reward them for their endeavours. They became bored and restless when they found themselves with nothing to do. In spite of their mother's resolve to remain at the bedside for the full duration of visiting time, the three went home much earlier as the exhausted woman gave up trying to control her sons, downbeat and defeated.

Emerald stood at the foot of Betty May's bed while flicking through her charts and listening to her deep, rasping, laboured breathing.

When she came to the word 'midazolam', she looked again at the patient, this time noting that beside a full, untouched glass of water was an inhaler. So Betty has breathing difficulties, she thought.

Emerald knew that no one was going to wake up to a tender shake when they were being given such powerful sedatives as midazolam in conjunction with morphine.

She knew that, unable to drink for herself, it was likely that soon Betty would receive fluids via an intravenous line. She knew that Betty would deteriorate through lack of food and fluid even before the bags were put up because she was already not receiving enough. She knew that as her condition worsened there would be condescending discussions with Betty's next of kin about her 'quality of life', and her family would be asked to confront the reality that she might be dying.

Such deterioration would be apparent to her loved ones who would grow anxious at the sight of Betty too drowsy to drink. They might insist that feeding tubes were inserted without delay. But only the truly vigilant would ensure that the intravenous bag was not deliberately set to run so slowly that it made little difference to the deadly process of dehydration.

The upshot would be that the patient would weaken to the point that doctors would assert that death was imminent. Intravenous feeding would be removed on the grounds it was unnecessary in such a patient, that the body was shutting down and fluids were superfluous or potentially harmful. Midazolam and morphine would continue to be administered via a syringe driver, perhaps in dangerously high doses.

Alone such drugs could be potent enough to cause death, but they made it a certainty when combined with the removal of fluids. Without fluids, every patient will die. It is axiomatic, there is no mystery to it. But those who are already elderly, sick and debilitated seldom last very long, most expiring within thirty-six hours of the withdrawal of their tubes.

Emerald put down Betty's notes and looked up 'midazolam and NICE' on her phone, seeking to check what the National Institute for Health and Care Excellence had to say about the drug. She found the reference then scrolled down to 'contra-indications'. She saw that midazolam could compromise airways and cause 'severe respiratory depression' in people with weak lungs or diminished capacity. A bad drug for Betty May.

The direction of travel for this patient was glaringly obvious to the nurse, though probably not yet to Betty's family, with their eyes still clouded by hope and trust in the system and in the medical profession. It would take a miracle for Betty to leave the hospital alive. Emerald knew that. Klein knew it. The family would discover it only later.

When it came to the dark art of the involuntary euthanasia of patients who were not dying, Emerald believed there was no one quite so skilled, ruthless or prolific as Dr Klein.

He had no equal: he was king. But in the death of Ray Parker he had been reckless, and had given his former lover—and a woman he had abused—a chance to act.

10

THE FIFTH BEATLE

Calvin watched the seagulls dive and bob on the wind as he stood in front of Andy Edwards's bronze sculpture of the Beatles on the Pier Head in Liverpool, waiting for 'Judith'.

His encounter with her in Tesco the previous Monday had been brief and, to him, needlessly and comically cloak-and-dagger. She said, 'Got them!' with open-eyed emphasis as she took the case of wine from him, and he replied 'Good, Beatles statue in Liverpool 3.45 on Thursday, if you can make it.' She nodded and hurried off. So overboard, he thought. Next time he would suggest they communicated by carrier pigeon.

As he waited, he turned his thoughts to the deeply satisfying meeting with the diocesan archivist that morning, exulting in the joy of his acceptance as part of the historical research team. Calvin had graduated with a first in History from the University of Liverpool and the subject remained very much his passion. His appointment meant the archdiocese had not only recognised his capabilities but was investing in them. It might well represent a first step in his rise to the office of diocesan archivist, the archbishop's official historian. That afternoon, with the moist sea air blowing in from the Mersey estuary, and the seagulls calling all around him, his mood could not have been more upbeat.

Turning to look at the Fab Four, frozen in that moment early in their career when they were leaving their home city to conquer the world, he felt, in his jubilation, strangely united with them, like a fifth member strolling toward limitless horizons.

He spotted Emerald coming towards him from the direction of the Royal Liver Building, which surprised him a little because he was expecting her to appear from the scenic riverside walk from the Albert Dock.

Her head was bowed and she moved quickly, as if she was in a rush, glancing furtively at passers-by. It dawned on Calvin that she must be nervous, careful about being seen by someone who might gossip about her. He zipped up his jacket over his clerical collar, ready to apologise for bringing her to a tourist attraction.

As they came face to face, her first smile at the priest conveyed warmth and vulnerability. She was every bit as stunning as he had expected her to be. He felt love for her. Drawn by her delicacy, by the sense that she was unique, he stifled his basest passions and told himself he desired only to protect her.

'Hi!' they said almost simultaneously. Emerald pulled up the fur collar of her coat to protect her neck from the bite of the breeze.

'If you're worried about being seen with me,' he said, 'we could go and have a coffee somewhere quiet and I'm also happy to give you a lift home. I assume it wouldn't be too far out of my way. It would give us a chance to talk.'

'I live in Wigan. Why don't we go and have something stronger?' she said. 'Where are you parked?'

They decided to walk up Dale Street towards the Queen's Square multi-storey car park where Calvin had left his Peugeot.

First, Emerald insisted on having a long look at the statue of the city's most famous sons, which she was seeing for the first time.

'I love the Beatles,' she said. 'Can you take a picture of me with them on my phone?'

'There you go, you tourist,' said Calvin, handing her back the device. 'It's great, isn't it? What I like best are the little symbols that the sculptor has included.'

He bent to show Emerald the L8 postcode on the sole of Ringo Starr's foot and the Indian mantra on George Harrison's belt. Then he pointed out the acorns carried by John Lennon as a symbol of world peace and the camera in Paul McCartney's hand, a reference to his marriage to Linda. He explained how the only hands visible were McCartney's left and Lennon's right, the ones they used to play their guitars.

'How do you know about all this?' asked Emerald, impressed.

'You wouldn't believe it,' said Calvin. 'Last year we had this national Eucharistic congress, just over at the Echo Arena, and I was asked to show a visiting cardinal from America around so I had to brush up on facts about public landmarks and so on. Anyway, he was dead interested in the role of Liverpool in the transatlantic slave trade and in the migration of the Irish to America after the Famine, but you should have seen him when we got to this statue. He was like a kid—ecstatic—sending selfies to his sisters and mates back in the States. I was struggling to get him away in the end.

'Mind you, I shouldn't be all that surprised. I've lost count the amount of times when I was growing up in London and was asked by visitors, pen pals, whoever, to take them to Abbey Road. Tower of London? British Museum? Nah, Abbey Road. It has to be the most photographed zebra crossing in the world. I'm sick of the sight of it.'

They walked down to The Strand, intending to cross over to Water Street. 'So, your cardinal wasn't bothered by Lennon's remark that the Beatles were more popular than Jesus, then?' asked Emerald.

'Evidently not. I discussed it with him and he took the view that Lennon didn't always choose his words wisely, and might not have meant that anyway. There must be some truth in that.

He tried to explain himself afterwards, but it just didn't stick in the United States, did it? The damage was already done. I see your point, though, and personally, I think *Imagine* is just daft.'

'What, you're joking me!' said Emerald. 'It's like a hymn, isn't it? He says all that stuff about equality and peace!'

She stopped and looked him in the face. 'Oh—I know why you don't like it.'

'Yeah, I find it a bit chilling, just as utopian any of the major ideologies of the 20th century, none of which was good,' replied Calvin, trying to hold firm. 'Lennon might have later changed his mind about some of the things he said, matured a bit. But we'll never know, sadly.'

They began walking again but Emerald was quiet. Calvin was worried that he had offended her.

'The point I'm making is that, in that famous Maureen Cleave interview in the Evening Standard, all Lennon was doing was predicting the decline of the Christianity in the West,' he said.

'It was just an observation. McCartney said the same thing— that the Church would diminish as it continued to lose relevance until, in the end, 'no one was saved'—remember *Eleanor Rigby*? But he was a bit more circumspect so he didn't cause the same fuss. In a way, he was right, the Church had to adapt. That's why we've got the 'new evangelisation', and that's what I'm all about.'

Emerald looked thoughtfully at Calvin and wondered if he was ahead of his time, like some kind of visionary, or trailing way behind it, an anachronism clinging to the idyll of a golden age which never was. 'What about that one there?' she said, pointing to *The Excelsior*.

It was a pub Calvin remembered from his student days. A decade later he found it hadn't changed a bit: shabby-chic furniture, polished oak parquet floorboards, a high ceiling creating a cavernous space and huge windows allowing buckets of light to flood in. He had often imagined the pub in its Victorian heyday and how beautiful it would have been filled with smoke, twisting in golden and silver plumes like incense rising to heaven in some Roman basilica.

He leaned on the bar, waiting to order a lime and soda for himself and a large wine and soda for Emerald, and began to reflect how he had changed personally all the while this lovely old building stood still.

Being there reminded him of some of the earliest and clumsiest parts of an interior journey on which he was still travelling. Back then, he had one foot in the new Jerusalem and the other dragging in the gutter.

His religious awakening was progressing rapidly during his time at university, making him the butt of the jokes of the fellow students who for a while continued to be his friends. They could not understand why a young man who was tall, blond and built like an athlete did not share their enthusiasm for hedonistic pursuits, especially since he could have surely exploited his natural gifts to glorious effect.

They marvelled that he was so evidently shy in the company of women, and were perplexed that he never seemed to want a girlfriend. When he admitted his virginity, some almost wept with laughter. They gave him the nickname 'Nonny' and taunted him relentlessly.

A lot of the time they pretended he was either gay or obsessed with pleasuring himself. He took their ribbing in good humour. It would usually start in a place like this pub, with the first or second pint of the night, as they were settling down. Typically, one of his companions would address him with a statement like: 'It will fall off, you know …'

'What will fall off?' he would ask.

The assembled company would roll about, collapsing into a contagion of ribaldry and bawdy jokes as they deployed the most comical euphemisms of the day to accuse him of an addiction to onanism.

'No, really, you ought to get yourself a girlfriend,' he'd hear as he blushed uncontrollably and their laughs descended into tearful, red-faced titters.

At that time, he tried to join the fun. He took their jibes on the chin, and compromised as much as he could, though daring not to admit to the raucous party that he never masturbated. That would be worse. It would have surely opened up a whole new seam of comic put-downs that would run for months. They would never have understood him if he had tried to explain to them that he had accomplished self-mastery over his passions by his early teens and that he believed he reigned as king over his body. It would have marked him out as a complete weirdo. Better to be called Nonny than the other names they might dream up for him if he came out with a line like that. It would be different now, of course. He would perceive any suggestion that he was anything less than chaste as an insult and would openly confess what he really thought of autoerotic behaviour: that it was a sin, an aberration. The one constant would be their wholly negative attitude to him and to what he stood for.

Calvin carefully navigated an archipelago of unoccupied stools, tables and benches, drinks in hand. Emerald had taken her coat off to reveal a cream woollen sweater following the curves of her breasts, tight jeans and heeled knee-length brown boots which made her legs appear even longer. She thanked him, took a sip then asked him to mind her bags and coat while she visited the ladies'. She stopped at the juke box on the way back and returned beaming while the sound of *Mind Games* filled the room.

'Now you'd better not tell me you don't like this,' she warned the priest.

'No, this one's okay,' he said, keen to appease her. As Lennon crooned out the words, 'Love is the answer, you know that for sure!' he nearly allowed himself to believe he was being sincere. Compromising again.

'Okay, in that case you can have the documents,' said Emerald, reaching for her bag. 'You'll make sure they'll reach that journalist, won't you? Don't show them to anyone else and don't reveal me as your source. But you can tell Jenny Bradshaigh that if the police ask her where the originals are, she can tell them to look in the Parker file. That's where I've left them.'

Calvin slid the envelope into the inside pocket of his jacket. 'I'll see Jenny on Tuesday. I'm marrying her—not like that—so she's coming round to discuss possible dates, that sort of thing. This will be a nice surprise for her.'

Emerald seemed relaxed so Calvin thought he could try changing the subject.

'So, you don't sound like you're from Wigan. If I'm not mistaken you sound a little bit like a London girl.'

'Correct, I'm not from Wigan,' she replied. 'I'm a bit of a mix. My mum's from Manchester, and my dad's French. They met in London when she was modelling there. He had a good job with a multi-national, and they fell in love, got married and settled in Chiswick, bought a house there. That's where we—me and my sisters—spent the early part of our childhood before my mum dragged us up North.

'I spent my teenage years trying to fake a northern accent so I could fit in, but never quite managed it. You're a Londoner too, aren't you?'

'Through and through. Grew up in Kilburn. Queens Park Rangers. What's your team?'

'Fulham—it didn't impress very much in the south Manchester secondary I ended up in, I can tell you.'

'So why did you move?'

'Mum and dad divorced. My dad was really good when we were kids but he was offered promotion that took him to Berlin and my mum didn't want to go—I think even London was too exotic for her—so they fought like cats then he went without her. He would come home regularly at first, and then less regularly after a while. Finally he stopped altogether and my mum told us in the end that he had a German girlfriend who was expecting a baby. It broke my heart.'

Calvin nodded sympathetically.

'That's when I stopped being a Catholic—after one Christmas when I was Mary in the school play and he didn't show up to watch me. He disappeared and all I got was uncle after uncle after uncle in a place I never got used to calling home. I got in with a bad crowd for a while but I went back to London at the first real chance that came along and worked at the Royal Free straight after my nursing degree.'

'Yeah, I know it.'

'Yet here I am again, bizarrely. I had some great years away but most of my friends moved on, and quite a few went abroad, places like Florida and Australia. I was tempted but, if the truth be told, I didn't want to leave my mum. So I ended up at Bethulia Park, out of sheer convenience. I know the area very well, so it's not a massive culture shock to me to be back here again.'

'How old are you?' inquired Calvin.

'Nearly twenty-eight,' she replied. 'I suppose I shouldn't be single by now, but I've been a bit unlucky and I've made a few mistakes. You know all my secrets anyway.'

'Your secrets? I don't even know your name.'

'It's not really Judith.'

'Why did you choose that? Is it because you're beautiful?' asked the priest before he could check himself.

He stared at the dregs at the bottom of the glass. Not bad going for just a lime and soda, he thought.

'What?' said Emerald.

'In the Bible, Judith was an exquisitely beautiful woman who saved the Israelites from annihilation. Did you know that?'

'No, I didn't know that. I plucked the name from thin air. I have absolutely no idea why I chose it.'

Seizing on his barely concealed embarrassment she decided to play with him. 'Father—or can I call you Calvin?—are you saying that you think I'm beautiful?'

'Well, you are beautiful,' he stammered helplessly. 'Sorry, I shouldn't have said that. I just thought it was obvious to everyone.'

The nurse leaned back and sat up, her sweater clinging to the undulations of her upper body. 'Don't worry, I take it as a compliment,' she said, setting down her empty glass. 'Shall we have another?'

Emerald wasn't usually attracted to men who thought they were good. But for some reason Calvin was different and as she sat opposite him, sipping her second generous wine and soda, she was trying to work out why she fancied him. It wasn't just his appearance, which obviously she liked. That was not a deal-breaker. She had suffered no shortage of good-looking men who had taken an interest in her. Many had let her down, turning out to be untrustworthy, vain or worst of all, boring; at least short or less attractive men would try to make her laugh or go the extra mile to make her feel special.

Fleetingly, she entertained the idea that she might be drawn to the priest because of his office, then brushed off the notion of being turned on by a clerical collar as simply ludicrous, and a bit perverted. Forbidden fruit. Then she recognised there was something about his goodness that appealed to her. She saw a childlike naivety in him, a freshness and an innocence she had seldom seen in men. As they talked, he listened to her attentively and respectfully, truly interested in what she had to say, and without judgement. His sincerity not only made it easy for her to open up to him, but left her fighting against the impulse to reveal to him facts about her past and the secrets of her innermost thoughts. Emerald felt she could have talked to him about anything. She felt him a soulmate.

He was so unmarked by emotional and ideological baggage, by the scars of heartbreak or rejection, or by the hardness and cruelty that comes from mistreating others. On the contrary, he exuded a sense of goodwill. It contrasted with the jaded cynicism of so many of the men she dated. Here was a person who carried hope in the better nature of humankind. How could he be so unspoilt?

'Are you a virgin?' she asked abruptly.

'Oh, don't you start as well,' he groaned. 'It must be something about this pub.'

'What do you mean?' she asked with a curious expression.

'In my student days I was the butt of quite a lot of jokes because I was—I am—a virgin, and a lot of the time it was when I was drinking with my friends here. Before you ask, no, it's not because I have sexual vices of any kind that makes me not like women—nothing like that.'

'So you're celibate? Don't you find it difficult, though?'

'Yes, I do. It's a daily challenge, but celibacy is something I've felt called to since my teenage years. It's one of the reasons I came to realise I had a vocation to the priesthood. It wasn't easy growing up with these convictions, and realising I was meant to be a priest was, in the end, liberating. Funny thing was, I decided to be a priest even before I became a Catholic. It usually happens the other way round.

'It was a rough ride, all the way through. Even my parents, they went ballistic. My old man's really Protestant, you know. More Glasgow Rangers than Queens Park Rangers in some ways. He wouldn't talk to me for months. Sometimes I think it would have been a bit easier if I was gay and came home with a boyfriend than to tell them I was going over to Rome. It was like a bereavement for them. They're okay now though.'

'How can you accept all that stuff the Church teaches about sex before marriage?' asked Emerald, frowning, 'and about the ban on contraception? Are you going to tell me you support that? It's bollocks.'

'I don't see things in terms of "bans'" but in the proposal of a better way, the one that results in the maximum of human flourishing,' said Calvin, straining to be as diplomatic as possible. He had been tested like this many times before. 'If you choose one particular route, then you can't follow the others, can you? And if you become aware that one route is superior to all the others, then it stands to reason that you follow it to the exclusion of the others, even if it is tough.'

Emerald was not smiling. 'I'm sure the rhythm method is very tough, but I'm not so sure it creates human flourishing—unless you're into big families. It doesn't sound like a lot of fun to me.'

Calvin came back at her quickly. 'The Church doesn't teach the rhythm method, that's a myth. Since the Sixties, there has been lots of research into new methods, which are easy to use, reliable, free and lacking medical side effects. Of course, Big Pharma doesn't want you to know about that. But more importantly, they allow couples to make the total and uninhibited gift of the self to the other—and that is what love is about, that's what the nature of God is.

'I'm convinced they're the key to the renewal of marriage and family life, and that's my interest. I want people to have happy marriages.'

'Okay, but what about all the single ladies?' asked Emerald. 'What if I'm out with my girls, clubbing,' she went on, simulating seductive dance moves from her seated position, 'and we're all sweaty on the dancefloor and a really fit guy comes over, all pumped, tanned and ripped, drop-dead gorgeous and wearing the latest drippy togs, lovely smile on his face, nice tattoos, and we start to get along, then I can't always rely on natural family planning if things moved on a bit a few hours later, can I?'

'No, not unless you've learned it weeks in advance, in the anticipation that you want to crack off with a total stranger. The

Church doesn't give advice on one-night stands other than to avoid them.'

'Thought so,' she said, dropping her smile. 'Then it ain't gonna work for everyone then, your natural family planning, is it?'

Calvin had the uncomfortable sense that a gulf was opening between them. 'Look,' he said, 'to me the difference is like someone with a gift for football having a spontaneous kickabout in the park with their mates, jumpers for goalposts and all that, which can be a lot of fun, or aspiring to play at their best in the Premier League, which has to be infinitely more rewarding.

'Most people don't realise it, but they are called to marriage—it's a noble and rewarding vocation—but they don't bother or it goes wrong when they do, and they give up on it. I want people to have happy marriages, that's all.'

'And to do that you've got to go bareback?' said Emerald, laughing as she tormented him, amused at her own vulgarity.

Then she sensed his awkwardness and realised that he was no match for her banter.

'Look, I've been married,' she said softly, 'I'm sorry to tell you it wasn't top of my must-do list. Mind you, it was only for three weeks, but you could say it lasted for life. I'm a widow. Actually, I like it that you care so much.'

Calvin's jaw dropped. 'A widow!' he said.

'Do you know what? Isn't it Aintree this week? It's the Grand National on Saturday, isn't it? We're going to get caught in racing traffic. I think we should stay for another.'

'Okay, but not in this pub. There's something about this place that seems to make people grill me about sex.'

They decided to head closer to the car park and arrived at *Doctor Duncan's*, an elaborately-tiled Edwardian pub occupying the former Pearl Insurance building, looking on to St John's Gardens and the cavernous mouth of the Mersey Tunnel leading out of the city to Birkenhead. The pub was largely empty but starting to fill up.

Calvin again refused an alcoholic drink while Emerald was beginning to feel a little warmer inside and slightly light-headed.

Their conversation turned back to Bethulia Park Hospital and to Jenny. Emerald was curious to know all about her—whether she was reliable.

The priest assured her the journalist was 'good news' and that she could be trusted. Drawing out his wallet, he pushed Jenny's business card across the table. 'You may as well have that in case you want to call her directly yourself,' he told Emerald. 'I've already made a note of her contact details. She's got a website anyway.'

As Emerald continued to drink, she volunteered more about her life, disarmed by her trust in the priest.

What she did not realise was that she was disarming him too. He was thoroughly enjoying her company, though their intimacy made him a little uncomfortable. This was a situation he had neither wished nor intended, and might have consciously avoided. A pub crawl was never on his mind.

Frequently she revealed the depth of her frustration about her job, at how her professional and personal integrity was being compromised by her participation, both passive and active, in acts she knew were wrong.

Calvin went along with her when she opened up, trying the best he could to understand, guide and support her. He could not stop being a priest, and did not wish to try.

He imparted the opinion that Emerald was being troubled by the voice of her conscience, the whisper of truth in her heart, what Cardinal John Henry Newman, his hero, once called the 'guide of life, implanted in our nature, discriminating right from wrong' in concrete situations. Though he did not say so, he could see in Emerald the living proof of Newman's teachings that conscience was 'severe and even stern', that it spoke not of 'forgiveness but of punishment'. It suggested 'a future judgement' to the person who dared to listen to its voice, though 'it does not tell him how he can avoid it'.

He pitied Emerald but he admired her too. It took guts to follow your conscience. It was something he knew only too well himself.

Emerald, for her part, was starting to recognise what she found so attractive about Calvin.

The fact that he was counter-cultural strangely gave him the bit of edge that had drawn her to other rebellious men. He was an oddity, yes, but she saw a person who was as brave as he was principled. They were qualities she found desirable in anyone. In spite of this celibacy thing, Calvin was fully man, not part weasel.

Emerald took her time with her final drink. They hoped that the majority of the racing and rush hour traffic had gone before them, but found themselves crawling along the streets of north Liverpool to the motorway.

They had been in the car together for more than an hour by the time they reached the exit slip road, just twenty miles away, with Emerald enduring something of a sermon on beauty as Calvin tried to recover from his faux pas earlier that afternoon

He was going on about the 'beauty of the soul', and telling Emerald about how he wished to visit a shrine in Wales where a Jesuit priest had written a fantastic poem about a woman who sounded notes of despair at a well there over the loss of beauty with advancing age only to hear another voice suggesting the cultivation of a different kind of beauty, an inner spiritual beauty which would never fade and die. Emerald felt her eyes stinging and beginning to close.

'Father, you don't have to feel bad just because you said I was beautiful,' she said in the end, slightly worn out, as the priest pulled up outside her apartment block. 'I really liked it,' she said. 'I also liked the stuff you said about bareback too. It sounds like lots of fun. I'd like to give it a go someday—er, I don't mean with you. What I mean to say is I'll try anything once. That sounds worse, doesn't it? I'm sorry.'

They laughed. Then Calvin looked nervously at Emerald.

'Thanks for the documents, you've been very courageous,' he said. 'I know they're going to make an enormous difference. I still don't know your name.'

Without answering, she leaned into him and kissed him gently on the mouth as he sat frozen, stunned. She pressed down on his thigh with her hand. 'I'll tell you next time,' she said, smiling. 'Thanks for everything, I've had a lovely day.'

The kiss was brief but a sudden and ecstatic warmth flooded Calvin's entire body at the touch and smell of her skin, and at the softness and moisture of her lips. It lit him up inside, as if she had run a magical finger across his soul and filled it with colour.

She got out of the car. Calvin looked straight ahead. At the back of his mind, he heard an echo of the taunts from years ago: 'You ought to get yourself a girlfriend ...'

He drove away with the sense of experiencing a very near miss, a brush with extreme risk.

The attraction of trouble, he knew, was another weakness for him. He was a little boy at a bonfire, enchanted by the glow and mystery of the flames, knowing the danger yet unable to stop himself from taking that extra step closer.

He was not having a very successful Lent.

Part II

Quod Scripsi, Scripsi
(What I have written, I have written)

Pontius Pilate

11

BREAKING THE STORY

After Jenny's newspaper report about the meeting at the Parkers' house, more families got in touch. She interviewed seven relatives who had lodged formal complaints with Lancashire police about the deaths of their loved ones at Bethulia Park Hospital, photographed them and collected pictures of the patients whose deaths had caused them such anger, upset and consternation. It was turning into a formidable dossier.

It was greatly strengthened by the Parker documents which Calvin handed over when she and Seb went to the presbytery to discuss plans for their marriage.

Calvin told her that he had received them from 'a contact' and emphasised his source's belief that Dr Klein was a serial killer.

'What he does is he dehydrates his patients to death,' said the priest. 'That's what the contact told me. They're not always his sickest patients either, apparently. This fellow uses a multitude of tricks to break down the health of a patient he has singled out so he can bring them to that point when the withdrawal of fluids seems not only a defensible but a sensible medical course of action. It's classed as treatment nowadays, food and fluid, you see.

'The contact says that people who are difficult to manage—the so-called "nuisance patients"—or those who don't have visitors are particularly vulnerable to the predations of this man.

'My contact said he does strange things with certain drugs and medicines. The contact said if drugs are—what's the phrase?—"contra-indicated" in patients with certain conditions, then often he'll use them, or dabble with their dosage, to make those patients more ill than they would be normally. It's horrible, isn't it? Really sinister. Families don't always get it because they seldom know one drug or medicine from another, let alone anything about the dosage. I certainly wouldn't.'

Listening to Calvin, Jenny was just as interested in visualising 'the contact' as she was in the *modus operandi* of Dr Klein. She was greedy for clues, but he was refusing to throw her the smallest of crumbs.

'So who's "the contact" then, Father Calvin?' she said. 'Are you going to tell me, or what? Please put me out of my misery.'

'No. The contact promised that I had to protect his or her identity at all times.'

'If you're that protective, my guess is that the contact is a woman. Is it that nurse Mrs Parker wanted to you to look for? C'mon, tell me.'

'I can't tell you anything, I really can't. Except that I did not find the contact. The contact found me. I can also tell you this: I don't know who the contact is. The person would not give me his or her name.'

'Wow! So are we sure these documents are real? I'd hate to be set up by someone planning revenge or a stunt of some sort.'

'Oh, they're definitely real,' said the priest. 'I'll let you in on another secret. I've met the contact. I know that the contact is reliable and that these copies are therefore authentic.'

Jenny nodded slowly, raising her eyebrows as she looked over at Seb, who was playing on his phone and did not catch her glance. He wasn't listening.

'Okay, so let me carry on about Klein,' said Calvin. 'The contact thinks you need to know a few other things.

'Once selected by Dr Klein for the death pathway, a patient's demise is a near certainty. By predicting death and then acting in a way which guarantees such an outcome, he always proves himself accurate in his prognoses—that's what the contact told me. It didn't matter if you are a stroke patient or have a degenerative disease, a broken leg, bed sores, pneumonia, whatever, if Dr Klein predicts you are going to die that is what will happen to you. This man holds power of life or death, like he's a god, so I'm told, and somehow he's found a way of doing it without being found out or being outed by his colleagues.'

'Your contact is on the inside, obviously, or you wouldn't know this in such detail,' remarked Jenny.

Calvin put a forefinger to his lips.

'Occasionally things can become awkward, so I'm told, like when families refuse to allow feeding tubes to be removed, or when a patient stubbornly hangs on to life. When that happens, he's suddenly in a bit of a spot, and he hates it.

'Incidentally, this point I know to be true from experience— I've seen it with my own eyes on several occasions. I've also witnessed patients crying for a drink through crusted lips as I've been doing the rounds late at night. So she's not lying about that. Nor are the Parkers, I'm sure of it.'

'She!' said the journalist. 'So it's a woman and she's on the inside. I'll have her mother's maiden name by the time I've finished with you, Father. This is getting easier now. Please carry on.'

Calvin ignored her. 'Surprisingly few relatives complain, though,' he said. 'It's strange, isn't it? Many are confused by what they see, or they are divided among themselves over the morality of the treatment—I've seen that too—and more than a few tacitly agree that the patient is better off dead, especially if there's an inheritance to be had. Some families are awful, believe me. Where there's a will, there's a relative.

'Then if you throw into the mix the possibility that the patient may be dying anyway, what does it matter? I suspect that's why the police don't seem terribly upset at what they're hearing—like that detective at the inquest. My bet is they think these people are on the way out anyway, and that families don't always understand what is happening in these cases. But what if the patients aren't always dying and the doctors don't always act in good faith? That's the question the contact raised. What if they would survive and go home if only they received good or even basic care?'

Jenny said: 'None of this explains what Dr Klein is getting out of it or how he is getting away with it. If he was doing it on his own he'd stick out like a sore thumb, surely. So what is it? Do they just let him crack on with it or is he in some sort of death cult that the rest of them are part of too? Are they all at it? It just doesn't add up.'

'The contact did explain a bit of that—it's sort of an abuse or a manipulation of the collegiality that they exercise—but I can't confidently tell you how it works. And on that note, I'm going to have to say that I'm glad to have done my bit but I'm going to wash my hands of all this from now on. This stuff isn't for me.'

'So at the moment there is no way of showing Dr Klein is a murderer,' said Jenny. 'We definitely can't accuse him of anything like that.'

'My contact says he is a murderer.'

Jenny yawned. She had heard the words "my contact" a few too many times for her liking.

'Tell us about your meeting with "the contact". It's intriguing.'
Calvin was silent.

'What happened? What's the contact like? Can I meet her?'

'Yes, she will be in touch with you directly next time,' he answered. 'I'm done with all of this. It's not for me—I'm a priest. She—the contact—will come straight to you from now on.'

The message was growing more unambiguous by the second:
Leave me out of it.

Reluctantly, Jenny accepted that she would get no further.
After a short silence they moved on to the wedding, and Seb
came alive again, joining the conversation for the first time as
they began to discuss their options.

The couple had plumped for the end of September if the
church was available. It would give them under six months to
organise the event, including marriage preparation courses, hen
and stag parties and a honeymoon, but they were confident they
could meet the challenge.

The priest, who moments earlier was on the verge of being
sullen, was cheerful as he pencilled Saturday September 28 into
his diary. 'Marriage is such a beautiful thing,' he told the couple.

Then he changed his tone as he began his first session of
instruction, warning the couple that they must not see marriage
as a way of mending problems in a relationship. 'If one of you
gambles, marriage will make the problem worse not better; if
one of you has a propensity for violence—hits the other—this
problem will not go away with marriage, it will get worse; if one
of you drinks heavily or uses drugs, marriage won't fix that but
is likely to make it worse. Do you understand me?'

They nodded.

'There's nothing in our relationship like that, I'm pleased to
say,' said Seb. 'What do you tell those people who have these kind
of problems, just out of curiosity?'

'I tell them that they mustn't be afraid to call the marriage
off,' the priest replied instantly. 'There is no greater commitment
you will ever make than marriage, and there is no greater responsibility than raising a child. You mustn't take these things lightly.'

Returning home, Jenny wasted no time in ringing Ralph Parker
to tell him that she had obtained the crucial documents.

Ralph sent a letter outlining his complaint to the police by registered post the next day, and by Thursday Jenny was ready to pitch the story to the national Press.

She sent an email to Ben Stanley, the news editor of the *Sunday News*, with 'Jenny Bradshaigh EXCLUSIVE', in the subject line. She made her proposal concise, knowing she had only a matter of seconds to grab his attention.

It did the trick. Within moments her former colleague was on the phone, wanting to know more about the story ahead of the editor's morning conference to talk through potential stories and features as planning entered its final stages.

'Hi Jen, Ben Stanley here. How you doin'? Look, I like the sound of this. Eight families, is that right? And it's all stood up, they're all on the record, pictures, everything? The boss is interested in this sort of stuff so I'm goin' to list it.'

'Thanks Ben, that's right, yeah. They're all pretty plausible to me, pretty keen to co-operate. They think the police aren't going to take them seriously so they want the publicity. I was hoping the editor would go for it. I remember him being quite big on this kind of thing when I was working for you. You've seen my note about the leaked documents too? Someone on the inside went to great lengths to get those to us.'

'I saw that, yes. Well done. Can you email them to me right away so I can take them into conference? Boss might want to see them for himself. These documents show a doctor lied at the inquest and it possibly swayed the decision of the coroner. That's right, isn't it? What's going on there, Jen? Is it dreadful care or, you know, is there more to it than that?'

'I can't say for certain and I don't want to promise what I can't deliver, but I'm trying to get to the bottom of it. I think this story might run and this is a good Day One. I'll give you everything I've got.'

'There's quite a lot already, I can see that. Cheers, Jen. It looks a cracker. I'll make sure you get paid properly for this, don't you worry, if the boss goes for it, which I think he will. Hey, and don't forget to give me a buzz next time you're down. Let's go for a coffee.'

The news editor abruptly hung up—no doubt, thought Jenny, to give another minute of his full attention to the next potential story on his list, and then the next. But he called her again two hours later to confirm the editor was keen on her proposal and would allocate the space to the story that it merited on Sunday.

In the three days that followed Jenny worked hard from her spare bedroom converted into an office, striving to deliver every scrap of information which the newspaper required to run the story about the complaints of the families as a 'special investigation'.

This, of course, involved approaching both Bethulia Park Hospital and the police for comments and incorporating their responses into the story. She did not reveal to either party the fact that she had obtained the missing medical records, in case an injunction was brought forbidding the newspaper from reporting information derived from a probably illegal leak. The public interest arguments in support of the inclusion of such revelations would be something the newspaper's lawyers would robustly defend later, if necessary.

However the Parker documents were central to Jenny's report that there was a serious scandal at the hospital. She wrote that the *Sunday News* could 'reveal exclusively' that the hospital trust had misled the coroner about Ray Parker's death and that the family were implacable in their demands that the police finally took seriously their claims of criminal negligence and unlawful killing.

By Friday evening her work was done, bar some last-minute queries from the sub-editors on Saturday ahead of the imminent deadline and publication.

Confident that she had left no stone unturned or no fact unsupported, Jenny treated herself to a large glass of Australian shiraz. She looked forward to her ride with Daphne next morning as a refreshing change of scene, a chance to exercise her body as well as her mind. She didn't even care if she ran into Dr Klein.

———

The following day, Angela Parker straightened out the broadsheet on her dining room table and looked at the spread. It occupied three-quarters of the page, comprising a main feature and sidebars about some of the deceased patients of Bethulia Park Hospital, with their pictures. They included Ray, leathery-skinned and grinning behind a pair of sunglasses on holiday in Spain more than a decade earlier. The headline read:

POLICE OPEN PROBE INTO SPATE OF 'UNLAWFUL KILLINGS' AT HOSPITAL

There was a picture byline of Jenny looking young, grave and important beside a subdeck which read:

Families accuse doctors of misdiagnosing patients to end their lives

The article was given the status of a 'special investigation' and included the claim that the Trust had lied to the coroner about Ray's death.

Mrs Parker surveyed the report with the reverence due to a hallowed text. It was more than she could have hoped for. It deserved to be framed.

'She's done a lovely job, that journalist, hasn't she?' she whispered to herself, as she sat down to read the article for the fifth time.

Mrs Parker would have preferred to have spent the rest of that Palm Sunday afternoon alone in the cosy warmth of her small living room with a couple of bottles of Guinness and her copy of the *Sunday News*, reading Jenny's article over and over again.

But her second son Michael, delighted by the coverage, had called her that morning to say that he had booked a table in an Indian restaurant where Ralph had been recently hired by Bob Torridge to sing regularly as an Elton John tribute act.

Ralph didn't look terribly similar to Elton John. He was bald and wiry with a moustache. He played the piano badly. But in front of the microphone he sounded just like the superstar. He much preferred to impersonate country singers, especially Glen Campbell, because he could play the guitar reasonably well. But Elton was the act for which he was best known in Crostbury's pubs and bars. Good entertainers give their fans exactly what they want—Ralph understood that—so most of the time he left his guitar at home.

Michael wanted his mother to join him, his wife Karen and their teenage children in celebrating their reversal of fortunes as Ralph sang to them. They could have some fun at last. Michael thought his mother would jump at the invitation, and he was surprised when she didn't.

'What's the matter, mum?' he asked. 'Ralph thought you'd love to see him.'

'I would, but I'm not so keen on spicy food—or on those Torridges. I'm a bit disappointed in Ralph. What's he doing going back to work for them again? I thought all that stuff was behind him.'

'Bob isn't like that any more, mum,' said Michael. 'He straightened himself out years and years ago. He's a nice fella these days, and a very successful businessman. Ralph's little mate Antony Geevarghese—you know, Toni G—he sings at his restaurant as well. The Asian Elvis. He says the tips are brilliant.

'C'mon, mum, be a bit more understanding. You know Ralph needs the cash.'

12

GOOD FRIDAY

Good Friday arrived, heralding the start of the Easter bank holiday weekend. Dr Klein would normally have joined his colleagues winding down their professional activities in the prospect of a well-earned rest. He might even have been happier than most given that on Easter Sunday he would be flying to Sardinia for a week in the sun with Jane and their daughters, Sophia and Philippa.

Yet he was more anxious than ever. As his shifts were drawing to an end, he found himself pitched forward over his desk, his head propped up by one hand and his heart so heavy there were intervals in which he was actively contemplating suicide.

He was thinking about injecting himself with a single but substantial bolus of either diamorphine or fentanyl so he could slip away painlessly. He was trying to work out what size of dose would kill a fit man such as himself and was pondering the potential difficulties in obtaining the drugs. Difficult, yes—but impossible, no. Klein had already discovered, to his satisfaction, that there were ways and means of secretly acquiring of a variety of drugs. One route was to create small surplus quantities, which he could hoard.

The more he dwelled upon the idea, the more it excited him. Yet his fantasy did not spur him on to end his own life. It had the reverse effect—it gave him the desire to live, to triumph. It revived his spirits and fired his imagination with the relish to experiment with the untried and untested. He remained low nonetheless. He had endured the worst week of a relatively brief but distinguished medical career.

It began last Sunday morning with a call from Dr Muhammad Baqri, the medical director of Bethulia Park Hospital NHS Trust, alerting him to the revelations in the *Sunday News* about how the coroner at the Ray Parker inquest was misled and how a group of families were pressing for a criminal inquiry into the possible murders of their relatives.

Within hours of the paper's publication, the police demanded the full medical files of all eight deceased patients named in the report, including Mr Parker's since Detective Inspector George Tarleton informed Dr Baqri that he would be examining this case again.

The medical director and DI Tarleton wanted to know from Dr Klein why the documents reproduced in the *Sunday News* were curiously absent from the Parker file the first time they had inspected it.

Dr Klein told both the detectives and the medical director that he still couldn't remember either the meeting with the Parkers or signing the documents, but now he did not rule out either as a possibility. As far as he knew, he declared, if the documents existed at all they must have been stolen. He also suggested the papers might have been simply misplaced during the filing process.

Full of contrived self-righteousness, Dr Klein haughtily invited the Trust and the police to search his office, and bluffed to the plain-clothed officers that they could raid his home too, if they wished. DI Tarleton did not take him up on the offer but coolly told him that the preliminary investigation would be thorough, and could take time, but would result in a full criminal inquiry only if there was evidence of serious wrong-doing by identifiable individuals. When Dr Klein assured him that he was certain such an outcome was extremely unlikely, the officer smiled and said nothing.

Relations between the two men had been superficially cordial for quite some time. They knew each other long before the police took an interest in possible criminal negligence at Bethulia Park Hospital. They belonged to the same country club and had played golf together a few times at the exclusive Crostbury course. Their familiarity meant that Klein felt comfortable in alerting the policeman to the possibility of other criminal activity at the hospital.

'What about investigating the likelihood of a person gaining unauthorised access to highly confidential medical documents in a restricted area in the hospital and then leaking them?' he suggested.

'Certainly, Dr Klein, this is also a very serious matter and I can assure you that my officers will be giving it their full attention too.'

Klein knew that in the coming weeks and months Dr Octavia Tarleton would be working tactfully on her husband, helping him with his analysis of highly complicated medical evidence, advising him about the significance of some aspects of the care of the patients, while dismissing others. Klein recognised that he could not have wished for a better friend at this time than his mistress, but simultaneously he was irritated that his reliance upon her might be adding an uncomfortable and unwelcome permanence to their relationship. He did not wish to rely on her for anything.

Dr Klein had always seen Octavia as a rare and valuable acquisition. He deeply admired her for her professionalism and her experience, and he could speak to her as someone who under-stood him because she was like-minded, though she was perhaps not as philosophical as he was, and carnally he found her irresistible.

He was under no illusion, however, that their affair was mutually self-serving and transient and this caused him to wonder, as he slumped over his desk, forcing his stiff fingers through his Beethoven flop of hair, if Octavia would stick around if he was beset by a scandal which threatened to engulf her too. He seriously doubted it. She might be an ally in the struggle opening up before him with the campaigning families, the journalist Jenny Bradshaigh and the insider who leaked the hospital records to her, but only if he was winning. To keep Octavia, he needed to sort out this mess, and quickly.

Of all the challenges confronting him at that moment it was the obvious presence of a traitor, or at least someone assisting the families from inside Bethulia Park Hospital, that worried Dr Klein more than anything. The wolves were circling the sleigh, and in the weeks ahead he must shoot them while maintaining the admiration and confidence of his superiors and the police. It was going to be a difficult balancing act. But which of the wolves was the closest? Who posed the greatest danger to him? It was harder to decide when he didn't know who to trust.

He raked the soil of his memory for any mistakes he might have made, while he searched assiduously for remedies and solutions. He had to get it right. The price of failure was too awful to contemplate, and it was this that brought him to the idea of suicide.

He could be confronted by the prospect of a fitness-to-practise panel; he could be struck off the medical register by the General Medical Council, or in the worst-case scenario he could face criminal charges, and possibly jail. He would wind up disgraced, ruined, divorced and friendless. He railed against the injustice of it. A man like him did not deserve any of that.

There was an unexpected knock at the door.

'Come.'

Emerald Essien entered the room.

'What's the matter?' Dr Klein asked, rising from his desk.

'Well, doctor, I was just wondering if you were all right,' she said. 'It looks like you've been having a tough time this week and I've been a bit worried about you. Are you okay?'

'Oh yes,' Dr Klein replied. 'Don't worry about me, or any of that business in the papers. It will all blow over. I don't think anything will come of it. I don't think the police can possibly find anything that will make them want to take it further because there hasn't been any criminal negligence at this hospital, as well you know, Emerald.'

He picked up his pen.

'Thanks for your concern. Is there anything else you want?'

'There is something I want to tell you, actually, yes,' she said sheepishly. 'Since that newspaper report came out that everyone's talking about—and I suppose I should have mentioned it to you earlier—but me and Nurse Sharyn Jones saw something a bit odd down at the records office a few weeks ago. Is that something that would concern you? I suppose you must be very concerned about how those documents ended up in the newspapers, or do you have an explanation for that already?'

'Are you kidding? It's upset me more than anything. I can't tell you … I've been lying in bed night after night, sometimes until four in the morning, thinking about what the hell went wrong there. Quite frankly, I'd even suspected that you might have leaked those documents out of spite, you know, as an act of revenge—payback.'

Emerald looked startled. 'What, you thought that it might have been me? Doctor, I would do no such thing!'

She moved closer.

'I'm not the vengeful type, you know that. It was ages ago. Why would I choose to do this to you now? Think about it, Reinhard. It doesn't make any sense. I'm loyal to you. You should know that by now. Why do you think that I'm not?'

He didn't reply.

'Look Reinhard, I mean Dr Klein, if you think I'm holding a grudge against you, you're wrong. It was fun but it didn't last. I'm over it. I'm a big girl. I've worked with you ever since, for goodness sake, and without complaint. Tell me when I've been off with you! I haven't. Look, I can work with you because I know you're the best doctor in this hospital—everyone knows that, including the medical director and Mrs Conway. Why the hell would I want to harm you?'

She paused but Klein said nothing.

'You're wrong about me,' said Emerald, her voice rising. 'It's not fair to accuse me like this. It's the very opposite of the truth. I feel sorry for you because you seem to be coming in for a lot of stick which you simply don't deserve and I wanted to help you out of this.'

Klein folded his arms and maintained an unmoving, solemn expression.

'These journalists, they don't know anything, do they?' she added. 'They don't have a clue about how good you are at your job. It's shameful the way they carry on. If only these people could see you the way I see you they would know that you deserve far more credit for what you do than anyone has ever given you. If there is anything I can do to help those families and the journalists see that too, then count me in. I'll promise I'll do whatever I can for you.'

'So what did you see?' asked Dr Klein.

'That priest,' said Emerald, 'you know, the new chaplain, the young fella. Me and Sharyn Jones were working on a Friday and we were sent down to the wing with a load of admin documents at the end our shifts—it was a good few weeks ago—and we saw him kicking the door of the records office and forcing the handle, like he was trying to break in. We challenged him and he said 'sorry' and that he was disorientated and then he walked away. We thought it was really weird at the time. In hindsight perhaps we should have reported it but we'd forgotten about it by the start of the following week. To be honest, I only remembered him when I was shown the article and it was then that I put two and two together.'

Klein licked his lips and frowned.

'Do you mean to say that this chaplain might have been looking for those documents because you saw him actively attempting to break into the area where they were kept? What do you think, Emerald? Do you think it was the chaplain that got into that office, one way or another, and took the documents then leaked them to the Press?'

'Well, you know he was at the inquest and at the meeting at the Parkers' house as well, don't you? Seems to have an interest in what's going on with the Parker lot. But it's not for me to say what he has or hasn't done. I can only tell you what I saw. Draw whatever conclusions you like. Seems a strange coincidence though, don't you think? You can check my story with Sharyn Jones.'

Dr Klein sat down and leaned back in his chair.

'It's interesting, but none of this explains how that chaplain got into the records office without someone here allowing him. It's passcode-protected and anyone other than authorised staff or police has to apply for access with our security people who log and record the visit. So, if none of them has done that then we can conclude that someone must have let him in. But you're saying he was trying to break in, right, but he didn't succeed?'

'That's what we saw, or at least that's what it looked like.'

'Then he must have obtained a passcode and gone back with it. It sounds a bit implausible to me, unless he's a very determined character. Do you know this chaplain, Emerald? Have you ever spoken with him apart from when you and Sharyn accosted him outside the records office?'

He eyed the nurse frostily.

'No, never,' she said, shaking her head. 'All I can tell you about him is what I saw and I saw him kicking the door of the records office, trying to get in.'

Dr Klein rose from his seat and came close to the nurse. 'So, Sharyn is going to vouch for your story, I suppose? You will both be interviewed by the police. You understand that don't you?'

'Yes, of course.'

'Good,' he said calmly, then he gave the nurse a devouring stare, his nostrils flaring. He was so close to her face she could feel his breath on her cheek.

'So why didn't you tell me about this?' he snarled. 'Why has it taken you so long to come forward with information about an attempted act of intrusion which was tantamount to a burglary? Why didn't you come to me earlier? Why come to me now? Are you covering your back, Emerald?'

'No!' she protested loudly. 'I wanted to help you!'

'Liar!' Klein shouted in her face. 'Don't ever cross me, Emerald. I warn you!'

She dropped her head and clenched her fists.

'I just didn't realise how serious it was. I just didn't make the connection and I'm really, really sorry for that. If I had any idea that what he might have been doing was part of all this stuff with those families, I'd have told you about it straight away, I swear. You've got to believe me. And you can ask Sharyn, she'll tell you I've been meaning to tell you about it since, but I've either forgotten or the opportunity didn't come up. I haven't seen that much of you, have I? Anyway, I'm telling you now. If you think I want payback, why would I do that? I'm telling you now.'

She dropped her voice. 'It is true that I want to help you and if I'm honest it's not only because I admire you professionally.'

Emerald raised her right knee so it brushed the inside of Dr Klein's leg. 'You can put it down to old time's sake. I'm doing an old friend a favour,' she said, their lips coming closer.

'Oh, I don't feel old,' said Dr Klein, his voice softening.

'Shame it ended like it did,' whispered Emerald. 'If you wanted to film me, you should have just asked. All you had to do was say "please".'

'I don't know what you're talking about,' said the doctor. 'But, yeah, it was good while it lasted. You know, I sometimes miss you too. I definitely would never rule out something in the future, for old time's sake, as you put it.'

'That would be nice.'

'Problem is, I've got another woman in my life right now. It doesn't mean you couldn't come over for drinks one night. I'm sure I could persuade her to welcome you. What do you think?'

'I'm not sure,' said Emerald, edging towards the door, 'but we'll see.'

Klein grinned as the door swung shut behind her. Retreating to his desk, he felt momentarily renewed, the cloud of darkness that hung over his head dissipating at last. Spring was returning to Bethulia Park. He reached for the phone.

'Hello, George, it's Reinhard. Yes, I'm fine, and I've got something very important to tell you ... '

Emerald left work thoroughly dejected and downcast, rebuking herself for behaving more like Judas than Judith.

She threw down her bags as she slammed shut the front door of her top floor flat and went straight to the fridge, taking out a bottle of wine and reaching for a glass. Still in her scrubs, she opened the french windows overlooking Trencherfield Mill, an enormous red-brick Edwardian edifice largely converted into luxury flats.

She stepped on to the tiny balcony and gazed across along the vast length of the building up to the northern and eastern sides of its pyramidal tower and to the box fastened directly beneath it by the Manchester Raptor Group to encourage peregrine falcons to nest.

Even with the naked eye she could see the heads of three fluffy chicks, with hooked beaks and saucer-like eyes. They were restless as they scoured the sky for their mother.

The hen came swooping in, calling a loud 'scraa, scraa, scraa', the grey and white barred underbelly obscured by the carcass of a pigeon grasped in its talons. After a few circuits of the mill the falcon came to rest on the sill of a broken window, her chicks bouncing up and down upon spotting her.

The mother sat with her kill for a few moments, panting with her beak open, its eyes staring from the black of their hangman's hood, the white shield on her breast heaving and shining in the evening light, its spots and bars like an intricate mass of hieroglyphics.

Responding to the cries of the chicks, the mother began to pluck her prey with her beak, sending down a blizzard of feathers. The peregrine dropped to the nest and ripped the pigeon into bloodied chunks, placing the morsels into the three hungry mouths in turn.

Emerald twirled the stem of the glass, marvelling at how beauty could be so deadly. 'Sorry, Calvin, but it was either me or you,' she thought. 'But I'll make it up to you, babe, I promise you.'

She hastily stepped back into the flat as she saw a familiar figure on the ground below, pointing up at the birds with a camera.

———

Dr Klein was still at work. A colleague had wished him a 'Happy Easter' which so infuriated him that he struggled to control his temper. After learning that a priest aligned with families determined to destroy his reputation had been skulking around his place of work, he was in no mood for religious festivals. He seldom was. He loathed Christmas as a day dedicated to religion, preferring to celebrate heartily on New Year's Eve. On this night, the very thought of Easter left him simmering.

Even the word 'happy' added to his rage. It was like a taunt to him, a man consumed by self-pity, disappointment, melancholy and, most profoundly, a persistent burning anger. A man like him deserved to be happier. Why should he, of all people, have to settle for occasional snatches of bliss? Why should other people have happiness when he did not?

As the evening calm descended on the wards, Reinhard Klein emerged from his office and began to prowl the corridors.

When he came to the door of a single room occupied by Pamela Worthington, he entered and quietly closed the door behind him.

Dr Klein was acquainted with the case. Seventy-five-year-old Mrs Worthington had been admitted on suspicion of a urinary tract infection and was put on a course of antibiotics and fed through a nasogastric tube.

After two days, Dr Klein diagnosed additional symptoms of pneumonia and sepsis. He and his multi-disciplinary team decided that it would be more appropriate to treat her as if she was dying, but her family objected. The patient's daughter, Mrs Torridge, was particularly aggressive and Klein walked away from her after she insulted him during an argument about her mother's care. The nurses then began to complain they were being intimidated. After that the family were repeatedly removed from the ward, first by hospital security and then the police. But Mrs Torridge had her way in the end, and her mother was sent home. A nuisance patient reunited with a nuisance family, thought Klein.

He was not surprised when Mrs Worthington arrived back in the hospital, given that he had halted the course of antibiotics part-way through and discharged her without the medication she needed. This time he would deal with her his way.

She was drowsy and offered no resistance as he slid the needle into her arm, assuring her that he required a small blood sample and he wouldn't hurt her a bit. Certainly, blood spat through the hub like a tiny party popper when Dr Klein hit a vein but soon it was pushed back into her body as he slowly and steadily emptied the contents. Mrs Worthington had stopped breathing before he withdrew the needle.

It was the first time that Dr Klein had killed a patient directly and, conscious that he had crossed a Rubicon, he paused to analyse how it felt. Not terribly different, was his first thought. The sky hadn't fallen in. But there was a new sense of elation, of satisfaction at having corrected the wrongs done to him by the families who questioned or opposed him. He was in control again—powerful, merciful and just, a moral authority with a moral purpose, a man ahead of his time.

He returned home to be welcomed at the door by Jane and the children. The girls were in their nighties but they didn't want to go to bed without seeing him. They giggled as Dr Klein embraced his wife and gave her a long kiss, then launched themselves into his arms for a hug.

Pippa, the younger, wanted him to read to her but first needed to ask about swimming in Sardinia. At five years of age, she had the ambition of divesting herself of her armbands and she wanted Dad to come in the water with her when she took them off. She was also set on an inflatable unicorn. 'Of course, darling,' he said, planting a big kiss on her cheek. 'We're going to have so much fun on our holiday.'

Sophia, who was eight, had some news from her piano teacher. 'Daddy, Miss Cooper says I'm good enough to be entered for my Grade Two and I've been practising. Can I play my piece for you before I go to bed? Please?'

Jane smiled at Dr Klein over their daughter's shoulder. 'She's really good,' she said. 'You have to hear this.'

'Yes, I'd love to hear you, sweetheart, of course I would. Just let me take my coat off.'

A few moments later they were in the large dining room where their Fridolin Schimmel upright piano was kept.

'It's from Joseph Haydn's Allegro—the fourth movement of Sonata in G,' announced Sophia. Jane leaned into her husband as their daughter began to play.

'Beautiful, beautiful,' said the doctor. He blinked hard as his eyes began to fill with tears.

In half an hour, both girls were in bed and Dr Klein and Jane were downstairs in the living room. They expected a few more interruptions before their daughters finally went to sleep because they were so excited about their holiday.

'It's been a tough week,' said Dr Klein.

'I know,' said Jane. 'You've been like a rhinoceros. I hope things have calmed down a little.'

'I think so. I think they're improving. Good Friday turned out to be not all that bad after all. I'll be okay, I'm sure of it.'

'Fantastic! Let's go and have a good holiday and forget about all that for a while.'

Without waiting to be invited, Jane reached into a drinks cabinet for a bottle of Lagavulin, Klein's favourite whisky. She poured a small glass and handed it him and he received it gratefully, giving his wife the appreciative smile she was seeking. She was pleased to see him relaxing at last.

'Aren't you having a drink?' he asked.

'Not tonight—I've got some news for you.'

She waited a second for his eyes to meet her own.

'I'm expecting! Let's hope it's that son you want so badly.'

Without speaking, Klein put down his whisky on the mantelpiece and embraced his wife, not wishing to release her. She revelled in his affection, euphoric that she had made him happy.

After a few moments she eased herself from his grip and smiled at him. He reciprocated warmly, then the line of his lips dropped a little.

'Jane, that's fantastic news,' he said. 'But there's just one thing.'

Jane braced herself, her smile waning too.

'This time, if it's a girl, I don't want it,' Dr Klein said. 'I think you should get rid of it.'

13

THE NAUGHTY STEP

The Easter weekend had been a high point of Father Calvin's brief ministry, a majestic and awe-inspiring celebration of the Easter Triduum—the liturgies of Maundy Thursday, Good Friday and the Easter Vigil—for the first time as the priest of his own parish.

All had gone exceedingly well, he thought, thanks to the lay volunteers gathered to help him with the preparation of the church, the choir, and a social reception in the hall on Sunday lunchtime, which would have been impossible without the help of Mrs Hoskins, his housekeeper.

He took Easter Monday off, and spent part of it walking along a fast-flowing river in the countryside close to his church, lush with wood anemones and the powerful stench of wild garlic, trying to relax after a tough and eventful Lent and a hectic Holy Week.

He had fancied himself walking in the footsteps of St Edmund Campion, the Elizabethan Jesuit and a convert from London like himself, who had fled to Lancashire in the winter of 1580 to escape the hysteria in the South created by the leaking of his 'Brag', his indiscreet assertion that the Catholic faith would prevail in England in spite of severe persecution. The missionary had made a huge impact on the people of the area. They were still talking about the sermons he had preached there on the Ten Lepers, the Last Judgement and the Hail Mary some eighty years after his martyrdom at Tyburn.

Although he wanted to emulate St Edmund, Calvin's mind was always elsewhere. All the time he was thinking about the nurse who said she was Judith. He was enchanted by her beauty and now he was also seized intellectually by the idea that she was an incarnation of the woman in the Bible, the holy and beautiful widow who beguiled and slew the Assyrian general Holofernes by his own sword: the original *femme fatale*.

Part of the reason for this was his discovery in the Old Testament Book of Judith that Holofernes murdered the Israelites by slowly dehydrating them to death. Was it a coincidence? He couldn't stop thinking about it.

Calvin had also been searching the internet for 'Judith' to see how she had been characterised in art. He was disturbed that her interpreters often chose to depict her as both violent and erotic. There were many of them: Botticelli, Caravaggio, Gentileschi, Rubens, Donatello, Furini, Reni, Allori and many more, even into the modern era, had been bewitched by her story. Like Calvin, they found her irresistible. He wondered if they, like him, had gone to bed thinking about Judith night after night until they were unable to think any more, and awakened to find she was still there at the forefront of their minds, slender, lithe and alluring, animated by an energy both deliciously sexual and horribly violent.

Judith, Judith, all the time Judith. Thoughts of her sucked the life out of him. They left him drained of intellectual vitality and unable to concentrate on his duties and obligations. Sometimes, at the altar, he felt he was an actor on a stage, that he wasn't really there, that he was going through the motions. It upset him and he would concentrate hard, but it would take only the slightest lapse to turn back to Judith.

The spell was broken at dawn on Easter Tuesday when a succession of thunderous bangs smashed through his sleep and made him leap out of bed confused and disorientated, barely conscious of who or where he was.

He pulled on a pair of tracksuit bottoms and a sweatshirt and opened his door to police officers who aggressively pushed past him and into his home. His mobile phone and computer were seized. They put him in a police car and drove him to a nearby station for questioning in connection with the suspected theft of medical records.

Calvin was at the police station almost all of that day. Initially, he was held in a cell on his own for a few hours while officers waited for a solicitor to arrive from the archdiocese, after being made to remove his shoes and surrender anything with which he might use to harm himself. He spent those hours in prayer, kneeling in front of the painted walls, sometimes wondering about the other people who had shared these small, dark and dingy confines before him, about what kind of criminals they were. 'A criminal. Is that what I am now?' he asked himself. 'A criminal?'

Shortly before lunchtime, a sour-faced and officious uniformed woman police officer fetched him from his cell and took him into a room sparsely furnished with a table and a few chairs and ordered him to sit down.

After a few minutes he was joined by Silvia Baldacchino from the archdiocesan legal team, and they spoke together for twenty minutes about what had happened and what he should say. Then the police came in and sat down.

Two detectives gave Calvin a tough grilling.

'I was sick and I'd been fasting all day and I was disorientated,' he told them. 'I didn't know where I was going, I was lost.'

'Rubbish!' said Detective Sergeant Amber Clarke. 'Lost people don't go around kicking the doors to restricted areas. You were trying to break into the records office. Why were you doing that? What were you looking for? The notes from Ray Parker's file?'

'No! I wouldn't know where to begin to look. I'm a priest, not a medical orderly. I couldn't find my way out of the hospital that day, never mind locate a file from a records office. How could I find a medical file?

'I was disorientated, I tell you. I strayed on to the wing because I mistook it for another identical in layout. It runs parallel to where I ended up that night. Check the plan of the hospital if you don't believe me. It's a massive place, it's a huge complex. I thought I was in one part of the hospital when really I was in another. I'm new to the place. I didn't know where I was. I was trying to find my way out. I wasn't going to nick anything. I pushed that door out of frustration because I expected it to open and it didn't. I was dizzy at the time and didn't realise, as I should have done, that it was the wrong door.'

He stuck to his guns and for the next two hours kept offering the same explanation as the questions from the police grew ever more speculative and ludicrous.

They even suggested that his alleged theft of the documents from the Parker file was the reason they could not be found in their initial investigation, and blamed him for their omission from the inquest.

'That's ridiculous,' said Calvin. 'I wasn't serving as a chaplain until a few weeks ago. It's preposterous even to suggest that I could have done that. I was in Liverpool at the time.'

Shortly afterwards, the police let him go.

So it was that on the Wednesday of the Easter octave Calvin found himself on 'the naughty step', the name the administrators at the Archdiocese of Liverpool gave to the stout leather chair reserved for errant priests.

As he waited to be called into the office of Monsignor David Wickham, the diocese's vicar general with responsibility for the care and discipline of the clergy, he was rehearsing in his mind the same explanations he had offered to the police.

A woman in her fifties stuck her head out from an adjacent room to tell Calvin that Monsignor Wickham was ready to see him. He entered to see a clean-shaven and balding middle-aged man at a desk, peering at him over the oblong spectacles that looked too small for his big head. His severe aspect and heavy build would not have looked out of place in a boardroom or a bank manager's office. Everything about him seemed to say: Don't mess with me.

'Good morning, Father Calvin, sit down,' said the priest, glancing down to reorder the papers that he had been examining. 'Unfortunately, the bishops have been called away on urgent business so I've been asked to deputise in your case. They want it sorted out now. So, let's begin. How long have you been at St Winefride's, about two months?'

'Yes, that's right, yes.'

'So where did it all go wrong?'

Calvin gave the monsignor his tailored version of events while the senior priest listened intently to the coherent and persuasive narrative and to his pleas of innocence, his claims to be a victim of a terrible misunderstanding.

Wickham waited in silence until Calvin had finished.

'Very interesting,' he said. 'In my job, Father Calvin, some-times people lie to me. It's what you expect them to do when they've been up to no good. The spirit of Judas, it manifests itself in so many different ways, you know—yet lying is the constant, it's the common denominator in all of these cases. I'm interested in the truth, and I promise you now that I will find out what it is.'

The two men looked at each other, Wickham allowing time for his words to sink in.

'Do you know what I used to be before I became a priest, Father?' he asked. 'A solicitor, and I dealt with a lot of criminal cases. There was one bloke, I'll never forget him, who came to me desperate for help because the police had arrested him on suspicion of sexually molesting a nine-year-old girl. This man was one slick customer. He was a well-heeled professional, nice house, car, wife, kids of his own, the lot, and he was absolutely insistent that he had been falsely accused, swore blind the police had it wrong.

'I was invited to the police station where he was being questioned one morning and I expected to be out by lunchtime. But the police kept me there, asking me to tell them "just one more time" why I thought my client was innocent. They did this about four or five times and by half past four they had me screaming at them, while they sat there asking me the same questions over and over again.

'Finally, at about six o'clock, the senior detective said to me, "We're going to let you go now, but we want you to see this first." Then he showed me this video of my client sexually abusing the girl. It was horrible. My client had made it himself. The cops sat there laughing at me.

'So, I've learned my lesson. No one is going to make a fool out of me like that again.'

He stared fiercely at Calvin.

'Thankfully, your case doesn't involve sexual misconduct. I'm happy to accept that at the present time. But if you have been downloading illicit images, that kind of thing, we will know about it soon enough because you can be sure the police will be looking for it now they have your computer.'

'I swear, Father, I have never in my life viewed pornography of any kind on the internet, or any media for that matter,' protested Calvin, wondering if Gustav Klimt's paintings of Judith flaunting her nipples from her 'robe of joy' would be of interest to the police.

'Okay, that's fine, that's not why you're here,' said Monsignor Wickham. 'I'm not accusing you of it, okay? If you were being investigated for that sort of thing, you'd have been ordered out of the presbytery immediately. You know that. My point is that

I'm not just going to accept what you have told me at face value. I'm not even going to waste my time picking holes in your story. But do you know what I think?'

Calvin shook his head.

'I think you are young, doctrinaire and conservative. What do you call it … *radically orthodox*? What even is that? And what was this, some sort of misguided pro-life activism? What have you done, blundered into a hospital, thinking you're some kind of knight on a white charger, tilting at the dragons of medical negligence? What were you doing at the inquest, for crying out loud?'

Calvin was stunned into silence by the realisation that the monsignor understood him far better than the police.

'Whatever it is you're getting caught up in, back away now,' said Monsignor Wickham. 'You are way out of your depth, boy. Leave all this kind of thing to the laity, even if the cause is just. The world's affairs, they're not for men like us. We're here to make Jesus Christ present to the world, not to try to change it by kicking in doors, for heaven's sake!'

Monsignor Wickham looked Calvin up and down. Seeing his dejection he changed his tone.

'Obviously, when we decided to send you into that parish on your own at your age and experience we discussed possible pitfalls because the archbishop was a bit worried about what could go wrong. Solitude drives many men mad, you know, but we thought we saw in you a certain mettle, a maturity, a conviction that might have carried you past all that—the drinking, the gambling, the women, the depression, that sort of thing. We didn't expect you to run off with the housekeeper, and we certainly didn't envisage this.'

It was impossible for Calvin to see himself eloping with Mrs Hoskins. He might have smiled at the thought if not for the Brussels sprout stuck in his throat: his superior, with piercing insight and intuition, had him cornered.

Feeling compelled to protest his innocence once more, he stressed with honesty that he had not seen the inside of the records office, that he had neither stolen nor photographed any medical records and that he was not source of the leak.

'Save your breath, Father,' interrupted Monsignor Wickham. 'We're going to let the police do their job and we are going to give them everything they ask for to help them in that, and we will decide what to do about you once they have completed their investigations. But let me tell you now—if it turns out that you have lied to me, then you are in serious trouble. If you are innocent, as you say you are, you have nothing to fear. The problem we've got in the meantime is what we are going to do with you.'

The two men stared deeply into each other's eyes, hesitating at the moment of truth. Calvin bit his lower lip.

'We think you should take some time out,' said Monsignor Wickham. 'You need to go on a mini-sabbatical. Don't take it personally.'

14

FIND THE KILLERS

Spilling out with the crowd from the Tube station on to Sloane Square, Jenny breathed in crisp spring air. She was so pleased to be back in London that the taste of the diesel fumes was almost sweet to her. She could have knelt down and kissed the ground. She loved living and working in the capital and she missed it sorely after sacrificing her way of life to join Seb in the North.

It was a consolation that her work often brought her back and she jumped at every opportunity of revisiting her favourite places and of going home laden with shopping bags.

She set off along the King's Road at a brisk pace, planning how to spend the afternoon once she concluded the interview. She was looking for Walpole Street to open up on her left and soon the Georgian terrace appeared, surprising her by its tranquillity given the proximity to the teeming thoroughfare.

Professor Arnold Silver, a hunched but bright-eyed man probably in his early seventies, wearing a dark suit and tie, answered the door to her.

Jenny was looking forward to meeting him. She had not heard of him until he wrote to her following her revelations in the *Sunday News*. She was fascinated by what she subsequently read about him, to discover that he was an eminent oncologist with an international reputation within medicine and a minor celebrity profile with the wider public, having successfully treated a number of politicians, actors, rock stars, entertainers and sports legends during their public battles with cancer. As a result he had been depicted in drama-documentaries on television which re-imagined the ordeals of such people in poignant and harrowing detail.

They shook hands warmly before Professor Silver led Jenny up a narrow staircase from the hallway to the comfortable front room of a first floor flat. She took in the high ornate ceilings and cornices, the majestic chandeliers. The walls were adorned with fine art from the 18th and 19th centuries. There were antiques everywhere.

'Tea or coffee?' asked the doctor in an East End accent.

'Tea would be lovely, thank you,' replied Jenny, her attention drawn to a huge cat asleep on the sofa.

Curled up and still, with its long cream fur streaked like the swirling top of a cappuccino, it had something of the appearance of a luxurious furnishing itself.

As the cat turned slightly on to its back, extending a stripy foreleg, Jenny could see better its lush white bib beneath its whiskered mouth, where a dainty triangular jaw drooped to reveal the tips of its teeth. It was blissfully asleep.

'Hello there!' Jenny whispered affectionately. The cat half-opened an eye the colour of a cornflower to dozily examine the visitor before deciding it was safe to drift off again.

'I love your cat,' she told Professor Silver as he returned with a plate piled with fruitcake and biscuits.

'Louis-Pierre, that is. He's going to be nineteen this year, can you believe it? He's in great shape. Mind you, he eats little else than premium tuna chunks in spring water—and he'll turn up his nose at anything but the most expensive brands. And he sleeps all day. Perhaps that's the secret to a long life. Maybe we should give it a try.'

'What is he?' asked Jenny.

'Mother was a Persian blue, don't know what the dad was. There was talk about this great big white farm cat that kept rolling up. I bet he was his old man.'

The doctor went to the kitchen again, returning with the tray of tea to find Jenny stroking, with the back of a finger, the cheek of the cat, which was purring loudly with satisfaction, its eyes tightly closed.

'I don't know, Louis—another tough day?' said the doctor. 'Let me check—are you sure twenty-three hours of sleep is really enough? I'd get more rest if I were you.'

He poured tea for himself and Jenny, and gestured to a sugar bowl.

'Thanks for coming to see me,' he said. 'I found your details on your website—very nice—after I read your article. I thought I might be able to help you in your work. It is very important, you know, what you're doing.'

'Thanks,' said Jenny.

'This is all off the record, mind, but I'll help you as much as I can.'

'I understand it's off the record but may I take notes for my own reference?'

'Of course. Mind if I smoke?' He heaved his skinny form out of the chair while he searched for his cigarettes. Jenny was bemused that a man who had spent his career fighting cancer seemed so careless about his own health.

'I see you've been played now by at least four actors,' said Jenny as he finally settled down opposite her.

'Yeah, they don't always get me right, though,' he said, lighting up. 'The last one they did, they seemed to suggest it was my fault the way that singer carried on. There was little said about all the drugs he was taking. They didn't help his prognosis, I can tell you. But anyway, most of these people have never heard of me until they get cancer. Then they seek me out for referrals even though

I'm not Harley Street, or anything like that. Word of mouth is a powerful medium, you know.

'I've worked for the health service all my life, apart from my teaching posts at Harvard and Yale, and I'm still doing it now although I'm not chief of cancer or anything like that no more. I love the health service, I believe in it, but I'll be retiring soon and in some ways I'll be glad.'

He looked at Jenny gravely. 'A lot of corruption has crept in in recent years—bad practices, you know, and they're having a big impact on life expectancy and on quality of care and on cancer recovery rates. Some of it's downright scandalous, like these disgraceful do-not-resuscitate forms. It has to be challenged.'

He blew out a long billow of smoke. Jenny scribbled away in Teeline shorthand.

'The amount of times I've been called on my mobile phone when I've been abroad by the family of a patient I've been treating for six or seven years, crying that they been sent to a hospice by some doctor who doesn't know them ... Honestly, I've had rows with people from car parks all over the world, screaming at them down my phone to get those patients out again. And there have been dozens—literally dozens—of times when I've ordered drips which have been taken down without my permission, because a patient was supposedly dying, to be put back up again, or when I've had to insist that my patients are removed from some death pathway or other. Their deaths were never imminent in more than a few cases. I looked after them, sent them home and they generally lived for a good while longer—eighteen months or so, on average, I'd say.'

He stopped speaking to give the reporter the time to catch up.

'We are not gods,' he continued, his voice trembling. 'This is such an arrogant position for doctors to take—to say, within a matter of seconds, that they know a patient will die. It is only in the final throes when we can say with certainty that death is imminent—you know, within the last two or three hours, and that's when a patient is extremely ill and we have no chance of resuscitating them. This is so dangerous. The prognostic tool to determine time of death with any precision is yet to be invented. But it's probably not too uncommon in most hospitals for a doctor from time to time to take just a quick look at a patient and decide they know what will happen.'

He slumped back into his armchair, watching Jenny down his aquiline nose until her pen went still.

'So what would you say is driving this then?' Jenny asked him. 'You mentioned arrogance. Does money have anything to do with it?'

'There is definitely a financial aspect,' said Professor Silver. 'Health care has become a bit like a conveyor belt, with too much emphasis for my liking on admission rates, targets, that kind of thing. It all comes right from the top. Of course they want the beds, but they'd never admit that. A few years ago hard-up trusts were being bribed with government cash to increase the percentage of patients dying on that dreadful Liverpool Care Pathway and they were also financially penalised if they failed to hit the targets. And what did Baroness Neuberger find out about that pathway when she reviewed it? That patients were being knocked out with "chemical coshes" then left to die without food and fluids. That's why they had to stop it. It didn't come as any surprise to me, I can tell you.'

'Isn't that precisely what's still happening at Bethulia Park?' Jenny inquired. 'How on earth are they getting away with it?'

'Possibly because the abolition of the pathway was a classic piece of political fudge. The brand was so badly damaged it had to go, but the mechanisms were all retained—predictive death, and the sedation, dehydration, and so on. Many doctors are now pretty cautious about going down that route and most of them don't want to kill their patients, but not, it seems, at the place you're talking about.

'So, to go back to your first question about what's driving this, it ain't just the money, I'm sure of that. It's this judgemental moral arrogance, which I mentioned first, and which by any objective criteria is creating bad medicine. Some people get a taste for power and it doesn't do them any good. This thing, it's taken on a huge dimension now—I think it's too powerful to stop. It's become like a belief system, complete with its own dogma. It's an ideology. It took more than a thousand families to get the Government to do anything about the Liverpool pathway. How many have you got? Eight? Well, anything you can do to push it back, do it. And good luck to you.'

Jenny put down her pen and sighed. She was starting to realise she had underestimated the scale of the problem. Clearly the doctor, with a lifetime of experience in the health service, was doubtful if her little group was going to change anything. Yet if he was fully despairing of the situation, Jenny wondered, why would he be bothering to talk to her about it at all? What, exactly, was he hoping for? Had he really brought her here just to tell her she was wasting her time?

'What would you suggest I do to push it back?' she asked

'It's good that the families have gone to the police, that's important, but I'm not sure you will see any doctors in the dock. It's been tried before. The police don't want to know. They hate this kind of thing. They're not doctors, and they're easily brow-beaten by our profession. The evidence threshold required to initiate a prosecution is also extremely high, and even when they get the go-ahead they find that they need a huge amount of resources—scores if not hundreds of officers, thousands of hours of detective work and millions of pounds of funds just to bring someone to trial.

'True, they got Shipman, but it was as if he wanted to be caught. He had his fingers in the till like he was begging them to notice.

'Think about this: what if there are others out there who are more careful than he was, who don't want to be caught, and who don't take the same chances? It's something that has troubled me for a few years now.'

He leaned forward.

'If you are to have any hope of stopping this thing, I think you would do better going after the killers than taking on the system. Find the killers. They're there—hiding among our great many excellent doctors, the chaff among the wheat. Root them out, expose them and there is a chance that many of the loopholes that allow them to get away with what they're doing will be closed afterwards.'

'Have you ever heard of Dr Reinhard Klein, professor?' said Jenny.

'No, never. Why?'

'He keeps coming up among the families I've been speaking to. The Parkers, in particular, blame him for the cancer misdiagnosis that was disputed at the inquest. I haven't enough to put the finger on him publicly but there's no one else in the frame.'

'I'm sorry to hear that—I was hoping you were going to tell me you'd found the woman who's being doing this for a long time.'

'Who?'

Professor Silver sighed and once more pulled himself forward to ensure he had the reporter's full attention.

'Going back more than a decade now there was this young doctor—very attractive blonde she was, could have been a model, simply gorgeous. She came to work at my hospital straight from qualifying and she was full of what she called "radical" and "innovative" ideas about end-of-life care in particular.

'Within no time they made her a manager. Of course, she didn't only impress the bosses, she was quite a hit with the younger male doctors and nurses—they were queuing for her attention. But after a while things changed, and doctor after doctor would come to me to complain about what she was doing to the patients.

'At first, I thought they were love rivals settling scores but then I saw it for myself. She would clear out all the beds; literally empty the wards, going through them at night and taking all the drips down, and doing many other things as well. I had fight after fight with her about it but she rocketed up the career ladder—they promoted her over and again even though her methods were patently unsound. Soon, she was being sent into trusts with low rates of deaths on these pathways to show them how to hit their targets. She has probably left quite a statistical trail behind her, and you should look for it.

'I'm not sure she is still working in the NHS now, after what happened to her with the ombudsman.'

'What do you mean?'

'Oh, they had words with her in the end. She doesn't take criticism very well—and I've also heard that she married so she probably changed her surname. I expect you will be able to find her quite easily, though. I was hoping that you had already done so, or I wouldn't have invited you all this way.'

'What gave you that idea?'

'Because the last place I know she worked was Bethulia Park Hospital,' answered Professor Silver. 'Octavia Topcliffe, her name was—at least at the time.'

Calvin had been back in London only a day and was already glad of the chance to escape from his parents' home. He arrived there the previous lunchtime, long-faced and sullen, only for his dad, with more than a hint of *schadenfreude*, to say condescendingly: 'Didn't take long for it all to go belly up, did it, son?'

It was hardly the consolation he needed. Feeling an abject failure and knowing his parents had never been fully supportive of his conversion and ordination, he could barely look at them, let alone talk openly about his difficulties.

The call from Jenny on the mobile phone loaned to him by the archdiocese jolted him from the trough of depression into which he had been sinking.

He looked forward to meeting her for a drink on Friday afternoon before she caught the train from Euston up the West Coast main line to Preston.

He strolled down Davies Street toward *The Running Horse*, the oldest pub in Mayfair, wondering if he should have a pint. He rarely allowed himself alcohol, conscious of the good example of the priesthood he sought to set—but it was Easter, he wasn't working and it was a social occasion.

'Why not?' he thought, the familiar, almost refreshing, malty aroma greeting him as the heavy saloon door gave way to the dark, panelled interior of the tiny pub, its walls set out with ancient pictures of racing and hunting horses.

Jenny was at a far table with four or five bags at her feet.

'I've got you a pint in.'

'Cheers, I need it.'

Calvin had rung Jenny on Wednesday to tell her he was effectively suspended and that it was being kept a secret from the parish in the expectation that he would be able to return before too long. Officially he was on a short sabbatical, and was hoping to carry out research for the archdiocese in his new capacity as associate archivist. He had not been expecting to see her quite so soon.

'How are you handling it?' asked Jenny.

'Badly,' said Calvin. 'I've been quite down, to be honest. I'm glad the vicar general told me I could go home, but it's hard, you know, everyone thinking I'm a loser, and that I've done something atrocious.'

He took a long pull of the beer.

'My folks think I'm a bit of weirdo anyway, and now added to that is the notion that even the Catholic Church thinks I'm a nutter. In some ways I am, I suppose. I'm not the most popular priest among the clergy. They can be a rebellious bunch, and I'm not, you see. I'm going to have to find something to keep myself occupied here or I'm going to go mad. Anyway, what about you, how did it go today?'

Jenny told him all about her meeting with Professor Silver. He listened, swigging his beer with increasing vigour.

'I'll have just one more,' he said, getting up to go to the bar. 'What would you like?'

Putting down a pint of bitter and a half of lager on the table, he said: 'You know, you've really cheered me up—I don't feel such an idiot any more, though I wish I hadn't been quite so reckless.'

Jenny looked puzzled. He hadn't told her about kicking the door of the records office.

'Shame your guy didn't have anything on Klein,' said Calvin.

'Yeah, but this Dr Topcliffe sounds interesting though, doesn't she?'

'But what's her significance if she wasn't involved in any of the deaths your families are complaining about?'

'We don't know that she wasn't yet. I could put her name to one or two of families of the older cases and they might just say, "Yes, that's the one." What matters is the professor has given me a lead, a name. Who knows? A little bit of investigative work might turn up a bit of context, like Bethulia Park was a normally functioning hospital until little Miss Doctor Death rocked up and made the killing of patients the norm. It all helps to build up the picture. It's about playing the long game with this sort of stuff. You don't always know where it will take you when you set out—perhaps nowhere—but it's worth a chuck of the dice.'

Calvin was impressed by her strategic, lateral thinking, her ability to recognise the smallest of leads and to explore them, to study new information from every aspect in a remote but persistent hope that whatever remained hidden for now would soon break out into the light of her understanding.

The conversation turned to Jenny's accident at the stables and her plans for Daphne, who was being kept in full livery until Jenny was fit enough to resume her usual routine.

'My back's still a bit crocked,' she told the priest. 'I can get around well enough, but I'm in some pain when I'm lying down. I'm lucky not to have broken my pelvis, or worse. It's going to be a little longer before I'm right again, but I'm getting there, thankfully. Actually, could I ask a favour? Could you possibly come to Euston with me with these bags? They're not really heavy but my back's beginning to hurt. I'll be okay at the other end. Seb's going to pick me up.'

'Yes, of course,' said Calvin. 'I take it you won't be going riding tomorrow then?'

'Just light stuff and not for too long. I've got some Freedom of Information requests to make if I'm going to learn anything about this Octavia Topcliffe, or whatever it is she calls herself.'

Jenny began to explain her proposed strategy for tracing the mysterious Dr Topcliffe but Calvin stopped hearing her words. They faded as if the sound was being turned down on a radio.

Judith stood at the bar, smiling and nodding at him, her hair tumbling down her neck and shoulders, but leaving her scar clearly visible. She gestured to him that he should have a drink and he lifted his pint glass, which had just two fingers of beer remaining. She shook her head mockingly and lifted a large glass of red wine. She pointed at the glass and then she pointed at Calvin. He nodded and she turned to order at the bar.

Jenny was still talking.

'Excuse me a moment,' Calvin interrupted. 'There's someone here I know. You've got to meet her. I'll be straight back.'

He lost sight of Judith as he apologetically squeezed and pushed his way through the drinkers packing the little room. When he made it to the bar she wasn't there. He scoured every corner but there was no sign of her. He dashed to the saloon doors, wrenched them open and almost flung himself into the street.

The road was straight and he could see clearly for hundreds of yards in either direction. But there was no sign of Judith, only a few office workers, chatting or entranced by their phones.

'Father Calvin, are you okay?'

It was Jenny. She had followed him outside, struggling to carry shopping bags in both hands.

'I don't know,' the priest replied. 'I'm really not sure if I am.'

15

CALVIN'S PROBLEM

The drumming of hooves drew closer. Calvin stepped off the sandy path to make room for the horses about to burst into view. There they were, led by a man sitting bolt upright as his large grey rocked beneath him in canter, its eyes dark and bright as anthracite, ears perked up and pointing forward. Behind him rode a woman on a smaller chestnut, smiling in exhilaration, her hands down by the mane, her shoulders relaxed and her pelvis swaying with the rhythm. Calvin thought of Jenny. Suddenly the pair slowed to a trot and Calvin twisted sideways to see a walker dash into their path to grab a terrier by its collar and haul it out of their way. The lead rider called out in gratitude and with an imperceptible squeeze of his calves he was in canter once more. Within seconds the horses were gone.

It wasn't quite silence that returned to Hyde Park. There was plenty of noise, but not the usual sounds of the city. Instead the air reverberated with the screeching of lime-green ring-necked parakeets flitting between the sweet chestnut trees, the cawing of crows and the 'tchaks' of the jackdaws that gave the birds their name. Tourists milled around statues and monuments. Children shouted and shrieked as they ran joyfully over grass dotted with daisies and buttercups.

Calvin slumped on a bench well away from other visitors. Mentally, he was tired. He'd had an exhausting week of doing nothing constructive; just battling himself. The park provided a respite, a place where he could escape.

He'd been to Mass earlier in the nearby Jesuit church in Mayfair, and soon he would head to the north-east corner of the park to the site of the Tyburn gallows upon which more than a hundred Catholic men and women died as martyrs between 1535 and 1681. He wished to conclude this last day of personal pilgrimages in the capital with an afternoon of prayer in Tyburn Convent. Soon he would leave London and take a break elsewhere, somewhere nice. With any luck by then he would be back to his old self. Through prayer and self-discipline he would shake off the black dog of depression spawned by his obsession with Judith.

Thoughts of the nurse had been more disconcerting to Calvin than his suspension by the archdiocese. He was unable to get her out of his mind. He had never felt this way about a woman before. She was in his dreams as well as all his waking moments, leaving him spiritually dry, struggling to pray. He was discouraged and worn out.

Yet there was something about the memory of her beauty that made him feel more fully alive. He craved it like an opiate, replaying their conversations over and over in his mind, savouring repeatedly the brief moments of personal intimacy he had so long denied himself.

The priest fought against his impulses at the same time as he scorned himself as preposterous. How could a religion which preaches love as its highest value lead him to battle against it with every sinew of his body, with the full mental effort of his mind and with the determined will of his soul? It made him resentful and rebellious.

But was it really love? It was not love as he had ever understood it, not like the love he felt for Jenny, for instance. It was not that ever-present disposition to give himself in service to all the people he encountered, in recognition of their dignity as sons and daughters of God and as his own brothers or sisters. This, if it was actually love, was not of that species. This was carnal love, *eros*. Calvin desired Judith sexually. He told himself he would not succumb to lust, but the ground on which he stood was shaky. It would take just a small push, an 'occasion of sin' like a few drinks in an intimate setting, a warm conversation and a romantic mood, and his defences would crumble and blow away to nothing like a sun-scorched sandcastle on a windy beach. He would be a virgin no more, the promise of celibacy he made to the archbishop evaporating as everything about him began to change.

Already, without realising it, he was beginning to find aspects of his ministry repugnant as he was moved by an inclination toward sensuality. He imagined himself shopping in Covent Garden for fashionable clothes and ditching his clerical collar. He fancied how he might look if he styled his hair and wondered if Judith would like him better for it. More and more, he desired that which he knew was obliged to avoid: thrilling intimacy with the nurse, to be alone with her.

Such thoughts made him burn. He was a heap of blazing embers from head to foot—fizzing, sizzling, spitting, smoking and about to burst into flames, impossible to cool down.

Yet Calvin hadn't quite lost his mind. He reasoned that he had spent the last decade convinced he was called by God to the priesthood. Consequently, he speculated that the nurse was a temptation placed before him by Satan to make him fall. He had inwardly chuckled at the thought that someone so lovely could be an accomplice in an evil design. But was he being deceived into mistaking an infatuation, an obsession, for love itself?

It was a serious question. Whatever the explanation, Calvin was sure the problem did not lie with Judith, but with his own appetites, and that it was only divine grace, and not human power, that could help him. He consciously decided to fortify himself by prayer and self-denial, asking God to come to his aid

when he felt forced to choose between madness or surrender—
to seek out the nurse and tell her how he felt. A third option was
taking root in his mind and it was appealing, simple but strangely
difficult: a return to sanity.

It meant not picking up his calls from Mrs Hoskins for fear of
being told about a message from a woman called Judith. It meant
a greater effort to fill his days, to distract himself. At first he spent
a lot of time with his parents. He went with his father to Loftus
Road to watch Rangers take on Nottingham Forest, but their team
lost to a single and impressive Karim Ansarifard goal, and both
came away miserable. Another time, he walked with his mother
on Hampstead Heath, a mild and ephemeral distraction.

Soon, he preferred solitude. He could lose himself in London
and its history. He toured churches, cathedrals and palaces,
walked in the footsteps of the saints and visited the sites where
martyrs shed their blood, constantly stimulated intellectually and
spiritually by the discovery of the secret world that existed on the
doorstep of his youth, seen anew through the eyes of his faith.

One afternoon Calvin found himself in Charterhouse
Square, peering through gaps in the masonry of the Carthusian
priory at the site of the altar where St John Houghton, the prior,
had celebrated a final Mass before refusing to take the oath
attached to the Act of Supremacy, the law that made it high
treason to deny King Henry VIII as the sole and supreme head
of the Church in England.

The King responded to his defiance in characteristic fashion,
and on the morning of May 4 1535 Thomas More watched from
the Tower of London as Houghton, three other priors and a
secular priest were drawn on hurdles by horses to Tyburn to be
hanged and quartered, remarking that they went as cheerfully to
their deaths 'as bridegrooms to their marriage'.

Houghton would soon tell the crowd assembled to watch him
die that his conscience made him 'willing to suffer every kind of
torture rather than to deny a single doctrine of the Church'. He

was still conscious when his beating heart was wrenched from his breast and held before his eyes. 'O Jesus, what wouldst thou do with my heart?' were reputed to be his final words.

From the same spot Calvin could see the arched entrance to the priory, the same doorway, presumably, where one of Houghton's quarters was subsequently nailed.

Walking a few hundred yards along a pavement opposite the old Smithfield meat market he arrived at the scene of the fires where forty-eight Protestants and one Catholic were burned under Henry VIII, Edward VI, his son, but mostly under Mary, his pyromaniac Catholic daughter.

Close by, the only statue of Henry in the entire capital gazed imperiously from a plinth over the place where in a single July day in 1540 three Catholic priests were disembowelled for fidelity to the Pope alongside three Protestants burned alive for heresy. What a way to make your point, reflected Calvin, grateful to be living in an era when playing God with human lives was seen as extraordinarily cruel. Yet human nature surely did not change with the times. Would it really be any better if, as John Lennon proposed, there was 'no religion'? Or would new and destructive ideologies rise up like the children of the Hydra's teeth to fill the void as they had in the last century? The 'end times' would be no sunlit upland of tolerance and social inclusion, of that much Calvin was sure. His faith told him so.

No, in his view the innate savagery would never go away. It would always be there, perhaps just below the surface—but always shifting, probing, searching and often finding new ways to burst forth and dominate, to enslave and destroy, like some kind of self-perpetuating and intelligent force. It demanded a response from every generation if humanity were not to be tipped once more into barbarism, the triumphs of civilisation unravelled and destroyed. Christ's ultimate victory was assured, but in the meantime evil sometimes won.

Calvin pulled at his collar, allowing the breeze to cool his neck, when he heard footsteps. He glanced sideways to see a fellow cleric, a snowy-haired man walking with a stick.

'Do you mind if I join you?' said the older priest.

'No, of course not,' said Calvin, shuffling along the bench to make room.

'I saw you in Mass this morning. You look like you had the weight of the entire world on your shoulders. I know an anguished soul when I see one. I don't recognise you. You're not one of the Westminster clergy, are you? Are you visiting?'

'Yes, my parents. I'm from this neck of the woods but I was ordained for Liverpool. Father Calvin Baines.'

The older priest accepted the outstretched hand.

'Pleased to meet you—Father Hugh Davenport, Society of Jesus. I'm a member of the community at Farm Street.'

Calvin shook Father Davenport's hand gently, conscious of its age and fragility, and he managed a smile before he looked away.

'Why are you really here?' asked the Jesuit.

Calvin was taken aback by the priest's forthright intuition. But he liked it. Someone to talk to at last. Someone who might just understand him.

'I landed myself in a bit of trouble. But I'm hoping to be reinstated soon.'

'Was it a woman?'

Here we go again, thought Calvin. 'Sort of, yes, but I haven't broken my vows or anything like that, though I have to admit that I'm so weak at the moment that it wouldn't take much to make me fall.'

'Temptation itself is not a sin,' replied Davenport. 'Surely you know you won't stop being tempted until you're in a box. It's part of our nature—and the struggle between good and evil will go on until the end of time. It's your response that matters.'

'That's what is troubling me, Father. I don't know if I'm strong enough to resist this woman, or what I should do. I can't do this any more, I'm worn out. I feel like I'm burning up all the time just at the thought of her.'

'Tested by fire. It could be good for you if you withstand it. Fire purifies metal. Don't be afraid. If you believe God called you to the priesthood, then you can be sure that he will give you the graces you need to persevere. He won't ask anything from you that you are unable to accomplish. It is a question of the will— your will, and God's will for you.'

'Can I talk to you in confidence?'

'Please do.'

'It's more than an infatuation with a woman, though I find her incredibly, almost irresistibly, beautiful. It's this idea that's in my head … that she's Judith out of the Bible, Judith of Bethulia.'

'Ooh, that's interesting,' said Davenport, twisting to face Calvin. 'And what brings you to that conclusion, other than her beauty?'

'I don't know her real name but she told me to call her Judith. She's a widow and she's trying to stop a bad man from dehydrating people to death, just like Holofernes did. I can't get her off my mind. I dream about her and I've experienced hallucinations of her. You know, I even had a beggar telling me she—er, well I think it was her—was going to cut my head off, at least I thought that's what he meant. I tell you, I think I'm going mad.'

'Cut your head off? You don't look like Holofernes.'

'No, but I do know what Holofernes looks like. I've seen him in my dreams too. What's weird is that I saw him in that scene from the Book of Judith, the one where it describes him in his tent, but I didn't recognise him, I didn't know who it was, until I read up on it later—and I did that only after this woman told me her name.'

'It's an unusual sequence of events. Are you sure you have it the right way round?'

'Yes, absolutely,' croaked Calvin, his voice breaking under stress.

'Have you spoken to a spiritual director or another priest about this?'

'No, no—I'm not supposed to know this woman. I'm protecting her identity. She could be in danger from the man she's up against. I mean, she could lose her job at the very least. She might even be prosecuted. I should go to confession, I suppose, but that's another thing—this whole business is weakening my faith. It's striking right at the heart of who I am as a priest, at my identity. It's a blessing being suspended, in some ways. It gets me out of that situation up there. I'm dreading going back.'

Father Davenport pressed down on to his stick with the palms of his hands while he thought about what Calvin told him.

'These experiences, do they feel extrinsic to you? Alien, like they don't belong to you—that's right, isn't it?'

Calvin nodded.

'This might not be a matter of psychology,' Father Davenport said. 'Did you do much spiritual theology at seminary, you know, the works of the mystics?'

'Bits and bobs.'

'Do you know anything about obsession, I mean the way we sometimes understand it—spiritually—rather than the mental illness that rightly concerns psychologists and psychiatrists?'

Calvin flashed a look at the old man to see that he was studying him intently, his face as solemn as a Crown Court judge.

'Are you aware of any of the writing of the mystical theologians—Tanquerey, Ribet, Royo Marin, people like that?'

'I can't say that I have.'

'Father Baines, listen to me,' the Jesuit whispered. 'I'm an exorcist. I know what I'm talking about. What you are experiencing may be just normal temptation, an infatuation like you say, but you may also be in very grave danger.'

'What?'

'Have you heard of diabolical obsession?'

Calvin blinked hard. He felt his pulse race.

'Isn't that where the Devil physically attacks holy people, striking them with unseen fists, appearing as dogs, spitting on them,' he said, 'the sort of thing that some saints said happened to them—Padre Pio and Gemma Galgani, people like that?'

'That's right, it's when the Devil attacks the virtuous ... well, usually the virtuous. Normal temptation is for everyone else, you see, but when you're not impressed by that he sometimes plays really dirty. The strategy is usually to attack you at your weakest point, get inside your mind and orientate you towards evil after breaking down your defences. The saints you've just mentioned experienced the external form of the phenomenon but what you've described to me about your fixation with Judith could be symptomatic of an internal obsession, though I can't be sure without examining you properly. It's a manifestation of essentially the same thing. Make no mistake, these could be violent assaults of the Devil, what is happening to you, though it might not always seem that way.'

The old man paused.

'I don't want scare you, but sometimes diabolical obsession can be worse than diabolical possession—when these spirits take over, usually as a result of something the person has done or wished for. You know what that is, of course, and that's simply terrible, I can assure you. That's why I said you might be in danger.'

Calvin drew away from Davenport and gave him an incredulous look. The Jesuit pressed harder.

'Do you know what M. J. Ribet said about this? Have you heard of him? He wrote this wonderful book about this kind of phenomena called *La Mystique Divine*—oh, it's ancient—but he makes the point very clearly that "obsession is more to be feared than possession, because the enslavement of the body is infinitely less fearful than that of the soul".'

'Thank you, Father,' said Calvin, swallowing hard. 'You've cheered me up no end—to add to all my other problems, I'm now possessed by the Devil, and it's a really bad form of it too. Great stuff. Just what I want to hear.'

'No, you might be a victim of obsession, not possession. Please get it right,' scolded Father Davenport. 'It's vitally important.'

'I apologise. The Devil's obsessed with me. Thanks for the clarification.'

'You're welcome. That's what I'm here for. But anyway I didn't say you were definitely experiencing this phenomenon. I can't say that. The signs are very mild. There might be a natural explanation for this. It's when the disturbance to your soul is so profound and the tendency to evil so violent that one can say without doubt that the explanation lies in an external force. It's something to be aware of—should this thing get worse. I suggest you acquaint yourselves with these spiritual writers if you are to discern accurately what might be happening to you.'

Calvin stared at the man. He wanted to put his hands over his ears. His life was turning into a nightmare. He pulled himself together.

'Who are they again?'

'Tanquerey, read Tanquerey. Like the others, he observed how the Devil can work on a person's senses, their imagination—how he can get inside their head. But Tanquerey also recognised how difficult it can be to decide whether the case is one of real obsession. Tanquerey said "when the temptations are at once sudden, violent, persistent and hard to account for by natural means, one may conclude that it is a special intervention on the part of the Devil". I wouldn't leave it too late if I were you. You have to discern what is happening to you and act to stop it, whatever it is.'

'Okay, I'll read Tanquerey,' sighed Calvin. 'And then what?'

'Resist the obsession via the normal defences of the Church is the simplest answer. You can start now—frequent recourse to the sacraments, prayer, a pilgrimage perhaps. Pray for deliverance. Holy obedience to Mother Church is crucial, more than austerity. Don't be afraid to be obedient. Obedience is the virtue of the good soldier. You must embrace it. It will set you free. Visit Jesus in the Blessed Sacrament, turn to Our Lady and invoke her maternal protection.

'Listen to St Paul in his letter to the Ephesians: "Put on the full armour of God so as to resist the Devil's tactics. For it is not against human enemies that we have to struggle, but against the principalities and the ruling forces who are masters of the darkness in this world, the spirits of evil in the heavens. That is why you must take up all God's armour or you will not be able to put up any resistance on the evil day or stand your ground even though you exert yourself to the full. So stand your ground with truth a belt around your waist and uprightness a breastplate, wearing for shoes on your feet the eagerness to spread the gospel of peace and always carrying the shield of faith so that you can use it to quench the burning arrows of the Evil One. And then you must take salvation as your helmet and the sword of the Spirit, that is, the word of God".

Calvin bowed his head and nodded along slowly as he listened to the old priest quoting Scripture to him.

'Don't be scared,' Davenport continued. 'God only allows these kinds of battles when a soul might grow in holiness through a triumphant struggle. See it as an opportunity to flourish but don't be caught off your guard, and if it becomes very serious, ask for help. I'll give you my card. Come to me whenever you need me.'

Calvin put the card into his pocket. 'And what's the price of failure, if indeed all of this is supernatural in its origin?' he asked. 'Her cutting my head off? Is that what she might do?'

'Let's hope it doesn't come to that. But corruption, evil, or complicity in evil are all possible outcomes. You could be ruined, or damned. Believe me, you definitely don't want to fail.'

Calvin felt as if he was about to be sick.

'Don't worry, don't be afraid,' said the older priest consolingly. 'You should be pleased that you've found help. A cure is only possible when the diagnosis is correct. I can help you.

'So let's talk about your specific problem. What you need to know first of all is that Judith was a real historical figure. You sometimes get biblical revisionists these days who will try to tell you that Judith is of dubious historicity—that even Bethulia never existed and that the Book of Judith is more of a morality tale than a record of historical facts. But I don't accept that. I think Judith lived and breathed and that she saved her people from the evil designs of a murderous opponent, a deeply dangerous man who would have exterminated them all.

'She's in the Bible for a reason and what emerges essentially from the Book of Judith is God's saving power, the assurance that the Almighty will deliver his people from even the greatest and most powerful of evils. The condition is that we must always stand firm in our faith and in our traditions. That's the crucial lesson. Judith showed to the Israelites that no enemy, however powerful, could crush them when they clung like children to God, when they put all their trust in the Almighty. Indeed, this continues to be a lesson for us all. Stand firm in the faith and put your trust in the Lord. Father Baines, this is what you have to do—and right now. Do you follow me?'

Calvin smiled weakly and nodded.

'You need to break this obsession and avoid whatever evil is being set up for you if there is infernal mischief at work here,' said the exorcist. 'I would suggest it ought to be an urgent priority for you. How are you keeping yourself busy?'

Calvin told him about his interest in history and his plans for a pilgrimage, possibly on his way back to Lancashire.

'May I make a suggestion?' said Davenport. 'We, by which I mean the Jesuits, have the head and a quarter of a martyr we can't identify. The relics have no provenance and I would dearly love to know who it is. They're in Holywell, in North Wales. It's a wonderful place. If you did a bit of research on the bones for me, while you're here, you could conclude your work with a pilgrimage. I'll let you have access to our library and our archives so you can work from here before you go. It will keep your mind occupied, which is very important for you, and you can use the church, visit the sacraments and you can rely on our help. I will never be far away. You'll have someone to talk to whom you can trust. You will have our prayers and our support and if you want to make some spiritual exercises that's fine by me too. You could see it as a mini-retreat, on the house.'

'That's really kind of you, Father. I've been wanting to go to Holywell for ages,' said Calvin. 'My parish is dedicated to St Winefride. Is it difficult to get there from London without a car?'

'No, it's easy for a young fellow like you,' said the Jesuit. 'Take the train to Shrewsbury and walk the rest of the way—you could follow the pilgrimage trail. It's only seventy miles and it's the perfect time of the year. You could do it in a week.'

16

WILD BOB'S BURGLAR

That afternoon, as Calvin settled down to hours of contemplative prayer before the Blessed Sacrament in the penumbral light of a cool London convent, Jenny was careering along a dual carriageway in her blue Audi 3, looking for the turn-off that would take her to the home of his 'contact'.

She passed a Go Outdoors centre on her left and tapped her brakes as she came to Domino's Pizza. She was looking for the entrance to Trencherfield Mill. Inside the complex, she crawled along the narrow drive, and took the turning on her left when she came to the fork, as instructed. She stopped in a car park away from the main buildings.

She was pleased that it was sunny because she did not look out of place in a big pair of sunglasses beneath a baseball hat pulled low—the contact had told her to be as discreet as poss-ible—and to watch out for Ralph Parker.

She was answered the moment she buzzed the intercom. She kept her shades on, even in the half-light of the lift taking her to the fourth floor, and along the empty corridor to an open door.

The nurse was standing in the living room wearing skinny jeans and a black V-neck sweater. Jenny was struck by her powerful natural elegance—as well by as the jagged scar that disfigured the left side of her throat.

The nurse held out a welcoming hand as Jenny swept off her cap and glasses.

'I'll never make a master of disguise,' she said, 'but I'm sure no one saw me—it's deserted out there.'

'I know I must have sounded over the top but I don't want to take any chances by drawing attention to myself. You don't know Dr Klein like I do. What can I get you?'

'I'd love a coffee please.'

'I'll grind some fresh,' said Emerald, walking into the kitchen. 'Would that be okay? I don't have any instant.'

'Perfect,' Jenny answered, wriggling out of her jacket as she scanned her surroundings. The front room was furnished with a thick cream rug cast over a polished pine floor, a white leather three-piece suite, a glass-top coffee table, a plasma TV and a low bookshelf full of detective fiction and adorned with pictures of the nurse, her family and friends. It was ordinary enough except for the south-facing french windows, framing the blue sky and allowing sunshine to suffuse the space with natural light.

Emerald returned with two mugs. Jenny held hers up to see the writing on the side. 'Emmy Essien, Fulham and Proud,' she read out loud.

'So you know my name,' the nurse said. 'You're already doing better than Father Calvin. I haven't told him it yet, but I will now you know it. Actually it's Emerald.'

She moved to the sofa and indicated one of the chairs to Jenny.

'I had to put the thumbscrews on him just to make him tell me if you were a man or a woman,' said Jenny. 'He's very protective of you.'

'Good. I knew I could trust him. If I'm identified, I'm dead. You must keep my name a secret.'

'You really think Dr Klein is so dangerous?'

'He is capable of doing anything he thinks he could get away with. You have to be very careful. I think he's in the mood for revenge. The police have been making frequent visits to the hospital—I've been interviewed—and there is this climate of fear among the staff. The nurses aren't even gossiping any more, they're too scared of Dr Klein. But I did hear a rumour about Father Calvin being suspended.'

'It's true. He's been suspected of leaking the documents, but he's hoping to be reinstated soon because he's sure the police don't have anything on him. That's a secret of course—officially he's on some sort of sabbatical or something.'

'Do you know where he is? I've been trying to get hold of him but no one at the church ever answers the phone.'

'He's in London, staying with his parents. I had a drink with him last week when I went to interview a doctor who contacted me. Calvin thought he saw you there—he had a funny turn. Were you down last week?'

'No, I haven't been for a while now.'

Jenny recounted her meeting with Professor Silver while Emerald wore a distant look, evidently affronted by the journalist's ability to contact Calvin when she could not. At times, Jenny wasn't quite sure if she was even listening to her.

Emerald relaxed a little when the reporter made it clear that she and Calvin were in touch only because he was preparing her for marriage. She answered questions about Klein, but frequently turned the conversation back to the subject of the priest.

'I've never heard of Dr Topcliffe, no,' she told Jenny. 'Must have been before my time. I'm glad you've spoken to Father Calvin, though. I've been very worried about him since it got back to Klein that he kicked the door. Do you think he'll talk to me?'

'I don't see why not. I'll send you the number of a phone his bosses have lent him while the police ... what door?'

'That's why they think he's the leak. Before I copied those documents for you, he tried to kick his way into the records office and was seen. It got back to Klein, and he told the police.'

'Gosh, what a hero! Or idiot. Fancy doing that! I don't know about him. Sometimes he worries me. He doesn't want to be involved in any of this any more, does he? He's told me he's done with it. He was probably panicking about getting himself into massive trouble because now he has.

'Anyway, he promised me you'd tell me everything. And what I most want to know is whether Klein is a murderer. Father Calvin seems to think that you believe he is. Is that right?'

Emerald shrugged her shoulders, then nodded.

'Is Dr Klein a killer?' Jenny asked her again, this time more emphatically. 'Should I be going after him? Are you sure there is no one else who's to blame for this?'

'It's Klein.'

'How's he getting away with it, then?'

'You've gotta understand him,' began Emerald. 'He's not your classic psychopath, whatever that is exactly. Don't get me wrong—he might well kill for pleasure—I'm sure he probably gets some satisfaction from it—but this guy, I think he does it more from conviction. He thinks he's thought everything through, you know, and he has all the answers, thinks he's doing the right thing. He thinks he knows it all. He's ice-cold and he's extremely clever. He thinks everyone else is wrong, that we're all idiots. Do you get what I'm saying?'

'Yeah, I've met the type.'

'Okay, you need to know that Reinhard is a great doctor. They revere him at Bethulia Park and Dr Baqri, our medical director, absolutely trusts him. They used to work together and he knows how good he is. He's excellent, in fact. He's saved a lot of lives, without a doubt, but the problem is that he discriminates too.

'Let's say, for argument's sake, you were in the flower of your youth and something bad happened to you and you needed emergency treatment. If Reinhard ending up looking after you, you could count yourself lucky. He likes them young and healthy even when they only have, say, a five per cent chance of survival. He'll fight for you and you might survive when you'd have died in the hands of a lesser professional. He really is the best I've seen when he's like that. He's pulled people back from the brink over and over again. That's why the staff love him at Bethulia Park, and so do the directors.

'But if you were a patient who was elderly or seriously ill or was appearing to be a nuisance, it might be different. You definitely wouldn't want him near you. He doesn't like disabled people either. All these people, you see, he reckons it's better for them, the health service, society, the country, everyone, if they are dead. He wouldn't openly admit that, of course, but I know him well and I've seen how it plays out.

'Honestly, you want to hear him drone on about such-and-such-a-body being a "voracious and unworthy consumer of the health service's finite resources".'

Emerald gave a booming imitation of the doctor's voice.

'I don't know what he bloody reads at night to come out with all that stuff. Thinks he's a philosopher, he does.

'You might take a negative view of opinions of that kind, as I do, but he's blind to criticism. I think he thinks he is "enlightened" or "progressive". It's not all bad, mind you, what he stands for. Sometimes listening to him is like hearing poetry, if I'm honest. You can just sit back and let him talk and he comes out with all these theories about fulfilment and being whoever you want to be in life, without any rules and parameters other than what's forbidden by law. Some of it's pretty compelling stuff.

'He makes more sense, in some ways, than I bet Calvin does with his universal moral laws and angels and saints. Klein will just tell you nice and casually to go out and find your own happiness—you know, that the meaning of life is something we create for ourselves. It's far easier to swallow. But it's a bit ironic that he's not the best advert for the utopia he's dreamed up. He's bloody morose a lot of the time, a right bullying miserable sod. I call him "Raging Reiny" when he's like that.'

Emerald explained to Jenny in detail how she had seen Dr Klein work. Her account corresponded with the stories the journalist had heard from the families she had interviewed. These people had invariably spoken about loved ones, mostly elderly, entering hospital with minor, seemingly treatable complaints, sometimes simply under observation, only to spend their nights crying out for a drink as they slowly dried up and withered away into weakness and death. They had described their awful feelings of impotence at watching their loved ones die and not being able to stop it. They'd told her in harrowing detail of their confusion and bewilderment when the causes of death that appeared on the official certificates did not reflect their experiences: dementia, emphysema, impaired swallowing, pneumonia, C. diff, the list was inexhaustible. But it never included the denial of food, fluids and antibiotics and the injections of painkillers and sedatives the families said they saw and which turned their memories into trauma.

'You know, that man has turned medical killing into a fine art,' Emerald told Jenny. 'Yeah, he's a murderer. If killing was a medical speciality, he'd be its leading light. One of his tricks is to leave an old dear by an open window with barely a sheet on the bed. He'd get a nurse to do it, one who wouldn't question him, and he'd forget to order her to close the window and move the bed back again for just as long as it might take for pneumonia to set in.

'A lot of the other stuff he gets away with because he hides behind collegiality and fabricated documentation. That should have worked for him with Ray Parker, but he chose to lie about cancer. That was off the scale. I can't believe he did that. Careless by his standards. He got cocky. But my bet is he'll get away with it again. He's made out of Teflon, I swear.'

'Silk' was the word that went through Jenny's mind, but she kept her counsel. 'Calvin mentioned collegiality,' she said. 'What did you mean by that exactly?'

'Well, in normal circumstances it would be part of the checks and balances for patient safety but Klein's gone and stood it on its head, in the same way that he's made pain relief and the management of symptoms into a pathway to death, dying or not, when ordinarily it's compassionate medicine at its most excellent.

'Did Calvin mention to you what I told him about his use of contra-indicated drugs?'

'Yes,' Jenny muttered.

'Well, normally doctors couldn't do that so easily, but Klein always seems to find a way. What I'm saying is that all medicines are prescribed and checked by the pharmacy, and contra-indicated combinations are withheld. The pharmacists don't give out drugs that might create an adverse side effect in a particular patient if they were administered at the same time.

'For some reason this doesn't seem to matter as much in end-of-life care because sometimes contra-indicated drugs are given together to these patients when they should not. Sadly, that's become medical practice. Klein steers his victims to the point where he can do this kind of thing without anyone questioning him.

'He starts with a forecast. Predicting death doesn't have an evidence base. It's guesswork until the very end, and Klein knows it. So he decides someone's dying then he makes it happen. He gets away with it by influencing the multi-disciplinary teams into agreeing with him, then fooling them into thinking they've made the decision collectively, or that his role was somehow minor.

'These teams are packed with people from peripheral medical backgrounds, like speech therapists, who would visit the patient sometimes only once. Most are not best qualified to make definitive life-or-death judgements of any kind, but Klein makes them all feel so knowledgeable and so important, and they're never going to argue with him even if they disagreed.'

Emerald looked hard at the reporter.

'Whatever happened to the all-crucial doctor-patient relationship in this, the essential knowledge of the patient? These teams don't offer that. They're no safeguard in the hands of that man. They're a convenience. He insinuates his malice into their judgements then hides behind this so-called principle of collegiality, shielding himself with other staff. The records always show that they shared in the process of reaching the conclusions he decided in advance. They're supposed to protect patients but, in Klein's case, they give him cover.'

She paused.

'I don't know what the hell went wrong with him but something did. From the outside, he's right where he should be but inside he's putrid. I mean, he's into this hard-core pornography for one, and it's shocking stuff. He showed me once … and what they were doing to these women—probably trafficked or abducted—it would turn your stomach. Vile, it was. Unspeakable, horrible. Women like pieces of meat. But he was loving it, the sick bastard. I'm no prude, I've got an open mind, but … that stuff, it depraves on contact and he was just soaking himself in it.'

Jenny gulped as she visualised Emerald watching pornography with Dr Klein, immediately wondering about the context. Why would they do that? What were they, swingers or something? Were they romantically involved? Were they having an affair at the time, or was it something as fleeting as a one-night stand? She was greedy to know more, but she dared not ask the nurse directly. She had only just met the girl. She had to be tactful.

'He didn't strike me as that type when I saw him with his kids at the stables,' said Jenny. 'Two daughters, is that right? I assume he's married then?'

'Oh yeah, he's married.'

'Does he have affairs?'

'Yes, all the time. He's having one right now, but I don't know who the girlfriend is.'

'And does he ever sleep with the nurses?'

'Sometimes.'

The two women stared at each other in awkward silence, eying each other with suspicion. Jenny changed the subject, first asking about her flat and whether she lived alone. Emerald nodded and asked the journalist why she wanted to know. Jenny pointed to a framed portrait on top of the bookshelf. It was of the nurse embracing a gangly man. Jenny said she thought the man might be her boyfriend.

Emerald smiled. 'No, that's Jim, my husband—well, he was my husband. He's dead now, and I miss him.'

'I'm sorry.'

'Don't worry. I'm okay now. We met in London when we were studying there. He was great fun. Then he got skin cancer—too much sunshine, I guess—and it spread. We got married in Camden register office and three weeks later he was so ill they rushed him to hospital. But they let me take him home and I gave him the best care I could, right to his last breath. I haven't met anyone quite like him since. He looked after me, still does now. All this you see here—this flat—Jimmy paid for this. Bloody short marriage, though. Another guy like him would be great. Can I let you in on a secret?'

'What? About Klein?'

'No. Not about Klein. I'm not into doctors. It's about Calvin. I quite like Calvin.'

'You can't! He's a priest!'

'I know, but he's my type. A guy like that—who wasn't a priest—now he would be the perfect man for me.'

'What's so wrong with the doctors?' asked Jenny. 'I saw at the inquest a few nurses who were behaving like Klein was their type.'

'I'm done with doctors—and Jenny, Klein's really dangerous. When you see him coming, walk the other way. That's my advice. Okay, Reinhard's a good-looking guy with edgy charm. He's naughty, and some people like that. We all know that some girls have an eye for the bad boys and me too once—I've been like those nurses, but I'm not any more.'

Emerald looked thoughtful.

'You know why I would prefer Calvin to Klein? Because of his integrity—that's what I like about him. It's not easy to find this quality so completely in any person, and to me it's attractive. People like him give me hope. They give me a reason to bother. When I'm up to my neck in wickedness all the time, it's people like Calvin who make me think that there is a good life out there somewhere, just waiting for me—and maybe a decent man too. It's just my luck that the first person I've come across who ticks all the boxes, since losing Jimmy, happens to be a priest. But Klein? A man like that? Not for me. Never again.'

Both women recognised their conversation had run its course and Jenny was relieved when Emerald sat up and gestured towards the mill opposite, telling her a falcon had just come in with a kill.

Jenny was striding towards the french windows when she felt Emerald's restraining hand gently slip into the crook of her elbow. 'Don't go too close to the window,' said the nurse. 'Ralph Parker's down there.'

'Well, why don't I ring him and invite him up?' said Jenny.

The journalist was studying the peregrine chicks and their attentive parents on the roof of the old mill when Ralph arrived at the door.

His eyes bulged at the sight of Emerald and Jenny together. He wiped his boots on the mat and entered the room cautiously, as if in disbelief. He wore a dark anorak and smelled of the fresh air outside. Around his neck were a pair of battered binoculars and he held a camera with a zoom lens.

'Fancy seeing you here!' he exclaimed, surveying the smiling faces.

'I see you found her, then,' he said in a low voice to Jenny, as if Emerald wasn't in the room.

'She found us, actually. It's a secret, though. Emerald, this is Ralph Parker, I think you've met.'

'We have,' said Ralph. Addressing the nurse directly, he said: 'Great to see you again. You were really good to my dad. If there's anything—anything—you want from me, just ask me, love. I owe you one.'

'Thanks, Mr Parker, I'll bear it in mind. Anyway, we've a treat for you. I think you can get some good snaps from up here. The peregrines are almost opposite. Just don't go so close to the window that others can see you. Remember what Jenny told you on the phone just then.'

'No problem at all—and it's "Ralph", by the way.'

Within seconds, Ralph was snapping away. 'Oh, lovely,' he kept saying to himself, 'Beautiful! Oh, that's a cracker. Go on, one more time. Oh, fantastic!'

The women looked at each other and chuckled. 'If you started charging them to come up here, you'd make a fortune,' Jenny said.

'Good idea. Maybe next year.'

Eventually, Ralph put down his camera and squinted the eye that had been doing the hard work. He sat at the table and showed the best of the pictures to Jenny, while Emerald brought him a cup of tea.

Between sips, he chatted enthusiastically about his hobby, apologising for the fact that he was using an antiquated second-hand 300mm lens.

'It's like being the littlest kid in the class again,' he said. 'For me, goin' into one of them hides with this little thing is like goin' into the shower block with all the bigger lads, all lookin' at yer and smilin'. Most of those buggers have lenses so big they have to pull 'em around in golf carts. A twitch goes up on one of them reserves and them hides are like Second World War pillboxes with bazookas and machine guns hanging out the windows. I can't compete with that so something local like this is just up my street, and being this close is amazing.'

'It's the expert hands that make all the difference anyway, hey Ralph?' said Jenny.

'Definitely. But I do want more range and I'm saving up for another lens. Sigma and Tamron are doing these 600mm lenses which are almost affordable for me, about a fifth or a sixth the price of a luxury lens of the same length, and I reckon I'll be able to get one soon now that I'm singing again.'

He registered the intrigue in the faces of both women. 'Yeah, Elton John, though I'm better at Glen Campbell,' he said. 'Boss won't have that, though. He says no one knows who Glen Campbell is any more and the punters love Elton John so I've got to do him all the time.

'I like Elton but I really love country. So me and me mate Toni, who does Elvis, we've come up with idea of doing a duet—an Elton-Elvis duet—in which I join him and we sing *Gentle on My Mind*. First time we did it, the boss went mad. "That's a Glen Campbell song", he was goin' on, effin' and jeffin' he was. "I told you to do Elton, not Glen effin' Campbell". I said, "No, Bob, it's an Elvis song. Elvis sang it as well, you can check. It's one of Toni's favourite Elvis songs".

'Ees' all right about it now. He'll be lettin' me do Glen Campbell after a while, once he sees the punters lovin' *Rhinestone Cowboy*. I've just got to find a way to sneak it in. I tell yer, I'm prayin' for the day when the real Elton does a country tribute album.'

'Who do you work for?' asked Emerald.

'Bob Torridge. Me and Toni sing in his new restaurant in Crostbury three days a week—but never on Fridays and Saturdays.'

'What, he's got a restaurant now? I know about his pub, The White Hart, but I never knew he had a restaurant.'

'He took over his dad's funeral parlour and—well, business is good around the Bethulia Park Hospital catchment area, innit?—no offence, Emerald. No, seriously, he's invested wisely and he's expanding all the time. Shrewd businessman now. Not the 'wild Bob' of his youth.'

'Wild Bob?' Jenny repeated.

'Oh, he had this reputation when he was younger. Ee was brawlin' all the time, then he was in big trouble for beating up some policemen and later for involvement in an armed robbery. That was the only time he went down. Tanya straightened him out soon after that—tough woman. He met his match there. He's behaved himself since. He's in his forties now, anyway. So all that was years ago.'

'So how is Tanya these days?' said Emerald.

'Oh, you know her! She's fine except that she lost her mum recently. Heart attack at your hospital on Good Friday, totally unexpected. They buried her last week. So it's been a bad time for the family lately. I haven't seen that much of her, to tell you the truth. I expect you know what Bob's like about Tanya so he's been pretty upset too.'

Emerald nodded knowingly, but Jenny appeared captivated. She looked pleadingly to Ralph to carry on.

'Oh, yeah, Tanya's the power behind the throne,' he told her. 'Keep this to yourself, but they say a few years ago when Bob's and Tanya's kids were little and they didn't have this big converted barn that they live in now, there was this low life going around burgling all the houses in their area. One day Tanya took the little 'uns to the shops in their prams or buggies, or whatever, and this guy breaks into 'er 'ouse. Nasty type by all accounts—horribly spiteful if he found himself in a nice 'ome. He'd wreck it, and more besides, if you know what I mean.

'Well, she comes 'ome from the shops and the back door's swinging open and there's broken glass all over the kitchen floor. She goes in and her living room's like a scene from the Blitz. This fella's gone to town all right, really enjoyed himself. He'd even turned the kids' rooms upside down, and ransacked the master bedroom. All Tanya's jewellery was gone along with a load of other stuff.

'So she calls Bob at work, bawling her eyes out, and the first thing he says is, "Don't call the police"'—well, this is what I've heard anyway—and he starts his own investigations. He starts asking around, on the quiet, to find out who's doing the burglaries. He's a very persuasive man, and he soon finds out who it is. He took care of it his way.'

'His way?' said Jenny, alarmed. 'What do you mean by that?'

'I mean I think that the burglar had to have a restful few weekends at home after running into Bob Torridge,' said Ralph.

'You mean no one's seen him since,' interrupted Emerald.

'He left town, as you would do, but it's not as bad as you're suggesting,' Ralph said, his eyes flicking toward the reporter. 'If it was like that, the police would have been involved and they never were. The upshot was that there were no more burglaries by him or anyone else around there after that, not for a long time, if ever. Bob did the police a favour. Not sure if Tanya got all of her jewellery back, though. I'll have to ask her one day. Anyway, I'd better get goin'. This is between ourselves, remember. Thanks for letting me up to take those pictures. Come and see me sing. I'll dedicate a few songs to yer.'

Jenny waited five minutes before departing, so she would not be seen leaving the building with Ralph. She chatted about her wedding plans and she told the nurse about her horse.

'Do you like horse racing, Emerald?'

'I wouldn't know, I've never been.'

'Oh, it's great fun. It's Seb's birthday soon and we're going to the races at Haydock, a group of us, for the meeting on the 25th. It should be a right knees-up. Why don't you come too? Fancy it? There's a few people I'd love you to meet.'

Emerald thought about it, weighing up the risks of being seen, but accepted and they talked through possible arrangements as Jenny put on her jacket, cap and shades.

As she walked towards the lift, the journalist took out her phone and began to scroll through the texts and emails.

There was one from Seb saying he was back from the gym and he was planning to spend the rest of the day gaming online with his mates.

There was also one from Dr Klein, inviting her to meet him.

17

NOTHING TO SEE HERE

The detectives were late for the meeting at Bethulia Park Hospital, leaving Dr Klein at the large table of the boardroom to make small talk with the chief executive, Anne Conway, and the medical director, Dr Muhammad Baqri. The constant rotation of his ball point pen between his forefinger and thumb was the only indication of his nervousness.

After a long fifteen minutes, the police arrived. Detective Inspector George Tarleton was smooth and dapper as usual, wearing aftershave over a face sooted by dark stubble that made him look, certainly through his own eyes, more ruggedly male.

He cheerfully made his apologies as he was followed into the room by two less senior detectives, who seemed to radiate an elevated sense of importance in the presence of their senior officer, as if it was a treat to be at his side.

With Mrs Conway at the head of the table and the two doctors adjacent on her left, the police officers naturally aimed for the other side and noisily dragged out chairs by their backrests. Tarleton directly faced Klein. The other two officers sat either side of him—Detective Sergeant Amber Clarke on his left, nodding warmly to the group, and Detective Constable Nick

Ramsbotham on his right, staring at Klein in undisguised contempt.

The chief executive called to her personal assistant for refreshments, but suggested that the meeting proceeded immediately because her medical staff were extremely busy and in demand elsewhere.

Tarleton took the hint and opened a cardboard folder, drawing out a pile of papers with some handwritten notes on top.

'The good news,' he said, 'is that we have got to the bottom of what really happened in the weeks before Ray Parker's death. We have managed to locate the missing notes—the same notes that the *Sunday News* has—and you know where we found them? In the Parker file.'

The three hospital officials looked at each other, bewildered, Klein appearing particularly confused.

'We have also traced and interviewed the Macmillan nurse who the Parker family maintained was present at the meeting,' Tarleton went on. 'She has not only confirmed it took place, as it was described by the Parkers, but she also made her own notes of the meeting, and filed them with the Somerset Cancer Register—you know, the NHS's electronic cancer patients record. She did that right after the meeting of September 11. They have that date on them. There is no doubt that the family's account is true.'

Klein felt the eyes of Conway and Baqri bore into him like lasers as he sat pinching his lower lip with a thumb and forefinger.

'Well?' said Conway addressing him directly with a ferocious stare. 'What do you have to say about that?'

'Anne, you know how damned busy we are,' he protested. 'I'm seeing patients and their families in these situations day in and day out and with all the hours I'm putting in and the pressures of the job, you can hardly blame me if I forget one or two of these meetings from time to time. It was a genuine failure of recollection.'

He jabbed a finger on the papers that Tarleton had set before them.

'You can see I haven't hidden the facts of the meeting. I signed those documents. I can only imagine that what happened was I forgot about the meeting, perhaps in the confidence that the documents existed if ever I needed to be reminded about it, and then they were misplaced. This is an unfortunate administrative error, that's what all this is about.'

Detective Sergeant Clarke gave the doctor a wintry look. 'How do you explain their omission from the file the first time we inspected it, Dr Klein?' she said. 'Surely you understand why the Parker family thinks the fact they were missing ahead of the inquest was extremely convenient for the Trust, with the way the inquest went in the end. Why were the documents missing then, but not now?'

'I simply can't answer that,' said Klein, shaking his head. 'It wasn't my job to file them away. I don't deal with admin matters like that. Perhaps they were misplaced, or misfiled, found again at a later date and put back where they should have always been, I just don't know.'

'Perhaps the person who gave them to the *Sunday News* put them back,' suggested Tarleton.

Silence momentarily descended on the group as they contemplated the differing scenarios, then Dr Baqri spoke.

'Dare I be so bold as to say this, detectives, but in my professional opinion the fuss over this meeting last September is something of a red herring. Mr Parker was so ill that he was going to die anyway. That was the view of the multi-disciplinary team who examined his case when cancer was suspected and who cared for the patient throughout his stay in hospital. It's in the records. With respect, Detective Sergeant Clarke, this meeting between Dr Klein and the family would have in no way altered the care and treatment that we gave to Mr Parker as he deteriorated without any prospect of recovery.

'The point I wish to make—and I wish to make it as emphatically as possible—is that the meeting recorded in the notes and confirmed by the Macmillan nurse would, I am absolutely sure, have had no bearing on the medical facts of his condition and ultimately the verdict of the inquest. It does not change a thing.

'The coroner had it right. He did his job well. There is absolutely no need at all for a second inquest. There was a failure of communication between us and the Parkers. We will make sure that won't ever happen again, I can assure you.'

Detective Inspector Tarleton thanked the doctor for his comments.

'I am sure you will be delighted to hear that the coroner has already indicated that he does not intend to open a fresh inquest,' he announced, his eyes shifting towards Conway, 'but he does want the Trust to apologise to him and to the Parker family as well.

'I strongly advise you to apologise. This matter is now in the public domain and it is important that the public sees that justice is being served, and that people have faith in the system, so we would also advise you to make your apology public as well.'

Mrs Conway promised the police officer that the coroner would receive an apology in writing without delay, and told Dr Baqri to draft a letter later that day.

Tarleton looked satisfied, Clarke and Ramsbotham less so.

'That takes us to the leak,' Tarleton began again. 'It was reported to us that a Roman Catholic hospital chaplain was seen behaving suspiciously outside the records office. Now that we have found the documents we can no longer consider the leak to be a theft, in the pure sense.

'We have searched the presbytery of St Winefride's Catholic Church, and we've been right through the phone and computer and other possessions of this Father Calvin Baines and found no copies of them, or correspondence with hospital staff—nothing whatsoever that links him. So we are going to eliminate him from this inquiry. In fact, we are no longer inclined to invest our time and resources into tracing a leak. We consider it to be an internal disciplinary matter for the Trust so we're going to leave it with you. It looks like an inside job. Of course, if you find evidence of criminal activity please come back to us.'

Dr Klein was angry. 'We can't have priests walking around, kicking doors at the hospital, surely!' he burst out, looking imploringly toward his superiors. 'I don't think he should be allowed back, at the very least.'

'I agree,' said Mrs Conway. 'Dr Baqri, could you contact the archdiocese and insist that this man is withdrawn from the chaplaincy rota at once?'

Tarleton then turned to the matter of eight complaints of unlawful killing and criminal negligence.

He explained that the arrangement with the coroner meant that the Parker case would proceed no further, before offering assurances that neither he nor his team had found any evidence in the medical notes of the other seven that would meet the threshold of a full criminal investigation.

'You will no doubt be glad to hear that I will be advising the Chief Constable that there is no evidence of criminal activity and therefore no further action should be taken in relation to any of them,' he said.

'We have a bit of tidying up to do but I expect that our investigations will be concluded by the end of May, and I am aiming to send final, concluding reports to both the Chief Constable and to you by a month from this day—June 7th—when the families will also be notified in writing of our decision.

'I can assure you that I am very sympathetic to you. I understand absolutely the pressures you are under and I, like so many of the general public, value the excellent work the health service does for this country and that this hospital does for this area. Personally, I think you are being unfairly criticised by a handful of disgruntled families and one or two mischievous journalists.

I think you deserve better. But please, please be careful. I don't want to be back here again. Nor, I'm sure, do you want the Care Quality Commission dropping in for a snap inspection on the back of all this publicity.'

Conway and the two doctors muttered their gratitude to the police officer, with Dr Klein also mentally praising the influence of the marvellous Dr Tarleton, who had evidently worked her magic. He was amused that she had fooled her husband into believing himself to be something of an expert on end-of-life care.

Dr Baqri was the most effusive. 'Thank you so much for your excellent work,' he told the Detective Inspector. 'There has been a problem with communication, like I said. We are fixing that.

'Another problem, of course, is that people don't understand that medical advances nowadays mean we can keep patients going long after they would normally have died. There must be a point in everyone's lives when we hold up our hands say 'enough is enough', but that is a debate society has to have.

'In the meantime, what we don't want to see is the spread of superbugs, or patients dying in surgery, or vegetating in bags suspended indefinitely over hospital beds because they can't lift themselves up off their bed sores. I am happy to assure you, Detective Inspector, that all patients who come into our care are given the highest standard of treatment, according to their best interests. End-of-life care allows us to do that extremely well within the law.'

'I'm delighted to hear that, Dr Baqri.'

As the meeting broke up, Dr Klein saw the chance to have a moment alone with Tarleton, who was standing by a large window overlooking a flower bed crafted to grow into the shape and colours of a rainbow around the white initials of the NHS. At its centre stood a pole with a rainbow flag.

'It's a great job, you've done, George, congratulations,' Klein said, adding with a smile: 'Tell me, does this deadline you've set have anything to do with the golfing trip to the Algarve on the eighth of June?'

'And here's me thinking I was the detective!' chuckled Tarleton. 'You could say so, yes. I want everything done by then. You should come with us one day.'

'I'd love to but I always seem to have too much on—family and work commitments. It's a difficult juggling act at times—two girls, long working hours, Jane always full of ideas about what she wants us all to do. One day, perhaps.'

'I've never had that problem. I'm not a family man like you. Octavia—you know her, right …?' Tarleton asked, raising his eyebrows.

'Vaguely. We worked together some time ago,' replied Dr Klein.

'Well, neither of us are too bothered about kids and it means we enjoy our money and enjoy our free time. It's how we like it. She does what she wants and I do what I want. We have loads of holidays. Sometimes she goes away on her own or with friends if I'm busy, but that means she isn't bothered if I want to go off with a gang of mates, get drunk and belt balls around in the sunshine for a week or so. I was never going to miss that trip to the Algarve.'

'It's a charmed life you lead, but family is everything to me, and my patients are just as important,' said Dr Klein, his attention distracted by the figure of Mrs Conway, waiting for him by the door. Her expression was grim.

18

THE STEAM ROOM

That evening Jenny relaxed alone in the steam room of the council-owned gym, rivulets of sweat running from her head and down her back and shoulders. She was saturated, her bikini top and shorts as wet as if she'd just climbed out of a swimming pool. For her, that final twelve or fifteen minutes of intense heat and humidity felt the best part of the workout and the reward for nearly two hours of aerobic exercise and weight-training. The small of her back still hurt a little from the fall so she was careful not to make the injury worse, but she had worked every other muscle group hard, especially her core, when she could, knowing the importance of good balance to riding well.

She leaned back and exhaled deeply through her mouth then breathed in slowly through her nose, the steam too hot on her throat to let it pass over her lips. There were pearls of sweat on every part of exposed flesh, and the heat was starting to make her feel a little light-headed.

She swigged water from a plastic bottle and poured a little over her forehead. It was blissfully cool.

Peering through the misted windows of the door she could see a clock in the shower area outside and she worked out that she had been in for eight minutes. Just five more minutes would be perfect. The heat was still bearable, and having the room all to herself bordered on luxury. She tried to time her visits carefully as there was always a risk of encountering men in the unisex sauna. She sought to avoid them: she never felt comfortable scantily clad and soaking wet before their prying eyes. It was like being trapped in a bathroom in your underwear with complete strangers.

The door opened and Jenny's heart sank as Dennis Clarence walked in. He honked out a slow laugh as she blinked back at him in disbelief.

'Dennis!'

'We'll have to stop running into each other like this,' he sniggered.

He was naked but for a pair of baggy red shorts which hung from his midriff like a hula skirt. His skin was sickly white and hairless, his muscles had few contours and gravity was not being kind to him in his indolence, leaving him not so much out of shape as misshapen. At least he was trying to get fit, Jenny thought, giving credit where it was due and recognising his effort to take care of himself. He sat down opposite her and within seconds sweat was dripping down his face and neck. Dennis was a melting snowman.

'I didn't know you were a member here,' Jenny said. 'What have you been doing?'

'Oh, I've just joined. I want to get fit. But I'm not ready to start on the machines just yet—thought I'd lose a few pounds in here, regular visits. I've just come for the steam room and sauna.'

'Don't overdo it, Den,' said Jenny sarcastically. 'Weren't you tempted to watch the game tonight? I thought every man for miles around her would be watching Liverpool and Barcelona in the semi-final. My guy's gone out for it with his mates and he isn't even into football. That's why there's hardly anyone here. It's the way I like it.'

'What is he, an egg-chaser?'

'A former semi-pro rugby league player, yes. Nearly made it but for injury. He's still mad about the game, though.'

'Is he a rough bugger?'

'Not with me.'

Dennis rubbed the sweat out of his eyes. 'Soccer's not much interest to me either, and I really don't give a damn about Liverpool. They've already lost 3–0 in the other leg, haven't they? They've got no chance, the pussies.'

His choice of word suddenly made Jenny feel even more self-conscious and deeply relieved to be wearing shorts instead of anything more revealing. Her bikini top concealed less, however, especially now it was soaked. Beads of sweat trickled across the exposed area of her breasts on to the thin nylon, tracing and delineating every part that remained out of sight. She could not have been more grateful to have chosen to wear black. She glanced again at the clock outside as Dennis sneakily looked her up and down.

'Been up to much?' he asked.

'Surveillance work, mostly,' she answered.

'Is that for the *Sunday News?*'

Jenny nodded.

'I saw your piece in the *News* the other week,' he said. 'You've been busy with those families—blimey! I thought about doing the same thing myself—especially after your advice—but I couldn't get my news editor interested. These people on the desk can drive you mad. They don't know what a good story is half the time. They get on your tits.'

Jenny squirmed.

'Of course, they're all interested now since you've done it. Because of that I've had to work on it all week and the week before that. So thanks a million. I still don't think they're going to go massive with it, you know—make it into a campaign. My information is that the investigation is going nowhere, that the cops won't act on the complaints. They're wrapping it up. We might go big on that line when the police announce it to the families officially next month. Sorry about that, Jenny.'

'Why are you sorry?'

'Because it makes your reports look a bit, well, you know—a bit made-up, a little bit fabricated.'

Jenny chose not to answer him.

'Did you know it was a non-starter when you pitched it to the *News*, Jenny?' said Dennis, one side of his mouth breaking into a smile. 'Kerr-ching! At least you get paid! Don't let the facts get in the way of a good story, eh? You not bothered about getting egg on yer face?'

'Are you bothered about getting a slap across yours?'

Clarence went into reverse. 'I didn't mean it like that. Just winding you up,' he stuttered.

'I stand by the facts,' said Jenny. 'It was a nice exclusive, that one. I'm pleased with it and so are the families.'

Dennis went quiet, then after some hesitation he said: 'I know what you mean. I love breaking exclusives.'

Sure you do, thought Jenny, looking away and wishing he would take off to Fleet Street to tell them how good he was. She was pretty sure he would not last long once the bruisers who staffed the news desks of the major titles began to scream 'EXCLUSIVES NOT EXCUSES!' at him, and that he would soon be back in the shires—privately with his tail between his legs, but with experience he could use as a springboard to the more lucrative world of public relations.

'No, I take it back about your reports. I have to hand it to you, you did a cracking job,' he said. 'Very thorough. Must have taken you ages. You know what I liked best? That stuff about the leaked documents. That was brilliant! I've not been able to get a lead on that, and I'd love to follow it up.'

He was unable to conceal a crafty look on his face.

'Who was your source? Do you think she'd speak to me?'

'Forget it, mate, I'm not telling you that,' replied Jenny.

Clarence bristled.

'Given the risks involved in getting hold of those documents, your contact must be a little scared now, I suppose,' he went on. 'So I understand your position. I bet it was that nurse with the scar who everyone was talking about at Angela Parker's. Was it her? I bet it was. I bet she'll be well upset when she finds the police investigation won't be going anywhere, that everything she did for you was for nothing. She failed. I feel for her. If they catch her, she'll be out of a job. Never mind, eh? It's all for a good cause, whistleblowing.'

'It wasn't her,' said Jenny. 'I don't know who she is, I don't know who you're talking about. And just so you truly understand my position, this isn't over yet. The families will pursue their grievances even if the police won't—you should stay in touch with them if you really want exclusives—and I don't think the *News* will necessarily accept it's a non-story just because the police won't investigate, that's if what you're saying is true.'

'Oh, it's true,' said Dennis. 'Last time we met, you asked me to give you a lead. Well, I'm giving you one now: there was a meeting today at the hospital with Detective Inspector Tarleton—remember him? Well, he told all the top people in the trust that the police will be dropping every one of the cases. All of them. It's over, Jenny, before it's even begun. It's going nowhere. Sorry I have to break it to you like this.

'I know it must annoy you to hear it from me, too, but it's not my fault if I'm ahead of the game, and you're not even playing.'

Jenny felt as if she had been hit in the face with a dustbin lid. Of course she remembered Tarleton from the inquest; the sooty-faced detective who brushed aside the family's request for a criminal investigation from the first moment, his evidence providing Dr Klein with everything he needed to be fully exonerated—until Jenny exposed the doctor as a liar. Hardly surprising that he wished to forget about the Parker case and brush all the subsequent complaints under the carpet too. She rallied herself.

'It isn't over, Dennis. It's just getting going. They can't just pretend this hasn't happened. The families won't let them, and I'm expecting more families to come forward. I'm going to carry on researching it too. I'm committed to this. No way has this run its course. Actually I've been working on a new line all week. Have you heard of Dr Octavia Topcliffe, Dennis? You've been working this patch longer than I have. You might know something.'

He shook his head. 'Why?'

'Apparently she has a long track record of getting waiting lists down by dumping patients on to end-of-life care by the truckload. I've heard the last place she worked was Bethulia Park and I'm dead interested to find out what she did there, and if she had any influence on the shaping of existing policy and practice.'

'Come again?' said Dennis.

'Well, I'm using the Freedom of Information Act as part of my research into how death rates might have changed in the time she was there, a lot of stuff along those lines. I should be receiving a few responses shortly. It would be interesting to know if she's part of this puzzle. With a bit of luck, you'll be able to read about it one day in the *Sunday News*.'

Jenny rose.

'Do please let me know if you remember her or come across her, and we could do some work together unless, of course, you're worried about the damage it might do to your glorious reputation. Now I've got to get out of here before I melt. See you around.'

As soon as the door closed, Clarence swore horribly, muttering all the things he wanted to say to her face but knew he never could. As soon as he was sure she had gone, he scrambled out of the steam room, with his head spinning and the sense he was about to keel over.

Jenny was of course reluctant to admit to Clarence that she believed his information to be true. A rumour had reached her that morning from a former colleague at the *News* who had been liaising with DI Tarleton over a police operation into people-trafficking in Blackburn, Burnley and Luton.

Evidence gathered by investigative reporters, including Jenny, helped the police to move swiftly against a Romanian gang and now convictions, jail sentences and deportations were expected.

Tarleton rang to thank the editor, then used the opportunity to whinge about the 'undue prominence' given by the newspaper to the deaths at Bethulia Park, assuring him that inquiries by his officers were routine and were unlikely to lead to anything. It was still a far cry from saying that the investigation was being decisively dropped, but it wounded Jenny to realise that Clarence was in the loop when she was not, and that what she received as hearsay he knew as a certainty.

Walking along a corridor from the changing rooms, she reached into her pocket for her phone to see if Seb had sent her any messages from the match. There were a few and she smiled at the soccer and beer emojis he'd attached. He seemed to be having a whale of a time. Liverpool were back on top.

She opened her email account to see another message from Dr Klein, the fourth he had sent via a portal on her website in as many days. She read it:

> Dear Jenny, As I said previously, I would dearly love the opportunity to talk to you about events at Bethulia Park. I want so badly to explain to you what is really happening there. You're a great professional but I am confident the accuracy of your reports will improve if you were to speak to me directly from time to time. I'm very willing to make myself available to you. How about a coffee, and the chance to see if we can co-operate? Yours affectionately, Reinhard.

Jenny mouthed the last three words of his message with a sneer and thrust the phone back into her pocket. Yet it was becoming abundantly clear to her that it would be a good idea to talk to Dr Klein.

Dennis Clarence clearly was already doing that and it meant he was getting stories when she was not. She couldn't allow that. She was also keen to hear Klein's side of the story beyond what he had told the inquest. It was true, furthermore, that she had seen no evidence of his culpability in any murder besides, perhaps, a shoddy attempt to mislead the coroner. But was there a more innocuous explanation for that? Fatigue, perhaps? Forgetfulness?

For all Emerald had told her, the nurse had yet to offer any proof of the accusations she made. All she had done, concluded Jenny, was try to explain why there was no proof. It was inadequate. Moreover, such claims were coming from a woman who admitted to watching pornography with Dr Klein and who was probably sleeping with him at the time. Was it really a wise move to invest all her trust in this person, who, for all she knew, might be motivated by a grudge, or a desire for revenge, without giving the doctor the chance to explain himself?

Jenny got into her car and slammed the door. She sat pensively for a moment. Then she dug into the pocket of her coat and took out the phone. She returned to the email from Dr Klein, hit the reply button and began to write:

Coffee would be lovely—Jenny

'Let's see where that takes us,' she thought.

19

SWALLOWED UP

The phone call from Monsignor David Wickham to inform Calvin that the police investigation had cleared him of any suspicion of stealing medical documents from Bethulia Park Hospital came as a massive relief.

His jubilation was immediately diminished by the vicar general's other news that Mrs Hoskins, his housekeeper, was in hospital after a suspected stroke.

'She's going to be all right, we think,' said Monsignor Wickham. 'She's under observation at the moment. You don't need to rush back to see her. In any case the Trust doesn't want you anywhere near the hospital. You're off the rota.'

Monsignor Wickham appeared delighted by Calvin's plan to go on pilgrimage to Holywell and gave him the time to do it, on the understanding that he would be back in the parish by May 19, the fifth Sunday of Easter. While Mrs Hoskins was out of action another widow, Margaret Edwards, a retired head teacher, would look after the presbytery and the church, and Father Frank McCarthy, a retired priest, would stand in for Calvin. The police, in the meantime, were going to return his possessions.

So on that morning of Friday May 10 Calvin took a train from Euston to Shrewsbury, wearing the clothes he intended to walk in during the week ahead, including, most importantly, sturdy boots and a waterproof anorak. The remainder of his belongings were stowed tightly in a backpack, to which he attached a lightweight one-person tent.

Leaving the station, he made his way past the 11th century castle and down the slope of St Mary's Street to the Severn. Mrs Hoskins was on his mind.

He was very fond of his housekeeper—they had become good friends. She fawned over him, kept his spirits up and she occasionally made him laugh. They watched TV and did crosswords together and she would give him the odd game of cards or chess, and helped him to perfect his magic acts.

Calvin thought she worked too hard and he would suggest she took things slightly easier, not mentioning, of course, his concerns over her weight. But Mrs Hoskins always volunteered to do more at the church, not less.

A yearning to be with her in her illness remained with Calvin as he arrived at Shrewsbury Abbey, the former Benedictine monastery that marked the starting point of the St Winefride Pilgrimage Trail. He stood beneath the red sandstone façade, gazing up at its crenelated tower and the smoke-blackened figures of St Peter and St Paul, smoothed by centuries of storms. He was consoled by the thought that every step he took from that point would bring him and the housekeeper that little bit closer. At last he was no longer thinking obsessively about the nurse who said her name was Judith. That was a consolation too.

He was nearly back to his old self, thinking about history and the things that interested him, at ease as he scanned the great building and pondered the deeds of men and women within its shadows and its sanctuary since its foundation almost a thousand years ago.

Calvin imagined himself standing on the very spot where Henry V commenced his own pilgrimage to Holywell 'with great reverence', according to the chronicle of Adam of Usk, in the spring of 1416. The journey was a thanksgiving for the crushing victory of 7,000 English soldiers over an army of 36,000 French troops in the mud of Agincourt the previous October.

Henry had placed his outnumbered forces under the protection of St Winefride, an immensely popular seventh century Welsh martyr whose relics were enshrined at Shrewsbury Abbey between the 12th and 16th centuries. There her mortal remains, believed by pilgrims to have been infused and animated by the Holy Spirit, served as a tangible and human connection with the saints. For centuries these relics held out the hope of the renewal of holiness among the people, and invited and inspired them to continued conversion of heart. In return pilgrims found a physical and spiritual presence to whom they could turn, a listening ear when they discharged their woes and worries, a friend who could approach God on their behalf in spite of their weaknesses and their sins, one of their own who could plead with the Almighty for miracles of healing among countless other favours.

By walking the 70 miles as a penitent to St Winefride's Well in Flintshire, Henry not only intended to show his gratitude for the saint's intercession. He also sought to atone for the wholesale slaughter of French prisoners after the battle for fear that they would regroup and overpower their captors. St Winefride helped him to wash his conscience clean.

Calvin took his first steps on the trip to Holywell, doubling back on himself to pace westwards toward the English Bridge and the town, telling himself that he would offer his own pilgrimage in penance for his errors. He would offer it up in atonement for the desire he harboured for the nurse and for allowing it to take hold of him in the way that it did, for his recklessness, for being a bad priest generally, and in the hope that he would find the strength to be better one. If the pilgrimage was good enough for King Henry V of England it was good enough for Calvin. It was an emphatic way to say he was sorry.

The destination was the well at Treffynnon, the place where, according to legend, Winefride, an exquisitely beautiful virgin who had eschewed marriage to dedicate her life to God, was decapitated by a spurned suitor, the Welsh chieftain Caradog, before she was miraculously restored to life by the prayers of her uncle, St Bueno.

Robert of Shrewsbury's life of the saint tells how Caradog was swallowed up by the earth, while at the spot where St Winefride's head tumbled to a halt, a sweet-smelling spring burst forth. According to this account, the pebbles and rocks in the bottom of the spring were streaked with red, as if by blood, and the moss that grew along the sides of the spring emitted a fragrant smell.

St Beuno was said to have placed his niece's severed head back on to her shoulders, and she was brought back to life and continued to live as if she had never lost it. The only sign of the virgin's decapitation was a white scar encircling her neck for the rest of her natural life. Upon reading the myth, Calvin was intrigued but sceptical. Maybe St Winefride had simply been mutilated but survived, he thought. He was aware that there were sources who scorned the theory that Caradog just disappeared, suggesting instead that he was slain in revenge for the attack by Winefride's brother, Owain. Such stories were surely to be taken with a gargantuan pinch of salt.

Calvin amused himself at the thought that perhaps the scar on the beautiful nurse's throat was supernatural proof of one such miracle. God of course could do anything, but very often a natural explanation could be found for the amazing and the miraculous, if only one knew where to look. St John Bosco, a priest and the patron saint of magicians, was such an accomplished illusionist that he devised a trick in which he made his head appear to fall from his shoulders before replacing it. Few magicians, even today, know how it is done and Calvin wondered what the saint would have made of the Winefride legend.

Although Calvin was on the mend spiritually, mentally and emotionally, he was nevertheless still on his guard following the sage advice of Father Davenport. Since his meeting with the nurse in Liverpool, he had read and re-read *The Leaden Echo and the Golden Echo*, the poem by Gerard Manley Hopkins about Holywell, as he searched for spiritual protection against the lure of the nurse's beauty.

One consequence of the episode had been to make him aware of himself as a sexual being and to be increasingly conscious of the reality that women were sometimes attracted to him. It had made him less naïve. One temptation would surely follow another, and new temptations would arise in the future. He had to fortify his points of weakness. 'Give beauty back, beauty, beauty, beauty, back to God, beauty's self and giver,' urged the golden echo of the well. That was what Calvin had to do—give his beauty back to God alone, as St Winefride had done many centuries ago, while not desiring that of another. Discipline, discipline, discipline.

Lost in his thoughts, Calvin looked down from the bridge to see a pair of swans leading a line of seven fluffy grey cygnets, bright against the graphite water. Then his phone rang.

'Calvin, it's me.'

'Judith?' he said, his heart leaping.

'Yes, but I'm not Judith. My name's Emerald—Emerald Essien. How are you? I've been worried sick about you. I've met Jenny and she said you were well upset about being suspended. She gave me your number. I hope you don't mind me giving you a call? Why didn't you ring me? I've left messages at your house but none of them were answered. Have you fallen out with me?'

'No, not at all. I'm fine, I've been reinstated. I'll be back in the parish a week tomorrow so don't worry about me. I'm okay. I haven't been checking my messages—I thought it would be best if I had a proper break. The other thing is Mrs Hoskins had to go to hospital so probably wasn't there to go through them.'

He shared his news from the vicar general and implored Emerald to look out for his housekeeper, to make sure she was in safe hands, until his return. 'I'm really worried about her, with all that I've heard about your place,' he said.

Emerald promised to do what she could, then told him the Parker documents landed Dr Klein in serious trouble with the chief executive.

'The rumour is that Conway wanted to investigate him and it could have led to internal disciplinary procedures, but the medical director talked her out of it, probably because he was never acting alone. Too many others are implicated in his decisions, that's what I reckon, and he still has Dr Baqri's trust. Still, it's a black mark on his record, especially at that hospital, and the man's furious.'

Calvin said nothing.

'Are you still in London?' Emerald asked. 'I'll come and see you, if you like? I'd love to take you around some of my old haunts.'

Calvin explained where he was and what he was doing, not without a little relief to be inaccessible given his emotional turmoil of recent weeks.

He heard her groan. Her disappointment was clear, and he had no wish to cause her any hurt or offence. It struck him that it was also ridiculous to fear her, and dishonourable to run from her or avoid her. They could meet again and this time he would ensure that he was better prepared for it. It was time to overcome his infatuation.

'You could come to meet me at some point along the way,' he suggested. 'Why not at the other end, next Friday, if you can make it? I could do with a lift home.'

Emerald said it sounded like a good day out and that she would take the day off and meet him at Holywell.

When the priest returned his phone to the inside pocket of his jacket he realised that his heart was thumping and he had broken into a mild sweat. He twisted his head nervously from side to side as he took a deep breath and told himself not to worry, that he could control his emotions, which at that moment were swinging wildly between delight and trepidation.

Calvin reached the opposite bank but instead of retracing his steps into the town he turned off the main road when he reached Beeches Lane and went up the hill to the Town Walls and to the Catholic cathedral, a small but splendid Pugin church. He wanted to pray for Mrs Hoskins before a statue of Our Lady Help of Christians, to whom the church was dedicated, and to see, on the recommendation of the nuns at Tyburn, the magnificent stained glass works of Margaret Rope, who was born in the town.

On leaving the neo-Gothic confines he descended the hill toward the river. He passed the garden of Charles Darwin's childhood home, went through a kissing gate and entered open countryside, with eight miles ahead of him until he reached Montford Bridge, the end of the first leg of his journey.

He had much to think about because over the past week he had taken up Father Davenport's challenge to examine the mystery of the martyr's remains. Rope's depictions of the saints in the cathedral helped to focus his mind on his task.

The Jesuit had framed his challenge in a single question: whose were the bones of the anonymous martyr?

To start Calvin off, Father Davenport provided him with a report from 1993 which was written following an inconclusive study by forensic pathologists hired by the Jesuits, who were hoping that the bones might have belonged to one of two Welsh martyrs who belonged to their order.

The Jesuits were keen to know if there was any evidence to support the theory advanced a century earlier by Dom Bede Camm, a learned Benedictine monk, who asserted the bones were those of either St John Lloyd or St Philip Evans. This was because they were found beside a second set of remains. Camm assumed the two men, who were close companions in life, were kept together in death.

The two Jesuit saints were quickly and emphatically ruled out, however, because just one set of remains bore signs of martyrdom, with the other showing no signs of violence. The Society of Jesus then explored a theory of one of their own members that the anonymous martyr might be the Welsh schoolteacher St Richard Gwyn, who was eviscerated for his loyalty to the Pope during the reign of Queen Elizabeth I.

But the garments in which the bones were wrapped dated from the Restoration era of Charles II, nearly a hundred years after Gwyn's execution. They offered circumstantial evidence that the bones belonged to a man from that time rather than Gwyn's. There were two priests martyred in the area in the late 17th century, victims of the Oates Plot hysteria. Perhaps it was one of them.

One was St John Plessington, who was hanged, drawn and quartered at Chester. Calvin initially ruled him out because he was buried by the Massey family, whom he served as chaplain. But the more Calvin read about him, the harder it was to shake off his suspicions that the bones might be his—especially after he learned that the man found in his grave following exhumation in the early 1960s could not have been the priest.

Calvin would have to wait until his return to the Archdiocese of Liverpool before he could locate a copy of the *Summary of the Findings of the Exhumation of 1962*, perhaps from its archives. In the meantime he read everything he could find out about Plessington, helped by the discovery that the priest distinguished himself from many other martyrs by writing down the speech he gave from the scaffold.

A full final testament, a photographic insight into Plessington's mind and soul was preserved for posterity. It made him stand out and it commended him for canonisation in 1970 as one of the 'forty martyrs of England and Wales' selected from nearly four hundred men and women who were put to death for their faith in turbulent times.

Plessington had died under Elizabethan statutes which made it an offence of high treason to serve as a Catholic priest in England. These had been revived almost a century after her reign because of the panic triggered by Titus Oates's fabricated plot of a conspiracy to assassinate Charles II and replace him with his Catholic brother, James.

Calvin brought every ounce of his skill as an historian into the task of studying each line and detail of the key points which this man, on the eve of his execution, wished to share with his contemporaries and with generations to come. He had printed a copy and perused it again and again on the train up to Shrewsbury, pondering each line for vital clues that might help to solve the mystery of the nameless martyr. He paused at a stile and took it from a pocket, thoughts galloping through his head. It read:

Dear Countrymen. I am here to be executed, neither for Theft, Murder, nor anything against the Law of God, nor any fact or Doctrine inconsistent with Monarchy or Civil Government. I suppose several now present heard my trial the last Assizes, and can testify that nothing was laid to my charge but Priesthood, and I am sure that you will find that Priesthood is neither against the Law of God nor Monarchy, or Civil Government. If you will consider either the Old or New Testament (for it is the Basis of Religion), for no priest no religion St Paul tells us in Hebrews 7:12 that the Priesthood being changed, there is made of necessity a change of the Law, and consequently the Priesthood being abolished, the Law and Religion is quite gone.

But I know it will be said that a Priest ordained by authority derived from the See of Rome is by the Law of Nation to die as a Traitor, but if that be so what must become of all the Clergymen or England, for the first Protestant Bishops had their Ordination from those of the Church of Rome, or none at all, as appears by their own writers, so that Ordination comes derivatively to those now living.

As in the Primitive times, Christians were esteemed Traitors, and suffered as such by National Law, so are the Priests of the Roman Church here esteemed, and suffer such. But as Christianity then was not against the law of God, Monarchy or Civil Policy, so now there is not any one Point of the Roman Catholic Faith (of which Faith I am) that is inconsistent there-with, as is evident by induction in each several point.

That the Pope hath power to depose or give licence to Murder Princes is no point of our Belief. And I protest in the sight of God and the Court of Heaven that I am abso-lutely innocent of the Plot so much discoursed of, and abhor such bloody and damnable designs. And although it be Nine Weeks since I was sentenced to die, there is not anything of that laid to my charge, so that I may take comfort in St. Peter's words, 1 Peter 14–16, 'Let none of you suffer as a Murderer, or as a Thief, or as an Evil doer, or as a Busy Body in other men's matters, yet if any man suffer as a Christian let him not be ashamed or sorry'. I have deserved a worse death, for though I have been a faithful and true Subject to my King, I have been a grievous sinner against God; Thieves and robbers that rob on highways would have served God in a greater perfection than I have done had they received so many favours and graces from Him as I have.

But as there was never sinner who truly repented and heartily called to Jesus for mercy, to whom He did not show mercy, so I hope by the merits of His Passion, He will have mercy on me, who am heartily sorry that ever I offended Him.

Bear witness, good hearers, that I profess that I undoubtedly and firmly believe all the Articles of the Roman Catholic Faith, and for the truth of any of them (by the assistance of God) I am willing to die, and I had rather die than doubt of any Point of Faith, taught by our Holy Mother the Roman Catholic Church.

In what condition Margaret Plat one of the chiefest witnesses against me was before, and after she was with me, let her nearest relations declare. George Massey, another witness, swore falsely when he swore I gave him the Sacrament, and said Mass at the time and place he mentioned, and [I] verily think that he never spoke to me, or I to him, or saw each other but at the Assizes week. The third witness, Robert Wood, was suddenly killed, but of the Dead why should I speak? These were all the witnesses against me, unless those that only declared what they heard from others. I heartily and freely forgive all that have been or are any way instrumental to my Death, and heartily desire that those that are living may heartily repent.

God bless the King and the Royal Family and grant his Majesty a prosperous Reign here and a crown of glory hereafter, God grant peace to the Subjects, and that they live and die in true Faith, Hope, and Charity. That which remains is that I recommend myself to the mercy of Jesus, by whose merits I hope for mercy. O Jesus, be to me a Jesus.

Calvin was captivated by the fact that Plessington named each of the three people who testified falsely against him: Margaret Plat, George Massey and Robert Wood. He reminded his audience that the first was unstable, even in the judgement of her family; that the second 'swore falsely' and that they had never met, and that the third had been 'suddenly killed'.

There was little that Calvin could discover about the three witnesses but what he did find out he thought was significant. Dodd's *Church History* recorded that they were paid by the family of a local Protestant man in revenge for objections made by the priest to his proposed marriage to a Catholic heiress. Two of the three died suddenly, it seemed, with Wood killed in an accident in a pigsty soon after he had given his testimony and

Plat 'crushed to death' not long after Plessington himself died. The fate of the third witness, George Massey, was mysterious, with Bishop Richard Challoner, the author of the *Memoirs of Missionary Priests*, saying only that he 'lingered away in anguish and misery'.

Lingered away? What did that mean? Did George Massey sit in a corner, outcast and sulking? Or did he disappear? It troubled Calvin like the myth about St Winefride. Did the earth open up and swallow Massey like Caradog, he wondered, pulling up his hood as he felt rain in the air. Or was there another explanation?

20

ST WINEFRIDE'S WELL

It had taken Emerald less than half an hour to conclude that Holywell was not going to provide the exciting day out she was hoping for.

'Can we go to the seaside?' she asked Calvin, stretching out her feet in the morning sunshine, her sandals beside her on the grassy slope by a towering Victorian building that served as a museum. 'The weather's gorgeous.'

Calvin had met Emerald on the car park first thing that morning. He loaded his back pack and one-man tent into the boot before escorting her down to the yawning Tudor arches of the 15th century building erected over St Winefride's Well by Margaret Beaufort, the mother of King Henry VII, and which had the aspect of a gatehouse of a Renaissance palace.

At the centre of the sanctuary, under the cover of the building, was the well that for more than a thousand years had been associated with the horrific murder and miraculous recovery of a beautiful Welsh maiden who became a nun.

It was the place visited by kings, queens and saints among the constant, uninterrupted flow of pilgrims over centuries, united in their attraction to the supposed healing properties of the waters and their promise of spiritual consolations.

The well itself was a pool of deep and clear water, overflowing into an outer bathing pool. It was boxed in by brick embanked walls, undulating like rose petals, and rising into Gothic pillars and arches. It reminded Calvin of the inverted shell in Sandro Botticelli's *Birth of Venus* and the beauty that Hopkins had spoken of in his poem.

Walking around the well and gazing into the still water, Emerald found the site mysteriously haunting, one of those rare places scarcely touched by time. A solemn and serene statue of St Winefride stood over it, a crozier in one hand to show she was an abbess and a crown and palm leaf to signify her status as a martyr. The saint bore a scar on her throat that was as clearly visible as her own.

The statue added to the mild sense of awe she was feeling as she circled the pool, affecting her in a way that left her reflecting about what it meant to be holy, what it meant to be a saint, and inspiring her to light candles and utter a few prayers, to Calvin's obvious approval.

Outside, Emerald paddled in the bathing pool of the sanctuary, Calvin watching her with amusement. He was in his clerical collar and wearing black trousers and a black shirt under a light waist-length jacket. He had no intention of undressing in front of her. He had already been in the water, but the previous afternoon. Emerald hoisted up her shorts as she paddled from the steps of the shallow, rectangular pool.

Sitting picking daisies from the grass afterwards while her feet dried, Emerald listened with great interest as Calvin told her about the legend of St Winefride and the supposed healing powers of the well, strangely consoled to have waded through its icy waters. But she laughed and shook her head when he told her of the saint's horrible death and restoration to life. 'No,' she said, 'that can't happen.'

'Something happened,' said Calvin. 'Something strange, possibly miraculous—I wouldn't rule it out—but what exactly it was, I'm not so sure.'

Emerald screwed up her face and withdrew from him slightly.

'Let me show you a card trick so you can see what I mean,' said Calvin. He took out a deck from his jacket pocket and began to riffle shuffle them, dovetailing the cards into each other. He cut the pack several times and held it out to Emerald, inviting her to take a card.

The top card was slightly dislodged and she lazily took it as she held his gaze, so far unimpressed.

Calvin said: 'I want you to imagine these cards are real people. What have you got in your hand?'

Emerald held up the queen of hearts and Calvin took it from her and showed it to her. 'This card is St Winefride,' he said.

Ripping the card into quarters, he said: 'Caradog chased her all the way out here because he wanted her to marry him. But she had dedicated herself to God and so she refused to yield to his demands. So he cut off her head.'

The priest held the pieces together in his fingers, passing them from hand to hand. 'Life for Winefride was over, just like it is for this card. But death is often an illusion.'

Holding the torn pieces of the card in his left hand, he reached into his jacket with his right and drew out a pen.

'Sometimes life continues in a different way,' he said, waving at the neat pile in his fingers with the pen, as if it were a magic wand. 'And sometimes life might not end at all.'

Calvin put the pen down and slowly unfolded a fully intact and undamaged queen of hearts. 'St Winefride, restored to life,' he declared.

Emerald ran her fingers through the grass and smirked mischievously. 'You think you're cool, don't you?' she said. 'Well, you're not.'

227

It wasn't the reaction Calvin was expecting. His eyebrows arched.

'Can I ask a question?' Emerald continued. 'If I hadn't taken that top card would I have ruined your trick for you?'

Calvin pretended not to understand.

'When you next wash your jacket make sure you take out all the torn up pieces of card or they'll make a right mess of the inside of your pocket,' she said.

He couldn't help but laugh.

'So, go on then—let's see you make Caradog disappear. That's the bit that interests me the most.'

She looked serious. Calvin's smile also faded when she asked him about going to the beach. The priest tried to look like he was considering her request, though he had no intention of going to any resort town that day. Ideally, he would have gone straight home, but he was sensitive to the fact that Emerald had just driven more than fifty miles and that it was reasonable for her to expect a little more from her trip.

'I think we should keep a low profile, for now,' he said. 'I don't want to have to explain what I was doing out with Gal Gadot next time I see the vicar general, and I'm sure you don't want to be caught with me either.'

'Father Calvin! You not supposed to know who Gal Gadot is.'

'I know,' he said, dropping his chin to his chest.

He suggested that, rather than drive up the coast to Prestatyn or Rhyl, as Emerald would have liked, they crossed over to the English side of the Dee and headed for Parkgate, a village overlooking the estuary where they could have lunch. He chose not to tell her he wanted to view the river and Welsh coast from the perspective of the Massey family of Puddington Hall.

She agreed and Calvin said: 'First, there is something I want to show you.'

He led her along the lawn to a stone staircase on the other side of the building. Reaching the top floor, he opened a door to a square room, filled with glass cases and smelling strongly of polish.

The largest exhibits of the tiny museum were arranged beneath glass panels of a table occupying the middle of the room—an array of ash-grey human bones, some wrapped in ancient garments.

The most striking was a skull placed at a corner of the cabinet, dusty as an old paving stone, with a diamond-shaped aperture in the crown, opening like a scream into the hollow.

'Oh dear,' said Emerald. 'If this chap rocked up on my ward I might find myself agreeing with Dr Klein that not a lot could be done for him.'

'He was hanged, drawn and quartered,' said Calvin. 'That was made by a pike driven through from the inside. They found all these bones in a chest in an attic in a pub nearby about a hundred and thirty years ago all wrapped up in a bodice from the late seventeenth century. It had been there for years and no one alive knew anything about it—except for the mice which used to use this chap's skull to nest in. One even died there—its little skeleton fell out, so I believe. Someone wrote a poem about it.'

Emerald examined skull closely then began to study a list next to the bones under the glass case and matching them to the corresponding number.

'You can see neck vertebrae one, two and three, and it says here that they appear to match the skull and reveal that a sharp heavy object—probably an axe—has been brought to bear on this area.

'And here we've got lumbar vertebrae three and four, a sacrum, an innominate bone—or a hip bone—and the femur, tibia, fibula, ankle bone and heel bone of a right leg, along with metatarsals one, two, three, four and five.'

She noticed that Calvin was silently impressed.

'I've done orthopaedics,' she said. 'In doorstep English what we are looking at is the head—minus the lower jaw—and an intact quarter of a man who was without any doubt executed in the way you said.'

She indicated a large dark bone.

'Look at this—this is the sacrum. It's located at the rear of the pelvis. It's usually triangular. With this one you can see clearly that it shows signs of being hacked in half. Someone's gone right through it. Yes, this fellow was chopped up. Who is it?'

'Good question. Someone set me a challenge to find out.'

'Oh—I like a murder-mystery. Can I help?'

'Someone of your forensic medical skills, courage and clear ability to get to the facts—well, how could I say no? As I've just come from Shrewsbury Abbey, I suppose I could be Cadfael and you could be … let's say—what was her name? That young widow, Mariam!'

There was a long pause. Then Emerald asked softly: 'Was she his girlfriend?'

She glanced up to meet Calvin's eyes but he quickly looked away and didn't answer, hoping she wouldn't see him turning pink.

As they set off in Emerald's white Volkswagen Golf 8, Calvin spoke enthusiastically about his research—explaining in detail the merits of various candidates whose lives he had investigated, why he liked some and discounted others.

'I keep coming back to one name but it doesn't add up—St John Plessington. He was buried in Burton, close to where we're going, and I thought it couldn't be him. Funny thing is, everyone you speak to in Holywell seems to think it is. I asked around last night and everyone seems to be of the same mind. It's like going into one of those remote villages in a horror film, where all the locals know the dark secret but won't tell—"You made me miss!"' he growled in a bluff and overcooked northern accent and began to chuckle, turning to see if Emerald recognised his reference but her face was straight, her eyes on the road ahead.

'They've even named the complex here after him. Plessington House, it's called. I don't know why they don't just come out and say the bones are his.'

'Why would they keep them anyway?' she asked. 'It's gross. They should have been buried long ago.'

Calvin twisted to face her. 'Well, he was a martyr and he's now a saint so his relics are holy. They belong in a tomb worthy of his status. That's why they tried to dig him up in the first place, back in the 1960s. You see, according to tradition, his body was buried in the Anglican churchyard of St Nicholas's in Burton, just down the road. But when they opened the grave they couldn't find him.

'They found someone else, though—a guy about fifteen years younger. He wasn't quartered like the chap you've just seen. His skeleton was intact, except that his neck was broken.'

Emerald shot Calvin a look of astonishment, her mouth opening as she tried to refocus her gaze on the road ahead.

'Yeah, he might have been hanged, or thrown from a horse, something like that because the rest of the skeleton was fine. Anyway, whoever it is, it isn't Plessington, and that's why they put him back in the ground, this time in a steel-lined coffin and in an unmarked grave which the Church of England has agreed to keep secret.'

Before long they arrived in the Cheshire village of Parkgate on the opposite side of the Dee estuary from Holywell. They parked near the Old Quay.

For Calvin, the location offered the prospect of surveying the distance between the English villages on one side of the river and the hallowed shrine on the other while he wondered how easy it would have been to convey the relics across the water, perhaps in a small boat in the dead of night.

Of course, he didn't sell it to Emerald on that basis, but rather as a place known for its beautiful promenade, home-made ice cream and historic baths which once drew such figures as Lady Hamilton, the mistress of Admiral Nelson, to immerse themselves in the healing waters.

They strolled in the sunshine along the promenade, which no longer overlooked the river but faced miles of salt-marshes. Birds were everywhere. Gulls squabbled over discarded chips and pie crusts along the roadside while further out herons, egrets and wildfowl of all kinds dipped in and out of pools as far as the eye could see.

Huge flocks of small birds took to the air in the distance and Emerald and Calvin stopped when a brown female marsh harrier floated into view, its head dipping to expose a cream-coloured crown—like a skull added to a mythical creature as an afterthought. The raptor zig-zagged low over the rank grasses with great sweeps of its vulturine wings in search of prey. Mighty yellow talons dangled beneath it like an undercarriage of a jet coming into land ready to grasp, crush and kill.

The pair began to walk again, and Emerald slipped her hand into the crook of Calvin's elbow and pulled near to him. He halted and faced her.

'Fancy an ice cream?' he asked.

They crossed the road, Calvin making sure, awkwardly, that he was a foot or two ahead of her. They sat at a table outside the shop and ten minutes later Emerald was reflecting on the visit to Holywell as she finished her rum and raisin waffle cone, with Calvin settling for a coffee.

'I can see why people were drawn to that well. Do you think water can really heal? I feel better for being there, definitely. There's something calming about being by water, don't you think—something therapeutic … like, it's good for the soul?'

'Yeah, I don't half miss the Thames.'

'Me too. When we were kids my mum and dad used to take us to Strand-on-the-Green and we would walk down the river from Kew to Richmond, or take the boat, and we'd all have fish and chips there, on the embankment near the bridge. I grew up along that river. I wish I was there now, if I'm honest. I still feel London's my home.'

'The well is more or less opposite us now,' said Calvin, pointing to the facing hills. 'What d'you reckon, seven or eight miles as the crow flies?'

He drained his cup.

'You know those bones you saw this morning,' he said, 'the priest who everyone at Holywell thinks they belong to—St John Plessington—well, he ministered on this side of the river as chaplain to the Masseys, a family of Catholic merchants and landowners who lived just a couple of miles down from here. It would have been easy for them to take him there. I don't have a problem thinking it was him. The body in his grave, though—that's still a mystery to me. I don't know what to make of that.'

Emerald crunched the last of the cone. 'Come on, Father Calvin—surely it's not that difficult.'

She reached for her bag, took out her purse and quickly counted out some coins. 'This is what happened,' she said, setting down two ten pence pieces at the top corners of the table and placing a one pound coin in each of the bottom corners.

She made Calvin hold his cup in his hand then pointed to the two ten pence pieces. 'Let's imagine that that one is this place, Burton, and that one is Holywell,' she said. 'And the pound coins are John Plessington, here on my left, and the mystery man found in his grave is this one on my right.'

Calvin signalled his understanding with an amused nod.

'Good,' said Emerald as she moved her left hand over the coin designated as Plessington. 'Now, let's suppose that the friends of John Plessington wanted to move his body, according to your theory, from this side of the river to Holywell without anyone knowing, of course.'

As she spoke the nurse slid her right hand toward the top corner of the table and wiggled her fingers over the coin that represented Holywell. When she withdrew both her hands the coin at the left corner had vanished, only to have appeared in the top right of the table.

'Wow, teleportation,' said Calvin, 'I love it.'

'Save your applause, I've not finished yet,' she said. 'Now, our mate with the broken neck,' she said, placing her hand over the pound coin in the bottom right corner. 'He needs to disappear too—and he's going to be hidden in a grave in Burton.'

She dragged her left hand up the far edge of the table and this time wiggled her fingers over the coin in the top corner. The coin at the bottom far right was gone when she dropped her hands, mysteriously relocating to the top left corner.

'Calvin, honey. We both know this isn't magic and I reckon within a few minutes you'll have worked out how I did that,' said Emerald, grinning. 'The thing is, what I'm trying to show you, is that all those years ago those people with dead bodies to hide and move about, for whatever reason—they just did this on a bigger scale.

'You can understand why they moved Plessington. You know their motives, and their means. What I'm saying is, this other guy, who was in his grave, might explain why they had an opportunity to pull all of this off.

'They wanted shot of someone. They killed him, stuck him in Plessington's coffin and smuggled the relics of the martyr to Holywell.

'The missing part of this puzzle can be explained by them, whoever they were, having to get rid of someone who was a threat, a real danger—someone perhaps so terrifying to them that they had to kill him. That's what I reckon happened. So go on, who's the guy in the grave? If you apply my theory, I bet you might have a good idea who he is.'

Calvin looked solemnly into Emerald's big blue eyes as she impatiently awaited his response. She found herself longing for his acknowledgement that she had solved the mystery, that she was his intellectually his equal.

'No,' he said eventually, shaking his head. 'It can't be right. You're expecting me to believe that the man in the grave was a villain lynched by local Catholics who disposed of his body in a saint's coffin just so they could get the priest's body out to Holywell without the authorities becoming suspicious?

'That theory doesn't work because killing anyone would go against the Ten Commandments. So you're wrong.'

'What's the matter with you?' she protested. 'You're so naïve! I didn't say just so they could shift the priest's body in secret. I think there must have been more going on and the execution of the priest might have given them an opportunity to get rid of someone extremely dangerous, at least to them.'

'Emerald, the teaching of the Church right from the time of the Apostles is that Christians can never commit evil with the intention of doing good,' Calvin said impatiently. 'The ends do not justify the means.'

'But people don't always abide by the high standards of Church teaching when they're tested, do they?'

'No, but I still don't go for your theory. Violent reprisals are not the Christian way, martyrdom is. That's how we testify to the truth in extreme circumstances. We're not sent out to be wolves among wolves.'

Calvin waited a moment before continuing.

'So,' he added calmly, 'is this all about Dr Klein? Is that what's on your mind?'

'No, it's not all about Dr bloody Klein!'

They very mention of the doctor's name sliced through their bonhomie with the force of a guillotine. Scowling, Emerald got up and paced away from the ice cream parlour with her arms folded. She was angry with Calvin because he refused even to consider the merits of her arguments and because he accused her of ulterior motives for advancing them. He was not treating her with the respect that was due to her. But he was right. She couldn't get Klein off her mind.

The priest caught up with her.

'Emerald, stop. What's the matter?'

She stopped and turned to face him.

'You won't listen to me. You dismiss what I say because you think I have secret reasons for saying it. Do you really think I'm so manipulative? Why can't you just accept that I'm telling you what I think because I believe it might be the truth? Not everyone is good like you, Father—and sometimes people who say they are Catholic do bad things too. If you want to get to the bottom of this mystery, I think you need to broaden your mind.'

'I'm sorry—I really am. I had no intention whatsoever to offend or upset you. Let me think about your theory. It's interesting. I'm sorry, Emerald.'

'It's okay, I shouldn't have been so tetchy. But I think I'm ready to go home.'

As they sped east along the M56 they were joking again, having agreed to share the secrets of their magic tricks.

Father Calvin humoured Emerald too, pretending she might be on track to solving the mystery of two sets of unidentified remains when decades of inquiries by forensic pathologists and historians were inconclusive, but without offering any of the information that he had uncovered.

'You're smart,' he told her, 'you're like Hong Kong Phooey's cat—that's what Mrs Hoskins would say about you.'

Emerald looked intrigued.

Then the priest quizzed Emerald about his 'narrow miss' with the police, asking her if she thought her colleague Sharyn had reported him.

'She didn't need to—lots of people already knew about you before this DI Tarleton turned up and began to ask questions.'

She paused. 'Listen, you were right before, I'm really worried about Klein. I'm in a bit of a bad situation with him. He suspects me of the leak, I'm sure of it. I've tried to buy myself a bit of time, but I can't keep up the pretence for ever. I'm going to have to start looking for a new job, maybe go abroad. Fancy coming with me, starting a new life, Calvin? You could be my man.'

'You're joking, right?'

Emerald took her eyes off the road to briefly face Calvin. She could see he was angry.

'Yes, of course I'm joking,' she said quietly.

'You're my friend, Emerald,' Calvin said. 'Let's keep it that way.'

She had failed spectacularly. She hoped they had a connection stronger than the pull of his vocation. She thought he would want her in the same way that she wanted him. She had misjudged him and now he had rebuffed her. How could she have been so wrong? She felt foolish and ashamed for imagining that he would drop everything to be with her. Hadn't she known in her heart, that he wasn't hers to take and that she shouldn't be tempting him away from his vocation? In some way she had feared him accepting her offer, perhaps, as she had fantasised, by placing his hand tenderly on the top of her thigh, and saying: 'I'd love that, baby.' But she wanted him nonetheless.

They sat in uncomfortable silence. Emerald turned the radio on, but kept the volume low.

Her eyes fixed on the road ahead, she chastised herself repeatedly for giving free rein to an illicit impulse she must have picked up like a contagious bug from Klein, a man whom she routinely blamed for many of her failures. Her next lover, she told herself adamantly, must be a single man, in every sense.

For his part, Calvin was mastering his emotions and passions with heroic determination, having steeled himself for that decisive moment when he would declare his intentions through continuous preparation, discipline and self-denial. He could say 'no' to Emerald because he was convinced it was right; and he would deal with whatever personal distress and anxiety that caused him later. If he ended up singed, it would be his own fault for having flown so close to the fire.

Perhaps he had prepared himself too well. Although he was reluctant to insult Emerald, he fought to restrain himself from exhibiting more forcefully the position he had chosen to adopt. He resolutely desired, against his baser masculine instincts, to be emotionally free of her, to wrest himself from the hold her beauty had exerted over him since he had set eyes upon her in that hospital corridor. He wished to break free from his obsession with her. She could no longer have any hold over him.

He began to ask about Mrs Hoskins again, though earlier Emerald reported that she was sleeping nearly all the time and seldom eating or drinking. There was a purpose to his inquiry, something else he wished to get off his chest.

'I'm really sorry to hear that,' he told the nurse as she elaborated on his housekeeper's condition. 'I'm going to visit her next week, first chance I get, even if they chuck me out.

'But about all that stuff that you say is happening at the hospital and all of your difficulties with Dr Klein, I hate to say it, Emerald, but I'm out. It's not right that I'm involved and I've learned my lesson. I remember you telling me once that I was part of it, like it or not. Well, I'm not part of it any more. I'm done. I want to be a holy priest. I don't want to be suspended again, or worse. So from now on I'm going to behave myself. All that stuff, it's not for me. I'm really sorry.'

She could not conceal her fury. 'You're a cheeky sod!' she exclaimed. 'I never asked you to go hunting me around the hospital, kicking doors. You wanted to be part of this, I didn't make you! I hope you're saying the same to your mate Jenny, and to the Parker family, or is it just me you want to stick this on?'

'I understand what you're saying,' said Calvin calmly. 'I just can't be part of it any more. I hope you get him, though.'

'Really? Think so, do you? We'll see.'

'What was that?'

'Oh, nothing.'

The atmosphere between them was curdled. Emerald felt utterly miserable, that she had wasted her time leaving her flat that day, and wished only to drop him off at his presbytery and forget about him for ever.

Eventually, Calvin broke the silence by asking her about Dr Klein, the man so obviously preoccupying her and whether she thought the risks she had taken had done any good.

Yes, she said, it was worth it. Klein had been shaken, his superiors were losing confidence in him, and the attention of the police had been drawn to him, although it was a tremendous disappointment to her that they were unlikely to pursue the case. It was also a shame that no more families were coming forward to complain about the doctor since she was aware that there were plenty who might have grievances about the care of their relatives. It was a missed opportunity and now it looked as if Klein was going to survive again.

'What do you think about Jenny's work in trying to find out about this woman Octavia?' asked Calvin.

'Between ourselves, I wouldn't be surprised if it leads her down a cul-de-sac,' replied Emerald. 'It smacks of desperation. She has nothing else to go on. The police aren't going to do anything about any of the cases, about anything.'

She turned off the radio.

'I want to be frank with you, Calvin, I'm scared to death of Klein and I've got a bad feeling about how this is going to work out. You're right to want to stay out of this, but I'm not sure you're going to be able to. Yeah, expect reprisals. This is his time now. The boot is on the other foot and he is going to kick us very hard.'

'Look, Emerald,' said Calvin, filled with remorse for speaking to her so harshly. 'I really want to say sorry for upsetting you— here I go again. I keep apologising. I shows you how hopeless I am around people like you.

'If I appeared hard it's because I like you too much for my own good. I sort of … well, I think love you—I never thought I'd say that to a woman in my life—and I'm terrified where this is going to take me. But I've made the decision to be a priest and I won't be any good to anyone if I'm a bad priest. Even to you, Emerald. If I became your man, I'd change and you wouldn't like me the way you do now. It wouldn't be for the better, please believe me.'

'I know,' she whispered, reaching across to squeeze the back of his hand. 'You're right. My mistake.'

'You have no idea,' sighed Calvin. 'I've been obsessed with you. I thought you were really the biblical Judith. I know, it's totally crackers.'

Emerald wanted to know more. Calvin told her most of the story, omitting what he had learned about diabolical obsession. By the time he had finished, she was flattered and smiling at him as readily as when they met that morning.

'Of course, you're right about not forcing me into this,' Calvin went on. 'I kicked the door of my own volition, but it was after being at the inquest, and hearing what those families said, I thought I had to do something. I was already part of it before you came to see me in the confessional.

'If anything it was meeting a woman called Tanya Torridge that was the tipping point for me. She ordered me to do something. She sort of taunted me at a time when I was most receptive to it. Just a chance encounter at the hospital.'

'You saw Tanya Torridge in the hospital?'

'Yes, on the women's ward, visiting her mum, the night I kicked the door.'

'Her mum's dead, did you know that?'

'No, I didn't. They aren't Catholics, as far as I'm aware. I was never asked to go and see her mother, though I remember her from when Tanya pulled me up. Jabbing me with her finger she was—jab, jab, jab—"You've got to do something!"'

'Do you remember her name, her mother's name? It's a big ask, I know. It's a long time ago and you say you weren't involved with the family.'

Calvin hesitated a moment.

'Funnily enough, I do,' he said. 'It was Pamela Worthington. I remember her name because St Edmund Campion—one of my other heroes, an Elizabethan martyr—took shelter with the Worthington family of Blainscough Hall when he fled to the North in 1580. The pursuivants nearly caught him there but one of the Worthington's maids saved his life by feigning a lover's tiff and pushing him into the duck pond. The priest-hunters rode past him on their horses, laughing at him. That's how I remembered her name.'

Heading north up the M6, Emerald was at peace with herself again; it hadn't been such a bad day in spite of some awful bumps.

Calvin too was at ease, convinced that by talking about his obsession he had broken it and nullified the evil that stalked him. The threat was over, the danger to his soul averted.

Emerald stopped the car about a quarter of a mile from St Winefride's presbytery. There would be no kissing as they parted on this occasion. Calvin looked anxious as he hoisted his backpack over his shoulders.

'So did you really mean it when you said you were thinking of getting job somewhere else or moving abroad?' he asked.

'I definitely need a plan B. I just don't know what Klein's going to do next,' replied Emerald. 'See you around, Calv. Take care.'

Emerald waved to the priest as he walked away. She couldn't help but like him. Life seemed just that bit better in his company. Friendship—yes, she could settle for that, if he would allow it to blossom. It wasn't as if there were any other women involved. It would be so good if he could make a little space for her in his life.

But as she headed for home on her own, she realised that she was simply rationalising failure. Slowly she confronted the stark reality that she had lost him.

Soon she was giving way to self-pity, furious at the thought that she might never see him again now that he was banned from the hospital. Why did it have to go so wrong? Why did he have to bail out, desert her when she needed him most?

She concluded that the line Calvin had drawn in the sand served only his interests. It did nothing for her and she resented him as selfish. Calvin's 'big news', as she was already calling his snub, did not change her own perilous situation an iota. She was still in danger.

She needed to deal with Dr Klein, and for that she needed allies. Her best bet, she told herself, was Jenny.

21

A WINNING STREAK

Four women stood drinking outside the *Bay Horse*, a pub on the main road leading south toward Haydock Park racecourse. Three of them were pulling on their cigarettes with relish. The fourth was wondering anxiously if another was ever going to show up.

The first race was due to start in less than half an hour and the last of the racegoers who had filled the pub and pavement were streaming away. Straggling groups of young men in suits, already half drunk, loitered and laughed rumbustiously as they joshed and joked among themselves, the excitement of the day mounting by the minute.

Most of the women, as well as the mixed groups, had already gone, and Jenny noticed the glances that she, Sarah, Olivia and Clara were starting to attract, along with a few passing jests, as they increasingly stood out to the male racegoers as good-looking and unaccompanied.

This was not strictly true. Jenny's fiancé Seb and her elder brother, Geoff, were inside the pub with two male friends.

Jenny spotted Emerald coming into view. The nurse walked tentatively across to the group, dressed in a floral tea dress and nude heels, a small Valentino handbag tucked under her arm.

She apologised for cutting it fine but explained that she had to catch a bus and that the journey had taken her far longer than expected.

'Let me get you a drink,' said Jenny, after introducing Emerald to her friends. She suggested that she and her guest would follow the others down to the track if her friends wanted to make it for the first race, but the other women happily agreed to wait for them

Jenny could see Emerald was nervous, looking around constantly, and was not surprised when she followed her into the pub. Perhaps her last-minute arrival was a little more deliberate than she'd admitted.

They saw that a large semi-circular seat had come free beneath the front bay window, and Jenny suggested it would be a good idea to move inside. Emerald went to fetch the others and soon they sat together amid stacks of empty pint glasses and discarded newspapers open at the racing pages. Jenny crossed the room with drinks squeezed together in her hands, the concentration of a tight-rope walker on her face.

She was shuffling toward the space left free for her on the seat when out of the corner of her eye she glimpsed a shock of blue hair. Curious, she turned to see Kai Nelson, Emerald's fellow nurse, walking away from the bar.

Emerald had seen him too. Kai had not noticed her, but she was fearful. Was this too much of a risk? Was she making a mistake in joining Jenny so publicly at a bank holiday weekend event attended by tens of thousands of people, many of them local? If Kai was at the races, who else might be there? She rolled her eyes toward Jenny and said: 'I work with a guy who's just walked outside.'

Jenny read the terror on her face and promised to be 'back in a sec' as she edged her way toward the open floor.

Two minutes later, she returned with four muscular men in their twenties, wearing skinny jeans and slim-fitted shirts so tight that their pectoral muscles threatened to burst through them. The curves of their tattooed forearms and biceps were so pronounced that it was wonder how they ever were able to push their arms through their tiny sleeves. Two were bearded—including one who was introduced to Emerald as Seb—and a third had stubble on his cheeks and chin. A fourth man, clean shaven, and by far the best-looking of the group, introduced himself to Emerald as Geoff, Jenny's brother.

'Jenny says you're coming with us,' he said with a friendly smile, 'having a day out with the lads. We can meet the girls at the track, but a bit more discreetly if that suits you better. Don't worry, they're good lads, these, and you'll probably have a better laugh with us anyway.'

Emerald was instantly relieved. She enjoyed the company of men, and she began to relax as Geoff chatted with her about the peregrines opposite her flat, fascinated to hear that the chicks were ready to fledge.

When the time came to depart, Seb left the men to join Jenny and her friends. Emerald remained at the pub with Geoff, Keith and Dave, after they agreed to reunite with Seb and the girls by the paddock in time for the second race.

Eventually, the men downed what was left of their pints and the group emerged into an overcast but dry day and began the short walk to the course.

The men laughed about how hard it was to heave themselves out of any bar, especially on a race day. Keith, the heaviest, recalled how the last time he went to Haydock he didn't leave the racecourse bar the entire afternoon, lumping on bet after bet at the adjacent kiosks.

Dave, who spoke with a broad Lancashire accent through buck teeth, upstaged him by boasting of a coach trip he had made to Royal Ascot one year. He described how most his companions were young people and they were overwhelmingly drunk by the time they reached the car park. There they ran into a group of women 'from Essex, or somewhere like that' who had set up a music system and were barbecuing burgers and sausages while knocking back the drink. The lads joined the party, sharing champagne, lager and their picnics. They drank, danced and feasted amorously all day in the car park, partying even more excessively on the seats of the coaches with the curtains closed. Not a single one of the revellers, he said, entered the race course precinct at any time, let alone ventured down to the track. Not one of them had a bet, and no one watched any of the races. But they thoroughly enjoyed themselves.

'It wur fantastic,' Keith said with a note of weepy nostalgia in his voice. 'It wur better'n Ibiza, or Glastonbury. I couldn't git ert o' bed fur three days after that.'

The straight avenue that took them down to the race course seemed to go on for ever. They passed scores of coaches lining the way, their excitement mounting as the sound of the crowd grew closer.

Emerald was immediately thrilled by the throng and the atmosphere, the hum of the beer gardens, the smell of onions frying with burgers and hotdogs, and of fish and chips, and the clouds of smoke issuing from thousands of cigarettes and cigars.

Once inside, the four headed toward the paddock, the men competing over how helpful they could be in instructing Emerald in the art of getting rich, and how to place a bet, which she understood without difficulty.

Haydock was a 'favourites' course', intoned Keith knowledgeably, explaining that its long flat home straight meant there were few obstacles that could cause unforeseen mishaps or other surprises to the on-form horses. If she plumped for one of the most fancied horses each time, he said, she was sure to enjoy a few wins.

Dave was trying to explain the difference between betting on the nose and betting each way, between betting at the Tote and with a bookie at the track. It was about trying to get the best price for your choice, he told her. She understood. For a woman who had never visited a racecourse she appeared well acquainted with the business end of gambling.

Geoff told her about Jenny's habit of going to view the horses before they went down to the track because she thought she could 'talk horse'. She believed herself able to discern which horses were 'up for it' and which might have an off-day. She would be at the paddock now, he said, studying their body language and expressions to divine a winner at a decent price.

'But what I do,' he confessed, 'is always back the greys or anything ridden by Frankie Dettori or the jockeys on form. After that it comes down to whether or not I like the name. It's not a science to me. The golden rule is to never chase your losses, and if you see your horse running last, look on the bright side—it means nothing's going to pass it.'

Emerald took his advice and placed £2 each way on Beatboxer simply because the name sounded fun. She smiled at Jenny, Seb and the girls when she and the lads bumped into them moving slowly through the crowd to watch the race from a barrier behind the finishing post.

The Amix Silver Bowl Handicap, the 2.50pm race, featured fourteen Class 2 horses running just over a mile. Beatboxer was ridden by one of four jockeys in green jerseys, leaving Emerald struggling to pick it out in the distance and at times even from the big screen.

As the thoroughbreds thundered down the straight to the roar of the crowd, the jockeys of both leading horses were wearing green, and Emerald found herself relying solely on the commentary to work out if her horse was one of them.

With four furlongs out, it sounded to her like Beatboxer was being soundly beaten by a horse called Munhamek, which was comfortably three lengths clear. She shrieked with excitement as she heard the frenzied voice of the commentator repeatedly speak of Beatboxer making a determined late challenge inside the final furlong—and the realisation that it might just have come first.

'Have I won? Have I won?' she almost shouted at the three straight-faced men around her, making little jumps from the tips of her toes, becoming aware that she was the only person in the vicinity who was celebrating.

'I've think you've nicked it by a short neck,' said Geoff. 'What was it, 20–1? You jammy thing—beginner's luck, that's what that is. Great race though!'

Emerald continued to bounce like a small child after she picked up her winnings, almost £60 from a £4 bet.

Then she saw Sharyn Jones. 'Oh, bloody hell,' she said under her breath. It was too late: her colleague had spotted her and was coming over.

'Hi Emmy, I didn't know you were into racing. You should have told me. You could come with us some time,' said Sharyn, gesturing with her head to a group of casually dressed men and women behind her, Kai Nelson in the midst of them. 'Any luck?'

'Yeah, I've just had the winner of the last race,' said Emerald, flashing the banknotes.

'Amazing! Very nice!' said Sharyn. 'So who are you here with?'

'Oh, just some guys I know. They asked me along and I've never been and I had nothing better to do so I said yes.'

Geoff and the other two men nodded politely at Sharyn, who, in the hope of tapping into Emerald's good fortune, pressed her for tips before scurrying back to her own friends, who were waiting with undisguised impatience.

'That's all I need,' Emerald told Geoff. 'I'm not sure my work-mate knows who your sister is but it's getting a bit too close, this. I can't really be seen with Jenny. Would you tell her for me, please? She'll understand. Can I stay with you, though?'

Geoff agreed and went away, returning some ten minutes later to say he'd had a word with Jenny who was with her friends near the parade ring.

'Seb's not there, though,' he added with some concern. 'He's gone off with some fellas he knows. Lovely, isn't it?'

Neither the third nor fourth races brought either Emerald or Geoff any luck. Geoff began to appear a little frustrated, his ego wounded in the company of his unexpected guest, who was by now more relaxed and determined to enjoy herself.

The alcohol was also working well; she was willing to admit to herself that she found Geoff attractive. Like his sister, he had wavy, dark brown hair and hazel eyes. He was tanned, broad across his shoulders with a thick neck and angular features. 'Take it easy with the booze,' Emerald reminded herself as she pressed herself against him to read the racing card in his hands.

Geoff badly wanted a win. When the horses were being led into the paddock ahead of the fourth race, a Class 1 fixture for fillies due off at 4.35pm, he suggested heading over to look at them to see if they included any greys. Observing how well Emerald and Geoff were connecting, Keith and Dave made their excuses to check prices of visiting bookmakers and to look for Seb, leaving the pair alone for the first time.

'You're in luck,' said Emerald. 'There are two greys in this one.'

Geoff was examining his racecard. 'Oh yes, that's Forever In Dreams, and the other, on the far side, is Gold Filigree.'

As they stood watching the horses parade around, Geoff turned to Emerald and said: 'It's beautiful here, don't you think? I've been to racecourses all over the country but I always think this paddock, here, is one of the nicest.'

He held his hand up to the overshadowing oaks.

'For me, it's these trees that do it. They're lovely, aren't they, especially this time of the year?'

After a pause he went on: 'Did you know this is where Dettori met his wife? She was a stable girl and when he saw her leading out his horse he fancied her straight away. So he says to her, "Allo, darling where have you been hiding?" and asks her for a date.

'That's exactly what I thought when I saw you in the *Bay Horse* earlier—"Where have you been hiding all these years?"'

Emerald interrupted him. 'Are you married, or got a girlfriend?'

'No ...'

'Okay, so what did this stable girl say?'

'Oh, she gives him her number and says if he can remember it by the end of the race she'll go out with him.'

Geoff leaned on the rail of the paddock with one arm, inhaled to lift up his pectorals and angled his face, trying to look his Hollywood best.

'So what's your number?' he said.

Emerald told him. 'Same deal,' she replied. 'If you can remember that after the next race, we'll have a date. So which of these two greys are you having? I'll take the other.'

'Of course now I'm going to have to pick Forever in Dreams.'

They made their way to a terrace and sat down in a row of seats about half way up.

The race was a sprint over six furlongs. As soon as the horses were out of the stalls Gold Filigree, Emerald's horse, shot to the front. Forever in Dreams settled off its shoulder just a length behind, with the rest of the pack staying in contention.

Emerald cheered on her horse. For the first five furlongs, it remained doggedly at the front.

The race changed dramatically in the final furlong when suddenly the others battled to win. It resembled a cavalry charge, with eight out of ten of the riders believing they could triumph.

Forever in Dreams gradually emerged from the pack with the advantage, the yellow jacket of the jockey edging to the front.

Gold Filigree faded completely as the other horses galloped faster, but none could catch Forever in Dreams. It seemed to fly over the finishing line.

Geoff was clenching his fists, growling 'Yes!' over and over again, then he began to laugh. 'D'you know how much I had on that, at 16–1?' he snorted, staring at Emerald. 'Fifty quid.'

'So you've just won 800?' she asked with astonishment.

Breathless, Geoff was bent double with his hands on his knees, but he looked up to nod. 'You know I said you should never chase your losses?' he panted. 'I always do it—and sometimes it pays off. Don't tell anyone.'

'Congratulations,' said Emerald, deadpan. 'So what's my number?'

'Damn, I've forgotten it already.'

Emerald faked an unforgiving expression for a second or two, then laughed.

'Never mind—you can still have a date so long as you get the champers in.'

From a table on a lawn, with a champagne bucket in front of them, Geoff was soon advising Emerald to place a double on the last two races which he thought would undoubtedly be taken by the favourites.

'We've both had outsiders today, but Keith's right about Haydock being a favourites' course, generally speaking.'

He said he would contribute £50 to her bet from his winnings, as a gift, and after he returned from the bookies, they spent the next hour drinking, chatting and laughing.

Geoff was swaying like a sailor by the end of the last race. Both favourites had romped home, netting each of them in the region of £350. He swerved into racegoers, apologising effusively as he made his way back from the pay-out desk.

'I don't know where I'm going to put all this bloody money,' he said, sitting down, then rising again and unfurling wads of notes from his side and back pockets and shoving some down his socks.

He dropped some notes on the ground and almost fell several times as he scrambled to pick them up. There was money everywhere.

Emerald, who was not quite so inebriated, helped him to collect and sort the notes, offering to put a few hundred pounds of his winnings in her purse for safe keeping. They counted out wad after wad, folded up the notes and put them away.

Becoming aware that they must look a sight, Emerald looked around and was embarrassed by the sheer number of mildly envious faces smiling at them, some of the spectators pointing in their direction as they laughed.

One of them was coming towards her, a tall, dark-haired and handsome man in a smart navy suit with a svelte blonde woman behind him. She was wearing a tight-fitting, expensive-looking lemon dress and high heels and was chuckling at Geoff's display of new-found wealth.

Emerald thought her heart was going to stop when she realised she was facing Detective Inspector Tarleton, Dr Klein's friend and the man who had overseen the investigation into the leak.

He and the woman were heading for the exit and as they drew level, he winked at Emerald and said with a smile: 'At least someone's had a good day. You look after him, love, make sure he gets home safely.'

The detective patted the seated drunk on the shoulder as he passed and the woman grinned at Emerald, showing perfect teeth gleaming against her tan, her make-up immaculate. 'Make sure he buys you something nice with all those winnings,' she said with a smile.

Emerald felt relief, thankful that Jenny was not with her because she suspected Tarleton recognised her.

She surmised the woman was Tarleton's wife, and reflected on how well the policeman had done for himself, pulling a looker like that. Sounded posh too. Then again, she had to admit, the copper was quite a dish himself.

Part III

'Corruptio optimi pessima'
(The corruption of the best is the worst)
Pope St Gregory the Great--

22

GAGGING FOR A DRINK

Calvin hadn't seen Mrs Hoskins for weeks, and at her bedside in Bethulia Park Hospital he barely recognised her. The big woman with the plump, ruddy face, who had always reminded him of a baker's or a farmer's wife, was gaunt and grey, her bedraggled hair draped over her forehead like seaweed on a rock at low tide.

She lay on her back, her head and upper body slightly propped up by two pillows. She was breathing heavily with her eyes closed. Her exposed forearms, a patchwork of bruises and plasters, rested on top of the sheets.

On the table next to her bed was a glass of water which appeared untouched. The priest pushed it to one side to make room for the box of chocolates and the small bunch of freesias he had brought. He pulled a chair to the bedside and sat down, his eyes never leaving her face. He was swallowed up in a cloud of anxiety and solicitude at the sight of her deterioration.

He put his left hand on the back of her right wrist and shook it gently, saying 'Hannah, Hannah,' as he tried to rouse her.

Two nurses walked through the ward and one stopped when she saw him. She recognised him from their encounter outside the records office.

'Are you supposed to be here?' she asked coldly.

'I'm visiting in a private capacity,' said Calvin. 'She's my house-keeper. Could you tell me how much she has had to eat and drink today, please?'

'She's always offered food and drink,' said Sharyn. 'We take good care of 'em in spite of what you might have read in the papers. But Hannah doesn't always eat because of the stroke. She struggles. She lost a lot of movement down the right side of her body and it makes it harder for her. She's asleep a lot of the time too.'

'Do you have anything I could give her now, if she wakes up? I've never thought she could be so thin.'

The nurse looked at Calvin distrustfully. 'I'll get you a yoghurt,' she said.

Calvin continued to talk to Mrs Hoskins, telling her tenderly he was worried about her, and that he had brought her some chocolates. After a while her eyes flickered open.

'Hannah! It's me, Father Calvin,' he said. 'I've come to see you!'

Her eyes widened as she strained to focus on him. 'Culva,' she muttered through distorted lips, one side of her jaw barely moving, as the priest patted and stroked her hand. 'Am tursta,' she said.

Knowing how partial Mrs Hoskins was to Ribena as well as to tea, Calvin had brought a bottle with him, and had also remembered some straws. He took them out of his bag and poured a splash of the blackcurrant cordial into the glass of water on the table, then adjusted the bed and the pillows so the patient was sufficiently upright to drink.

He placed the straw in her mouth and held the glass while she sucked in a third of its contents, soon signalling to him that she was confident enough to hold the glass herself. The nurse returned with the yoghurt and a teaspoon and placed them on the table, departing without a word. Calvin spoon-fed his housekeeper tiny mouthfuls, all the time promising to get her out of the hospital as soon as he could.

'I can see you've not been eating well,' he told her. 'It's usually you who's saying that to me. It's funny how it's suddenly the other way around. I need you back at St Winefride's, so you'd better make a full recovery. I'm hopeless without you, I can't cook for myself—I keep getting the beans stuck in the toaster!'

It was agonising for Calvin to see only one side of Mrs Hoskins's mouth rise in an attempted smile, then fall again almost instantly.

'We'll get you out of here and into rehabilitation and as soon as you're well enough you can come back to work. I'll keep your position open for you. We're a team.'

With the care of a mother for an infant, Calvin gently scraped yoghurt from the edges of his housekeeper's lips as she strained to gulp another mouthful, most of the small plastic pot now empty.

Mrs Hoskins said: 'Fav Culva, a won you to 'ave pow of attorney. Cun a give it you?'

'You want me to have power of attorney?' said Calvin. 'Yes, I'm sure we can sort that out. I'll get on to the solicitors. It might take some time, and I guess you'll probably be out of here before we need you to sign anything.'

She weakly shook her head. 'Am not comin' out o''ere. Am gonna die 'ere. Doctor said, doctor wit long err.'

'No, don't think like that!' he pleaded. 'You have to be positive. You've had a stroke but it doesn't mean you're going to die. You're going to get better, you have to believe that. You can't let despair get the upper hand.'

She shook her head again and said: 'A won you to give me laz rye—now, an confesh'n.'

Calvin sighed. He had brought a consecrated Host with him because the duty chaplain, to whom he had spoken the previous evening, told him Mrs Hoskins was asleep when he had visited the ward to give her Holy Communion on Sunday afternoon.

It was in the bag at his side, along with the stole, consecrated oil, prayer books and other items required for him to confer the Sacrament of the Sick. He unzipped it, and began to take them out. He could not refuse a request for last rites from his friend.

He was midway through the ritual when he became aware of the presence of the nurse at the end of the bed, hands on hips, regarding him with open hostility. She wheeled around and walked swiftly up the ward to the doors at the far end.

Calvin packed everything away and sat listening to the entreaties of Mrs Hoskins, who was struggling to make herself understood though it was clear that the stroke had done nothing to impair her mental capacity.

She told him that she had made a will and that the church would be among the beneficiaries. She had also been paying into a funeral plan. In spite of every attempt he made to lift her spirits, to divert her from her preoccupation with her demise, she returned doggedly to the subject, insistent that she was going to die in the hospital and asking the priest to spend whatever was necessary on her funeral, with her bequest to cover any additional expenditure.

Mrs Hoskins also asked him to have her coffin taken into the church the evening before her funeral so her friends—whom she regarded with the affection of close family members—could spend time at her side, praying in a vigil for the eternal repose of her soul. She wanted to go to heaven, she said.

Nodding, Calvin gave her the assurances she was seeking as noisy footsteps approached. He looked sharply over his shoulder to see Sharyn with a security guard.

The uniformed official pointed at Calvin. 'You,' he said, 'out!'

Within two minutes he was being escorted from the hospital premises, with the nurse telling him crossly that he had no right to be on the wards functioning as a hospital chaplain because, as everyone knew, he had been removed from the rota on suspicion of trying to force an entry into a restricted area of the hospital.

Calvin made no attempt to defend himself against the accusation. Instead, he went on the counter offensive.

'For all the good care you say is given to the patients here, I must say that I'm surprised at how thin my housekeeper is. It looks like she has lost about three stone or something. Are you really feeding her?'

'Of course we are! What are you trying to say? I've already told you—she's refusing to eat a lot of the time.'

'I managed to feed her and give her a drink—why can't you? The first thing she did when she woke up was tell me she was thirsty.'

'I refuse to have this conversation with you,' said the nurse as the hospital exit came into view.

'You should perhaps try that little bit harder when it comes to giving them a drink. You never know what might happen,' Calvin continued, the three of them halting before the double doors that opened on to a driveway leading to a car park. 'If anyone gives so much as a cup of water to one of these little ones … she most certainly will not go without her reward.'

'What?' answered the nurse, flushing at his temerity in quoting Scripture to her.

'Matthew 10, paraphrased. You should read it sometime.'

Opening the door, the security guard gave the priest a hard and unexpected shove to his shoulder.

'Shut up and get out, you creep,' the guard said, watching with satisfaction as Calvin tripped on the pavement and scrambled to regain his footing.

The priest walked alone towards his car, distraught about the condition and hopelessness of his housekeeper and the realisation that he had little chance of visiting her in hospital again.

23

KLEIN SHOWS HIS HAND

'Where are we going?' Emerald asked as she slid on to the leather passenger seat of Dr Klein's black Jaguar XF that Wednesday evening.

'I thought it would be nice to have a ride to St Winefride's Catholic Church. I thought you might be able to show me the way.'

'Er, no—but I'll find a postcode for you,' she said, thumbing her phone into life.

They travelled in awkward silence, Emerald leaning toward the passenger door as they rolled between lush fields, her elbow on the sill so her left hand could support her head, while the doctor was rigid and expressionless, his eyes staring ahead in single-minded determination.

He swerved the car sharply left on to a gravel driveway that led down to the 19th century neo-Gothic country church. They headed toward the presbytery instead of following the track to the main car park.

Klein stopped in front of the big red-brick Victorian house, and the pair got out of the car. Emerald stood beside the vehicle as the doctor marched past a bank of blue hydrangeas and mounted three steps to ring the bell.

The door opened and Calvin appeared, dressed in black as usual, but without his clerical collar. He was holding a pack of playing cards and he was obviously shocked to find in front of him the smart, tanned, clean-shaven figure of Dr Klein, a smile spreading across his face while his eyes remained cold and unmoving. Emerald stood on the gravel, her arms folded, her face frozen.

'Father Baines, isn't it?' said Klein. 'I think we've met briefly at Bethulia Park. This is Emerald Essien, one of our finest nurses. Perhaps you're already acquainted?'

He glanced over his shoulder to indicate that his assertion applied as much to Emerald as it did to the priest. As Klein turned back to face the priest, Emerald was tempted to signal to Calvin with a few short and frantic shakes of her head. But she realised that the doctor was watching her in a reflection from a high front room window.

'Hello, doctor, how can I help you?' said Calvin.

'You can help me by reading this,' said Klein, producing a folded sheet of paper from the inside pocket of his jacket.

'This is a copy of a letter from the coroner accepting the explanation from our medical director that the loss of documents relating to the care of Ray Parker was accidental. I want to show you that it's the end of the matter. In a couple of weeks, the police are going to announce publicly the same conclusion in relation to the families who have complained about criminal negligence and unlawful killing. It means that you have lost and I have won.'

'That's a very strange conclusion to draw, doctor,' said Calvin.

'Is it? Surely you don't expect me to accept that you are somehow impartial in this matter. You're up to your neck in it. You've been questioned by the police yet you still show up at the hospital when you're not supposed to be there and harangue my staff with quotes from the Bible. How dare you!'

'I was visiting Hannah Hoskins, my housekeeper, as a private individual and she was thirsty when she woke up. I'm worried about her. I wanted to impress on the nurse that she might do a bit more to make sure she has enough to drink. That's all it was.'

Klein rubbed his eyes, slowly nodding, frowning and puckering his lips in the show of sympathy he had perfected over the years.

'Sure, I understand,' he said, stroking his chin. 'It is a terrible, terrible thing, thirst, very distressing for the patient. Dehydration can cause intense suffering, yes. Several studies have shown that and we hear it time and again from people who have recovered from severe illness in intensive care units. They describe how extreme thirst was among the most agonising sensations they experienced throughout their ordeal.

'Anyone with a heart would wish to alleviate the symptoms of thirst. As a man of science and medicine, thirst interests me from a scientific perspective. One day I might conduct my own research into thirst. We simply don't know enough about it, in my opinion.

'We know it is a primitive sensation, rooted in the hypothalamus, one of the deepest levels of the brain, and that it has the power to dominate all others. Sedatives probably don't take it away, no matter how drowsy a patient might appear to be. I would admit that we don't always have it right in our hospitals, especially with the wetting of patients' mouths when they can neither drink nor take fluids intravenously. The only research ever done on that—carried out on dogs and horses—shows that it actually aggravates thirst rather than alleviates it. But we can't change the world, can we?

'You're right, Father Baines, the only thing that can truly remedy thirst is the correction of bodily water depletion—a good drink. But you are rudely mistaken if you think that gives you a licence to conspire to steal from my hospital and abuse my staff.'

'I haven't …'

'Shut up. Don't lie to me. That would not be the correct response. The right answer would be an apology and then a confession. You can confess to me who you were working with on the inside. Does that make sense to you, Emmy?' he growled, glancing behind him.

The nurse remained still and silent, not daring to utter a word.

'You were at the Parker inquest, you were at that meeting of families who claimed we treated their relatives criminally, you get yourself put on the rota and walk around the hospital asking for Emmy here. I wonder, did you ever find her?

'Then you were seen trying to force your way into our records office, interviewed by the police, taken off the chaplaincy rota, and suspended by your Church. Then you come back to the hospital, without authorisation, behave like you think you're a chaplain again and quote scripture at my staff. What are you, an idiot? Do you think I'm an idiot?

'I don't know much about the Bible, but I'd love to hear you quote some scripture at me. Go on, give it your best shot. I'm all ears.'

Klein stood studiously, his hands joined together in front of his crotch and wearing a stupidly pious expression, while Emerald raised her eyes to the sky, wishing she could be transported to any other place in the world.

Calvin breathed deeply, then looked Klein in the face.

'All right then,' he said. 'Lord, when did we see you hungry and feed you, or thirsty and give you drink? In truth I tell you, in so far as you did it to one of the least of these brethren of mine, you did it to me.'

Klein rocked back on his heels, laughed and started to clap in slow applause. 'Very good!' he enthused condescendingly. 'I read lots of stories to my daughters but I don't recognise that line. Which book's that from? Harry Potter and the imaginary friend?'

'I think our conversation is over,' replied Calvin. 'I'm not going to stand here and listen to you blaspheme. Why don't you stop playing the big man, jump back in your car and go and do something useful, like save someone's life?'

'Who says we're finished here?' said Klein, unshifting. 'What's up, are you in a hurry? Have you got someone in there?'

He turned to Emerald then pointed at the cards clenched in the priest's hand so tightly that his knuckles were like pearls.

'I bet he's got a houseful of eight-year-old boys, teaching them Strip Jack Naked or something. Filthy, these people!'

Calvin was bright red.

'Don't worry, you've got all day,' said Klein. 'Hannah Hoskins isn't coming back any time soon to catch you at it, that's for sure.' He moved his face close to Calvin's, so he could whisper in his ear. 'I'm going to see to it that your housekeeper dies slowly and in pain and alone, and you can't see her.'

Calvin threw down the cards and grabbed the lapels of the doctor's jacket with both hands. He pushed him backwards down the steps on to the path without letting go, his teeth gritted and exposed.

Klein bowed his head and smashed a punch into the priest's ribcage with his right hand, following it with an identical punch from his left, then a right again.

Winded, Calvin released the doctor, who immediately swung a right hook into the priest's gasping mouth.

Calvin's head was jerked sideways and before he could regain his balance Klein hit him on the side of his nose, busting it immediately. Blood sprayed in an arc.

Emerald threw herself between them, shouting at Klein to stop, while Calvin sank to his knees, nose and mouth streaming with blood.

The nurse's fingers were splayed across Klein's chest, pushing him back. She begged him to calm down as he pressed forward, not quite finished.

'You saw him, Tavy, he hit me first,' said the doctor, glowering at Calvin with fists still clenched and raised. 'I was acting in self-defence.'

He dropped his hands when he recognised that he had hurt the priest, pleased that he retained one of the proudest talents of his youth. It had been more than ten years since he had last punched someone in anger. He'd missed it.

Watching Calvin still on one knee and wiping away blood with a saturated handkerchief, he began to laugh almost uncontrollably. 'I think you ought to see a doctor about that,' he jeered, pointing at the priest's swollen, blotched face.

Feeling Klein's body relax and seeing that she no longer had to restrain him, Emerald walked over to Calvin. She bent down and cradled his cheeks with her hands to inspect the damage to his mouth and to see if his nose was broken.

'I'm sorry,' she mouthed to her friend, as Klein's laughter rang in their ears.

'Did you hear that?' Calvin whispered, trying to stand.

'What?'

'He called you 'Tavy'.'

Klein's triumphant joy was suddenly checked by fear of recriminations.

'So, you're going to go crying to the police now, are you?' he sneered. 'Are you going to tell them I've beaten you up? Are you going to report me to the hospital? Well, you started it, don't forget that. You attacked me for no reason whatsoever, totally unprovoked. I've got a witness to prove it. That's right, isn't it, Emmy?'

'No, I'm not going to report you,' said Calvin nasally through his tears. 'I'm going to offer it up.'

'Offer it what? Ha! And here's me thinking I'd finally seen the man within, the one willing to pick a fight with someone his own size instead of bullying the little nurses. If ever he pops out again, let me know. I'll give him a second round. Let's go, Emerald, let's get out of here.'

Klein watched from the driver's seat as Calvin bent stiffly to collect up his playing cards before retreating into the presbytery. He looked down at his hands, extending his bloodstained fingers repeatedly to check them for damage or bruising. Satisfied that his fists were only slightly swollen, he started the car and smiled as he reversed, the nurse beside him stunned into speechless despondency.

The contrast between his new mood and the volcanic anger that he had struggled to contain on his way to the presbytery was profound.

He emitted short, low and ecstatic bursts of laughter as he replayed the fight in his mind repeatedly. 'I wish you'd filmed it,' he kept saying to Emerald.

He switched on the radio and the sound of Rose Royce and *Is It Love You're After* filled the car. Klein began to sing along, and Emerald cringed.

'Definitely a good time, that's what I'm after,' he said to the nurse. 'What about you?'

She didn't answer. Her attention was focused on the detour Klein was taking, his Jaguar bouncing over the potholes as he crawled along a hawthorn-lined country lane, thick with white blooms.

He pulled on to a dusty field entrance flanked by birch trees. Although it was still bright there was no one around.

'I have to admit it, I feel great after that,' Klein said, stretching his fingers as he surveyed Emerald's face, entranced as ever by her beauty.

'C'mon, babe, for old time's sake, like you said,' he said, unbuckling his seatbelt.

'It's my period,' said Emerald quickly.

Klein sat back, wondering if he could trust Emerald as he had done in the past or if his hunch that she was out to destroy him was justified. It was she who reported the priest and who proposed that they reignited their affair. Was she playing him, or did she mean it? He would call her bluff. He snaked a hand around the back of her neck.

'I'm burning up, honey, you've got to help me out,' he said, starting to undo the buckle of his belt. He leaned over to kiss her. She reciprocated reluctantly, then pulled away.

'Are we going to get this thing going again, me and you, like you wanted?' he said. 'It would help me forget.'

'Forget what?'

'About who was responsible for the leak.'

Dr Klein reached into the glove compartment and took out a phone in a white case. 'I'm definitely gonna make a film of us this time,' he breathed excitedly. 'Is that okay?'

Klein held his phone low in camera mode, greedily anticipating the moment when he would capture their sexual intimacy, close up and on film—when he would take away from her whatever scraps remained of her self-respect.

Emerald became starkly aware of the weight of self-revulsion that had crushed her for so long. This time, it would be worse. She would not forgive herself. Nothing would shift the bitterness and regret. Anything, at that moment, seemed preferable to what Klein had in mind—even death.

She sat bold upright, her spine locked.

'I can't do this,' she said.

'What do you mean?' demanded Klein. 'I thought we were back on?'

'No, I don't want to. Not here, not like this. It doesn't feel right. You're covered in that man's blood, for God's sake. What's the matter with you, Reinhard? This isn't fun. You're really scaring me!'

She bit her lower lip as Klein fastened his trousers and put away his phone. His dark mood was returning, and she was braced for the worst, having no idea about what he might do next.

He sat in silence, then started the car.

'I don't want to disappoint you, honey, really I don't. I'm just not in the mood today,' said Emerald.

'I don't want to hear it,' interrupted Klein. 'I think it's time we were a little more honest with each other, darling, don't you? I don't think you've been very honest with me.'

Emerald tried to say something but the doctor cut her off. 'Let me finish!' he snapped. 'You haven't been honest with me, Emerald. For all you say, you've never moved on from our affair. You've never forgiven me, have you? And secondly, I have a gut feeling that you've been co-operating with some of those people who have caused me so much trouble lately, who have done me so much harm. You're quite vengeful and vindictive, aren't you?'

'No, you're wrong.'

'It's time to give up, Emerald. It isn't working. The campaign by the families has fallen at the first hurdle. It can't go any further, but I don't trust you. Have you thought about your future?'

'What do you mean?'

'Well, things are not likely to get much better between us, are they, realistically?'

'I don't know what you mean. I've been honest when I say you're a wonderful doctor and I really thought maybe we could be friends again.'

Emerald knew she sounded unconvincing. She saw the side of Klein's mouth twitch as he tried to suppress the shadow of a grin.

'There might be some merit in perhaps thinking of your time at Bethulia Park a little like staying in a hotel while you're on a good holiday,' he said. 'You've had some great experiences, a lot of fun, met some lovely people and seen the sights but now maybe it's time to move on. But first you have to pay the bill. So I'll take you up on your offer of friendship as settlement in full of the debt

269

between us—one night of friendship with me and perhaps a friend of mine, without complaint, and we'll call it quits. That and an agreement to get out of this campaign for good. And Bethulia Park Hospital. After our night of friendship you go your way—without delay, without hanging around—and I, well, I'll stay where I am. That's the deal.'

Back behind the wheel of her own car some thirty minutes later, Emerald was trembling at the shock of seeing Calvin beaten up, and the prospect of Klein's 'deal'. She was also annoyed to have *Is It Love You're After* stuck in her head.

She turned on her radio in the hope of purging it from her mind but switched it off within seconds, the DJs and their song choices irritating her beyond measure.

Why, she wondered, had the musicians decided to put love and a good time at the opposite ends of a spectrum when surely they were complementary aspects of a healthy relationship that would occupy essentially the same place?

It would have been a much wider spectrum if she had composed the song, she told herself. Love would be at one end, and at the other she would have included betrayal, lies, duplicity, sexual violence, defilement and the abuse of power. They were not her idea of a good time.

As she sped back to St Winefride's, her hands shaking on the steering wheel, she was infinitely relieved to have resisted the doctor's advances without him turning exceptionally nasty. She had escaped violence and disgrace. Yet it brought her no peace: she might have only delayed the inevitable.

Emerald arrived back at the presbytery to discover several playing cards still fluttering around on the gravel. Some were splashed with Calvin's blood.

Emerald picked the cards up and looked at them. Among them were the king and queen of spades and the queen of diamonds. The others she shoved into her pocket, meaning to return them to the priest, but she kept hold of the three. Before she rang the doorbell, she placed the two black cards in her left hand and the red in her right. For a moment she alternately contemplated all three, concentrating hard.

'Why did you call me 'Davy'?' she muttered as she stared down her sleeve at the king. At least that's what she thought Calvin had said. Her focus shifted to the black queen.

'And who are you?'

24

RED RIDING HOOD

It had been three weeks and two days since I had agreed to meet Dr Klein. We'd exchanged phone numbers and I was surprised when he didn't call. His apparent lack of urgency added to my suspicion that the police investigation wasn't going anywhere. Why would he need to speak to me if he knew he had won? Everything I heard from the families throughout May convinced me that the information imparted by Dennis Clarence in the steam room was true: the campaign by the families was scuppered before it was off the ground.

It was as if the police were merely going through the motions. One woman, Gayle Turner, rang me to tell me that two detective constables had been to her home to speak to her about the death of her mother. She was angry and upset because she didn't feel the detectives had taken her seriously. She said she explained to them how her 86-year-old mum was bright and talkative (though immobile without her Zimmer frame) before she was admitted to Bethulia Park with a suspected stroke and that she was 'tortured and killed' before her eyes. She said her mother was reduced to someone who 'looked like an Egyptian mummy'.

According to Gayle, the officers assured her they would inspect her mother's medical records thoroughly but departed suggesting she made a formal complaint to the healthcare ombudsman. She took it as a sign the police had given up before they had even opened the files. I was reluctant to admit it to Gayle, but that's how I saw it too. Similar stories of such a perfunctory approach by the police reached me from other families. It didn't make me relish the prospect of sitting opposite Dr Klein and watching him gloat and boast, so on balance I was relieved not to hear from him.

Something must have happened to make Dr Klein decide to ring me in the final week of that month. Maybe he'd learned of the Freedom of Information requests I had made to Bethulia Park Hospital Trust about the death rates there over the last decade, and the corresponding use of end-of-life pathways and similar protocols. Perhaps it was something else. But I was pretty sure he realised that I hoped to match up any possible revelations with the career path of the mysterious Octavia Topcliffe—or 'Doc Ock' as Seb called her, laughing, when I told him what I was doing. A character from bloody Spiderman. Seb's so stupid and childish at times that it makes me wonder why I bother.

It was the Tuesday, the day after the second May bank holiday, when Dr Klein phoned and suggested we finally went for that coffee. We agreed to meet in Manchester city centre two days later when he had a day off. It was easy for me to get to there on the train; I often went there to shop. Klein told me he went there frequently too because it was a city he loved and knew well, having spent much of his childhood in one of its affluent southern suburbs.

It was a relief that he wasn't gloating when he sat down opposite me in Starbucks on Peter Street that Thursday. He was chipper, cheerful and modest. He was affable Dr Silk, cracking jokes and telling me what it was like to ride with the hunt. The ice between us melted.

As he talked, he would sip his cappuccino and snatch the occasional glance of shoppers passing the windows. He seemed easily distracted, as if he was registering everything that went on around him, making a mental record of every person he saw. Sometimes the passers-by returned his stares, especially the younger women. Did they see what I saw? A charismatic man, toned and tanned like a lifeguard. Could his magnetism really penetrate reinforced glass?

It wasn't surprising that women looked at him. With his long hair swept back, impeccably styled and held in place by a gel so strong that the Gucci sunglasses he wore on his head failed to shift a single strand, he was gorgeous. More than that. He was perfected and polished. I bet if all the worms in China were to get together to create a man from silk they could not make anyone quite so smooth as Dr Reinhard Klein.

He wasn't wearing a suit this time. He was dressed in expensive designer clothes, casually, like they were his birthright. His white collarless seersucker shirt was by Armani and his light blue blouson was Stefano Ricci. I asked what it was made from and he told me it was lambskin. A wolf in sheep's clothing. Yeah, there was definitely something of the wolf about Dr Klein. A wolf who kills grannies.

I'd often wondered about his name, and decided to put him to the test.

'*Es ist mir eine große Freude, Sie endlich kennenzulernen,*' I said, smiling, when there was a break in the conversation.

'*Ich habe schon nicht mehr daran geglaubt, dass wir uns einmal treffen würden,*' he replied. '*Auf Formalitäten können wir verzichten. Sie können mich als Freund betrachten.*'

He was growing silkier by the second. He eyed me curiously, as if to demand an explanation, and I laughed and said: '*Ich habe an der Universität Cambridge Sprachen studiert. Ich spreche Spanisch und Französisch und mein Italienisch ist auch nicht schlecht.*'

From the outset he made it clear that he would not talk about individual cases and I accepted that. I didn't expect him to dis-cuss them. Indeed, I was lucky in many respects to have a doctor willing to give me an off-the-record briefing at all. Normally, I would put my inquiries through the Trust's press office and would receive nothing more than an anodyne response so predictable I could have written it myself backwards in Braille.

'It's over, Jenny,' Dr Klein told me, deadly serious. 'The police aren't going to do anything about the complaints about Bethulia Park.'

I shrugged my shoulders resignedly.

'So what's with the Freedom of Information requests about death rates? Are you hoping to keep your campaign going?'

'It's not strictly my campaign, Dr Klein. The families are driving all this. My job as a journalist is to report what is happening.'

'Oh, the families, yes.'

He rocked back and fixed his gaze over my head, looking into space as he disappeared into his thoughts.

'I am so sorry for these people. It sounds like they have had terrible experiences and it's all very regrettable. I'd like every patient to have nothing but a perfect experience at Bethulia Park. But it's a hospital, not a five-star hotel—that's the reality.

'Also, I'm not quite sure I would agree with their versions of events—which I can't discuss with you for obvious reasons. I don't think it surprises you to hear that. But I do want to express to you nonetheless that I think much of the problem lies in miscommunication and in the misunderstandings of their families about the limits of medicine—about what we can and can't do for patients. It's about their expectations, in many cases, and how they respond when they meet with disappointment or failure. As a society, we're no longer conversant with death in the same way our forebears were. People don't talk about it and they no longer cope very well when it arrives, as it inevitably does. It's a fact of life. But are we deliberately killing patients, or shortening their lives? Absolutely not. It's outrageous to even think that.'

He leaned forward and fixed his gaze on me.

'Please listen to me because this is important. If I, or anyone else, had been killing patients at Bethulia Park, the police would have found a case against us—and they've barely been away from the hospital in the last six months. The Care Quality Commission would also be all over us. But the police have closed their investigation because there is not a single case to answer. They have looked and they have found none. That's the bottom line. It is that straightforward.

'Sure, there are a handful of families who have grievances, and perhaps some of them may have some degree of legitimacy—poor care does happen from time to time and I regret that. With the best will in the world we don't always get it right and our staff are occasionally susceptible to human error like everyone else. I am. I forgot about the meeting with the Parker family. But these new cases, even if they have any merit, are a drop in the ocean compared to the vast numbers of people—the tens of thousands—who we treat each year and who go home happy, grateful and praising us for the standards of our care.'

I said: 'It has been put to me that some of these complaints have arisen because you game the system to perhaps hurry people along when they're not quite ready. What do you say to that?'

He thought about it for a moment and smiled as he answered. 'I don't game the system to kill my patients or "hurry them along", as you put it. Perhaps, what some people fail to recognise, is that the system is designed with a degree of flexibility so that the medics who work within it can exercise judgement in every instance. This allows us to use our best knowledge, expertise and wisdom—acquired over years—to sometimes determine when it is time to stop, when treatment is futile and when we can no longer help patients. Instead, we make them as comfortable as we can. Sometimes the best thing is to let nature take its course. We're not meant to live for ever.

'The system gives us that flexibility to deliver the highest quality of care on a case-by-case basis. It does not give us a licence to kill our patients and none of us do that. There's nothing wrong with the system and there's nothing I've done, Jenny, that's broken the law. I say that with absolute sincerity.'

Dr Klein reached into his jacket pocket and took out a piece of paper. He unfolded it and passed it to me. I noticed grey and violet bruising on his knuckles.

'Oh, what have you done?'

'Oh, that. Nothing really. Household accident,' he replied, trying to conceal a smirk. 'I was helping my wife move this huge antique dresser she inherited from her uncle—a big heavy thing, carved black oak—and I whacked my hand against a wall shifting it from one room to another.

'Anyway, please read on. You need to know that none of these investigations are going anywhere. That letter in front of you is from the coroner and when you read it you will see that he has accepted that the hospital did not mislead him by failing to disclose the full medical records at the inquest. He recognised it for what it was—a regrettable human error, an accidental omission.

'He also understands that the missing records were irrelevant to case. Mr Parker was a dying man. I wish I could have kept him alive, but I couldn't, and I can't bring him back either. It really is time to move on, Jenny. Bethulia Park Hospital does not deserve all this bad publicity. It's a good place, staffed by caring, dedicated people who do their jobs often in difficult circumstances. But right now, we're finding a lot of our patients are coming in terrified about what we might do to them all because of this egregious campaign by a disaffected group of families which is making its way into the Press. It's not fair to us and it's not fair to them.'

I felt embarrassed and a little angry. He made it sound as if I was personally to blame for this perceived injustice. But did I really have it so dreadfully wrong? Was I complicit in smearing a sound institution by giving a platform to people who had somehow got hold of the wrong end of the stick? I took a moment to read the letter from the coroner so I didn't have to look Dr Klein in the face. I did not want him to see that I was doubting myself, but my shame deepened with each word I read. It was true. The letter explicitly absolved Bethulia Park Hospital and Dr Klein of any fault whatsoever, the coroner categorically accepting both the explanation and the apology offered by Anne Conway, the chief executive of the Trust.

As I handed back the letter, I forced my lips into a smile, wishing to show Dr Klein that I too was ready to accept the judgement of the coroner. I didn't feel I was in a position to argue. He sensed my weakness.

'So, Jenny, why are you continuing your investigations? Why have you submitted those Freedom of Information requests? I hope you don't mind me asking.'

'Because I have heard multiple testimonies from a good few families who are adamant that their relatives died as a result of shocking care at Bethulia Park and that the treatment of their loved ones bordered on deliberate criminal negligence. That's why I'm doing it. I wouldn't be doing my job properly if I failed to determine, to my own satisfaction, the truth of these allegations that have been brought to my attention. I'm sure you agree, Dr Klein, that patient safety is clearly a matter of the public interest. That's one of the reasons why we have a free Press, it's why the Press is so important.'

'Yes, of course I'm happy to accept that. But I'm curious about the Freedom of Information requests? What are you up to?'

'You don't need to worry, it doesn't concern you.'

'Why not tell me, then?'

'Okay, I will. Do you remember a doctor called Octavia Topcliffe?'

'No, I've never heard of her, why?'

'That's surprising. She was at Bethulia Park from 2015 to 2017 and you've been there since—what is it?—2009. Are you sure you don't know her?'

Dr Klein paused. I sipped my coffee while I watched him ruminate, wondering how he would answer. I felt a little stronger as he grew suddenly uncertain.

'Oh, hang on a minute, I do know who you mean,' he said with a chuckle. 'Yes, I remember her, but only vaguely. Why do you ask? How do your investigations have anything to do with her?'

'I'm not sure yet. Why did she leave, Dr Klein? Whatever happened to her?'

Dr Klein blew air into his cheeks, puffing them up, and released it in a blast as he began to answer.

'I think, but I'm not a hundred per cent sure, that she went abroad. I think she went off to Canada. I didn't really know her so I can't say for sure. She was very idealistic, as I remember. She had a lot of radical ideas about patient care which were also a bit revolutionary, a bit ahead of her time. I've heard it said that she was even a bit wacko. My understanding is that she became rather excited by the euthanasia law passed in Canada and migrated there when she married because she wanted to work in a country with a more progressive attitude. I think she married a professor with a strange Russian or Polish name. Anyway, she went to Canada and as far as I know, that's where she lives and works today.'

'What is her married name? Do you know?'

'I don't, I'm sorry. I'd never remember a name like that and, like I said, I barely knew her. A journalist of your standing could find that out. You don't need my help for that. I'm still not sure I understand how it's relevant to anything that has happened at the hospital lately. You must appreciate that Octavia Topcliffe left Bethulia Park quite a while ago. But please keep me up to date with how you get along. I'm very interested to know if you find anything out about what she is doing now.'

'I'll bear that in mind, doctor.'

'Thanks. But these really are big "ifs" and "buts", if you don't mind me saying so. I think you're barking up the wrong tree. That's just my opinion, of course. Time will tell. I'm most interested in what has happened over the last six months or so and what might happen next. That's most important to me. I really want this business to end.'

He took a long breath.

'I asked you to meet me because there are a few things I think you need to know, stuff you really need to be aware of if you were to have what I think is a much more rounded view of the difficulties we've been going through.

'I think some of your sources are bit *parti pris*, a little bit untrustworthy, shall we say—and I'm not talking about the families. You need to beware of them.'

'Who exactly?'

'The nurse who leaked the document to you, especially.'

'How do you know it was a nurse? I never said it was a nurse.'

'I know the rules of the game and I don't expect you to reveal your sources—though you can if you like—but my suspicion is that the leak was a nurse. For argument's sake, I'm going to call her Scarlett.'

I avoided eye contact as I did my best to keep my face straight. He began to laugh and it was painful for me not to smile.

'Why are you laughing?' he said.

'I'm not laughing.'

'Yes you are, you're laughing. What's so funny about "Scarlett"?'

'Nothing. I'm laughing at you laughing.'

He'd trapped me. His mirth masked a serious ploy. He wished to see how I would react to the name he'd invented, and he caught me off guard.

'Scarlett? I don't know anyone called Scarlett,' I said, collecting myself. 'But you're correct on one point—I'm not going to reveal my sources. So if I were you, I wouldn't bother trying to play mind games with me in the hope that I'll slip up. It isn't going to happen.'

'Accepted. But please listen to what I have to say. Scarlett is not telling you the truth. Scarlett is a fantasist and a liar. Scarlett has an agenda and she will do anything to advance that agenda. You would be a fool to trust Scarlett.'

'Do you have any evidence for these accusations against this person you call Scarlett?'

'Plenty. But I don't have a file on her to leak to you. Let me tell you something about Scarlett. When she passed over those documents to you she tried to cover herself by coming to me and blaming a Roman Catholic hospital chaplain for stealing them. She did so knowing that this man, who would have thought of her as his friend, would be arrested and investigated by the police. Father Calvin Baines, his name is. I suspect you've come across him, a weird young chap who's very involved with the Parker family. Well, he was suspended because Scarlett chose to betray him. I bet she didn't tell you that.'

I felt as if I was about to pass out. I said nothing.

'No, she didn't, did she?' Dr Klein went on. 'Well, I think there was even more to it than that. I think she recruited this gullible fellow with the purpose of using him as a shield if she felt she had to. And you accuse me of making pawns out of people? Do you really think Scarlett is someone you should trust? I wouldn't, if I were you. She's a fantasist and a compulsive liar. I think she's a bit unhinged, actually—possibly because of her difficult upbringing and then this violent attack that she suffered. She could have died, you know—she was very lucky to survive. Losing her husband probably didn't do much for her mental health either.

'Jenny, I'm not settling old scores here, I don't have an axe to grind against this person, and I don't feel comfortable discussing anyone's medical history, even those who are anonymous to us. It's unethical. But her history is relevant in this case. You need to know that Scarlett enters into fantasies—no, honestly, she does—in which she thinks she's a famous person. She role-plays, she self-identifies, call it what you will. Of course, it's all the rage now—men saying they're women, women saying they're men, and that's just the uncomplicated end of the trend. You know, I've even heard of someone self-identifying as a dragon. With Scarlett, it's usually historical figures she goes for—movie stars, famous dead people, characters from books. It's hard to guess who she is from one month to the next. It's harmless, but sometimes it's borderline madness. It's not that I'm against any of this stuff. In many ways, I admire her. I agree with it. Creating your own reality represents another step on the march of progress, the victory of Post-Modern man over suffering and death, with which I strongly identify.'

As he preached to me, I remembered Emerald's description of Dr Klein as a cod philosopher and poet.

'What is reality? What is truth? There is no real truth,' he went on. 'It's what we make it and Emerald—sorry, Scarlett— creates her own truth and finds happiness from that. We all create our own truth and when we die the dreams and ideas we have made for ourselves blow away with the dust of our lives. She does it a little bit more extravagantly than most.

'I wouldn't mind so much if she wasn't out for revenge. That's the other thing you need to know.'

'Why would Scarlett seek revenge against you, Dr Klein?'

'Because I wouldn't desert my wife and children for her,' he said curtly. 'This is off the record.'

'I get that,' I said. 'So you admit to an affair with the person you call Scarlett?'

'I admit to being human. Look, I love my wife and my daughters dearly—you've seen my girls at the stables, right?'

'Yes, they're lovely.'

'They are lovely, you're right. I wouldn't want to hurt them or my wife. I let this nurse into my life for a brief period and I had to let her go when she was going to wreck my marriage. Now it's payback time. I was a fool, I should never have had an affair, but I was weak. Does that make me a killer? No. But this woman is out to convince everybody that I am.'

I looked out of the window, trying to hide my anger with Emerald. I didn't know what to believe any more.

Dr Klein carried on talking as I stared into the street. 'She's totally brazen, and she will not let go,' he said. 'She is still making sexual advances toward me even now. She tried it on with me again yesterday. It's the last time I get in a car alone with her, I can tell you.'

'Poor you, all these women chasing you,' I thought, looking at him again and admiring the way he was able to channel vulnerability and regret in his expression. He was presenting himself as a victim. What was he asking me for? Sympathy, comfort, an apology for having judged him so rashly? The acknowledgement of his version of events?

I wasn't taken in by him and I was immediately sure he'd barraged me with a mixture of truths and half-truths and barefaced lies, leaving me confused and unable to discern the real from the illusory. I knew that whatever I threw at him, however grave or damning it might be, he would come back with a benign and convincing explanation. I felt like Little Red Riding Hood with the wolf. *What big pointy ears you have!* All the better for hearing you with, my dear. *What big eyes you have!* All the better for seeing you with, my dear.

We could go on all day. It was amusing in some ways. There he was in front of me, this big wolf—great-looking and funny, charming, intelligent, accomplished—claiming to be the injured party and looking sorry for himself. A wolf made from silk.

'Did your wife ever find out about your affair?' I asked.

'No, so please don't let on if ever you meet—for the sake of my girls.'

'Your daughters are lovely. How are they doing in their riding lessons?'

'Very well indeed. The younger is still a little rough in canter and hasn't quite grasped the finer points of lateral work. She tends to drive those ponies around with her heels, kicking all the time, but I expect it is something she'll grow out of. The older girl,

Sophia, though—well, she's great. Absolutely fearless. I swear she could jump fences blindfolded, she's such a natural.'

He paused.

'I haven't seen you at the stables lately. Where've you been?'

'Oh, I still go there. I'm going to be moving soon, though. My horse is going to my parents' farm once my dad's renovated the stable block. It shouldn't be too long, now. I'll still see my mare nearly every day but I need a bit of extra help because I have so much on my plate at present. I've not been in the arena on Saturdays because we hack out every week in spring and summer, usually very early.'

'Where do you go?'

'I usually do a circuit passing the edge of Crostbury Golf Course and back down through the fields, sometimes much further if the weather's nice and I've got the time. If my horse tires on the long trip, I jump off and walk with her, chatting, just the two of us.'

'Is it the work that's making you so busy?'

'Yes, and I'm getting married in September. I had no idea it would be so complicated.'

'Who's the lucky fellow?'

'Preston's answer to Nick Knowles, but I doubt you'll know him.'

'Congratulations in advance. I see it's going to be a big and special year for you. You must let me buy you a wedding present as a token of my goodwill after all this is over. Y'know, I love being married. Twelve years now for us. I married my childhood sweetheart who is now also a successful commercial solicitor as well as a very busy mother.'

'So you must regret your affair in that case?'

'I regret becoming entangled with Scarlett, for obvious reasons, but I don't really regret having an affair, no. It's no big deal if no one gets hurt. A lot of people do it. You might understand where I'm coming from after, say, three, five, seven years of being married yourself. We crave a bit of excitement sometimes, a break with routine. I honestly believe a bit of sexual adventure can make marriages stronger. I still love my wife.

'I also think it's perfectly reasonable for young people to have a bit of fun before they eventually tie the knot, to sleep around a bit. In fact, I would recommend it. I know one lady doctor who had a fling right up to the eve of her wedding day. It hasn't caused any harm to her marriage whatsoever. It's just a bit of harmless fun, a bit of sport. Don't you agree?'

I said nothing. I was speechless. We had concluded our discussion about Bethulia Park and we were entering perilous new territory. *What big teeth you have!*

Dr Klein licked his lips.

'How about lunch?' he said.

I looked out of the window at the Midland Hotel across the street. Rolling around on a large double bed with Dr Klein would undoubtedly be an extremely enjoyable way to spend an afternoon. I could see he was bad but I liked it. I liked that about Seb too; it was the same quality that had first attracted me to him. But here before me was a man far more my type than my own fiancé, who now seemed desperately limited and lacklustre in comparison, and our engagement a hasty and reckless mismatch. I fancied Klein too. Far more than Seb. As the doctor waited for me to give him an answer, I searched for a rational response, my mind working at the speed of light. But everything seemed to be prefaced with the words: 'If I slept with Dr Klein …

'If I slept with Dr Klein, it would only be once; if I slept with Dr Klein, I would want silk or satin sheets on the bed; if I slept with Dr Klein I would want to be able to see him as well as touch him …' I was getting closer to saying: 'Yes, I'm starving.' I had to pinch myself.

He must have seen I was flustered. I paused again, still not sure what I wanted to say.

'So you'd like me to undress for you, would you, Dr Klein?' I muttered eventually.

'I wouldn't mind,' he said.

So casual, and so compelling. A step closer and I would give in. I would be his. I stood up quickly, picked up my bag and pushed my chair under the table. I was running away from the same intense and awful persuasive charm to which Emerald had once succumbed. I was no longer angry with her. I understood her. I wanted to keep my head. Seb annoyed me but I had no desire to cheat on him and I knew in my heart that a fling with the doctor, however brief, could ruin everything between us at a time in our lives when we were meant to be most happy. Nor did I have any conscious urge to sleep with someone else's husband. Until that moment, the very idea had been repugnant to me.

'Thanks for the coffee, Dr Klein,' I said, hoisting my bag on to my shoulder. 'But it's time I got going.' I moved toward the door.

Then I turned round. I should have been angry with him and myself but I wasn't. I was overcome by excitement, consumed by desire. I should have been afraid but I feared only the prospect of a missed opportunity which I might regret. Klein was watching me from over his shoulder.

'Italian,' I said.

'What?'

'My favourite food—it's Italian.'

I walked back to the table and sat down, crossing my legs. A smile of satisfaction unfolded on Dr Klein's face. Where was a woodcutter when you needed one?

25

A NEW HOUSEKEEPER

Emerald had not cried so much since the day her throat was cut. She had been thoroughly miserable since Wednesday evening when she had watched Dr Klein batter Calvin and returned to the priest to find him sobbing, his nose swollen and the left side of his upper lip gashed and protruding, sagging like the mouth of a basset hound.

It was not so much the injuries that were causing such distress to the priest but the fact that the next day was Ascension Thursday, a holy day of obligation when all of the people of the parish were summoned to Mass, and he would be at the altar looking as if he'd gone five rounds with Tyson Fury.

They wept together while Emerald did her best to console him and patch him up, telling him she would be back early in the morning, before her shift, with her make-up bag to cover up most of the marks on his face. At home, she cried alone late into the night.

She did a pretty good job of masking the worst of his cuts and bruises the following morning and she went back after work to apply more concealer ahead of the evening Mass, which she attended. She stayed with Calvin for two hours afterwards, stricken with worry and with guilt for having betrayed him to

Dr Klein, something which she had yet to admit to him. She wept again when she went home that night—full of grief for Calvin, and shame for betraying him and leading him into violence, and convulsed with fear of what Dr Klein might have in store for them.

Mrs Edwards, who was standing in for Mrs Hoskins, had asked to be released from her duties because she had become a grandmother for the fifth time and her daughter needed her assistance. Emerald had noticed from the moment she set foot inside the presbytery that it was a mess. Papers and books were strewn everywhere, there was dust on the furniture, soil on the carpets, grime on the worktops and dishes piled up, a typical bachelor pad. On Friday she made Calvin clean it up, helping and directing him but refusing to shift the bulk of the work herself. But she empathised with him: it was not easy living alone. People were not made for that, she was convinced of it. She felt loneliness keenly herself when she returned to her flat that evening and drank a bottle and a half of Spanish Albariño in solitude, wiping tears from her face for the third night in a row.

However that evening was not as bad as the previous two, thanks to the passage of time and a couple of interesting developments.

First, Calvin had yielded to her insistence that she would visit the presbytery several times a week to help with the running of the house and with mundane administrative and secretarial tasks until Mrs Hoskins could return or a new housekeeper could be found. She was also willing to learn to look after the church whenever he needed assistance. Calvin agreed that she would become his de facto housekeeper, with very little resistance. Emerald was looking forward to spending some time in his company. She had her friend back.

She had been open with him about her forthcoming date with Geoff, Jenny's farmer brother, that Saturday, and she felt that this helped Calvin not to consider her as a threat any longer, that she was some sort of incarnation of Judith who was out to seduce him and cut off his head. Her announcement had the effect of reducing the tension between them presented by their mutual attraction. Having a boyfriend and being seen with him publicly from time to time would remove any suspicion from the minds of the priest and his parishioners that her practical goodwill and solicitude flowed from ulterior motives.

Although Calvin greeted the news of her date with muted relief, and by saying he was keen to meet Geoff, he privately experienced an awkward sense of personal loss, which made him feel a little guilty. It pleased him enormously, nevertheless, that Emerald remained in his life. He wanted her there. He had tried to pull away from her for good on the way back from Parkgate but she was closer to him now, at least physically, if not emotionally, than ever before. Reunited by Dr Klein, of all people.

Of course, her frequent visits to the parish dramatically increased the risk of Dr Klein discovering her association with the priest. But in some ways, Emerald was almost past caring. Klein was already convinced of her guilt.

She believed that the truth, in most cases, has an uncanny knack of fighting its way to the surface and she reckoned that the truth about her friendship with Calvin would probably not stay hidden no matter what she did. Why bother fighting a rear-guard action she was destined to lose?

If only exposing the truth about Dr Klein could be so easy. The campaign by the families and the Press had borne fruit, certainly. The doctor was, for the first time in his life, seriously sullied in the eyes of his superiors and the police were now familiar with his name and the poorer side of his reputation. But Detective Inspector Tarleton was not going to act on the complaints by these families. Not this time. That particular battle was lost. He and his team had all but concluded their inquiries, and Emerald knew it. She doubted if her friend Jenny, in spite of her determined efforts to win justice for the families, could do anything more to help them in the absence of any new and damning information about Dr Klein personally.

So her discovery that Dr Klein was probably the last person to see Mrs Worthington alive was the second development that helped her to dry her eyes. Emerald had learned from the patient's medical records on Friday that Dr Klein was the physician who confirmed Mrs Worthington's death from an unexpected cardiac arrest. There had been no post-mortem and Ralph Parker said she was buried after a funeral service at St Oswald's Anglican Church in Crostbury, where she worshipped. The circumstances of her death gave Emerald the hope that she perhaps had one last card to play, just one more desperate throw of the dice, before she left the country to escape Dr Klein.

Emerald had decided that she must go. There was no way she would agree to 'pay the bill' on the doctor's terms. She had a very good idea of what it might involve—probably torments similar to those inflicted upon those poor women in the sick and disgusting films Dr Klein took so much pleasure in watching. A home movie directed by and starring Klein himself, probably masked, with Emerald featuring as a slab of meat. It was too terrible to contemplate. Some bill.

She wasn't sure she would be safe from Dr Klein unless she went very far indeed. France was her first and immediate choice, the country of her father whose language she could speak almost fluently. She had lots of relatives in the Burgundy region and they would welcome her there. But she was also thinking about applying for work in the United States, Canada, Australia and New Zealand.

Alternatively, Emerald could politely decline Dr Klein's proposition and stay where she was, but a long and subtle campaign with the objective of forcing her out of her job, and possibly destroying her, would surely follow.

So it was with a heavy heart that she left her flat to meet Geoff for their first date that Saturday morning.

She took a train from Wigan Wallgate to Southport, feeling self-consciously scruffy in the clothes she normally put on for the gym—shorts, a T-shirt, and trainers with ankle socks—with other belongings in a small backpack.

She found Geoff leaning on the barrier in the sunshine at the end of the town's pier at noon, as they had arranged. He had cycled to the resort from his parents' farm an hour earlier to meet a friend who was lending him a bike and a helmet for Emerald, and he handed both to her with a grin.

It was the first day of June, and Geoff had the grand plan of cycling from 'pier to pier', a 21-mile route from the resort's majestic Victorian iron pier, at 1,300 yards the second longest in the country, via various pubs to Wigan Pier, the famous but runty coal-loading staithe that now appeared as a wooden jetty embedded with railway sleepers jutting out just a few pathetic feet over the Leeds-Liverpool Canal. Conveniently, it was situated around the corner from Emerald's flat where they could get cleaned up after the ride before going out again for a few drinks locally. That was the idea—a long and jolly day of non-stop carousing and fun. To Emerald the thought was as alien, at that moment, as being on another planet.

Geoff knew from the instant he saw her that she was feeling low, so he talked to her consolingly as they walked with their bikes through the bustle of Saturday shoppers and day trippers toward the outskirts of the town. He promised her that she would feel better once they were out in the countryside.

The first part of the ride was on the back roads through farmland as flat as a prairie, making it possible to see any vehicle approaching from miles away.

Because Emerald had not cycled since childhood, Geoff advised her it would be safest nevertheless for that part of the trip if she stuck close to his tail in single file and tight to the roadside unless they could be sure there was no traffic around. 'You can't trust motorists,' he warned her. 'They're idiots.'

It meant they could chat only occasionally, at junctions, or when their senses told them there was absolutely nothing around and they could briefly pull level. For the most part they ploughed ahead in silence, working hard to reach the safety of the Leeds-Liverpool Canal where Geoff knew they could relax and begin the minor pub crawl he had always found a tremendous hoot. Pedalling in silence at the start of the trip gave Emerald the time she needed to gather her thoughts, to get herself together, but she could not help but reflect on Dr Klein's demands. She plunged into hopelessness and desperation. She cursed herself for making such a mess of things, for taking him on and then allowing him to win.

By the time she and Geoff arrived for their first stop at the *Farmers Arms*, a canalside pub outside Burscough, Emerald could no longer contain her emotions. She burst into tears the moment she came to a standstill, sobbing as she straddled the bike, her hands on her face in embarrassment, unable even to dismount.

Geoff was stunned by her breakdown. He hesitated at first, not knowing what to do, then jumped off his bike and ran over to her. She pushed him away when he put his arm around her, and he stood silently with his hands on his hips waiting for her sadness to run its course.

Eventually, she wiped away the tears with the back of her fingers and threw down the bike angrily on to the gravel. As Geoff bent to pick it up, she stamped towards one of the wooden tables in the beer garden, saying: 'I'm sorry, I'm sorry, I'm sorry.'

'Why don't you just go to the police?' asked Geoff as he put down a pint of lager and a wine and soda on the table five minutes later.

She gazed at him in disbelief through puffy eyes. 'What do you think these families, and your sister, have been doing all this time? The police don't care a jot. They're part of the problem.'

'I meant, well, you know—about him beating up that priest?'

'It's complicated,' she said. 'Father Calvin's fighting for his life to stay in his post after his suspension and he doesn't want the police, the archdiocese or the Press involved. He most certainly doesn't want his superiors to know about this. That's why I can't tell Jenny yet. Promise me you won't say anything to her about it, will you? Please don't tell her. He doesn't want it in the papers. It will be the end for him. Leave it to me. I'll tell her when the time's right. She'll understand.'

Emerald dropped her chin at the thought that she must also tell Jenny about Dr Klein calling her 'Davy', or something like that, in the heat of the action, which she was reluctant to do because she would have to invent some sort of false context to protect Calvin, at least at the present time. It could wait for now.

'But this is an opportunity to get this doctor, isn't it?'

Emerald dabbed her eyes with a tissue.

'Perhaps, but we'd have to lie and Father Calvin isn't the lying type. He grabbed the doctor first, that much is true, so technically he assaulted him—and he might have hit him too if Dr Klein hadn't smacked him first. If anyone deserves it, it's that doctor, so I don't blame Calvin one bit. He provoked Father Calvin as well, by threatening to kill his housekeeper. That's what Calvin told me. I never heard Dr Klein say it, but it doesn't mean he didn't.'

'Do you think he will do away with his housekeeper?'

'Yes, I think he would. But he wouldn't leave his fingerprints, that's for sure.'

Geoff didn't quite understand. Nor did he wish for an explanation. He wanted a good time and he wanted Emerald to enjoy herself too. 'C'mon, gorgeous, drink up, we're not even half way there yet—let's get going. There's another pub five hundred yards away. You've got to see this one.'

After washing her face in the ladies, Emerald got back on the bike. It was only about a minute before they reached *The Slipway*, another canalside pub. Geoff bought a round and the alcohol started to work as intended. Emerald began to smile, and to laugh at his jokes. She took an interest in their surroundings and reflected on the distance they had covered and the effort involved. It had included one seemingly never-ending and physically taxing ascent as they neared the canal which left them sweating, breathless and their thighs throbbing.

'It would have been better fun flying down that hill than cycling up it,' she said.

'That's the spirit,' said Geoff, 'you're getting the taste for speed, you're going to be a great cyclist.'

He was interrupted by a slap on the shoulder and turned to see three men in shorts with lagers in their fists.

'Hi Geoff, you a'right, lad?' said the man closest to him. 'Mind if we join yer?'

They were some of his drinking buddies, out for their regular Saturday afternoon session, and curious to see his new girlfriend.

Emerald smiled as Geoff introduced her to each of them, the last of whom simply stared at her and groaned: 'Have you got any sisters?'

His comment set the tone for the next half an hour, with Geoff relentlessly ribbed and Emerald grilled salaciously, every new conversation ending at the same conclusion—a lewd or suggestive remark then raucous laughter.

'So you're the lass who's got peregrines outside your flat?' asked a ginger-haired man.

Emerald began to give a serious answer but another friend cut in. 'Can you see 'em from the bedroom, Geoff?'

Ultimately the banter became tedious so the pair were glad to depart. Stopping for lunch in Burscough, they took their time. They ate outdoors, warmed by sunshine but cooled by a breeze fluttering in from the Irish Sea. After one more glass of wine, Emerald switched to soft drinks but Geoff washed down his steak pie and chips with three pints of San Miguel.

A little bloated, slightly light-headed and having lost the motivation to exercise, they struggled to tackle the next long, rural stretch of tow-path that led them to the village of Parbold.

Geoff suggested going to *The Windmill* pub where Emerald opted for another soft drink while he continued on the lager. She noticed he was slurring his words, like the previous week.

The final five miles featured some of the most scenic parts of the route. The canal cut between steep hills and meandered through fields and woodland. Willows bent as if to drink from the pine green water while poplars gazed like Narcissus upon their own reflections. The stillness of the ancient waterway was broken only by leaping roach or kingfishers diving from the over-hanging branches. The cyclists joked and laughed heartily, Emerald forgetting her worries for the first time in days.

The route became busier as they approached the residential areas. Emerald wanted to slow down and take more care, cautious about hitting a child, an elderly walker or a dog.

Geoff, on the other hand, was showing off, weaving in and out of unoccupied iron moorings embedded along the bank for canal barges. Then he hit one concealed in lush grass and was launched headfirst over the handlebars into the pungent dark water of the canal, his bike following him and missing him by inches.

He emerged gagging, spitting out water and shaking his head to clear his ears. He wore a look of panic, which disappeared the moment he realised he could touch the bottom and stand up.

Embarrassed but laughing at himself, he waded to the bank dragging his bike behind him with a single hand as he stretched forward with the other. He fell back into the water three times as he attempted to haul himself out. Emerald buckled over as she watched him, almost falling from her own bike. With each failed attempt to get out of the canal she shrieked louder than before. She wanted to help him but she could barely move.

It was some time later when the pair trundled up the cobbled towpath to Wigan Pier, still sniggering. Geoff was dripping and cold, but that didn't trouble him as much as the discovery that canal water had flooded the backpack in which he carried a change of clothes. He was filthy from head to foot, with nothing clean to wear.

As they neared the converted mill, Geoff was thinking about what might happen when they reached Emerald's flat. Would she ask him inside? Could he perhaps wear one of her dressing gowns after taking a shower, while they watched television and ate pizza? Why bother to go out again? They could have more fun if they stayed in.

'I was wondering if I could come in and see your peregrine chicks?' he asked outside the complex.

'They've fledged,' she said, looking him up and down with more pity than lust. 'I've had a great time, Geoff, and I'd love to let you in. But you stink. Let's go out again tomorrow instead. I'll call you. Is that all right, darling?'

Emerald kissed him briefly then closed the door, leaving Geoff to squelch clumsily up the hill to the station, a bike in each hand, their pedals bashing his grubby shins and ankles as he battled to straighten them up. The good luck of the previous week had clearly run out.

Emerald put on some coffee, undressed and stepped into the shower, tired yet refreshed from the exercise. After drying and straightening her hair, she brushed her teeth. In the bedroom she looked for something to wear, finally opting for a little black dress and a pair of stiletto heels. She chose her jewellery, her watch and picked out *J'Adore* by Christian Dior as her scent. She applied her make-up and stood before the full-length mirror for a moment to admire the transformation. 'That will do,' she thought. She picked up her phone and called Ralph Parker.

26

THE CINCINNATI KID

Groups of men, mostly young, streamed into the *White Hart* and began to crowd around the bar and to fill up tables arranged around a huge screen at the back of the room. One party followed another, the doors swinging open every ten seconds or so. Emerald sat with Ralph at a table in the corner, taking little sips from a glass of orange juice and growing visibly more nervous with each fresh arrival.

'Why are there so many people here at this time?' she asked. 'It's barely gone half past seven. I thought the place would be empty.'

'Champions League final, Liverpool against Spurs, all-England contest. It's absolutely massive. You don't get bigger than this. The match kicks off in Madrid a couple of hours from now and by that time this lot will be well on their way and it will be crammed in 'ere. It will be banging. It'll be a good night. My dad would have loved this.'

Ralph looked around.

'Don't worry, if he's gonna see yer, he'll see yer well before it gets goin'. Ee'll be watchin' it himself.'

Emerald could barely take her eyes from the door. She scruti-nised every person who passed through it with thinly-veiled suspicion. Every now and then she would glance at her watch to check the time.

'You said he'd see me about seven.'

'Stop worrying.'

No sooner had Ralph spoken than a portly man with a shaven head, wearing grey trousers, a white short-sleeved shirt unbuttoned at the collar and a tie hanging loosely about his neck, appeared in the middle of the room, having arrived from another doorway on the far side which led to a staircase. He looked over to the barmaid who nodded in the direction of Emerald and Ralph. He signalled with his head for them to follow him and Emerald rose quickly to her feet, picked up her bag and hurried toward him, Ralph following her.

He led them up a dark staircase that wound between wood-panelled walls decorated with a gallery of pictures of stags at their most majestic. They stepped on to a landing where the head of a white fallow buck was mounted high on the wall, its face locked in a permanent belch and its antlers extending into an empty embrace.

'This way,' said the man, turning to the right. He opened a door further down the corridor and ushered the pair into a long room, which Emerald guessed was reserved for functions and receptions. A dozen circular tables ran to the windows at the far end, but most were clustered around another large screen. On the opposite wall was a row of square tables, pushed together and laid with plates and bowls covered by tea towels and silver foil.

To Emerald's left, at the end furthest from the windows, was a bar where a group of four strong-looking men with tattoos on their thick arms and necks stood chatting idly while drinking pints of bitter, paying barely any attention to Emerald and Ralph as they arrived with their guide.

'Wait here,' said the man in the tie when they reached the bar. 'Give these two a drink—whatever they want,' he called to a barman before he vanished through a door marked 'Private'.

'I'll have a vodka, lime and soda—tall glass, please,' said Emerald. She wanted to calm her nerves. It had been a long time since she had seen Bob Torridge.

Five minutes later the door to the restricted area swung open. The shaven-headed man beckoned toward Emerald but held up a hand to Ralph when he moved to follow her. 'Not you, sausage fingers,' he said.

'Have you ever heard him play the piano?' the man asked the nurse as she followed him into a corridor. 'He's crap. Sings like an angel though—the voice of angel, the fingers of Les Dawson, that's Ralph Parker.'

They passed a couple of closed doors on their right before she was shown into a room near the end of the passage.

Bob Torridge was sitting behind an antique desk; a casually dressed man with a shallow beard in his early forties was in a chair to his left.

Torridge put down his pen on the green leather desktop and looked up.

'Bob,' she said meekly.

'Emerald. It's been such a long time,' said Bob, waving away the minion, who closed the door behind him. 'Look at you, you look amazing. What is it? It must be nearly ten years. You're all grown up.'

Bob looked older too, thought Emerald, but she did not say so. He was still as broad as a wardrobe like she remembered him but his face was fuller, his chest and stomach a little rounder, his eyes a little more tired and his dark hair was beginning to turn grey.

He gestured to the other man.

'This here is Harry—Harry Worthington, my brother-in-law, the youngest and smartest of all my wife's brothers. You remember Tanya, don't you? This is her brother, and now he's a partner in the business.'

Emerald started to speak but Torridge cut her off. He was on his feet.

'Do you know who this is, Harry?' he declared excitedly. 'Do you have any idea who this is?'

Harry shrugged.

'It's Emerald Essien—the great Emerald Essien, the world's finest croupier.'

Harry raised his eyebrows as he tried to look impressed.

'Oh, Bob, you don't have to over-egg it,' Emerald said with an embarrassed giggle. 'There's no need to flatter me, really. Ignore him, Harry, he's pulling your leg.'

'Did you hear that, Harry? That's modesty, that is—that's humility. She pretends she's not much good when really she knows she's the best. It's the poker face, that's what it is. It's what makes her such a good banker, such a good player. She's made us a lot of money, you know. No one can work tables like she can. She's like the Cincinnati Kid.

'Maybe she can give you a demonstration, but there's no point. You wouldn't be able to see what she was doing with the deck. You wouldn't know what she was doing. She can run, jog, throw, cull, crimp, palm, deal from the bottom—you name it, she can do it. Such sleight of hand! There is no trick this girl doesn't know.'

He turned to Emerald again.

'It's great to see you here after so long. But to what do I owe the pleasure? I'm pretty damn sure this isn't a social visit after what happened to you. I'm intrigued.'

Emerald shifted uneasily.

'Let's have a look, then,' said Bob.

He came round from the other side of his desk. Emerald felt his powerfully masculine presence as he hung over her, as ominous and as deadly as a grizzly bear, all 6ft 4in of him. She felt a pang of fear and she was relieved to see him smile.

He angled his face as she lowered the top of her jacket and tilted her head back to reveal the jagged scar on her throat.

'Cor, it's not got much better, has it, love?' he whispered as he inspected the vivid raised lines. 'Terrible business that.'

He beckoned to Harry and Emerald showed him the scar too. He winced then went back to his seat.

'Do you know who I mean now?'

'Aye, Bob,' said Harry, eyeing Emerald with mixture of awe and respect. Bob sat on the edge of his desk and folded his arms.

'So, how can I help you, Emerald? I didn't expect you to come back and ask me for a job after all that. Is it a job you want? I hope it is. I'll give you a job. I'd love you to come back and work for me again.'

'Thanks, Bob, but I'm a nurse now. I can't relive my teenage years. It was fun at the time but I've moved on.'

'A nurse! Yes, that's right. You always said you were going to be a nurse and no one believed you. We all thought you'd end up in hospital, though.'

Bob laughed loudly at his own joke and Harry chuckled deferentially.

Emerald smiled bleakly.

'But you've made it. Of course you did. Where do you work, Emerald?'

'Bethulia Park.'

Both men were suddenly solemn. They exchanged sideways, knowing glances.

'That's why I've come to see you. It's about Bethulia Park. I've some information for you that I think you will find very useful.'

'What information?' barked Bob.

Emerald turned to the bearded man.

'How did your mother die, Harry?'

'She had a heart attack in hospital on Good Friday. Why?'

'Would it matter to you if I told you the last person who saw her alive was Dr Reinhard Klein? Would that mean anything to you?'

'The doctor with the long hair?'

'Yes, him.'

'I think it would, yes,' said Harry. 'It would definitely mean a lot to Ralph Parker too. He's convinced this guy's on the rampage. He says he killed his dad.'

Emerald fished in her handbag and pulled out a memory stick. She offered it to Bob and invited him to turn on his desktop computer.

'On here are photographs of the files that will prove to you that Dr Klein was the physician who confirmed her death that night. They show that he found her dead. Now I think that's suspicious. I think it is also highly suspicious that there was no postmortem. It might be that Dr Klein is trying to hide something about the death of your mother-in-law—and your mother—from the pathologist, something he did which he doesn't want the authorities to know about.

'Bob, what I have come here to ask you to do is to go to the authorities and demand that your mother-in-law is exhumed and tested for toxins, particularly opiates which will still be in her body, or overdoses of medication. I think she might have been poisoned.'

'What authorities?' drawled Bob, putting the stick down on his desk. 'Make demands of who exactly?'

'The coroner and the police.'

Bob turned to Harry and they sniggered disdainfully.

Harry said: 'The last time I visited my mother in Bethulia Park the police threw me out and they threatened to arrest me. They did the same with my other brothers and my sister. Are you saying that they're going to take me seriously if I go and tell them that my mother was poisoned by a doctor? I'm sorry, Emerald, I don't think that's going to happen.'

'They will act if the coroner tells them they have to,' she said. 'You need to kick off about it and demand a post-mortem is performed on your mother. Why wasn't there one at the time? Why didn't you ask for one?'

The two men fell silent. 'Perhaps we should have said something,' conceded Harry eventually, 'but we're not on the best of terms with the authorities, as you call 'em. We told ourselves that my mother was unlucky. It's what kept us from going in there and smashing the place up. I've felt that way often enough, I can tell you. We never supposed that the hospital would poison her. They can't just put people down like you would a sick dog, can they? They wouldn't do that, would they? But is that what you're saying happened to my mum?'

'It isn't the hospital that's the problem,' said Emerald. 'You're right, they wouldn't do that. But Klein would. The death of your mother might be murder and it might be the best chance families like yours and Ralph Parker's have had to see this monster put behind bars.'

'This Dr Klein's a killer, is he?' asked Bob.

'Yes, he's a killer. At last, somebody gets it!'

'And you think that if the cops dig up my mother-in-law and test for these drugs they can prove it was him who put her in the ground?'

'They can prove that you mother died suspiciously. Then they've got to find the evidence to link it to Klein, which might not be impossible given that he was one of the few doctors working in that part of the hospital on a Friday evening of a Bank Holiday weekend.'

'Very interesting,' said Bob, looking over to Harry. 'But if the cops say "no" and the coroner says "no" then it's back to square one, after digging up his mum—my wife's mum. We wouldn't be able to do anything if that didn't work. But if they say "yes" then there is a chance, but not a certainty, that they can sort this doctor out. But he could still get off with it. There's probably still a good chance of him getting off with it.'

'Yes, he's got away with lots of things. But good luck runs out. You and I know that, Bob. The positive thing is that the police, the coroner and his own bosses must, by now, be suspicious about him. He must be on their radar. He's been badly discredited by a campaign by families who say he murdered their relatives in Bethulia Park. The police took no notice but they know what lots of people are saying about him. It's been in the *Sunday News*. I thought you might have seen it. He wasn't named but he's the man who's behind all this. Take it from me. I know. I work there. I work with him. It might only take one more push to make him fall. Just one more time in the crosshairs might be his last. Please, Bob, I beg you. Please don't let this opportunity pass you by. Think about the people who have suffered at the hands of this man. You'll be a hero to them, Bob. Go to the coroner to demand the exhumation of your mother-in-law and a full post-mortem.'

Running a hand through his thinning hair, Bob took his time to answer. 'You have no idea how upset Tanya has been about all this,' he said softly. 'I don't know how she'll cope if her mother is exhumed—especially if they find nothing and the doctor gets off with it. She'll see it as disrespectful. It will be traumatic for her. It will break her heart. One funeral's been bad enough for this family. I don't want to have to do it twice.'

'But what if her mother's been poisoned?'

Bob drummed a finger on his chin then stood to his full height. He glanced at Harry then turned back to Emerald.

'Wait in the bar,' he told her. 'Don't go anywhere. I want a few words with Harry in private. And those files on your memory stick—are they clearly marked?'

'Yes, they're marked "Pamela Worthington", and you didn't get them from me.'

The shaven-headed man appeared in the function room after fifteen minutes. He gave Ralph a ten-pound note and told him to go home. He said Emerald would be staying for a social drink with Bob, and a taxi would take her back to her flat.

Emerald was led down the corridor again but this time passed the door to Bob's office and arrived at a room at the end of the passage. She had been there many times in her late teens: it was the card room.

In it were four card tables of different sizes and shapes, each covered in green felt. Bob and Harry were seated at a circular table in the centre of the room. Bob held a pack of cards. He invited Emerald to sit down with them.

'Harry never saw you work,' Bob said to her, smiling, 'and he was wondering if you'd be so kind as show him a few of your skills.'

Harry sat with his arms folded as Bob held up the pack of cards to Emerald, the back of the deck facing her.

She reached out to take the deck from him but he held it firmly in his grip, his face locked in a cruel and mischievous frown. He wrapped his left hand around hers.

'Look at these fingers, Harry—so delicate, so clever. Lovely fingers! Expert fingers, these, so skilful!'

Emerald realised that as Bob spoke he was deliberately positioning her fingers on the pack, encouraging her to hold it in a certain way. He directed her to clasp it firmly by her fingertips, her thumb on the top edge.

Bob dropped his hands to the table top as she held the deck in front of him. Then he slammed his hand on to the top of the deck, a karate chop that sent cards flying out over the table and on to the floor.

Harry laughed hard when he saw Emerald jump. It was true that Emerald was a little shocked by the blow to the deck, but not too much. She had seen this trick performed before, and Bob had executed it well. Just one card remained in her hand, as he intended, and it was facing her. It was the king of spades.

Her mouth opened slightly. She looked at Bob who caught her gaze and held it with a horrid concentration.

'My and Harry have had a chat, Emerald, and that's what we want you to do for us. Do you understand me?'

Emerald was speechless.

'We want you to get this doctor on his own. We want you to find out where and when this Dr Klein will be on his own and then we want you to tell me all about it.'

Her lip trembled, and slowly she shook her head as her eyes filled with tears. 'Bob, no.'

'What do you mean, 'no'?' he snapped. 'You don't come to me and tell me I have to go to the police. You know that, and I don't believe for a minute that that was what you really expected me to do.'

'Bob, believe me, I was sincere. If it was about any other patient I would be saying the same thing to their relatives as I would be to you. I was being honest with you. Why does it have to be you, Bob? God, I wish it wasn't. I wish it was someone else's mother-in-law. It would be so much easier for me if it was.

'Bob—I don't want you to kill Dr Klein. I've too much blood on my hands already. I'm done with all this. I can't carry on like this. I don't want you to hurt him.'

She dropped the card on the table top. Tears ran down her cheeks, messing up her makeup.

'Are you crying, Emerald? Harry, look she's crying. Go and get her a tissue, will you, there's a good chap.' Harry left the room.

'Bob, you have no idea,' Emerald sobbed. 'I've barely stopped crying for four days. I've never been so upset.'

She pulled her chair back from the table so her tears would not fall on the green felt surface and mark it.

Harry came back moments later with a box of tissues. Bob was staring hard at Emerald.

'Listen to me, love, no one has said anything about killing anyone,' he said. 'I'm not going to do that. We don't do that. We haven't said anything about killing the doctor, have we, Harry? I've not said that I'm even going to hurt him. But I want to talk to him and I can assure you of this: he's going to tell me the truth.

'So, Emerald, you're not going to have blood on your hands. You'll be a link in a chain, that's all. Anyway, you're already up to your neck in this. The time has come to see it through. You know I have my own way of doing things. All you have to do is get me the information I'm looking for. That's all I ask. Then call me on this number.'

Bob took his pen from his jacket pocket and scribbled a phone number on the king of spades. He pushed the card towards Emerald. After a second or two she picked it up and put it in her bag. She shook her head again.

'I can't do it, Bob,' she said. 'I can't have any more blood on my hands. Can I go now?'

27

BABY RATS

Octavia's three dogs attacked Klein the moment she left him alone with them in her living room on Sunday morning when he went round to discuss developments at Bethulia Park.

He knew they hated him, and so did she, but she went into the kitchen anyway. She would not let him walk on her thick white carpets in his shoes, insisting that he took them off and left them by the front door as soon as he came in. He stood in his stocking feet as still as a lamppost, hoping her pets would ignore him in her absence.

But the unusual white pug curled up on a cream chaise longue in the corner of the room decided he should not be there. It lifted its head to look at him while emitting a low growl, its bulging eyes appearing to look in different directions. Its hostility acted as a battle cry to the two white Pomeranians, which launched themselves from satin cushions to yap furiously at Klein between snaps at his calves and ankles. At this point the pug joined the fray.

Klein swore violently at the small barking fiends, roaring threats as he kicked at them. 'You too,' he bellowed at one of the Pomeranians, which had momentarily retreated before pouncing forwards to try to bite him again. 'Go on, get out of it!'

Octavia came back into the room to see Klein hopping from foot to foot to escape them.

'You pig!' she screamed at him. 'Why are you upsetting my babies? You don't talk to my babies that way! Now apologise!'

Klein stared incredulously at Octavia.

'I mean it, apologise now, or you can get out of that door!' she screeched, her right arm extending and a finger pointing towards the hall. 'Do it!'

Klein had never seen Octavia so angry. Her face was twisted with a dark and terrible rage. It made him afraid. He had dealt with livid women on many occasions, both in his career and his private life, but something about Octavia was different from all of them; something about her body language told him that her fury was at the low end of a scale and what lay beyond threatened to exceed the rules, the ordinary boundaries and norms of behaviour. It was her eyes. They were black, hollow and murderous, a killer's eyes—and they told him that she would be prepared to do anything. They dared him to push her, to see how far she would go.

'You really want me to apologise to three dogs?' he asked her coolly, hoping she would recognise the unreasonableness of her demand.

'You bet I do,' she said resolutely, then mimicking his casual tone she said: 'Now apologise ...'

Octavia knelt to kiss, caress and comfort the dogs, all crawling over each other to cover her face with slobbery licks.

'Okay, I'll apologise,' said Klein softly. 'What are their names again?'

'This baby is Whitey Bulger,' said Octavia. Klein screwed up his face as she kissed the pug on its mouth. 'And these babies are Ronnie and Reggie.'

Klein had no idea that he was tapping into tension between Octavia and her husband as she put on a vulgar show of meeting the tongues of her pets with her lips. George, who was golfing that day, had as little interest in animals as she had in children. For a long time he answered her pestering for a toy pedigree with his standard refrain, that he would always 'prefer a burglar to a dog'. So she bought three, naming them after notorious gangsters. They could both be happy, she told him, because it meant he had his criminals and she had the dogs she wanted. In this way George discovered there was no point in arguing with her. Klein would learn his lesson too.

'Ronnie, Reggie and Whitey Bulger, I apologise unreservedly for shaking your teeth from my trousers with undue vigour while using intemperate language,' said Dr Klein to the dogs. He turned to Octavia. 'Will that do?'

'Don't be sarcastic or it won't count.'

'Tavy, what do want me to say? Give me a number for Interflora and I'll send out for flowers and chocolates, if you like. Would that cut it? If you don't mind, your babies were trying to bite me.'

Octavia threw him a black look as she rose slowly to her feet. Klein was grateful that the dogs turned their interest to each other, Reggie trying to mount Ronnie, and Whitey Bulger licking away between its hind legs.

He could not restrain his disgust.

'Some babies!' he exclaimed, his mouth contorting at the sight of Whitey plastering its nether region in spittle.

'Look at that one—the dirty little sod—and you've just been kissing that thing on the lips. It's rank. I'm sorry, darling, but I'm not going near you until you've brushed your teeth with chlor-hexidine gluconate. Bloody ugly dogs! For goodness sake!'

Octavia was not going to take the insult to her pets.

'Get out!' she snarled, pointing to the door.

They spoke by telephone an hour later when Octavia had calmed down a little, each agreeing that the work of Jenny Bradshaigh was so important that they needed to sit down together and discuss it. They would put the drama of that morning behind them and cooperate.

It was shortly after 2pm when Octavia turned up at Klein's cottage. Klein had been gardening since arriving there and he was pleased to see her. But he knew from the first second she swung her legs from her red BMW Z4 sports car that she was still in a foul mood. And she had Whitey Bulger with her. It was going to be a difficult afternoon.

Octavia sat on a wooden chair on the stone-flagged patio at the rear of Klein's cottage. She was wearing white jeans, sandals, and a thin white cardigan over a turquoise camisole top. Much of her face was concealed by a huge pair of Coco Chanel sunglasses. She barely spoke to Klein for half an hour, leaving him to tidy away his tools while she fussed over Whitey, assuring the pug that she would not let that 'mean, horrible man' swear at him ever again.

House martins were feeding chicks popping out their heads from a row of five mud nests.

Octavia watched them for a while.

When she was bored with that, she went into the house and came back with Klein's air rifle.

Systematically, she shot the adult birds when they landed at their nests, beaks full of insects for their young. She reloaded and shot at the chicks leaning out of the nests in anticipation of their parents' return.

Klein emerged from the house with cold drinks and put them down on the table. He saw the dead martins beneath his kitchen window. A look of disgust opened up on his face.

'Do you have to do that? It's a criminal offence, you know, disturbing wild birds while they're nesting.'

'They're pests,' said Octavia, putting down the rifle and picking up her lemonade. 'You may as well be keeping rats—boxes of baby rats on the side of your house. Can't you see I'm doing you a favour?'

'Not really, and now you've been shooting into the nests, there is going to be a load of rotting dead birds above my kitchen window as well as below it. I'm going to have to take the lot down now. They'll stink.'

Klein disappeared and returned a moment or two later with a long Dutch hoe. He pulled one of the three unoccupied garden chairs over to the wall and climbed on to it, then used the hoe to smash each of the five nests to pieces, sending them falling to the floor in a cloud of dirt, dust and feathers, oblivious to the distress of the surviving parents and the cries of their dying chicks.

'I think you should help me clear that up,' he said brusquely to Octavia when he had finished.

'No, I'm not doing that,' she said.

After the massacre of the house martins, Octavia watched with satisfaction as Dr Klein brushed the mud, straw and dead birds into a pan and, over several trips, took them away to a large green bin at the side of the cottage. She was at last placated, feeling she had achieved a victory over him. She was ready to talk when he finally sat down.

'Sorry about your birds, Hardy. Let's call it quits for you insulting my babies. But you still owe me for helping get you out of trouble. I've done my bit. The investigations haven't gone anywhere. Now what about the information you received from that journalist friend of yours? Is it Clarence? Have you been able to check if it's true?'

It was indeed Dennis Clarence who tipped off Dr Klein about Jenny's investigations into Dr Octavia Topcliffe, complete with an explanation for his motives. Clarence wished to distance himself from 'right-wing' journalists like Bradshaigh who, he said, were attempting to drive forward an unjustifiable agenda to undermine or destroy the accomplishments of the great Aneurin Bevan, the founder of the National Health Service. The campaign against Bethulia Park was deeply political, Clarence asserted. He went on to paint it as some sort of fascist conspiracy.

The least he could do for the good doctor was tell him what Bradshaigh was up to. Klein thanked him profusely.

Octavia had been so shocked when he first passed on the information that she had to sit down for fear of fainting. Dr Klein told her that Jenny had not only named her specifically to Dennis Clarence but was researching information about her career path and collecting comparative data about mortality rates in the places she had worked.

'It's certainly true in the case of Bethulia Park,' Klein told Octavia as he put on his sunglasses that afternoon. 'I checked with Dr Baqri and he confirmed that we're dealing with at least one Freedom of Information request from Bradshaigh exactly along the lines described by Clarence. But better than that, I've met the journalist and she's admitted to me that she's trying to find out all about you. The good news is that it seems to be nothing more than a fishing trip. I can't see what she can possibly do with any information she can get hold of. At the moment, she doesn't even know who you are or where you work. I told her you married a Russian and waltzed off to Canada. That will slow her down a bit. It might put her off altogether.'

He expected Octavia to laugh but the blood leached from her face and she trembled. Then she started to hyperventilate, struggling to regain her self-control. 'Bitch!' she said, her hands shaking on the wooden table. 'I'm scared, Hardy. What are we going to do?'

'We don't have to do anything. It's all taken care of. I've taken care of the journalist already.'

'What?'

'Are you aware of the saying, "the way to defeat your enemy is to make him your friend"?'

'No.'

'Do you know who said that?'

'No, I've never heard it. Was it one of your chums at the Sally Army? I'm worrying about you, Hardy. You're losing your edge.'

'Octavia, don't ever accuse me of being a Christian. I won't stand for it, you know that. It was probably Abraham Lincoln, though some people attribute it to Mark Twain. I prefer to think it was Lincoln. Anyway, whoever said it had a point.'

'So you've made this journalist your friend? Wait a minute—does she happen to be young and pretty? Why do I bother with you? You must be a walking plague pit, you're so promiscuous. And you call my dogs filthy! They've got nothing on you! Have you slept with her?'

'I'm a lover, not a fighter.'

'You bastard!'

'No, I haven't slept with her,' said Klein quickly, seeing the thunder clouds gathering. 'I've just brought her around to seeing things our way a little bit and I think she'll change sides soon. There's no reason for you to be scared. What are you scared of? I've taken care of the threat.'

'You don't see it, do you?' she said. 'You say she can't do anything with the information she finds out about me. But what if she finds out everything I've done, and who I am now, and she puts it all together? My name's all over that damn ruling by the ombudsman. What if she finds out that I'm married to the detective in charge of this investigation into these families, which you say she helped to initiate? She's got a long way to travel before she changes sides, Hardy, even if you have slept with her, which you probably have, you liar—you bastard! Don't you forget that I know you. I know who you are. And what are you going to do now that you've slept with her? Sleep with her again? Sleep with her regularly? Are you going to dump me for her after everything that I've done for you? You'd do that, wouldn't you? You don't care!'

Klein stared at Octavia open-mouthed. 'You're jealous,' he said with a tone of surprise and triumph.

Octavia rose, grabbed her drink and threw the contents into Klein's face. She went to hit him across the head with the empty glass but he blocked the incoming blow with a forearm and the glass bounced off, flew over the patio and landed harmlessly on the lawn a few feet away. Whitey was on his feet, growling.

'How dare you betray me with the woman who is out to get me!' screamed Octavia. 'How could you do that to me?'

'Get a grip of yourself!' Klein shouted. 'Octavia, darling, I haven't betrayed you. I haven't slept with her. We just got along fine, that's all. She's beginning to see things from our point of view. Okay, I flirted a little. But just to maintain her interest. It keeps her liking me, that's all.'

'Do you think she'll like you if she finds out that I'm your mistress and you've lied to her? The mistress of the doctor who everyone around here now knows lost, or hid, those records about the Parker family.

'My theory is she isn't going to like you any more than that nurse who you say leaked the records to her. My theory is that this journalist and her friends in Fleet Street are really going to come after us when they finally discover everything.

'George has complained to the editor of the *Sunday News* about the reports into Bethulia Park, you know. They're going to be furious if they find all this out, and George will be back on to you too. You have no idea of the lengths I've already gone to protect you from my husband.'

She paused for breath.

'You idiot! What have you started? What are we going to do? I'm really frightened, Reinhard, and you should be too.'

She started to sob. She sat down and wrung her hands repeatedly.

'Octavia, no one knows about our affair, so don't worry about that,' said Klein, standing over her and wiping himself. 'The investigation into the families' complaints is over, thanks largely to you, and I'm grateful, and before long everyone will have forgotten all about it, the same with Ray Parker.

'To be honest, I don't think the newspapers would give a damn about who you are married to and what you did previously and even if they did they'd have to tread very carefully or you could sue them for defamation. They can't just publish vague allegations. I think you're over-reacting. This journalist can't hurt you, so calm down!'

He looked thoughtful.

'But we've got to do something about her, just to be sure. I agree with you. We've got to make her safe. That's all I'm doing. That's all I've done, and I'm doing it for you. What else can I do? I can't punch her in the face like I did with that priest. That would bring the newspapers down on us, without question. Just leave her to me. We're going to be all right. You should be pleased.'

Seeing Octavia relax, he decided the time was ripe to tackle another issue.

'You might want to get off the white stuff too, Tavy. It's turning your mind to mush. It's making you paranoid.'

Octavia stood up and swore horribly at Dr Klein. 'I'll do what I want when I want and you won't judge me for it!'

'You'd cope better if you cleaned yourself up.'

'I have cleaned myself up—I stopped injecting ages ago. Anyway, that's none of your business! Now, you listen to me: you better be right about this journalist or we're going to do things my way. You've not done very well at getting yourself out of trouble lately, Hardy, have you? Why should I trust you any more?'

'What's your way?'

Octavia didn't answer.

'Thought so,' said Klein. 'As I said, leave the reporter to me. It will be fine. You don't need to worry about her.'

He smoothed back his hair.

'Now, about the priest,' he continued. 'He's not going to bother us. I gave him a bit of a shock and he's not allowed into the hospital anyway. What you do need to know is that his housekeeper came in with a stroke about three weeks ago and on Thursday we started to withdraw her treatment. I don't think it's going to be complicated. I don't think the priest even knows that's she's now on the pathway and she will be gone soon. He can't see her, and his friendly nurse isn't involved in her care.'

Octavia let out a little laugh. The tears on her cheeks were drying.

'The best thing is that he's probably going to think it's me who's killed her. I told him that I would. He'll think that it's part of his punishment for crossing me, and indeed it is. But I'm making sure I can't be connected with this death, don't you worry. If the priest gets on to your husband about it I'm confident George will dismiss him as a one hundred per cent crank. They won't be able to find anything that would incriminate either me or any of my team. Any complaint will only weaken whatever credibility these campaigners still have. No one will take them seriously again.'

Octavia smiled and nodded. She asked Klein to fetch her a chilled sauvignon blanc, promising not to hit him with the glass this time. When he returned with it, and one for himself, he found her the calmest she had been all day.

'But what about that person on the inside, the one who's being handing out the records from the hospital?' she asked. 'Have you sorted that one out yet? I bet you haven't.'

'I have given her her marching orders and I don't think she will want to hang around. Obviously, the sooner that happens the better, from our perspective.'

He sipped from his wine while he watched Octavia lift Whitey on to her knee and begin to stroke him.

'As I've told you, this nurse is an old flame of mine and I'm sure she's partly motivated by revenge.'

'Well, that's what can happen when you sleep with women, treat them badly and dump them. Bear that in mind, Hardy, before you cross me or hop into bed with that journalist.'

'Quite. But this one has put herself in quite a compromising position with me. She knew all the time that I suspected her of being the leak so she's been trying to put me off the scent by offering to sleep with me again. She's so stupid, honestly. But it's a good offer because she's really quite a beauty. So I've suggested that we have a threesome, see if she means it.'

'You've done what?' said Octavia, almost throwing Whitey to the ground and standing up so suddenly that Klein reared back in alarm. 'Are you completely off your head? You've just told me that no one knows about our affair—are you really so dense that you can't see that by inviting people to join us we might be helping to spread the word? I hope you haven't given her my name!'

'I'm calling her bluff, Octavia. I'm putting the frighteners on her. I want her out of Bethulia Park and I want her out soon. Every time she tries to appease me in this way, I'm going to turn up the pressure. She'll go soon, believe me. I don't expect her to accept my offer. I think she hates me. I'm driving her out. I've already isolated her.'

'But what if she says "yes"?'

'If she says "yes" then we can have great fun with her, and I guarantee that afterwards she will go very far away from here and very quickly too.'

'Great fun? You dirty bastard. Is it just me, or does your strategy for resolving the problems at Bethulia Park involve you sleeping with every woman you come across? You never asked me about women. I'm not going to have sex with another woman. You want to set up a threesome, get me a man, not one of your old slags.'

'I couldn't do that, darling. I don't want to watch you have sex with another man, and if a man ever tried to touch me sexually

I think I'd kill him. Now, I know it's Pride month, and I'm all for inclusion, diversity, equal rights and all that, but wearing my rainbow lanyard's the limit as far as I'm concerned. I'm old-fashioned that way. Keep it to myself, mind you.'

'But you think it's all right for me to do it with a woman? You hypocrite—you should be ashamed of yourself. Honestly, I've never met anyone so egotistical.'

'You have to see her though,' said Klein. 'Do you want to see her?'

He went into the cottage and emerged five minutes later with a mobile phone in a white case.

Octavia oohed and aahed as she watched the film of Klein and Emerald together.

'I know this girl,' she said. 'I've seen her somewhere before. D'you think you could persuade her to make another film with us?'

'That's exactly what I have in mind.'

Octavia looked at Klein thoughtfully and he winced as, just for a second, he glimpsed that deep blackness within her eyes once more. It was like a void, a pit, like looking into death, and it filled him with fear.

In an instant the impression faded and Octavia was back down to earth—voluptuous, sultry and pouting.

'Shall we go inside, darling?' she said.

Klein walked over to the back door and opened it. 'Come on, Whitey, you can come too,' he said, smiling. 'He's such a cute little guy.'

28

HACKING OUT

The shrill bleeping of the alarm on Jenny's mobile phone woke her at 5.30am the following Saturday. It was already light and she rolled reluctantly out of bed, doing her best not to wake Seb, who was facing away from her, the sharply-defined triangle of trapezia muscles of his naked back heaving with each deep breath.

'You must be mad,' he grumbled, 'getting up at this time.'

She ignored him. He said that nearly every week. Jenny dressed quickly, trying not to make a sound so her fiancé could drift back to sleep. She pulled on her tan breeches, feeling them tight across her thighs, buttocks and around her waist. She buttoned up the front and went to the door.

Some five miles away Octavia was also getting up, unusually early for her. George barely stirred as she explained that she was taking out the dogs because she couldn't sleep and that she would be using their Audi SQ8 instead of her sports car because they needed the room.

She tied up her hair and applied some light make-up. She dressed in black jeans, low-heeled black boots and her olive Harkila shooting jacket—bought for her trips to the moors with Dr Klein—over a black vest top.

323

After a slice of buttered toast and an espresso, she opened the door from the kitchen to the garage. As quietly as she could, she dragged a rusted tool box from under a shelf, opened it and took out a silver plastic bag, shoving it into a large black canvas tote bag.

Soon she was parked among a row of vehicles close to the junction of a lane that led down to the riding school and stables used by Dr Klein's daughters. She put on a pair of dark glasses and sat low in the front seat. She watched the junction through the rear view mirror hoping that she hadn't missed Jenny turning up in her blue Audi 3.

Octavia did not have to wait too long. The journalist arrived as expected, the only car on the road, indicating to turn right.

As soon as Jenny was out of sight, Octavia drove a short distance to a deserted lane and parked again. Telling her dogs to behave themselves while mummy was gone, she took the canvas bag from the passenger seat and stepped out, gently closing the door. She walked back to the main road and headed in the direction from which the blue car had approached, before crossing over a stile which gave her access to open countryside. She followed a public footpath to a patch of woodland about a mile away.

With her sights set on a two-hour hack starting from about 7am, Jenny wasted no time in grooming Daphne. Except for rhythmic munching at her hay net, the big mare was almost inert, allowing Jenny to wipe dust, grease and dried manure from the brown hair of her body, and to pick out straw from her black forelock, mane and tail. When the brushing was done, Daphne obediently lifted each leg so Jenny could pick out packed manure from her hooves with an iron hook.

Jenny fitted the saddle and bridle and led her horse out into the golden haze of the morning. It had been raining during the night but the sun was coming out. The pathways were spotted with shining shallow puddles and steaming dew curled up from the fields. Chiffchaffs tick-tocked in the trees around them.

Wearing a hi-vis yellow jacket, Jenny positioned the horse by the mounting block and slipped her left foot into a stirrup, swinging herself on to Daphne's back in a single sweeping movement. She leaned down to tighten the girth and checked her stirrups were of equal length. A squeeze of her legs made the horse walk on.

Daphne plodded forward into Eden. Everywhere was so wonderfully green, so lush, so fresh, so perfect and so alive. But Jenny had a sense that she was saying goodbye to it all.

Certainly, it would be a different scene that would greet her and Daphne when they hacked out in a fortnight's time after she moved her horse to her parents' farm about ten miles away. Her father, Mick, had already bought two riding school geldings which were retiring, and they were going to be delivered the following Saturday. Daphne would join them a week later, no doubt taking charge of the small herd as dominant mares tended to.

Jenny would have all summer to rediscover the bridleways of her childhood, to make it a new home for Daphne. She was hoping she might be able to persuade her brother Geoff to go hacking with her every now and then. Perhaps she might introduce Emerald to horses, and they could ride together too if all went well. The two women already had more in common that Jenny was prepared to admit to anyone.

There was much to look forward to in the changes that were under way, not least in the fact that she would not run into Dr Klein every week. She didn't want to see him again for as long as she lived.

The horse walked away from the stables along a well-worn earthy path, the soil hardened by the daily treading of hooves. They proceeded at a leisurely pace at first, with Jenny more than happy for Daphne to take her time as long as she remained responsive to the instructions from her legs and seat and didn't naughtily snatch mouthfuls of bracken, Himalayan balsam and leaves from the low branches of trees.

She would of course trot Daphne that morning and she knew where there were gentle grassy slopes, free of rabbit burrows and mole hills, which would be perfect for short canters. Jenny would put the horse through her paces as long as she felt safe enough, given her continuing nagging injury. She wanted to renew her sense of unity with her horse, their shared purpose and their single mind. They had to be partners again. There would be a full recovery.

For the most part, their usual route involved simply walking the horse along established bridleways with few hazards. Her friend Sarah did not always like to get up early on Saturday mornings and Jenny increasingly found herself going out alone. She didn't mind. She had done it often enough and it gave her the time and space to think. This was important to her because in recent weeks she had grown increasingly preoccupied with plans for her wedding, with her mother Carole encouraging her to make the big decision about a dress.

Jenny reached a gate that opened on to a path along the hedgerow leading towards the wood and she remembered that the last time she was there she was wondering if she could persuade her mother to spend a day shopping for the dress in London. It would be a day in which she was certain her mother would fuss embarrassingly, even shed a tear. Best to get it over with in one go, Jenny had thought, and have some fun while they were at it. They would come home with more than a wedding dress, Jenny was sure of that. Their trip was now planned for the first Friday in July. She closed the gate behind her, turning her horse with her legs so she did not have to dismount, but this time, as she executed the manoeuvre, she was thinking about her hen party.

Since Seb proposed to her at Christmas she imagined that she would take off for a weekend with her friends and the women of her family. High on her list of options was a day at one of the racecourses within reach of London such as Sandown or Ascot followed by a meal, drinks and possibly a show in the West End. She also considered attending one of the big equestrian meetings, perhaps eventing at Burghley or Blenheim, or dressage at Somerford Park. But now she was entertaining new thoughts about her hen do. What if she could have two parties instead of one? There could be the one for her wider group of friends and relations, including her mother and her cousins, somewhere horsey, as planned. Then there could be another with just a few girls she knew—girls who liked a party. They could fly to Ibiza, Crete or the Costa Del Sol—somewhere lively, somewhere sizzling—for a mini-break of four or five nights of sunbathing, dancing and drinking. Just a bit of luxury, a bit of raucous fun before a lifetime of marriage. It could be a hen party to remember or to forget quickly, depending on what might happen. The thought excited her.

She leaned forwards to duck under the branch of a young beech tree.

Another new thought crossed her mind. How would she feel if Seb was to do something similar with his friends, to take off to Benidorm for a week? Could she trust him? The words 'Do I care?' raced into her head followed by a sense of shame. 'I suppose he can please himself, it's up to him,' she told herself more deliberately as she fought to moderate and correct emotions she recognised as callous. Such sentiments reminded her that no matter how hard she was struggling to restore her internal equilibrium, her feelings for her fiancé had been redefined by her day with Dr Klein. She was hostage to a memory which could never be erased. It changed the way she felt both about herself and about other people.

Jenny pressed her horse forward with her calves and shortened her reins a little so Daphne was made to raise her head. She wanted a bit more energy in the walk.

She returned to her thoughts, to the stark new reality with which she wrestled every minute of her waking day since that afternoon in Manchester. That evening she lay in her bath until it went cold. Her head had finally resumed control of her heart and she was overwhelmed by awful disbelief. She didn't want to get out, to come face to face with Seb. She had never cheated on him before. She lay there, asking herself repeatedly: 'What have I done?'

Of course, the afternoon with Klein was all she expected it to be. Yet it had not enriched her life, or left it the same as before, but had changed it in a way she had not quite foreseen. In the days that followed, she was tetchy and short-tempered with her fiancé, picking fights and criticising him about faults which previously had barely mattered to her at all. It could be anything—the way he coughed, a dropped sock, a tune he was humming that was driving her mad. Besides Seb, she was irritable toward others whom she knew would be sorely hurt or scandalised by her tryst. She sneered at the cocooned values of her parents. She scoffed contemptuously at the thought of Calvin tut-tutting about her 'sin', and laughed about Emerald when she heard from her mother about how she dragged Geoff off to church. 'That girl is truly off her head,' she thought.

In truth, her attitude to Emerald was more complex and ambivalent. She retained some respect for her but wondered how much she should trust her. The nurse represented a paradox, and Jenny deliberated upon just how much of Klein's character assassination was justifiable. Was Emerald a brave and principled defender of the vulnerable or was she, as Dr Klein argued with apparent conviction, a fantasist? Was she a bit of both?

Her mind turned fully to Dr Klein, as her horse entered the wood and trod a path so narrow that it would have been difficult for two people to have walked it side by side. She wanted nothing more to do with him and she was glad she had told him so. She associated him most directly with the sense that she had let herself down, both personally and professionally, when she was honest enough to allow herself to feel any remorse for her infidelity. She blamed him for everything. She was also deeply upset with him for lying to her about Octavia Topcliffe, and it was the anger of a personal and intimate kind, like a slight from a lover. It accentuated her sense of being detached from her real self, infuriating her all the more. She had become emotionally involved with Dr Klein. This was not how she was supposed to be either as a journalist or as a woman about to marry. Why had she ever let herself get into such a mess? She should have done her job properly and she would have been okay. She should have listened to Emerald's warnings. She should have checked the public records on marriages long before she met Dr Klein. If only she had done so, she would have known straight away that he was lying to her. She was sure she would have walked away from him when he did. The doctor must have taken her for a fool. He must have thought she was easy. So sloppy, so unprofessional, so unforgiveable. Alone in the woods, with no one to see her, she blushed.

When they came to a narrow bridge over a fast-flowing stream, Jenny raised her ankles to her saddle to prevent her legs from banging into the metal rails. They progressed through the little winding wooded valley and she leaned forward, standing on her stirrups to relieve the horse of her weight on its back as it powered up steep inclines, and leaned backwards while pushing down into her heels as the horse carefully picked its way over roots and mud during dangerous, twisting descents. But whenever she did not have to work with her horse she was thinking continuously about her failures.

She was trying to figure out why she had not checked the marriage records straight away. She concluded it was because she never seriously felt her investigations would lead to anything like a big story until last week. Her hunch was that she was wasting her time, that it was really just an exercise conducted as a favour for Professor Silver. She lost interest in Octavia after an early burst of activity in the days that followed her trip to London, although she asked people about her from time to time.

Indeed, she might not have looked at the public records at all if it was not for some fascinating results which began to arrive from those early inquiries. Her Freedom of Information requests in particular were bearing fruit. They helped to show that wherever and whenever this doctor had worked the numbers of patients who died on end-of-life care in those locations had risen sharply. Jenny's interest was piqued once more. She compared the doctor's career path more generally with data on mortality rates at her former places of employment. Jenny looked at how such rates fluctuated in the years before, during and after Octavia's involvement to see if they revealed any identifiable patterns. Jenny was able to conclude that patients died in greater numbers and at higher rates whenever and wherever Octavia was present.

Jenny had also discovered, again within the last week, that Octavia had been rebuked by the healthcare ombudsman for putting two patients on the Liverpool Care Pathway long after its abolition by the Government as 'a national disgrace'. The families of those deceased patients, who were in the care of a Manchester healthcare trust, complained about the way their relatives died. The ombudsman concluded that not only had Dr Topcliffe acted unlawfully but there was also a realistic supposition that the patients would not have died had she not imposed the discredited regime upon them.

Her train of thought was broken when she arrived at the stream a second time, at a point where it was bubbling and surging into a shallow and noisy ford. She concentrated as Daphne crossed it, giving the horse a longer rein as it felt its way across the slippery rocks, always alert to the possibility of a sudden skid and a subsequent dive on to sharp rocks below. It was such little diversions as these—the thrill of ever-present danger—that made a hack so rewarding. On the dark earth of the opposite bank, it also thrilled her to think that Octavia was no longer in

Manchester when the ombudsman's ruling was issued, but at Bethulia Park. As far as Jenny could see, there was nothing to show that she had been disciplined for her behaviour, with neither the police nor the General Medical Council involved at any stage. Any punishment must have been very light, nothing more than a slap on the wrist. Yet Octavia left the hospital shortly afterwards.

She decided to check the marriage records when her discoveries made her want to know more—and she found out that Octavia Topcliffe married George Tarleton in Crostbury Register Office on Saturday August 20, 2016. She also found out that Dr Octavia Tarleton still worked in the area, as the medical director of Crostbury Park Hospice. But she could locate no pictures of her in any of her internet searches.

Jenny and her horse continued along the path, both knowing they were nearing the exit to the wood and that soon they would be joining a farm track. This would take them to a road and they would turn right and walk a few hundred yards uphill, cars and vans overtaking them at intervals, before they turned right again on to another track at the top.

Jenny reflected on her last exchange with Dr Klein. She began by recalling how, when they parted company in Manchester, they agreed not to contact each other frequently in the mutual fear that texts, phone calls or WhatsApp messages might create grave domestic problems. But she called him when she discovered that his story about what happened to Octavia failed to correspond with the facts.

'What the hell are you protecting her for? What are you playing at?'

Klein did not answer at first. Then he denied knowing Octavia very well and said he must have been misinformed—and then he asked to see Jenny again.

'We'll see,' she said. 'I'm not sure I can trust you.'

She hung up before he could say another word.

Now she felt her heart pound. She had worked herself up and wondered if the horse was able to sense her anger. She was looking forward to emerging from the woodland. It was dense at that time of the year and she was wet from leaves that brushed over every part of her body as they ambled along. Her high emotions left her energised and she was in the mood for a trot and a little canter.

She would have to wait until after she turned off the road ahead to the second track. This one was bounded by a hedgerow on one side, with occasional gaps offering panoramic views over the woods and fields. There was dense scrubby woodland on the other, which eventually would give way to the immaculate lawns of Crostbury Golf Course. On the side of the track there were numerous long, straight and flat grassy surfaces, perfect for picking up the pace and letting her horse run freely. They would follow the track for a mile and a half, trotting and cantering occasionally, to the point when a bridleway would open up on their right and present them with the opportunity to wind slowly down through fields and coverts toward the lower ground and back toward the stables. She was looking forward to it.

They were still in the wood when Daphne suddenly stopped. This usually meant a dog walker and Jenny was preparing to politely ask the owner to put their pet on a lead. Not all horses were as confident as Daphne. Their powerful herd instinct meant that few were comfortable hacking out alone because they felt insecure when they were isolated. Daphne was more dependable but large, strange dogs could make her nervous and there was always a risk that she would simply turn around and run.

Jenny screwed up her eyes and saw a figure coming towards her. She could see it was a woman—slim, blonde, her hair tied up, carrying a bag on her shoulder and dressed way too fashionably to be walking in woodland. She could not see a dog.

'Do you have a dog?' called Jenny. 'My horse is looking for your dog.'

'I have got a dog, a German shepherd, but he's not with me today,' replied Octavia. 'He's a bit off-colour. But I needed to get out. It's been a long week at work. I must admit that I do feel a little odd not having him with me. Wow, your horse is a beauty, isn't he?'

'It's a she—Daphne.'

'Oh, I'm sorry, Daphne. May I stroke her?' said Octavia, raising her hand towards the animal's neck.

The horse grunted, lifted her head, and took several steps backwards deliberately to avoid the open palm coming towards her.

'Daphne, don't be so rude,' said Jenny with a laugh. 'She's not always like this.'

'I should have brought some Polos,' said Octavia. 'What is she? She's huge.'

'She's an Irish sports horse—she's a good girl. She's over sixteen hands so it is a little bit high from up here, but you get used to it.'

'Yes, I wouldn't like to come off her. Does she spook easily?'

'Not really, she trusts me. But horses can be funny. It can be the littlest of things—like a crisp bag floating on the wind, a pheasant flapping up out of a bush, or a falling twig—that sets them off. So I still have to be careful with her. I did come off her, by the way, a few months ago. It still hurts.'

'Oh really? What happened?' asked Octavia. 'I trust you are okay now?'

'Yeah, I'm okay. On reflection, I think it was a breakdown in communication. I wanted one thing, she wanted another. I didn't ask the right way, or didn't allow her to do what I was asking, probably hanging too much on to her mouth, which she didn't like. When all these little things came together we had an accident. But we got away with it, that's what counts. It's all experience. Long way down, though.'

'Communication's so important, isn't it?' said Octavia thoughtfully. 'Even for humans. Everyone on their phones all the time, Twitter this, Facebook that, fake news everywhere. I think we'd all better off without all that, and I'd hate to work in the media.'

'Oh, it's not that bad,' said Jenny. 'Speaking from experience I can assure you there is still a lot of integrity in journalism. It's true though that you can't say that about social media.'

'You're a journalist? Gosh!' said Octavia. 'You must have a lot of enemies, then?'

'Not that I'm aware of, no.'

'You sure you're not being a little too brave, coming down here on your own, on a big spooky horse—what, with all those people who must hate your guts? You must have absolutely loads of them, all wanting to do you in.'

Jenny was puzzled by this turn in the conversation.

'No, I don't think so.'

'Oh, come on, are you sure?' Octavia pressed on, pleased to see Jenny's smile fade. 'I'm only joking, dear. If anyone's a little foolhardy, it's me, coming down here on my own, without my dog. I'm starting to get a little nervous now, I must say. It can be a bit lonely, can't it? I think I'd better get going.'

Jenny squeezed her calves gently on the girth beneath the saddle and her horse began to walk forward. 'Nice to talk to you, have a lovely day,' she said.

'You too,' called Octavia. 'Ride safely, Jenny, you don't want to be falling off again, now, do you?'

The journalist's heart skipped a beat and she asked herself who the hell that woman was, and how she could know her name.

Should she turn her horse on the forehand, spinning the mare 180 degrees in a standing position, and go after the woman, demanding an answer? No. She decided to carry on pushing Daphne forward, telling herself that soon she and the horse would be back at the stables and that she could look forward in the weeks ahead to the security of her parents' farm.

But as she emerged from the woods on to the track, she felt isolated and vulnerable. She thought about dismounting and walking beside Daphne but opted to ask the horse to walk faster as a priority took shape in her mind and became increasingly insistent: she wanted to go home.

Octavia was also walking with enhanced vigour. She was now pacing along a line of hedges at the edge of a field, up the hill and in the direction of the golf course. She made it to the wood at the side of the course long before Jenny had turned Daphne off the main road. She sat behind a small thicket, breathing deeply and listening carefully to the noises around her. When she was satisfied that no one else was in the vicinity, she reached into her tote bag, took out a pair of black leather gloves and put them on. Then she drew out the silver plastic bag and removed a powerful hunting catapult that belonged to Klein.

He had taught her to use the weapon in the afternoons when they were lazing around the garden of his cottage the previous summer, assuring her it was perfect for stealth hunting and if handled properly it was as accurate and as lethal as a rifle. This model was Octavia's favourite. It had a moulded grip handle like a machine gun, a wrist support to steady the hands and aim, and long and dependably strong surgical rubber bands attached to either side of an industrial steel fork which branched out so widely that a variety of objects could be accommodated as ammunition.

In the hours spent in Klein's back garden, Octavia had learned to fire pebbles and stones with precision but today she planned to use something different. From the accessory pocket of her bag, she drew out a brand new golf ball, one of three she had taken from her husband's golf bag the previous evening. She placed it centrally into the slingshot.

She heard the approaching clip-clop of hooves, and knew without looking that it must be Jenny.

Horse and rider passed. Octavia darted to the left of the thicket where an opening in the foliage gave her a clear view. She took aim and unleashed a golf ball at the horse's hindquarter, leaping back into the greenery as Daphne bucked, then reared.

Jenny, shrieking, lost her stirrups, her balance and her seat. She thrust her arms around the horse's neck, attempting to use her weight to force the animal forward in the fear that it would otherwise fall backwards and crush her beneath its tumbling bulk.

But it was she who fell to the ground, landing with a crack on her left shoulder. The squealing, terrified horse bucked and reared around her, stamping on her and kicking her repeatedly as she tried to twist out of the way. She screamed for her horse to stop until a powerful kick to the head left her suddenly motionless.

The horse stopped rearing and bolted back towards the road.

Satisfied and smiling, Octavia pushed the catapult back into the bag and jogged along an overgrown footpath through the woodland, emerging much further down the track and crossing it only when she was sure no one would see her.

She walked back to her car over the fields, using the shadows of hedgerows and the natural screens formed by an archipelago of copses and coverts to conceal herself.

She threw her bag in the boot and jumped into the driver's seat, greeted by the drool and the stench of her restless pets.

'Okay babies, that's enough,' she said, pushing off the three dogs. 'Mummy's going to take you on that little walk she promised you now and you can all help mummy to get rid of something she doesn't need any more, and then we can all go home and we can all have a nice bath. That nasty journalist has gone! Hooray!'

Octavia was home with time to fry breakfast for her husband before he decided to get up. George was having a very long lie-in, but was planning to spend the rest of the day with his wife before they dined out that evening. He was determined to share the full weekend with her ahead of his golfing trip to the Algarve the following Saturday. Octavia sipped tea and read the papers in the luxurious comfort of her home as George showered.

At the same time, doctors at Bethulia Park were fighting to save Jenny from death or paralysis. She had a broken neck and the medics decided to put her into an induced coma. Ultimately, she would be transferred to the intensive care unit, with instructions that she was kept under extremely close observation.

Daphne was euthanised at the roadside by a vet after she was struck by a wagon coming round a blind bend into which she was charging in panic.

Police officers and ambulance crews discovered Jenny unconscious on the track after the truck driver alerted them to the horse struggling unsuccessfully to get up at the roadside.

Uniformed officers visited Jenny's parents to tell them about her riding accident.

No-one, however, visited Hannah Hoskins as she lay on her back in a private room that same morning, now a skeletal figure. Her eyes were closed but her mouth was wide open, issuing horrible 'death rattles' over a shrivelled tongue.

Nurses would enter the room every now and again to check her condition and administer more diamorphine if she showed signs of distress.

But it was just a waiting game. The housekeeper was unconscious and in the throes of death. Those closest to her had no idea how much she had deteriorated in such short a period of time. If they had, someone might have been at her side to hold her hand and accompany her departure from the material world with their prayers. In the event, she died alone.

29

JUDITH'S PRAYER

Four days after Jenny fell from her horse a crisis summit was held at the Bradshaigh family farm. It was not how Emerald had imagined she would meet the parents of her new boyfriend, Geoff.

Jenny's mother Carole seemed perilously close to a mental breakdown when they shook hands. She was clearly exhausted, sickened by worry and deprived of sleep, and was losing the capacity to think rationally. Her husband Mick constantly hauled her back to reality as she ranted about worst-case scenarios and imagined wildly what might have happened.

Mick, a silver-haired farmer with a barrel chest and a hint of sagginess in his florid cheeks, tried to appear strong but would fall into long silences, with lips quivering, as he sought to restrain powerful emotions of his own.

Jenny's fiancé Seb, the taciturn carpet fitter and ex-rugby league player, was there too. He spent most the time shifting restlessly along the kitchen units, gnawing at his fingernails and, like Geoff, refused to sit down at the oak table with Emerald and Jenny's parents.

Emerald had not seen Geoff since the previous week. She had not visited Jenny in hospital because she would have been unable to justify her presence on the intensive care unit unless she was working there. She did not wish to further arouse the suspicion of Dr Klein of her complicity in the work of the journalist, which she still denied. So that evening she was learning of the full extent of Jenny's injuries.

Seb and Geoff explained to her that a number of vertebrae in Jenny's neck were fractured in the fall, although the good news was that doctors were confident that her spinal cord remained intact.

They had stabilised her neck by fitting a metal halo to her skull and attaching it by rods to her upper body. She would not be able to move her head until doctors were satisfied the bones of her neck were fully healed and this could take five or six months. She had also broken her left collar bone, several ribs and her left arm, and she had suffered a collapsed lung.

Of more immediate concern to the consultant neurologist was the severe blow to the head inflicted by Daphne's kick. Geoff told Emerald the doctor had been candid with the family about his serious reservations concerning her prospects of overcoming the trauma.

'She's in a coma,' he said. 'The doctor says her situation isn't hopeless but he can't tell us when she might come out of it. So I put it to him, "What? Days, weeks, months?" And he said to me that it could be days or it could be years, or it might never happen. That's why none of us can sleep.'

'Wedding's off,' added Seb. 'She was so looking forward to it—so excited. She was talking about it all the time, always making plans. She'll be back, though, don't you worry—I know she will—and we'll do it then. We'll do it next year.'

The family and Seb began to share the information they had individually learned from investigating police officers as they tried to piece together what had happened.

Mick was particularly knowledgeable.

'The police sealed off the whole area—taped it off and kept everyone away—and they brought in a forensic unit and combed the whole area,' he said. 'They went over every blade of grass, checked everything, took stuff away to be tested. They were there for at least two days, maybe longer.

'But all they've found so far is a bloody golf ball. So now they're working on the theory that the horse was hit by a stray golf ball smashed from one of the greens on the other side of the woodland. That's what made it go mad. That's what the police reckon.'

Emerald spoke up. 'What time was the accident? It was between seven and eight in the morning, wasn't it? The golf course wouldn't even have opened at that time, would it? Surely that can't be right.'

'That's the problem,' said Mick. 'That's why they can't prove it. If it had been during opening hours they would be able to track everyone who was on the course at that time and would probably work out very quickly who'd done it.

'It's a lot harder for them when they have to put out an appeal for people who shouldn't have been on the course in the first place to come forward with evidence when they know they're gonna be in trouble for being there and especially if they think they'll be blamed for knocking a woman off her horse as well.'

Emerald was puzzled and Seb came to her rescue.

'What Mick's saying is that the golf course has a problem with teenagers and young fellas sneaking on to the greens when the club's closed and playing a few holes without paying. It's dead easy to do. I've done it myself once or twice when I was younger. This time of year it's light just after five. So the cops are thinking it might be one o' them kids who've gone on the greens when they weren't allowed.

'The club officials are going to be in big trouble over this because they should have stopped it ages ago. They don't do much because it's easier for them to turn a blind eye to it, especially if there's no damage to the course. They just chase them away every now and then, and leave it at that.'

Mick said: 'So the police found a ball at the scene, and they're planning to make a general appeal. They'll ask dog walkers and anyone else who was about at that time if they saw anything or anyone suspicious.'

'Is that all they've got to work on, a golf ball and a poxy appeal to the public?' said Emerald, scowling. 'I just don't buy it.'

'Why do you say that?' said Geoff.

'I've got a bad feeling about this.'

'We all have.'

'No, I don't mean like that. I'm wondering if it had anything to do with Dr Klein.'

Geoff rolled his eyes.

'I've thought about that too,' said Seb. 'The police were asking me if there was anything that Jenny was doing that might make someone want to hurt her. But she was always up to something, weren't she? I told them about some of the jobs she'd been working on lately, surveillance stuff mostly. But she said it was really boring, and that her news editors didn't want her to confront any of the types she was watching. Police seem to think that it's unlikely that someone's going to attack her if they didn't know they were being watched in the first place, or even to go to great lengths to plan something like that. Stray golf ball is far more likely. That's what they said. I told them about this Dr Klein too, I told them that she was still investigating Bethulia Park Hospital.'

'What did they say to that?' said Emerald.

'Well, they listened. But they weren't sympathetic at all. I think they thought it was a bit of a conspiracy theory. One of them laughed at me. When he could see I was mad about it he promised he would talk to Dr Klein and his wife but I think it was just to keep us quiet. He said there's no motive for Klein to hurt her. The investigation into the hospital's been dropped and he was never in any bother anyway, he probably just didn't like what she wrote.

'Then this same copper told me later that Klein was having breakfast with his wife and kids at the time of the accident. He also said Jenny had been exchanging texts and phone calls with Dr Klein and that they all seemed very friendly. They've got her phone, you know. He said they went for a coffee. I knew that. They were actually smiling at me when they were tellin' me all this, the detectives. They weren't havin' any of it.'

Emerald turned white.

Geoff said: 'Did they say anything else about the horse, what made it panic like it did? Have they got any proof it was a golf ball? What else could it be?'

Carole took her sodden handkerchief away from her puffed, reddened face, and her chapped nostrils. She sniffed and said: 'There was something wrong with that animal. It threw her three months ago. She should never have got back on. It couldn't have been Jenny's fault, she was too good a rider. That horse was a wrong 'un. She should have got rid of it when she fell off the first time.'

'It's right that she fell off, yeah,' said Mick. 'But it was only because the horse dropped its head and yanked her forward by the reins. Just unbalanced her, that's all. She wasn't chucked off like she was this time. You're right, though—Jenny's too experienced to be caught out by a horse playing up so I don't think it's mischief from Daphne. I think something's hit that horse. It could've been a golf ball but what if it was something else?'

'They must have checked for airgun pellets, things like that,' said Emerald.

'They've had a proper look, yeah, that's what they told me,' said Mick, 'and they're still checking but they haven't found anything yet that would change their theory that the horse was struck by the golf ball.

'The horse was a mess. It bounced off the side of that wagon—it weren't a head-on collision. Driver might have been killed if that happened. It was more of a sideways, glancing impact, but the horse was thrown to the roadside and broke all kinds of bones. There was blood everywhere. From what they tell me, I think they're gonna struggle to pick out a single injury and say for sure that that was what did it. That's what they're telling me anyway.'

'My theory is that Dr Klein is somehow involved in this,' said Emerald doggedly.

The room went silent. Seb and Jenny's family were unconvinced. Her assertion seemed so out of kilter with everything else they had heard. She tried to justify her suspicions but eventually she clammed up, feeling a little stupid and guessing from the wearied looks of the others that she was beginning to sound like an obsessive. She wondered if she sounded selfish to them too, more concerned about the campaign of the families, of which she was a part, than of the plight of Jenny herself.

As the evening wore on Emerald was more and more like a stranger, an outsider, who was barely tolerated by this close and devastated family circle. Yet privately she could not escape the conviction that Dr Klein was mixed up in Jenny's fall. *Cui bono?* Clearly Dr Klein. If Jenny was continuing her investigations, as she said she was, her mishap was highly convenient for the doctor.

But what on earth was she doing talking to him? Why had she ignored Emerald's advice? What had passed between them? What information had they shared that might have precipitated this awful incident? Emerald grew more disconcerted, more fretful, by the minute.

She did not hang around to spend time with Geoff when the meeting broke up. She went straight home, unsettled and anxious, a night of troubled sleep ahead of her and more fearful of Dr Klein than ever.

The following day was Thursday 13 June and Emerald visited the presbytery in the afternoon to do some paperwork while Father Calvin went to St Winefride's Catholic Primary School to catechise children with new magic tricks she had helped him to perfect. Most of the bruising around his eyes was disappearing but he still relied on the nurse to apply a little bit of concealer when in proximity to the public.

He left Emerald with the important task of arranging Mrs Hoskins's funeral and she gladly took responsibility for it. She could see Calvin was deeply grieved by the death of his house-keeper at Bethulia Park and that he was in a dreadful state emo-tionally, heartbroken and blaming himself for Mrs Hoskins's lonely demise. He was further distraught about the news that Jenny was fighting for her life.

The funeral had been set for the following week, Thursday 20 June, and Emerald had been liaising with Tanya Torridge, who managed Torridge Family Funerals. They spoke frequently by phone. That afternoon Emerald rang Tanya to order Mrs Hoskins's coffin.

'Yes, she was a big woman,' said Emerald as she spun from side to side in a brown leather upholstered chair at the desk in Calvin's study. 'Taller than six feet, yeah, I'd say so. I'm not sure exactly, so I'll go for the last one you mentioned to me.

'Oh yes, and we definitely want her to be delivered to the church the afternoon before the funeral. It was one of her last wishes that we have a prayer vigil for her before we send her off … Thanks, Tanya, sure … That would be fine, thanks. See you Monday.'

You can't fuss too much about the size of a coffin, thought Emerald as she put the handset back. Six foot two, six foot five, six foot eight—was there really that big a difference? In the end she had plumped for a coffin that was six foot five inches in length, twenty-six inches across and fourteen inches deep. Plenty of room.

Emerald had arranged to go into the funeral parlour on Monday to discuss the finer points of the arrangements, and to hand over a list of readings and hymns and a picture of Mrs Hoskins for the order of service, which she would also help to design and proof-read before she signed it off.

All that remained for her to do before heading off for a late shift was to lock up the church.

She entered the darkness of the sanctuary and instantly felt herself in the presence of God. She was startled by her own sudden religiosity. What was this? Was it simply the atmosphere of an empty church? There was no one there but her. The solitude, the shadows and the gloomy neo-Gothic arches certainly evoked something which transcended the ages—something sacred, infinite and all-powerful. It might be her imagination, but she doubted it. It might be an echo of the ages, of all those of people who had gathered there over many decades to pray together, to hear the muttering of the Mass amid billows of incense, to baptise their children, to marry, to bid farewell to their dead and to mourn.

Yet Emerald was not touched by a sense of history like she had been at the well in North Wales. There was something more than that. There was something alive within that church, something present but unseen, something too beautiful to put into words, something ineffable, something holy—something like a burning bush.

She walked into the church and the carved faces of saints gazed at her. She felt their presence in the stained glass windows, almost intimately, as if they knew her. She halted before one statue with the sense of a profound and instantaneous connection, the force of a personal encounter. It was a life-size St Winefride, the patron of the parish, standing above a rack of blazing candles left by the faithful with their prayerful entreaties. The saint wore a crown and she held a crozier in her left hand, a model of an abbey in her right. Her expression was serene, the scar across her neck vivid and raised, just like the one on Emerald's throat.

The nurse knelt on a leather rest beneath the statue. She joined her hands and offered a short prayer for Jenny, looking up at the statue as she said it, addressing the saint as if she were a friend, and finding her strangely beautiful.

'Please don't let her die, please rescue us from him. Please, St Winefride, if you can, stop this. You are a woman like me. You know what it's like to be pursued by an evil man. You had your throat cut like me. I think you know me. Please listen to me. Please, please help me. If you can, please hear my cries—hear my prayer.'

Suddenly embarrassed by this onset of uncharacteristic fervour, she hauled herself from her knees. She blew out all the candles, nipping the smoking wicks between her forefinger and thumb to make sure they were extinguished. As she did, she tried to turn her mind from the supernatural but could not help but wonder if she was being warned. Did the impulse to seek help come from Heaven or from her imagination? Was she being affected by the suggestive power of statues with kind faces or was she really in danger?

Such thoughts proved irresistible. She dropped to her knees again and this time she bowed her head as she began to think about Judith. She knew her story well, even before Calvin had told her about his obsession. She had known all about Judith's beauty, her wit, and her power many months before she set eyes on the priest. She knew that Judith, the holy widow of the Old Testament, was also a woman like her.

She reached into her bag and drew out a small Bible. She turned to a page she had marked in the Book of Judith and began to read aloud a passage as if she had written it herself.

'Break their pride by a woman's hand,' she said. 'Your strength does not lie in numbers, nor your might in strong men; since you are the God of the humble, the help of the oppressed, the support of the weak, the refuge of the forsaken, the Saviour of the despairing. Please, please, God of my father, God of the heritage of Israel, Master of heaven and earth, Creator of the waters, King of your whole creation, hear my prayer. Give me a beguiling tongue to wound and kill those who have formed such cruel designs against your covenant.'

She thrust the Bible back into her bag as if it was subversive literature. She rose from her knees to walk round the church. She locked the main doors and checked the others. She turned off the lights and left the building through the sacristy, joined by a passage to the priest's house. Finally she locked the presbytery and set off for the hospital.

In the car she slumped a little, physically tired and drained, and made an extra effort to concentrate on her driving. She was dreading a busy night ahead. Yet despite her fatigue her mind was racing.

She had often felt like killing Dr Klein. It was partly why the story of Judith appealed to her, why she had sometimes drawn solace from it, taken refuge there. She had even seen herself as the biblical Judith, fantasised about it. But cutting off Dr Klein's head was not something she would ever do. She was not really Judith and he was not Holofernes.

Furthermore, she was convinced that deliberate killing was wrong. It was one of the reasons why she had taken great personal risks to expose Dr Klein. She had listened to the voice of her conscience and she had come to the conclusion that what he was doing could not be justified by any objective criteria. Her conversations with Calvin had reinforced this view. If God had created her for 'some definite service', as the priest said Cardinal Newman had taught, if God had committed to her some special work 'which has not committed to another', she was certain that it did not involve murdering Dr Klein. God makes the sun shine on the good and the wicked alike, she told herself, and only He has the right to judge, to condemn and to punish. She knew that much. Yet defeat Klein she must, and for that she had to be strong. The situation in which she found herself was a battle for survival, akin to warfare. That was why Jenny was in intensive care. She was a casualty of the conflict, Emerald was sure of it. As the nurse drove to work that afternoon, she slowly came to the conclusion that she would not take any option from the table.

Besides stress and the exhaustion, the possibility that she might run into Dr Klein made her apprehensive about work. Of course, she would be forced against all her contrary emotions to smile at him, to act as if nothing had happened. She did that all the time, there was nothing difficult about it, though it might be harder with Jenny in a coma and the doctor breathing down her neck about her outstanding 'bill'. He was the last person on earth she wished to meet.

Luck would have it that Dr Klein was the first person she saw as she entered the hospital. He was standing talking to security personnel and he broke away from the group as soon as he spotted her.

'Could I have a word, Emerald?' he called. 'My office, five minutes.'

When she entered she was so tense she felt she might snap. Klein, at his desk studying some documentation, looked up at her with a friendly smile and invited her to take a seat.

He was not the angry and menacing Dr Klein of the previous weeks and months but was composed and relaxed.

He pretended not to notice the coldness of her attitude towards him. He was a better actor than Emerald and he chatted warmly as he attempted to analyse her reaction.

'Awful business about that journalist,' he said eventually.

'Which journalist?'

'The one in intensive care. You must have heard about her. It's been in all the papers. Thrown from her horse on Saturday. Her helmet saved her life, apparently. Did you know her?'

'The one who did the stories about us? No, I've never met her.'

'She's the one, all right. She covered the inquest and wrote biased reports about it then she received leaked information about the Trust which she then went and sold to the *Sunday News*. Charming, eh? Of course you know about it. She needs us now that's she in the ICU.'

'So that's why you're in a good mood, because she's in intensive care?'

'I'm in a good mood because she is alive. Are you upset about her, Emerald?'

'I've told you, I don't know her. I've never met her. Is this why you've asked me to come to see you?'

'No. Nothing to do with that at all.'

Emerald made a show of looking at her watch, signalling to the doctor to hurry up because her shift was about to begin.

'Have you ever heard of pancuronium bromide?' asked Dr Klein.

'Yes, isn't it used in intubation, that kind of thing? To relax muscles. It's a paralysing agent, isn't it?'

Dr Klein picked up the notes on his desk and waved them at the nurse. 'I'm brushing up. Do you want to know why?'

Emerald braced herself.

'Yes, it's a paralysing agent. It's like curare. Do you know, it's one of the drugs used to judicially execute criminals in the United States and also for euthanasia in the Low Countries. We make it here but we can't export it to America, only to Europe, because we're against capital punishment. We're on a crusade to stamp it out around the world. It's an odd distinction to me, because we're supposed to be against euthanasia too, but I digress. A large dose stops the heart, hence its use in capital punishment and in euthanasia, but smaller doses simply make it impossible to move. At the same time, patients retain their senses. They can hear, smell, see, taste and they'd be conscious, able to think, if they weren't brain dead, of course.

'They retain their sense of touch too, and they can feel pain. Think about that. Imagine feeling intense pain, and not being able to move away from it, or do anything about it whatsoever. It must be terrifying, don't you agree?'

'Why are you trying to scare me?' protested Emerald.

Klein sniggered.

'Sorry, I didn't mean to scare you, nor was I trying. The only reason I'm telling you this, Emerald, is because I think you'd be fascinated to know that if this journalist deteriorates, the one whom you don't know nor have never met, she probably isn't going to slip away quietly in the night. It is more likely that she will die during surgery to remove organs for transplants. If that eventuality should arise I am likely to be part of the team that takes out her heart and lungs. I expect the family to consent, don't you? I would be very interested to know what reasons they might have for refusing to help other patients waiting for a donor.

'Of course, if Jenny Bradshaigh is kept alive until February next year it won't matter what they think because they won't have a choice in the matter. It's going to be mandatory soon. Unless you've opted out of organ donation in advance, you're going to be in—consent will be assumed—and we may be able to harvest her organs whether her family likes it or not. It is terribly sad but at least some good will come out of this awful, tragic accident and the waste of such a promising young life.'

Klein leaned forward.

'Have you ever taken part in one of those procedures, Emerald, where they remove the organs from patients who are brain dead?'

Damp heat issued along Emerald's spine as she moved fractionally with discomfort, the tension returning to her shoulders. She said nothing.

'This medical report I have in front of me explains that in theatre brain-dead patients seldom behave like they're dead. We wash them, we shave them, we hook them up with tubes and wires to all the machines and they don't move a muscle but as soon as we cut them, they react to the pain—their pulse rates and blood pressure shoot up, their arms and legs thrash about, torsos jerk, and sometimes they even make co-ordinated attempts to grab the knife. It's all in here.'

He held up the documents again.

'We have to use pancuronium to stop the surgeons and the nurses from throwing up, or from going home with post-traumatic stress disorder. That's another purpose for this drug, it's what we use it for. But what I want to know, what I want to find out, is just how much pancuronium I will need to calm a patient's muscles while permitting maximum sensory perception. I want to know that if I was to slice open that journalist, to take out her heart and her lungs, that I've given her the precise amount to stop her from kicking, but no more than that. Do you understand what I'm saying?'

Emerald felt sick.

'Of course, we all hope it won't ever come to that. You know, and you have often said, that I'm a good doctor. I could help that journalist to get back on her feet. With my involvement, I'm sure she'd have an improved chance of recovery. I've also grown very fond of Jenny. We've met, you know, we've become good friends. I am emotionally invested in her full and swift return to health. I sincerely want to help her. I want to see her back in the saddle. I'm looking forward to our next lunch.'

He watched Emerald keenly. She looked straight ahead and did nothing more than blink.

'Why don't you help her, then? What's stopping you? What's all this ridiculous talk about pancuronium bromide and transplant surgery? What's with the horror story, Reinhard? Just help her!'

'You can help her.'

They stared at each other.

'Settle the bill.'

Emerald was silent for a few seconds.

'Okay, I'll do it. I'll settle the bill.'

'Yes!' exulted Dr Klein, rocking back in his chair. 'It's better that we all draw a line under this business. Emerald, irrespective of what you keep telling me, you are the leak.'

'I'm not the leak.'

'Come on, I know you are. Why else would you care? Anyway, I think we have a great opportunity next week. I'm supposed to be on a golfing trip to the Algarve but actually I'm going to be with my friend. Her husband is on that trip. You could join us for one night. Same terms, plus a guarantee of my care for Jenny. Sunday evening after eight at my country retreat would be good, so would Monday or Tuesday, same time. I'm out of the country from Wednesday because I'll need a tan. When can you manage it?'

'I'm sure I'll be able to make it on one of those dates. I'll have to check my diary and get back to you. I'll send you a text.'

'Oh, no. Don't text me, ring me, nothing like that. I mean, you don't have to. Just knock on the door. Just turn up, but don't leave it too late. I'll think you're a burglar and I'd have to shoot you.'

'Let's go for Sunday,' said Emerald. 'I take it you're providing the bubbly?'

'Sure, it's all on me.'

30

DRESSED TO KILL

Octavia turned on the lamp on the bedside table while Klein closed the blinds of the back bedroom, casting an eye over the closely cropped lawn and neat flowerbeds below.

'Why do I have to be the one who gets tied up first?' she huffed, walking to the foot of the bed.

'I've told you already,' Klein answered. 'She doesn't fully trust me, and she isn't willingly going to slip into handcuffs, do this whole bondage thing, unless she sees that you've done it first and it was enjoyable. I don't want to have to drug her, or club her, just so I can tie her up. We can do that later.'

They both laughed.

Klein was in a claret silk dressing gown with black collar, cuffs and belt, and black Armani slides, and he was drenched in *Very Sexy: For Him* by Victoria's Secret, which Octavia had bought for him after reading that it was a favourite scent of Liam Gallagher.

His skin glowed from his afternoon in the sun and his hair glistened, not a strand out of place. If he was going to be in a home movie, he had to look his best.

Octavia had made even more of an effort, her hair cut, styled and coloured the previous day, and now dropping in golden locks over the see-through lace shoulders of a short red kimono she had picked up in Paris the last time she was there with her husband. Her lipstick was the exact shade of the garment and was also a match for the rubies inlaid into her white gold ear-rings. The hem of the kimono fell about two inches below her buttocks, revealing the red lace tops of nude-colour stockings that covered her slender legs down to her cream high-heeled shoes. Under her robe, she was wearing a red suspender belt, 'lipstick' hip-hugger pants and a red lace camisole. Around her neck was a Tiffany graduated ball necklace from a shopping trip to New York.

A tripod set up for a camera with a wide-angle lens was positioned at the corner of a wrought iron frame bed made up with rose-coloured faux satin sheets, one end piled with cushions and small pillows of a similar colour. A smaller tripod held a phone on the other side of the bed. A device in a white case was on the bedside table nearest the window.

Octavia surveyed the mattress, then folded her arms. 'She's a bit late, isn't she? What time is it? It must be way past nine. D'ya think she'll come tonight?'

'Give it a few more minutes, babe, then we can have a dress rehearsal, if you like. I can't be bothered waiting around all night myself. More champagne?'

Octavia smiled and held out her glass as Klein reached for the bottle chilling in a silver bucket beside the bed.

She took a sip, looked again at Dr Klein and the bed, then put down the flute, marked by her lipstick, on a coaster on a tall chest of drawers behind her. She took care not to knock the glass against a free-standing full-length mirror.

'C'mon, honey,' she said eagerly.

Emerald was at that moment speeding along twilit country lanes in her white Golf, her face steely hard and still. She was deliberately late. She wanted it to be almost dark before she showed up. She flicked on her side lights, releasing a hand that had been gripping the steering wheel so tightly that the skin of her knuckles was taut. She felt pins and needles in her fingertips and her palms were damp with sweat.

Arriving at the driveway to Dr Klein's cottage, she braked and took a sharp left. Gravel crunched beneath her wheels as she rolled up to the house.

A magnolia arched over the driveway in front of the house and Emerald parked beneath it. The spot was well out of view from the main road. On the other side of the drive Klein's Jaguar and a sporty BMW were similarly tucked out of the sight of anyone who might peer up the driveway.

As she swung her legs out of the car, she pulled her figure-hugging electric blue hour-glass dress straight before reaching into the vehicle for a large cream leather shoulder bag.

Commanding herself to focus, Emerald walked up two shallow steps flanked by deep pots of pink geraniums. Breathing deeply, she banged hard on the knocker of the thick wooden front door, a recent coat of gloss black paint gleaming in the half-light.

The sound of the car arriving was enough for Klein to leap from the bed and hastily grab his dressing gown. He slipped on his slides and almost ran from the room, ignoring the protests of Octavia, who was handcuffed to the bedposts and blindfolded.

Klein dashed to the master bedroom at the front of the house and looked out. He was relieved to see that Emerald had come alone. He didn't trust her and wanted to be sure she wasn't followed. He opened his wardrobe and drew out a double-barrelled shotgun, which he was not licensed to keep at the cottage, but had brought with him just in case. He wanted to be sure there was no mischief.

He called to Octavia that he would be straight back as soon as he had let Emerald in. He hurried down the stairs and unbolted and opened the front door. His guest put a hand to her chest in fright when he stood before her holding a powerful firearm.

'Had to make sure it's just you, Emerald. You never know. Country life makes you like that. Always on your guard.'

'Who else could it be? Are you expecting anyone else?'

'No, absolutely not. Come on in. You're a bit late so we've started the party without you, but have a drink and meet Octavia. Loosen up a little. She'll be down in a minute. She's just a little tied up at present.'

He smirked at his own joke.

'Thanks, Reiny. I could murder a drink. That reminds me, I've brought a few bottles of wine and bubbly with me. If we're going to have a party, let's make it a good one! That's what I think. They're in the boot. Would you mind helping me carry them in? My overnight bag's there too. I could do with a hand.'

'Sure, no problem.'

Emerald stopped for a second on the step to adjust one of her shoes while Klein walked to the Golf, carrying the gun with both hands at waist height. As she came up behind him she glanced at the cottage windows to make sure no one was watching, then reached into her bag and took out a pistol.

She halted, raised the gun with two hands and looked down the sights as she levelled it at the back of the doctor's head.

'Put down the gun, Reinhard!'

He turned, and jumped when he found himself looking directly into the barrel of the pistol.

'Put down the gun now, or I'll kill you. I swear—don't make me do it. I want to do it! If you want to live put the gun down now!'

He lowered the shotgun gently on to the gravel at his feet and stood up straight, raising his hands above his shoulders.

'Good boy. Now get my stuff out of the boot.'

As Klein edged closer to the car, Emerald picked up the shotgun, still keeping her pistol on the doctor. The boot swung open and Klein leapt backwards. A man wearing a balaclava unfolded himself and climbed out, pointing a gun at the doctor's face all the time. The rear car door opened and a second man, also masked, emerged from under a dark blanket and pointed his pistol at the doctor.

'On your knees,' said the man from the boot in a low voice.

Klein stood motionless, glaring at Emerald with perfect hatred. The other man approached him from his side and without warning smashed down the grip of his weapon on to the doctor's collar bone. Klein screamed and buckled and the man hit him again in the same place.

'Do as you're told!' he snarled.

As Klein knelt, gasping, Emerald took a pair of plastic medical gloves from her bag and pulled them on. She propped up the shotgun on the wall by the open front door and went in, the pistol in her right hand and her bag over her shoulder. She knew that if another person had seen what had happened outside she should have to be quick if she was going to prevent them from alerting the police.

She paced swiftly along the hall and up the stairs, knowing that Octavia was there somewhere, but not sure what to expect from her. There was a light on in the back bedroom and the door was ajar. Emerald kicked it open and jumped into the room, her hand outstretched and pointing the pistol, ready to shoot. She lowered the weapon and chuckled when she saw Octavia shackled to the bed, lying naked on her stomach and shivering like a wet dog.

'I know you,' she whispered to Octavia as she observed the face behind the blindfold. 'I know where I've seen you. How fascinating!'

Octavia issued a torrent of four-letter words and curses. They were directed principally at Dr Klein.

'Where is he? Let me go! This is it! I've had it, I've had enough of him! It's over, I'm going home! Let me go!'

She pulled at the cuffs so strenuously that the bed began to shake, but there was no chance that she could break free.

'Shhhhh, calm down,' said Emerald softly, putting gun into her bag. 'Dr Klein's going for a ride to see a man who wants to talk to him about some of the bad things he's done, and if you're nice and quiet for me I might be able to save your life. My friends are outside now. If you swear and shout, they'll come and take you too. So be quiet.'

Octavia opened her mouth and panted deeply as the reality of her predicament sank in. 'They're taking him away. Who? Taking him where? Which man?'

'The king of clubs.'

Emerald looked at the tripods. It was just as she expected. Then she switched her attention to the white phone on the bedside table, recognising it instantly from the dashboard of Klein's car. She dropped it into her bag. Then she pulled open a deep drawer in the dressing table and looked inside. She grimaced and swore, cursing Klein as vividly as Octavia, as she inspected a range of objects which the doctor had probably placed inside for that evening's entertainment. Most were surely meant for her, thought Emerald. She stopped at the sight of a small bottle. She withdrew it and frowned as she read the label out loud.

'Pancuronium bromide.'

She walked around the bed and bent down to Octavia. 'Was this meant for me?' she said an inch from her ear. 'Was that the plan? That I would be tied up while he injected me with curare? And then what?'

Octavia bit her lip. Emerald saw it bleed.

The nurse put the bottle back into the drawer and strode angrily out of the room. She crossed the landing into the master bedroom where she found Klein's other phone, the one in a black case, on top of a chest of drawers. Against a wall was a holdall packed with clothes. Emerald rummaged through it until she located the passport in a side pocket. She shoved the clothes back and carried the bag downstairs.

Still furious after her discovery of the paralysing agent, she went into the kitchen. There was a wooden knife block on the worktop. Emerald drew out a couple until she found a 20cm carving knife.

Klein was still on his knees near the passenger door of her car when she emerged from the house, his wrists bound behind him. Emerald hurled his holdall on to the ground near the boot, and told one of the masked men to put it in.

'His phone, probably with his plane tickets downloaded, is in the side pocket along with his passport, if he should be lucky enough to live. After what I've just found in that house I'm not sure he's going to make it off this driveway.'

'What's up?' asked one of the men.

'Nothing I can't handle myself. Don't worry. You don't need to go in.'

Emerald went to over to Klein and squatted so she could face him.

'Hello, Reiny,' she said, smiling at him, but with her eyes screwed up. 'Raging Reiny, Reiny the rhino. Not so tough now, are you? How does it feel to be vulnerable? Do you want mercy yet? You'll be screaming out for it soon.'

He stared past her as if she wasn't there.

'Why did you have pancuronium in your bedroom, Reiny? Was that for me? Was I going to be your guinea pig? I always knew you were going to hurt me. But were you going to murder me too? Was that the plan?'

Dr Klein looked over his shoulder to the two men. 'Take no notice of her,' he said loudly. 'She's off her head. She's mad. Utterly barking. I've never hurt anybody and I wasn't going to hurt her either.'

He sneered at the nurse. 'You are a nutcase, aren't you, Emerald? Go on, who are you play-acting at tonight? You fantasist!'

The nurse reached inside her bag and took out the carving knife. She showed it to him then quickly placed the point under his chin, near his Adam's apple, forcing him to look up. He twisted his head backwards from the sharp tip of the knife but watched the nurse keenly from the corner of one bulging eye.

'Tonight, Reiny, I'm Judith. Do you know who she is? No? She killed this awfully bad man—he was a bit like you—by cutting off his head with his own sword. Do you recognise this knife, Reiny? It's yours. Do you know what it's like to have your throat sliced? I do, and you're about to find out.'

Behind the doctor, one of the men frantically shook his head, signalling to Emerald not to go through with her threat.

'Boss wants him alive,' he muttered.

She ignored him.

'What really happened to Jenny? You can tell me that as well.'

She aligned the knife so he could feel the length of blade on his skin of his throat. Just a little extra pressure, or the slightest of sideways movements, and he would be bleeding. But Klein kept quiet.

Emerald was strongly tempted just to cut him and to keep cutting, sawing down deeper and deeper through muscle, fat and bone, while he shrieked and sputtered, blood spurting out of severed arteries in torrents. She wouldn't stop until she could lift his decapitated head by its hair in her fist. She wouldn't just be Judith. She would be a female Perseus slaying a modern-day Medusa. She had thought about it when she fantasised darkly about ending the doctor's hold over her. But in the cold light of day she was no Judith, and nor did she want to be. When it came to the bloodlust of Dr Klein, she had no wish to be his equal. She was better than that. But now she was having second thoughts after concluding the doctor intended to kill her.

'The pancuronium wasn't for you, Emerald,' he pleaded. 'I'm studying it and I took it upstairs by mistake and shoved it in the drawer to get it out of the way. If I was going to use it to paralyse or kill you why would I want to film myself doing it? It would be madness, it would be suicidal. Think about it, Emerald. It wouldn't make sense.'

She stood up and contemplated his appeal while she studied the knife in her hand. She dropped it into her bag.

'Don't worry,' she said, looking up at the men in the masks. 'I'm not really Judith. He's the one making things up, not me. But before you take him off to see your boss I want this man to tell me the access code to this phone.'

She drew the mobile in the white case from her bag.

'Are you going to tell me the code, Reiny?'

Dr Klein stared silently at the ground in front of him.

'No, I didn't think you would.'

She fixed her attention on the two men, still aiming their pistols at Dr Klein.

'Get your boss to get that code off him before he asks him about anything else and get someone to send it to me tonight. I'll check it works straight away to make sure he isn't lying. I need to know what is on that phone.'

'Are you not coming with us?' one said.

'No, I'm going to stay here and make sure everything is in order, then I'll make my own way home. I'll speak to your boss tomorrow. I can walk down to the village and I'll call a cab when I'm there.'

Emerald went behind the car and opened the boot. A moment later she came around to Klein with a hypodermic in her hand. She pushed it into his shoulder and emptied the barrel of its contents.

'Goodbye, doctor. It's been a blast. If you're good and behave yourself then, who knows, we might meet again in better circumstances. We could have a laugh and a drink about all this. Can you imagine?'

She giggled.

Emerald returned to the boot to dispose of the needle then tossed her car keys to one of the men.

'Give it back to me tomorrow,' she said.

The two men bundled the doctor, already feeling the effects of the sedative, on to the back seat of the car and covered him with the blanket. Emerald went back into the house, collecting the shotgun on the way, and gently closing the front door behind her.

Octavia was still chained safely to the bed. She was still shivering, although it wasn't cold. She was convulsed by an agony of fear. Emerald felt a little sorry for her.

She had seen Octavia's handbag in the master bedroom and she fetched it. She dragged a chair close to the bed and sat down as she riffled through the bag. She found her purse and took it out.

'Octavia Tarleton,' she said, reading a credit card. 'I thought so. You were at the races with that bobby who looks like he needs to shave five times a day. He's your husband, obviously. Have you been married long, Octavia? Who were you before this? Were you Octavia Topcliffe?'

'What are you going to do to me?'

'Tell me something. I call Reinhard Klein "Reiny" for short. What do you call him?'

'Hardy, why? Can you let me go?'

'He calls me Emmy when he's being friendly. What does he call you for short?'

'He calls me Tavy.'

'I'm so stupid at times. He's probably told you that, hasn't he? That I'm stupid. So you were Octavia Topcliffe, weren't you?'

'Yes, that's my maiden name. Are you going to kill me? Don't forget I'm married to a detective.'

'Should I kill you? What would you do to me if I was in your position and you were in mine?'

Octavia bit her lip again. Emerald put the purse back into the bag and continued to sift through the contents. She took out a phone.

'Ah, another one that's password-protected. I need you to tell me the code.'

Octavia didn't answer her.

'Look, darling, this is really simple. You either tell me the code and I might let you go, if you co-operate nicely with all my other questions, or you clam up like you're some kind of secret agent and I kill you. Don't think I won't do it. It would be easy for me to make it appear as if Hardy did it to you. It looks like he has just done it to you, if you don't mind me saying. George would think that was rape, wouldn't he? And an overdose of pancuronium—well, only a doctor would think that one up. It would be easy for me to stick it in you now. No struggle, no mess. I just walk out of here. I would never be a suspect. They'd look for Klein and they'd never find him. He'd be on the run for ever. He's not the sharpest sheriff that's ever rode into town, is he, your husband? Are they all like him? Is it that he's simply overworked and understaffed? Either way, killing you is an easy option for me to take. No doubt Hardy had thought up similar arrangements for me. Come on, Octavia. We both know what it's like to have blood on our hands, me and you, and when you've done it once we know we can do it again. So tell me the code in the next ten seconds or you're brown bread. What's the code?'

'It's 2268.'

'Very good. You made the right choice.'

Emerald made a note of the number with a pen and a small pad she pulled from her own bag. She also drew out a Roland R-07 audio recording device, about the size of a deck of cards. She activated it, hit the record button and put it on the floor under the bed. She looked through Octavia's phone in silence. She flicked through the contacts, read a few emails, some texts and had a look in the photo album. She stood up, pulled the chair to one side and stepped back so the whole of Octavia's body was in the frame. She clicked away.

'I'm going to take off your blindfold now, is that okay? And I want you to smile for the camera … I said smile.'

The eyes of the two women met for the second time.

'I'll have this,' said Emerald, dropping Octavia's phone into her own bag. 'Don't worry, it's off.'

She sat down.

Octavia blinked hard as she raised her head from the bed to observe Emerald closely. She smiled at the nurse, revealing her perfect teeth.

'Wow, you've got a scar, how exciting.'

'That's nothing,' said Emerald pulling out her pistol and holding it up to her right cheek. She wore a sultry, menacing expression, like a Bond girl. 'How do I look?'

'I like it. It's a good look. Very sexy. You're a very beautiful woman. I like your gun too. What is it?'

'I believe this is a Biretta 9000. Your husband would probably say it's a standard criminal gang weapon. So it suits me?'

'Yeah, it does. You look hot. Do you know how to use it?'

'Of course I do.'

'Have you shot anyone?'

'Not yet. I was tempted to tonight though. I put it on Reinhard when he was walking away from me and if I'd pulled the trigger when he turned to face me I'd have slotted him right between the eyes. I so wanted to kill him. You don't know how hard it was for me to control myself.'

Octavia cackled and raised her head from the pillow. 'I'd have shot him,' she said. 'I'd have emptied that gun into him. I wouldn't have wasted a single bullet. You're so lucky to have that chance. He'll be sorry for crossing me, if I get my chance.'

'I believe you.'

Octavia's head dropped to the pillow again.

'I wasn't going to kill you tonight, Emerald. I think Klein wanted to. But I had another plan. I was hoping we could have turned on him. He's a nasty piece of work. He has used me to protect him through all the problems he's made for himself over the last year, and I have. I've helped him. I didn't have to. He's been an idiot and I have been an idiot in helping him. I know that because of the way he's repaid me. He went off and slept with that wretched journalist. Did you know he'd done that? He's all gooey and soft about her now. He wants her to be his new girlfriend. I just know it. I can see the love hearts in his eyes. What a creep! So I was hoping that we might have made a team tonight, sorted him out. You should have shot him.'

'Someone else is sorting him out. No need to worry. Let me ask you, why would he kill me and film himself doing it at the same time? Wouldn't the existence of a film increase his risk of getting caught and the certainty of life behind bars if he did? He just pointed that out to me and I think he was right. It doesn't make sense.'

'Oh dear! You still don't know Hardy well enough, do you? Emerald, sweetheart, these cameras weren't for you. Well, they are in a way. He was going to film me, not you. We didn't bother in the end. But it was part of this plan of his that he would leave them up to give you the impression that whatever happened in here you would walk away afterwards. They were there to help to lure you into a trap. Once you had these cuffs on, I doubt the cameras would roll and you were right first time—the pancuronium would come out.'

'Thanks, Octavia. I appreciate you telling me this,' Emerald said quietly. She was almost dizzy with shock.

'No problem. Bear that in mind when you think about killing me—that I'm helping you. Do you think he'll kill Hardy, this king of clubs?'

'I really don't know. Could he kill him, does he have what it takes? Absolutely, yes. And Klein probably murdered a close member of this guy's family, so he is pretty angry with him. That doesn't put Klein in a very strong position. But will he kill him? I've no idea. I'd rather he didn't. The king of clubs is full of surprises. You don't know what he's got up his sleeve, what he's going to do next. It's what makes him so dangerous, so effective. It's how he stays out of trouble.'

Emerald stood up.

'Oh, by the way, do you want me to cover you? You look freezing.'

Emerald covered Octavia's body with her kimono and sat down again.

'Thank you.'

'You're welcome. Once a nurse, always a nurse.'

'Why don't you let me go? We could leave as friends. I like you a lot and I think we have a lot in common. We could have a lot of fun.'

'There is a lot I like about you too. I thought I liked you when I saw you at the races. But there is a gulf between us. This doesn't mean I'm against letting you go. I'm not. I'd rather let you go than kill you. But I want a few more honest answers from you first. If I think you're lying—I'm going to do one of two things: I'll either hand you over to the king of clubs or jab you up myself. Cooperate with me, like you've just shown me you can, and I'll let you go—most probably. But I'm not releasing you now, so we can chat over a glass of bubbly, if that's what you mean. I think you might kill me. Come on, Octavia, you know I have absolutely no reason to trust you.'

'So what do you want to know?'

'Klein told me earlier that it was you who attacked Jenny and put her in intensive care. Is that true?'

'No!'

Emerald gave Octavia a grave look.

'I fired the golf ball but he made me do it.'

'You fired the golf ball. What did you use?'

'His catapult.'

'You've just told me Klein had gone soft about Jenny after sleeping with her. So why would he want to kill her?'

Octavia thought about the question for a moment.

'Because he thought she didn't feel the same way about him. He'd lied to her and he thought she was mad with him about it. He was worried she would carry on pursuing both of us in one way or another. He was panicking. You think I did this out of jealousy, don't you? Well, how would I know the route of that journalist's ride if Hardy hadn't told me? The journalist told him where she went when they met in Manchester and he told me so I could get rid of her. But he was so pleased when she survived—I mean he was ecstatic. He obviously regretted wanting to hurt her, and I could see he was in love with her. That's the truth of it. That's the way it happened. If it was just about my jealousy I would have had to think of something else.'

'But you quite willingly shot at her? Why do you kill?'

'It's a habit, I guess, an addiction. You're a dangerous woman, you know what I'm talking about. I think you would kill me and I bet you want to now that I've told you all this. This journalist was a friend of yours, I can see that. But I've been honest with you, like you asked, and you said you will let me go. We made a deal. I hope you're going to honour it.'

'You say we're alike, but we're not,' said Emerald. 'On the most important things, we couldn't be more different. The only reason you're still alive is because I am not like you. I couldn't think of anything worse than being like you. But, yes, I'll keep my word, with a few conditions.'

The nurse bent down and picked up the recording device under the bed. She held it up in front of Octavia's face.

'Your confession is on here and if, when your husband comes to get you, you fail to follow the instructions I am now going to give you, to the letter, then this information will send you to jail for life.

'Octavia, you have got to stop killing people. If I hear of you doing it again it would take only a word from me and the king of clubs will come for you. Or I'll hand this recording to the police. Agreed?'

'Yes, I agree.'

Emerald slipped Octavia's blindfold back over her eyes.

'Secondly, I'm not going to let you go until you've had a taste of your own medicine—literally. It isn't going to be nice but you should accept it as punishment for what you have done to others. I'm going to throw some clothes around, leave out a shotgun for the police to find, and wash your champagne flute so it looks like it's been a party for one, obliterate every trace of me being here, and then I'm on my way. So this is what I want you to tell the police when they come to get you …'

A little over an hour later, Emerald reached a village nearly two miles from Klein's cottage. She sat on a bench outside a pub and waited for a drinker to emerge. She selected a half-inebriated middle-aged man who came out alone and asked him nicely if she could borrow his phone. Then she rang for a taxi.

Her own phone was at home, left on, and when she arrived back at her flat she was a little disappointed to see she had not received the code she needed to unlock the device in the white case at the bottom of her bag. She was impressed that Dr Klein appeared to be holding out against Wild Bob for so long, and slightly worried that he might be talking his way out of trouble again.

31

KISS ME LIKE THIS

Mrs Hoskins's coffin was so big that the small pine trestle provided by the funeral directors appeared barely strong enough to support it.

The coffin was arranged in the nave of St Winefride's at the point where the four limbs of the cruciform church met, in front of the sanctuary and at a right angle to the altar. A golden crucifix and a Bible were placed on its lid with a picture of a smiling, happy and fashionable woman taken some forty years previously. Six bolts ran along each of the long edges, their pointed ornamental coverings sparkling in the amber glow of the wall lights like big brass bullets.

Mrs Hoskins had asked for mourners to pray for her on the eve of her funeral but few people had come to the church that Wednesday night. It was almost nine o'clock and Calvin alone knelt on the cushion of a pew directly alongside the coffin, feverishly running the beads of a rosary through his fingers as he muttered one Hail Mary after another.

The priest expected to be on his knees for almost an hour before he finished. He intended then to move on to other meditations and prayers for the repose of his housekeeper's soul. He was determined to make a night of it. Mrs Hoskins, in his opinion, deserved nothing less. He loved her dearly and his failure to prevent her death filled him with remorse, his heart darkened by the despair that grew from his powerlessness to secure justice for her or to stop others from dying needlessly. Going to the police would be pointless, Calvin knew that, but he hated himself for not trying.

He heard footsteps approaching from the sacristy and he knew it was Emerald. The nurse had been at the church since she had finished her shift and had told him she wanted to stay quite late. He was glad to have her around, not least because he was worried about her, noticing how exhausted, haggard, stressed and thin she had suddenly become. She needed to take more care of herself, he thought, and to stop fretting over him and how badly he was taking the death of Mrs Hoskins.

Squeezing past the coffin, she came close and bent to speak quietly to him. 'Father Calvin, there's a phone call for you. It's Father Davenport from London. He says you've been trying to get hold of him.'

Having completed the last of the joyful mysteries of the rosary, Calvin saw that it was an opportune moment to break briefly away. He shrugged in acceptance and silently made the sign of the cross, coiling the white beads of his rosary into a small plastic box and retreating into the house while Emerald remained in the church.

The nurse listened to Calvin walk away and looked around. There was no one else there. She approached the coffin, kissed the open fingers of her left hand and transferred the kiss to the lid.

'Reinhard, I'm so sorry,' she said. 'I didn't want them to kill you. I begged them to send you away. I never wanted your blood on my hands. Wherever you are, if you can hear me, please forgive me.'

The following morning Calvin vested himself in purple robes in preparation for the Requiem Mass.

St Winefride's was less than a third full for the funeral. Most of the mourners were elderly friends of Mrs Hoskins, many of them widows, who wept as the priest preached about the mercy of God.

The Parker brothers were there with their mother, Angela, in the same suits that they wore for their father's inquest. Ralph was again in his trainers.

None of Mrs Hoskins's remaining family had been able to make the trip from Australia.

Emerald, her hair tied up in a French braid, sat by herself in a pew toward the rear of the church in a smart slim-fitting black midi dress which covered her shoulders and dropped to the swell of her calves, matched by stylish flat heels and a black leather Donna Karan handbag at her side.

Father Calvin spoke movingly about how holiness could be obtained through doing the little things in life with love, consoling the congregation that the gates of heaven stood wide open to housekeepers as well as to the greatest of the saints.

He told them that Mrs Hoskins was among 'the least of these little ones' for whom Jesus had shown such affection and solicitude. Our Lord called everyone to be saints and housekeepers were no exception, he said.

He kept his homily short and Emerald could see that Calvin was trying to conceal his heartbreak. Every time his voice faltered, tears of her own crept into the corners of her eyes.

Emerald recognised the casket-bearers as the big men who were drinking upstairs in the *White Hart* the night she went to see Bob Torridge about Mrs Worthington's suspicious death.

At the end of the Mass, she stood and watched nervously as they puffed and strained under the weight of the coffin, making her more sure than ever that 'Wild Bob' had managed to squeeze the tortured corpse of Dr Klein alongside the emaciated body of the housekeeper. But as a funeral director, Bob surely had many ways of disposing of bodies and she couldn't be certain that Klein was there unless he or one of his gang confirmed it to her—and that was not likely to happen.

Emerald was indeed lucky to find out anything about Klein's fate. The morning after he was taken away, she had received an anonymous telephone call giving her the phone code she'd asked for. Her car was dropped off at her flat at lunchtime, the keys pushed through her letter box in a blank envelope.

That would have been the end of the matter had she not been dealing with Tanya, whom she had known for some years. Shortly before the funeral, when they met to talk through the last details, she leaned into Emerald's ear.

'You don't need to worry about that doctor any more,' she whispered. 'He's gone and he won't be coming back. That's it, Emerald.'

'Gone? Gone how?'

Tanya held up two fingers to signify a pistol and tapped her temple. 'Very gone. Dead. It's a secret. Don't ask any more questions. I know I can trust you, Emerald. Thanks for giving me my mother's killer.'

That was usually Bob's way when he turned extremely violent. A single bullet to either the chest or the head delivered as a *coup de grâce* to end some horrible suffering. The mercy killing of Dr Klein.

The casket-bearers made no further complaint as they shuffled down the aisle. Emerald felt nauseous when they drew level with her pew. If she had had her way, Klein would still be alive but permanently somewhere else, even on a beach working on his tan with a cocktail in his fist. Her spinning head and the sickness in her stomach came not only from the knowledge that he was dead and she was partly to blame but also from anguish she felt for Mrs Hoskins if it was truly the case that the housekeeper would have to share millennia in a grave with her murderer.

None of the mourners went to the cemetery. It was Father Calvin and Emerald alone who watched as the coffin was lowered into the ground and who cast the first lumps of dirt over the top of it. Dr Klein was gone, and so was Mrs Hoskins.

Calvin hadn't bothered to use a trowel but scooped earth from the nearby mound with his fingers. Watching him wipe the soil from his hands reminded Emerald of the words in *Eleanor Rigby*, the song they had talked about when they met in Liverpool. The lyrics 'no one was saved' rang in her head.

She had tried to save Klein from death but she couldn't. Now she was complicit in his murder. Dr Octavia Tarleton was, however, to the best of Emerald's knowledge, still shackled to the bed in the back room of his cottage.

Octavia could still be saved. But it was now Thursday afternoon. Nearly four days had elapsed since Emerald abandoned her and if she was not freed soon she would die from dehydration. Perhaps she deserved it for all those times she had condemned others to similar terrible deaths, and not least for what she had admitted she had done to Jenny.

But as she listened to Calvin preach at the funeral that morning, Emerald was more certain than she had ever been that she could not kill her. She was sick of killing and death. She did not wish to be a murderer. She wanted to be honourable and to have integrity. She had made a deal with Octavia and she would be true to her word. Let God be her judge instead.

Staring hard at the pine box in the grave, Emerald said final prayers in her mind for both Klein and Mrs Hoskins and also goodbye to them while Calvin muttered a few prayers of his own. Emerald could see by the way he was blinking hard and repeatedly that he was trying to stop himself from sobbing. 'Give me a few minutes,' he said to her. He did not wish his friend to see him weep.

Emerald crossed the lawns that separated the tombstones and halted beneath the boughs of a giant oak tree close to the main avenue some thirty feet away to wait for Calvin. He had his back to her but she guessed he was releasing some of the profound and private grief that he had kept hidden from the congregation during the Requiem Mass an hour earlier. She wanted to console him but she felt it would be better to leave him alone. He would detest her seeing him so wounded and vulnerable. She would give him as long as he needed.

Emerald saw Calvin lift a handkerchief to his face. He turned and walked toward her with his head bowed. In spite of his efforts, his cheeks were streaked with tears, and his eyes pink. His chin began to wobble as he stood in front of her.

'Baby, come here,' Emerald said, moving swiftly forward, her arms opening to embrace him.

They held each other tightly and the contours and curves of their bodies fitted together as parts of the same whole. Calvin squeezed Emerald and felt her breasts push into his ribs. She ran her left arm around his lower back and reached around with her right to caress the back of his neck. She stroked his hair and pushed his head down into her shoulder. Her cheek and neck became wet with his tears.

'It's okay, it's okay,' she whispered like a mother to an injured child. But her desire to console him was soon being overtaken by the thrill of being wrapped in his arms. She had ached for this moment. Why did it have to be an occasion like this?

She prised herself slightly from him so he would look into her face. She couldn't help but kiss him—just as she had done after their day in Liverpool some three months earlier. Calvin received the kiss passively so she kissed him again, and the third time he reciprocated. He was as clumsy as a schoolboy.

Emerald tipped her head back.

'When you kiss me, kiss me like this,' she said.

She brushed her lips lightly against his own, bringing him into a prolonged, unhurried and gentle kiss of great tenderness.

They let each other go and stared at one another, utterly startled by the transport of their shared pleasure, their hearts racing.

'What now?' asked Emerald, breaking the silence.

Calvin stared at the ground then lifted his face to look into the nurse's eyes.

'Haven't you got a boyfriend?'

'Not any more. Geoff's got a lot on his plate. I wasn't interested in him anyway. It's you, Calvin. It's you I love. You're a good man. I love you and partly it's because you're a good man. I wish I'd met you before you were a priest.'

'We shouldn't have done that. I'm such a bad priest.'

'No, you're not. You're a good priest, and a good man.'

'The problem for us is that I couldn't be good if we started an affair. Would you really be satisfied with life as the mistress of a priest, the bit on the side of a man who is cheating on God? You're worth more than that, Emerald. And what if I left the priesthood to be with you or even to marry you, would you really respect me in the same way you do now?'

Silence fell again. Emerald wanted to say 'yes' but stopped herself. It would have sounded selfish.

'I'm not sure you would,' continued Calvin. 'We'd end up like Edward and Mrs Simpson, you and I. You might think you'd be getting a good man but you'd lament losing the man you once admired and were attracted to. You'd end up with something you never really wanted. You'd lose respect for me and you'd end up despising me, and I might resent you for taking me away from my priestly ministry. I know this is my vocation and, difficult as it is, it's where I'm going to find happiness and salvation. So nothing can change between us. I'm sorry.'

'I accept that,' said Emerald. 'Don't apologise. I'm just a bloody fool. But we can't keep doing this, I mean me tempting you like this. I'm sorry I kissed you.'

'Perhaps we tempt each other.'

'Do you think it would be easier for each of us if we went our separate ways?'

Calvin thought about her question, then fixed Emerald with an agonised look. There was sadness in his voice when he finally spoke.

'St Augustine said that for some people complete abstinence is easier than perfect moderation.'

Emerald took Calvin's hand and squeezed it gently, pleadingly. This time there was no positive response. He left his hand limply in her own. She implored him with her eyes to think about what he was saying, to reconsider his position. He gazed over her shoulder. She understood.

'Goodbye, Father,' she said.

Calvin watched her as she walked along the avenue away from him, committing every second to his memory. It struck him that this could be the last time he would ever see her. His heart was breaking all over again.

Emerald couldn't bring herself to look back at the lone figure of the priest, but stared ahead.

When she had disappeared from his view, Calvin went back to the graveside to offer more prayers and to say goodbye to Mrs Hoskins one last time before the gravediggers moved in to finish their work.

32

ON THE RUN

It was the evening of the following day, Friday June 21, the longest of the year, and Emerald was sitting on a bench at the top of Ashurst Beacon, looking across the Lancashire plain to the Irish Sea.

A light offshore breeze was chasing away wispy clouds, leaving the view below sharp and clear. Looking west from the hillside that formed the country park it was easy to pick out the enormous red cranes of the Liverpool docklands. Emerald could trace the coastline south to the city centre with St John's Beacon, the Radio City Tower, sticking up like a giant pin thrust into the landscape.

Beyond the Mersey estuary she could see the cliffs of Helsby Hill near Chester, and the contours of the Welsh hills behind, rising and falling into the horizon.

Looking to her right, Emerald was able to gaze north across miles of farmland and open countryside to the faint outline of Blackpool Tower, knowing that somewhere down there, amid the patchwork of fields, was the Bradshaigh farm. Turning to her left she could look upon the cooling towers of Fiddlers Ferry power station. That way lay the south and Emerald felt its pull, its attraction. Where, exactly, did she belong?

Crossing her outstretched legs and sitting back, she observed the etiquette of dog walkers moving aside to let each other pass on narrow paths, while their pets pulled on leads with unremitting enthusiasm. At the foot of the hill two boys rolled around in the long grass while a golden retriever jumped around them, overjoyed to the point of ecstasy simply to be outdoors.

Emerald was relaxed yet alert. There were sufficient numbers of people around for her to feel safe and secure from any potential harm, but not so many that they were encroaching upon her or could observe what she was doing. She was about to watch pornography, and she didn't want spectators.

Her problem was that once mobile phones were activated they could be traced, so she wasn't going to do it at home.

Glancing over each shoulder, the nurse reached into her bag and took out the phone in the white case. She entered the access code and scrolled through the photos library until she found what she was searching for.

It was the first time she had seen the film. She blushed, filled with a sickening sense of regret and remorse, and deeply ashamed at the thought that Klein could have shown this awful thing to others.

The liaison was an occasion she remembered well. Klein, friskier, pushier and more energetic than he had ever been, persuaded her into engaging in some of the most adventurous sex of their affair.

She had no idea at the time that he was filming it. She didn't know then what he was really like. Had she just the slightest idea of his true character she would never have entered a house with him, let alone a bedroom. Emerald blamed herself. After all, she knew the man was married.

She turned off the device and put it back into her bag, glancing around again as she fished out Octavia's phone.

This held her curiosity for longer as she painstakingly went through the address book, and the contacts, the emails, texts and photographs, before stopping at the pictures she had taken of Octavia, blindfolded and tied to a bed.

Emerald selected the best of the images, the one in which she thought Octavia was looking most vampish. She forwarded it in a text to the phone number held for Detective Inspector Tarleton accompanied by a message which read:

> You can come and get me now baby. I've had enough. I'm at Dr Klein's. Hurry up or I'll die xxx

Immediately, Emerald turned off the phone, dropped it in her bag and walked up the hill to the car park.

She drove over the top of the Beacon and through the quaint village of Dalton, the Vale of the River Douglas opening spectacularly on her right. The landmarks of Wigan were clearly distinguishable below—the Heinz factory, the football and rugby stadium, the towers and spires of the churches and the high rises of the town centre and the pyramidal peak of the mill that overshadowed her own flat.

Even though she had worked a full shift, cooked a light meal for herself and spent more than hour at the Beacon, the sun was far from setting. She estimated there was at least an hour of daylight before it would sink into a tangerine sky beyond the Bay of Liverpool.

She descended the hill into Parbold, the village at the northern end of the slope, crossed a bridge over the Leeds-Liverpool Canal and picked up speed as she climbed a hill at the other side. When she reached the summit, a popular beauty spot, she parked in a lay-by and got out of the car.

There were still plenty of people on Parbold Hill that evening, most of them walkers at the end of their excursions. Others had driven there for the scenery and nothing more. Nearly all would leave as the evening drew in.

Pulling the strap of her bag over her shoulder, Emerald left the main road to follow a steep downhill path that took her along the edge of a field into woodland. After about twenty minutes she emerged on to an ancient, sloping stone bridge that straddled a rustic stretch of the canal at the foot of the slope.

It was only three weeks since she and Geoff had cycled cheerfully in the sunshine along the towpath at the end of the bridge. It seemed as if an eternity had passed since then, the ride like a memory from a foreign holiday.

She was a little sad that their relationship had not worked out. It was over very quickly, and without acrimony. The relationship had no chance to blossom. It was simply the wrong time. Jenny's fall had killed it off. They parted after a 15-minute long phone call in which Geoff explained to Emerald that he was so crushed with worry for his sister that he could focus emotionally on little else. He was also struggling to control his drinking. Emerald told him that perhaps one day, in better times, they would get together again, but in her heart she accepted that their romance was over.

The sun was dipping. Emerald leaned on the stone ramparts of the bridge, inhaling the rich country air and swatting away the odd horsefly. She was waiting until she was sure there was no one around. Because of the arc of the canal and the dense foliage along its banks, she could see a few hundred yards of towpath in each direction. It was hard for anyone approaching to see her until they were close, or to draw near through the woodland without making a sound.

Putting her hand in her bag, she grasped both of the phones. She held them over the edge of the bridge and let them drop together into the murky green water below. That was it. Done.

Driving home from Parbold Hill, all Emerald wanted to do was settle down for the night in front of the television with a chilled bottle of wine.

Tomorrow night would be just the same. In a month she would turn twenty-eight and it would not surprise her if she found herself still spending her weekends stuck at home, unless she went to visit her mum in Manchester. She couldn't even go to see Calvin any more.

Perhaps, thought Emerald as she sank into her sofa, the time had come to start that new life somewhere else.

She had few close friends, no boyfriend, no appetite for online dating, and a job she was struggling to face.

It was at times like this that she missed Jimmy the most, when she mourned the death of her husband as if she had only just lost him, when she talked to him as if he was still there with her.

At present there was no one around who could come within a mile of filling that space in her soul.

———

It was Saturday night when police officers forced their way into Dr Klein's cottage. Detective Inspector Tarleton was still in Portugal when the text was sent to inform him that his wife was in serious trouble. He had been checking his phone only inter-mittently and saw the message for the first time on Saturday morning. Officers were confused about what was meant by 'Dr Klein's', and Jane Klein and her two children were horrified to see squad cars screech to a halt outside their home and police officers storming up the path toward their front door.

The police reached the doctor's cottage just in time to save Octavia. She was severely wasted, her body feeding off itself for days as every part of her screamed for water.

The early mental torments of panic attacks, insomnia and sheer terror had been compounded by the gradual physical agonies of severe headaches, nausea, stomach cramps and muscle spasms so intense that she shook violently all over.

Then the hallucinations started. The first was simply an enduring sensation of the bed swinging like a hammock. They soon progressed to imagined conversations and visitations, some of them inescapable and vividly horrible, like nightmares from which she could not awaken.

Among the figures she thought she had seen was Dr Klein, soaked in blood. He was pointing at her and laughing hysterically. She saw the faces of people she had killed down the years, looming out of the gloom like balloons, smiling at her or cursing her, and then popping.

When the officers pulled away the gag that Emerald put over her mouth just before she left, Octavia babbled incoherently through a dried and swollen throat and tongue over blackened and cracked lips, unable to see her rescuers although they had taken off her blindfold. Then she vomited blood.

She was taken to hospital in an ambulance blasting its siren as it made a racetrack of the country streets and lanes.

While paramedics strove to rehydrate her, she recovered sufficient mental strength to stop herself from slipping into unconsciousness. She fought against succumbing to the euphoric warm cocoon enveloping her, inviting her to give up. She knew from her own experience that death would inevitably follow if she took the path of least resistance.

Soon she was placed on intravenous glucose-based fluids in the intensive care unit only a few beds away from Jenny Bradshaigh, the woman whom she had attempted to murder two weeks earlier, and who was still in a coma.

Detective Inspector George Tarleton was told by doctors later that his wife would have died within twenty-four hours if she had not been found. They were optimistic that she would recover to some extent, but feared that she had suffered damage to her central nervous system, her heart and her kidneys. She would be in hospital for several weeks at the very least.

At the end of July, Octavia was moved to a recovery unit at the hospital and then to a secure mental health unit. There, in the moments when her medication for a range of severe problems rendered her sufficiently calm to talk to detectives, she answered questions about what had happened to her and to Dr Klein.

In spite of the repeated changes to her story, and her frequent nonsensical contradictions, police eventually pieced together a coherent version of events, a horrific and tragic case of a successful female doctor lured to a house on false pretences where she was held at gunpoint, drugged, raped, and left to die of thirst.

Police announced that Dr Reinhard Klein was wanted in connection with kidnap, rape and attempted murder. They said there was a possibility he had already left the country.

At the same time, a police advisory was sent to news desks reminding the media that on no account must the victim be identified because of her right to anonymity under Section 1 of the Sexual Offences (Amendment) Act 1992.

A number of journalists knew privately, however, that the woman was Dr Octavia Tarleton, the medical director of Crostbury Hospice and the wife of a senior detective.

Among the millions who watched television reports of the press conference that day in late July was Jenny Bradshaigh. She had emerged from her coma but was still recovering from multiple fractures and the trauma from the kick to her head.

Father Calvin was thrilled to hear that she could have visitors and that he was allowed back into Bethulia Park Hospital to see her. At her bedside he sometimes ran into Jenny's family. Her fiancé Seb told him that they were hoping they could get married in spring or summer of the following year. He had some other news too: Jenny was seven or eight weeks pregnant.

33

HALO GOODBYE

I was in a coma for a good few weeks after I fell for the second time in a year, and I am not exaggerating when I say that when I woke up I didn't know my own name. It was as if I existed as some kind of ethereal presence, a disembodied spirit trapped in an unending shimmering clash of a cymbal. I had to wait for the rattle to fade out and expire before I could breath, think or rationalise, start to be human again.

Awareness returned with the realisation that I could barely move. I was in a 'halo', a metal ring fixed into my skull with pins and held in place by stabilisation bars attached to a vest, designed to keep my head still so the bones in my broken neck could heal.

I lay in bed, a railway sleeper, watching the lights come back on slowly, like a dimmer switch being turned up in imperceptible increments. Along with the five senses came pain, discomfort, hunger and thirst, the primeval sensations. The pain! It was agonising even to blink.

I would sob in sadness and deep grief without knowing why, or I'd be convulsed by fear like a child who wakes up in the middle of the night terrified of the dark and starkly aware of her own awful solitude. But I learned gradually to understand my world again through my feelings. I asked myself what they signified, what they could teach me, and it was through them that I began to make sense of my existence again. I would feel a certain warmth when I saw Seb by my bed reading, talking to me and telling me stories and there would be joy and consolation at the sight of my mum and dad and Geoff although I can honestly say I don't think I knew who any of them were in the earliest days.

As my powers of analysis returned, one of things which constantly mystified me was the sense of undue anxiety I would often experience, especially when I was on my own. There was this enduring trepidation and expectation which I felt did not simply originate from my condition, or from the worry about the disruption my accident has caused to my life. It was different. It worked at a much deeper level, and I knew it spoke to me of something prior to the accident. I was waiting for someone to come to my bed and was certain they would show up. But I didn't know who that person was and I had no idea if they would help me or do me harm.

As I lay there in the semi-darkness I would ask myself what power they possessed that could make me watch for them, why my locked-away self was so constantly alert for their arrival, at times panicky, my eyes flickering habitually toward the door. How did this person cause a chaos of contradictory emotions so overwhelming that they could assert themselves in spite of my injuries? Fear and awe, anger and adulation, attraction and repulsion—a powerful, exciting sensuality one day and a fear so intense the next that if I didn't have my head fixed inside a steel cage I'd have hurled myself from my bed and run screaming down the corridor in my pyjamas and out into the street to flag down the first taxi I saw. Who on earth can do all that?

Then out of a foxhole in my subconscious crawled the name Dr Reinhard Klein. I wanted to know why he mattered so much.

Seb wouldn't talk about Klein. He told me I didn't have to worry about him because he was 'not on the scene any more'. He promised that when I was out of hospital and fully recovered, he'd tell me more about him. In hindsight I can understand why in those early days he was a bit concerned about my emotional state, always trying to concentrate on what he saw as the good things in our life, like the plans for our wedding and our hopes for a baby who would make us a family. He's terse at the best of times and, to be fair, I don't think he knew anything about Klein. I don't think he ever saw him and could rely only on what I told him before my fall and, even then, I bet half the time he wasn't even listening.

Father Calvin wasn't much better. He never liked to speak of Klein either. He'd sometimes give you this look like he didn't know who you're talking about whenever I mentioned him. But I know he did. He's a terrible liar, and a worse actor.

I've got to know Father Calvin quite well. He visited me regularly after I was discharged from hospital and because he was preparing us for our marriage he was around a fair bit. Seb wanted a church wedding but initially I wasn't religious myself, so the process was an eye-opener for me, quite a journey, especially to be instructed by a priest like Father Calvin. He's quite deep and can talk endlessly about history and philosophy as well as religion. He's idealistic and driven, and I like that about him. We became good friends and we'd chat often about all kinds of things once the formalities were over. He was on my level intellectually and I was encouraged to think I was close to full recovery when I was able to follow and understand everything he was saying to me.

He loved nothing more than to talk about Cardinal Newman, his hero. He went out to Rome for his canonisation by Pope Francis and for weeks afterwards he would speak of little else. As usual, Seb would retreat into his own little world, often with the assistance of some hand-held device, while Calvin and I chatted together.

One time, for instance, Calvin brought it up about Newman having this view of history and progress which was a little bit outside the norm. Calvin said Newman saw history advancing not in a linear fashion but in a series of expanding concentric circles, like the ripples sent out by a stone plopping into a lake, except the ripples grow stronger as they spread out rather than weaker. It's an interesting concept, I'll give him that. Calvin went on to say that Jesus entered history following this model, arriving after a succession of prophets prefigured and promised a Messiah. The same would go for the Antichrist, he claimed, the iniquitous figure who will come during the 'end times' but only after a series of ante-types ripple out ahead of him, preparing the way, so to speak. Cardinal Newman couldn't have known about Adolf Hitler, Calvin pointed out, yet he certainly expected his arrival.

It was stimulating stuff, typical of Calvin. But it was Newman's 'theology of conscience' which I found the most fascinating of all his reflections, partly because he would sometimes, in the same breath, talk about Germany, a country I know and love.

We were discussing philosophy and Calvin was telling me how the school of phenomenology, established by the German philosopher and mathematician Edward Husserl, prepared the ground for the reception of Newman's teachings uniquely among German academics who were seeking an alternative to Georg Hegel. Later Newman appealed to German academics opposed to Martin Heidegger and other philosophers who supported the Nazi Party.

According to Calvin, Newman was the antidote that was searched for by people like Theodor Haecker, who spoke of the Nazi years as 'the German apostasy'. Other such luminaries as Edith Stein, Matthias Laros, Dietrich von Hildebrand, Erich Przywara, Romano Guardini and Otto Karrer also drew strength from his writings as Germany descended into a neo-pagan totalitarian state. They ordered Newman's works to be sent from England and translated them into German and they were used to fuel the underground anti-Nazi resistance with an intellectual, philosophical, moral and spiritual vitality.

Calvin told me that such teachings found their fullest expression in the rise of the White Rose resistance group whose tracts, disseminated anonymously throughout Nazi Germany and inviting people to rise up against 'Nazi terror', were underpinned by a theological content he described as 'pure Newman'.

'A good conscience sometimes comes at a heavy price,' he declared after he told me about Sophie Scholl's tragic end at the age of just twenty-two. 'What they did was vital to bringing the evil of those times to an end and for restoring the self-respect of the Germany people,' he said. 'The world is so much better for their heroism.'

At that point, he inadvertently mentioned Dr Klein's name as he mused out loud. 'I wonder, Dr Klein had a Germanic name, didn't he? I wonder what his background was.'

'His grandfather was from Berlin—from a long line of doctors—and he moved here when he married an English girl,' I blurted out helpfully without thinking. 'Then their son married a German girl. So he has a German mother and a German grandfather.'

'Gosh, I knew you were investigating him once but I never expected you to be so thorough, Jenny. I am impressed.'

'Yes, I am thorough,' I said, blushing. 'You know I'm a German speaker. His name was interesting to me too and it was one of the first things I looked into. Do you have anything on the White Rose I could look at? I'd love to know a bit more about them.'

Calvin disappeared and came back after a few minutes with a DVD of a film called *Sophie Scholl—Die letzten Tage* (the final days), and I took it home with me to watch on one of the many days or nights I would be on my own.

Of course, Dr Klein had made me more interested in Germany than I might ordinarily have been. By the time of my conversation with Calvin, I'd remembered nearly everything about him, including the day I spent with him in Manchester and the time I rang him after I thought he lied to me about Dr Octavia Tarleton. I also remember thinking about how I would have liked to have seen him again and that I was almost ready to tell him I would.

It seems weird, but the one black hole in my memory is of the morning of my accident. Sarah says it's not uncommon to have irretrievable memory loss about events that immediately precede a bang on the head. A few sports stars, including those in equestrianism, have written about this, she assured me. So I accept that I might never know what really happened. Occasionally, I'm sure I get glimpses of what look like clues. Every now and then into my mind seeps an image of a strange and pretty woman in the woods, for instance, and a sensation of fear, a desperate desire to go home. I see myself on Daphne when this happens so I assume it must have been that day. The woman spoke to me but I can't remember what she said. Was all this connected? I raised it with Seb and he said he, my dad and Geoff went over the possibilities of an attack with the police at the time and officers weren't interested and closed the case after concluding that my fall was a freak accident. They did not suspect foul play. I decided to wait to see if I remember anything else before I attempt to talk to officers. Besides, stirring things up might do more harm than good. I didn't want Seb to know I'd been unfaithful. My fiancé didn't deserve that.

All the time I was in hospital Seb was at my side and while I was at home with the cage still on my head he did everything for me. He bathed me, he washed my hair, dressed and fed me and daily treated the entry sites of the pins to my skull with antiseptic to prevent infection. It's not only that I depended on him, but I also came to recognise a strength of character which I hadn't seen before. His kindness made me believe I could spend my life with him. But it broke my heart to see his love for a child yet to be born—the way he ran around, decorating the baby's room on his own—all the time knowing that the son within my womb was not his but Dr Klein's. How could I break it to him that he was not the child's father? I couldn't.

By December I was cursing my foolishness and the bad luck that had led to so much unhappiness. Months of physiotherapy lay before me once the screws were gone from my head. No job and no horse, yet always the burden of a dirty secret. Every good deed that flowed from Seb's big heart was met with a sharp pain of remorse and a sense of betrayal and, though I looked forward to being rid of the halo, I was dreading the arrival of 2020 as much as I had come to hate 2019.

Luckily for me it was only a week later that a CT scan showed the bones in my neck were healed and doctors announced they could take the halo away.

It was the boost I needed and Christmas wasn't nearly as bad as I'd been expecting. I was home, I was making a full recovery, I was slowly active again and I was working. I could snuggle into Seb and rest on his shoulder like I used to. My release from the prison cell around my head called for champagne but because I had a baby inside me I had to take it easy. We were nearly happy again. But my liberation was not complete. Klein continued to secretly and irresistibly squat in my imagination like an abscess which would not heal until it was lanced. He was jammed inside my head as rigidly as the cage had been stuck to the outside of it. At least I knew that one day they were going to take the cage away. I didn't know if I would ever be free of Klein.

It was simply impossible for me to forget that he was the father of the son I was expecting in March or April and I struggled to find a way of reconciling that internally. I craved legitimacy. I didn't want to hurt Seb and I didn't want to deceive him either. In the end I opted for a radical solution and one after-

393

noon in January I told Father Calvin that I wanted to become a Catholic. Seb almost fell off his chair since I had said nothing to him about my intentions.

'I can arrange for you to be baptised and fully received into the Church at Easter,' said the priest when we went to see him. 'It's going to be a wonderful year for you—a new faith, a baby, and a marriage on September 26th. My goodness!'

'Would you baptise our son too? I think I want to call him Matthew.'

Again, Seb sat there stunned, his mouth half open. I had discussed names with him but never mentioned Matthew.

'Why Matthew?' he asked, exasperated.

'Why not? You got to name the cat, so it's my turn. Okay, seriously—I like Matthew because he was bit naughty. People were astonished, you know, when Jesus called him to be an Apostle.'

'That's right,' said Calvin, smiling. 'There's that great picture of Jesus calling St Matthew by Caravaggio, isn't there? How did he explain it to the Jews? "Those who are well have no need of a physician, but those who are sick; I came not to call the righteous, but sinners". That's what he said. I suppose you feel a lot of solidarity with sick people after everything you've been through.'

'Yes, I do but there is also this sense of gratitude for the mercy of God that permeates the entirety of his Gospel. I like that very much too.'

This time they both gawped at me. I was content to let them ponder my words without explanation. I was never going to tell them about the inner turbulence that had led me to this point.

Neither had any idea of just how important it is to me to raise my son as a Christian. In my darkest moments I envisaged the child as a punishment for my lust for the rest of my life. Yet in better moods I saw him as a heart to love, my own flesh and blood—my son, my boy. I chose to keep it that way. I resolved to teach him that love is our highest value and that he could do no better than to love God and neighbour. I did not want him to be like Klein, who was never far from my thoughts. Gradually I was becoming convinced that the doctor was somehow mixed up in my accident, that somehow my neck had been broken by his hand. I didn't know precisely how but one day, I promised myself, I would find out.

Seb thought my decision to become a Catholic signified that I was coming round to seeing things from his point of view and it would bring us closer. I've never seen him more effusive than he was that day, going on about how he and his boy would watch all the *Star Wars* films together, how he would coach him to play rugby like a pro, and how we could transform a spare room into a gaming suite when the child was old enough to play with his friends online.

He gushed not only about this baby but about all the others he predicted we were going to have—two boys and a girl. I was happy to see him like that. Better than the sullen and sometimes selfish man I resented. I'd always wanted a family and now it was happening. There were other things I could be grateful for too, including the prospect of a return to work if I could balance my career with the demands of motherhood, like other young women in my situation. I was still on good terms with the *Sunday News* and my former colleagues, who sent me flowers after my fall, were now giving me bits and pieces to do from home. It made me confident that money would keep coming in. Seb and I were planning to redecorate the house and were thinking about where we would go on holiday. I had survived my accident and life had returned to something I could consider normal. I could have been grateful.

But normal didn't feel good enough. Normal, for me, had gone. Seb thought it would return once the halo was off and he reverted slowly to his former lifestyle, leaving me on my own to read and watch movies while he was gaming, in the gym all day or out with his friends. When he was around he was quiet to the point of dull. My old resentments crept back. I was often gloomy and in the midst of my melancholy Klein was there in my thoughts, like he'd moved into my mind and made himself at home. The fleeting moments of happiness I shared with Seb, when they came, were always marred by his memory and by the guilt that I was carrying his baby and not Seb's. The more excited Seb became by the prospect of fatherhood, the worse I felt. Klein would not go away.

It was on a Sunday afternoon late in February when Seb was in the gym and I had a few hours to spare that I put on the film that Father Calvin had lent me. I watched it without sub-titles because I'm fluent in German. I love foreign cinema and I was surprised that this one had slipped my attention. It might have been because I thought it was a war film, which I hate. But this acclaimed historical drama by Marc Rothemund was not like that. It told the true story about the final days of the student named Sophie Scholl who, with her brother Hans and a friend, Christoph Probst, were among a group of civilians who defied the tyranny of the Nazi regime at the cost of their lives, each of the three decapitated by guillotine, one after the other, in a Munich prison on February 22, 1943.

The movie was shocking because those people were so like us, practically of our times. It made me see how the seemingly abstract theology that my priest friend would talk about had been realised in Germany in extreme and extraordinary circumstances. It made me reflect afterwards what conscience was and what it did. It was true, as Newman said, that conscience doesn't offer easy solutions and perhaps makes demands that sometimes require supernatural levels of fortitude to fulfil— that there is 'nothing gentle, nothing of mercy in its tone ... it is severe and even stern .... [that] it does not speak of forgiveness but of punishment'. Conscience suggests 'only a future judgment' and it does not tell the person how he or she can avoid it. I began to think quite keenly about my own conscience.

Then Seb came home. He was sweaty and exhilarated, a big muscly man, and he was raving about the forthcoming release of some video game for Xbox called *Assassin's Creed Valhalla*, in which he could play at being a Viking raider.

'Oh, that's lovely,' I said. 'I'll get it for you for Christmas.'

'Nah, I want it well before then. I'm havin' it as soon as it comes out. What's for tea?'

'Why don't we dine out tonight? It will be a change, and we can spend some quality time together.'

'But I told the lads …'

The sulkiest look I could muster seemed to do the trick and he agreed to an evening at our favourite Italian restaurant, *La Via Appia Antica*, a family-run business on the outskirts of Crostbury.

I drove so Seb could have a drink and I asked for a candlelit table in the corner where we could speak privately without being easily overheard. I have to admit it, he looked and smelled wonderful that night, and I was attracted to him as he happily went on about the things he loved, the same things I've heard about so many times before.

I waited until he finished his last mouthful of ice cream and put down his spoon before I stared him in the eyes and said to him: 'Seb, I have something very, very important to tell you and you're not going to like it.

'The baby isn't yours. It's another man's. I'm not marrying you. It's over between us. I'm going back to my mum and dad's.'

An eternity seemed to pass while he tried to make sense of my words. He really struggled.

'Not my baby? Whose baby?'

'Dr Klein's—the day we met in Manchester. It was May 30. Work it out. I slept with him that day and I didn't sleep with you all of that week, or around that week. We were both mad busy and we weren't getting along. Remember?'

'You slept with him? You slept with Dr Klein? What, you've been having an affair with that man? You said he was a monster!'

'I slept with him once.'

'How could you?'

He began to sob, slowly and reluctantly, and he kept repeating himself and he sniffled and pushed the tears away from his eyes as soon as they appeared.

'How could you do this to me?'

He was saying it over and over again.

'Why did you do that? We were happy. How could you?'

'No, Seb. We weren't happy. We were comfortable at best. We really need to be honest with ourselves about this. I bore you as much as you bore me, probably more. We have hardly anything in common. We never have and I fear we never will. The whole of our relationship was built around physical attraction—it's because I went to bed with you without taking the time to think it through properly. It's been great but now we have to do the right thing before it's too late for us and we make each other very unhappy.'

'What do you mean, do the right thing? What are you talking about? Jumping into bed with a doctor, is that what you call the right thing? I can't believe what I'm hearing. How could you do that to me?'

'I mean I can't marry you, Seb,' I hissed. 'Ending this now is the right thing. It won't work. It would be a disaster. It would end in divorce.

'I'm not saying that what I did with Dr Klein was right—I'm not saying that at all—but I don't think I would have gone with him if things were, or could have been, better between us—and they can't ever be right between us because we're not right together. Can't you see that? I don't want to hurt you, and I'm sorry that I have.

'I'm leaving you, Seb. I'm very sorry it's ended this way, but it's over. It's better for both of us if we stop now. I'm sorry, but that's it.'

His face was bright red and beads of sweat from his forehead were beginning to mingle with his tears. His eyes became cold and hard and his lips taut as his initial shock subsided and gave way to fury.

'I tell you what I can see—I can see you are a slut,' he said in a low and menacing voice. 'You're a filthy good-for-nothing cheap little slut. You're no better than a whore. I hate your guts.'

He stood up so abruptly I thought for a moment his chair would fly backwards or he might try to punch me. But he grabbed his coat and stormed out into the freezing rain without another word.

I sat alone for nearly half an hour, stunned by what I had done, before I asked for the bill and paid it. In the end, I'd realised I had to tell Seb about Klein and the truth about the baby. For me, it was a matter of integrity. I had to be honest with him. I couldn't carry this secret for ever. To my mind, it is a wicked thing to deceive a man into raising a child which is not his own. I had to move past Klein.

Lord knows, I was grateful for all that Seb had done for me, and I loved him in my own way, but I couldn't let him raise my son in the mistaken belief that he was the father. Also, I didn't love Seb in the way I knew I should. He was never going to be a soulmate, my trusted partner for the long journey of my life. If we had set out on that road together I fear that we might have parted long before we'd reached our destination. We just weren't right together. I knew, too, that I could not deceive Calvin. Nor, in the end, could I deceive my conscience.

I'd expected Seb to be extremely upset and was braced for a few insults. I was thankful that he was man enough not to make a scene. He would be inconsolable, and there was no way I could return to our house any time soon. He was a powerful man and just in case he was still around I asked Mario, the head waiter, to escort me to my car. The last thing I wanted was another broken neck.

Seb was nowhere to be seen and soon I was driving to my parents' farm, where my mum and dad were waiting for me, determined that it would be from there that I would rebuild my shattered life. I was consoled by a sense of peace. I felt that in my private life I had turned a corner and at last I was doing the right thing. No more mistakes.

It wouldn't be easy for me, I knew that. In about a month I would be a single mother, sharing my parents' home with my boozy brother while scratching around for stories to keep my career as a freelance journalist afloat in this semi-rural corner of the country where nothing ever seems to happen.

34

HEY JUDITH

It was Saturday 29 February, a year almost to the day since Ray Parker's inquest, when Emerald entered the confessional, coming in as Father Calvin was about to lock up, like the first time.

He did not have to see her, hear her voice or smell her perfume to know it was her. He sensed her presence as soon as she closed the door behind her.

She invited him to open the curtain and as ever he found himself struck by her beauty. He had never seen a woman as lovely as Emerald.

'I've been away,' she said.

She made the sign of the cross and told the priest her last confession was in France shortly before Christmas.

'There are a few other things I want to get off my chest, to put straight with you …'

Calvin interrupted her.

'Emerald, please don't be upset but I don't think this is a confession that I am able to hear given the circumstances.'

'What do you mean?'

'Under the *Code of Canon Law* I can't give you absolution for any sin we've committed together that breaks the Sixth Commandment.'

Emerald looked at Calvin quizzically.

'That's adultery. The commandment against adultery covers all sexual sins.'

'But it was only a kiss!' she protested.

'I know, but it means I have been romantically involved with you the code might apply. If you would like to see another confessor, I can arrange it for you.'

'No, it's okay. It's the seal of the confessional that's especially important for me today. I wanted to tell you everything about Dr Klein, but now I can't. But it's okay.'

Calvin was intrigued. 'You still could. Our conversation could be protected as a professional secret.'

'Let me think about it,' said Emerald, rising from her knees.

'Wait!' exclaimed Calvin as she pressed down on the brass door handle.

'Please don't go—I really must talk to you.'

She slipped through the door.

Calvin dashed out of the confessional and through the sacristy into the main body of the church, relieved to see there was no one else there, to catch sight of Emerald blessing herself with holy water from a stone stoup by the entrance, her face downcast. A bar of winter sunshine illuminated the church as she pushed open the heavy wooden door.

'Please!' shouted Calvin.

Emerald let the door swing shut and turned towards the priest. Calvin came face to face with her and touched the points of her elbows lightly with his fingertips.

'I've missed you so much,' he told her. 'I don't want to lose you again. I want you in my life. I can see that now. Please don't go. Please let me at least make you a cup of tea, let me talk to you.'

He took his hands away from her and slowly opened his arms in an invitation to embrace. They hugged each other tightly.

'I've missed you so much,' Calvin said again.

'I've missed you too,' she whispered in reply.

In the presbytery kitchen, Emerald leaned against the worktop as Calvin filled the kettle and rooted around for a couple of clean cups, inspecting them for interior traces of ancient coffee. It was clear to Emerald that he had not replaced Mrs Hoskins.

'Take your coat off, and your scarf,' he cheerfully beckoned over his shoulder. 'Make yourself at home.'

'Thanks, but I'm not sure how long you'll want me here once I've told you a bit about what went on.'

Calvin spun round to face her. 'You can tell me anything, Emerald,' he assured her. 'You're my friend.'

Emerald took off her coat and placed it with the scarf over the back of a chair by the kitchen table. Wearing a red sweater and jeans, she followed Calvin into the living room. There were books, papers and magazines on every surface, and on the coffee table they'd accumulated into piles. Emerald wondered if she'd been the last person to use a duster in there.

She sat cross-legged on the couch, while Calvin perched in an armchair at the far end of the coffee table, in black trousers and jumper and a clerical collar.

'It's lovely to see you,' he said a little nervously. 'Did you go anywhere nice?'

'Yes, I felt like I needed a good break after Mrs Hoskins's funeral so I left my job at the hospital and went to France to stay with my grandmother for a while. I spent Christmas with my father's family—and the best bit was that Dad came and joined us for a few days. It was the first time I've seen him since I was a girl. It was quite an emotional reunion, and I did give him a piece of my mind, all right, for walking out on us like that. He told me he was sorry and we sort of patched things up. We had a lot of catching up to do. It's brought me a lot of healing. My mum can't believe it.'

'That's wonderful. Was it nice where you were?'

'It's lovely—a small village in the Burgundy countryside, sur-rounded by forests, rolling hills, fields and valleys. I'd say the nearest places most people might have heard of are Dijon and Langres. The food's sensational. I mean, wow! The cheeses … oh, Calvin—you'd love it.'

Emerald reached for her tea and took a sip.

When she faced the priest again, her expression was serious, that of a woman brought to greater maturity and wisdom by suf-fering.

'I've never really been one for guilt,' she said quietly. 'But I left this country in September with a tremendous burden. I did a few bad things. I wasn't sorry at first because I felt I had to do the things that I did. But I am now—I am sorry. I went to con-fession in France, so I feel I have put things straight to some extent—in French, of course. *La torture et le meurtre*. That poor country *curé* mustn't have heard anything quite like it in his life. I think he was wondering why the walls didn't crack when I dropped that one.'

'Torture and murder? What are you talking about?'

'Dr Klein, he's dead.'

Calvin slammed his tea down. He threw himself back into his chair and raised his eyes to the ceiling.

At first he was dumbstruck. Eventually he mumbled: 'The Lord has struck him down by the hand of a woman.'

'What was that? Oh no, I'm not really Judith and I didn't kill Dr Klein. Those people—Klein and the other one—they tried to kill Jenny and they were planning to kill me as well. But I didn't want him dead. I'm not going to say anything more about this. I don't want you to be implicated by what you'll find out from me, and I don't want the police involved. You must promise me that you repeat this to no one.'

'I promise, absolutely. But you say "they". Who are you talking about?'

'Klein's mistress—"Tavy", remember? She's Octavia Tarleton—Topcliffe before she was married—the woman Jenny was looking for. She took Jenny off her horse. Don't even think about telling anyone about this, including Jenny. Octavia's married to Detective Inspector …

'George Tarleton,' gasped Calvin.

'Yes. Quite the love triangle, wasn't it? Well, I stopped her too, but she's alive. All hell will break loose if you tell anyone. I've had my throat cut once already, thank you. I've had enough of all that. It is better that this was ended now. You must promise not to tell …'

'Your secret is safe with me.'

'Thanks, Calvin. I'm trusting you with my life.'

She cleared her throat and leaned forward, her knees tightly together.

'But none of this is what I really wanted to tell you today— I think I owe you the truth about what I did to you in particular. That's more important to me.'

She cast Calvin a severe look and he thought she looked older again.

'It was me who reported you for kicking the door.'

She waited for the priest to react.

'You mean you told Dr Klein?'

'Yes, I blamed you. I let you take a hit for the team. But I didn't expect Klein to attack you and I'm sorry your bishops sent you away. You were always going to be reported, though. You weren't going to get away with kicking that door.'

The priest let out a low 'humph' in implied agreement.

'You didn't do it vindictively, though, did you?' he asked. 'You were protecting yourself, that's right, isn't it?'

'Yes, that's right, but I still feel I shouldn't have betrayed you in the way I did. I can understand you hating me for this because of what happened to you afterwards but at least now I can sleep easier knowing I have been honest with you. I'm so sorry.'

Calvin went quiet. He stared coolly at Emerald and she felt herself unnerved. She began to cry silently.

'Do you want me to go?'

Calvin shook his head resolutely. 'I don't hate you, Emerald. Goodness, no! And, no, I don't want you to go. No, please stay.'

'Are you sure?' she asked plaintively, her tears trickling in an almost continuous torrent.

Calvin crossed the room and sat beside her. He put his arm around her back and heaved her gently into him. 'I couldn't be more sure,' he said. 'Come on, don't be sad. There's no need to worry. I'm not going to judge you for what you did.'

Emerald sank her head on his chest and he cradled her as she wept, asking himself all the time if Jesus would have done the same, wondering if this was how it might have been with St Mary Magdalene.

Emerald kept telling the priest she was sorry and he kept reassuring her there was no need to apologise to him, that he had forgiven her.

They were like that for what felt like an age. Then Emerald sat up and remarked that her tea was cold.

Calvin pulled away from her. 'So, what are you doing now?' he asked as she leaned on him and rested her head on his shoulder. 'Are you staying in the area or just passing through?'

'I'm staying. I'm going back to Bethulia Park. Dr Baqri, the medical director, wants to give me my old job back. He says I'm a great nurse.'

'I think that too, for what it's worth, and I'm delighted for you—and if I'm honest also for myself. It means we can be friends.'

She raised her head and looked curiously at the priest, who adjusted his position so he could face her directly.

'I mean it,' said Calvin. 'I've given this so much thought since we parted. I've prayed for us, and I kept asking the Lord for guidance. I've been waiting for you to come back, looking out for you like—I don't know—like a castaway searches the sea for a ship. Every day I've waited for you. I'm certain that there's something special about our friendship. I think it's meant to endure. I think it's right that we're together in a certain way. Have you ever felt that too?'

'I've always felt it,' she said.

Calvin was suddenly emboldened.

'But I'm still convinced I'm called to be a priest. Frankly, I'm going to have to confess to you that I am always going to be attracted to you, and perhaps you might have feelings for me for a little while. Maybe we should just accept that and be grown up about it, just deal with it. We can go much further if we're not lovers. "Perfect moderation"—let's give it a go, that's what I say. True friendship can be such a beautiful thing.'

He smiled in the hope she would smile too.

'But if we keep kissing we'll end up married so we'd better be careful about that, I think. You know, I would like to marry you one day,' he went on with a short laugh, 'but it will be to your husband and I will be the presiding priest and later I might baptise your babies too. That's what I hope for. We could be friends for many, many years. There's no reason we can't be friends. With all my heart, that's what I want. That's what you mean to me. What do you say?'

'You're already my best friend,' she answered. 'Judith doesn't marry a second time, don't you know that?'

Calvin sitting there aghast, clearly taking her answer seriously, amused her. 'I'm joking,' she said, and laughed at him.

'Friends, hey?' said Emerald as she looked disapprovingly around the room.

'This place is a dump,' she suddenly announced in a tone of authority. 'I think you need a new housekeeper.'

Her eyes were lit with a mischief which made her look youthful again, and which caused Calvin to grin broadly.

'You're hired,' he said.

———

Emerald wanted to celebrate their reunion by cooking a meal for Calvin at her flat that evening. Although she didn't say so, she was resolved not to do anything in his kitchen until she had made him clean it up. Besides, the priest had never visited her in her own home and she thought it was the right time to introduce him a little to her world.

A buzz signalled his arrival and she let him into the block. He took a lift to her floor but had no need to look for the number to her apartment. All he had to do was follow delicious aromas wafting down the corridor from an open doorway at the end from which he could also hear *Hey Jude* playing on a music system. 'Hey Judith' would have been more appropriate, Calvin jested to himself.

She answered in an apron and beamed when he handed her a bunch of daffodils he'd picked up from a Tesco supermarket on his way over from St Winefride's and a 2018 bottle of Bourgogne, a French pinot noir by the Maison Louis Latour, which he had chosen because of its Burgundy grape and because, at £15 a bottle, it was most of the expensive reds on the shelf. He wanted to bring a bottle of a decent quality.

Emerald offered him both cheeks to peck and invited him inside. 'I'm using another wine from the region tonight,' she said as she read the label, which boasted of how Louis Latour 'harvests, vinifies, ages and bottles the finest wines of Burgundy'.

'I'm cooking boeuf bourguignon, following a traditional recipe given to me by ma *mémé*—my granny—and I'm using a red for that. I had just enough time to buy the ingredients and get it in after seeing you today. We'll have it with boulangère potatoes. Are you happy with that? Don't worry—I'm taking it easy with the garlic. I know you've got to meet people after Mass tomorrow. It's still in the oven so you may as well relax for a bit.'

She glanced at the music system.

'Do you want me to skip this? It's just an old playlist—I know you're not mad about the Beatles.'

'No, honestly, it's fine. I don't mind at all. It reminds me of when we met that time in Liverpool—seems ages ago, getting on for a year surely.'

Emerald took his coat and offered him a drink. Calvin agreed to a single glass of wine because he would be driving home.

'I was thinking the same,' she said as she pressed the glass into his hand and turned to sit down. 'Those birds came back last week, the peregrines. That's what did it for me. It's a pity it's dark or you could see them. They nest opposite, the same pair. They stay together for life. Well, throughout all that trouble last year I watched them every day. They made me think and they helped me, in a strange way, to stay sane. The day I betrayed you to Dr Klein I remember how that evening the mother came in with a big pigeon, and plucked it and fed it to her chicks. The law of tooth and claw can be a terrible thing—but sometimes that's life. I expect those birds are going to bring back a lot of memories for me.'

'So how did you do it in the end? How did you stop him?'

'You helped me to find the final scrap of evidence I needed to prove that he was a killer but it wasn't the police who took care of him, regrettably. I can't tell you any more than that right now—but us two, we stopped him as a team, even if you don't realise it.'

'You're quite the detective, aren't you? Do you think we're a bit like Holmes and Watson?'

She giggled.

'More like Hong Kong Phooey and his cat—I looked them up after you said Mrs Hoskins used to joke about them. Have you ever seen those cartoons?'

Calvin shook his head, mystified.

'Oh, it's this dog from the 1970s called Jenry. He's a janitor in the day time but a super-hero at night, but quite an awful one. He thinks he's cool but he gets everything wrong but lucky for him he's got this big blue cat called Spot and that's who solves all the mysteries for him.'

'So who's Hong Kong Phooey and who's the cat?'

'You're Hong Kong Phooey, obviously. He'd do something stupid like kick a door to a records office and get caught. I'm the cat.'

'It's an interesting concept but I was thinking more along the lines of me as a Lord Peter Wimsey—you know, a gentleman detective—and you as Harriet Vane.'

Emerald almost choked on her wine, but gulped it down her throat as Calvin waited for her to answer.

'Aren't you forgetting something, Father?' she asked him. 'Harriet became Lord Peter's wife.'

'Oh, yes—of course,' the priest stuttered, blushing. 'I can see now that you're the cleverer half in this partnership of ours. I'd better up my game.'

'You're not that bad. You just need to listen to me more.'

Calvin smiled. 'I have failed to appreciate you fully. I'll give you that. I'll try to make it up to you.'

Emerald dropped her eyes, a little embarrassed at how easily the priest had read her hidden thoughts.

'Did you ever work out who those bones belonged to, the ones we saw in Holywell?' she asked, keen to move the conversation on.

'I have advanced a written theory,' said Calvin, his brow furrowing, 'and it's based largely on your idea—see, I don't dismiss what you say to me all that easily. I was going to tell you about it, probably later this evening. But anyway, I wrote up a report for Father Davenport and I gave it to him three or four months ago. It's on my computer so you can read it whenever you want.'

'So what did you tell him?'

'I said that there was strong circumstantial evidence to support the notion that the bones probably belonged to St John Plessington but that further scientific tests would be required to confirm that.

'I also said that the body in that grave, the younger man with the broken neck—I said it was probably George Massey.'

EPILOGUE

WOLF IN THE SHEEPFOLD

Wednesday July 19th, 1679

William Massey rested his buttocks on the top of a barrel at the end of the Burton riverfront pier. He puffed on a clay pipe and looked out to sea while the sun sank over the horizon.

He was surrounded by five men, who like him wore stockings and breeches and buckled shoes with raised heels. Some shielded themselves from the cool offshore breeze with long coats over their shirts and a couple wore broad-rimmed black hats.

All were watching the spreading copper tones of the fading summer sunshine that told them the time like the hands of a clock.

'Are you sure Captain Talbott's going to return?' said one of the men anxiously to Massey. 'It's been quite a while now. What are we going to do with the prisoner if he doesn't come back? Does he come back with us?'

The two looked down at a figure sitting crossed-legged between the barrels. He was bound with rope and had a sack over his head. The only sign that he was alive was an occasional shiver and the slow rise and fall of his chest.

'Oh, he'll be back, even if he has to come alone,' said the squire. 'This fellow has already done enough to die but Captain Talbott wants to be sure he's the person he thinks he is. He doesn't like to hang innocent men so he'll be back and he'll bring a second opinion with him. I want to talk to the prisoner myself before he arrives—as soon as it's dark enough.'

They stood, waiting intently for that moment of dusk when it was still bright enough to see yet dark enough to not be clearly seen, particularly from a distance.

Massey finally crouched level, curious to see closely, and without the help of a lantern, the man whose false testimony had led to the execution of his chaplain. He removed the sack.

He felt slightly frightened to find himself staring into the face of a strong, fit and fierce-looking man, at least ten years older than himself. The prisoner's black hair fell untidily over his shoulders and his tapered beard was matted with blood, his face cut and bruised, probably in his struggle to escape Captain Talbott, who grabbed him from a privy beside a tavern in Chester that morning and eventually brought him bound to Puddington Hall via a different route from that taken by Captain Wild. There were smears of blood on his torn shirt, which, like his stockings, were caked in dust and dung.

He raised his face and the two men glared at each other in mutual loathing and contempt. The squire retreated a little then rallied himself.

'So here he is,' said Massey, 'the man of straw. My friend says you might be a former soldier, is that true?'

The man said nothing.

'How much did they pay you to lie in court so they could murder my priest?'

Again he was met with silence.

'Go on, what was it?' urged Massey. 'What price can you put on a man's life? You do know what they did to him, don't you?

Of course you do. Some of my people said they saw you laughing about it afterwards.'

The man's eyes suddenly widened and his lips pursed slightly. 'Plessington was a traitor, and you are too,' he said. 'He was plotting to kill the King. That was the judgement of the court. I was a witness in the service of the King.'

'There is no plot!' growled Massey through gritted teeth, his eyes flaming. 'And you say he was a traitor! Is that so? I don't believe it! You know nothing of the man you helped to murder. Do you know who his father was, what he sacrificed for King Charles during the siege of Greenhalgh Castle up in Lancashire? How he was punished for it by the Puritans? And you are telling me, that his son, this man who you had killed, one of the most peaceable and orderly men I have ever known, was part of a plot to murder the next Charles Stuart, after all that his family suffered for their loyalty to the Crown during the war? A traitor, him? Do you have any idea of how preposterous that sounds to me? I know of no family more loyal to the King than his.'

The prisoner stared at the wooden timbers of the pier floor, his fists clenching behind his back and pulling on the cords that tied his wrists together.

'The judge said he was a traitor,' he sneered. 'You're a traitor too!'

The man tried to rise to his feet but he was pushed down by heavy hands on his shoulders. He spat at Massey. 'Traitor!' he snarled.

Ignoring the provocation, Massey moved closer to the prisoner. 'You're a wolf which has entered into my sheepfold, a dangerous man who seeks to grow rich on the blood of the innocent. We're not animals to be slaughtered and our meat traded from the shelves of a butcher's shop. I won't allow my people to be robbed or murdered by men like you. That goes for my chaplains, and it goes for myself. I know about your plan to steal my name and then worm your way into taking my place at

Puddington Hall. You're as fake as Oates himself. What's your real name? Who are you?'

The man looked at the ground.

'Look at me!' demanded Massey, snapping his fingers. 'I want to know your name, I want to know who killed my chaplain.'

The squire took a deep breath.

'Soon you are going to die,' he told the prisoner. 'My chaplain would have abhorred that. But him and I, we're different. I must involve myself in the world's affairs. I have responsibility for the families who live and work on my land along this waterfront. Business is going well for us, trade from the colonies is growing and this river is a gateway to the New World. We don't want to live in Lord Baltimore's colony. We'd rather stay here than go to Maryland. Oh, yes—I've heard all the talk about how soon these waters will be running with gold. Perhaps it's true. Perhaps, before too long, a great city will rise right here on these banks— right here.'

Massey stretched a hand towards the darkness of the shore, inviting the man to imagine what might be.

'We want to be part of all this,' he continued in a quiet but earnest tone. 'We want a share of it. We won't let you take it from us.'

'Please let me go, and I swear you'll never see me again,' the prisoner whimpered suddenly. 'Let me live, please! They put me up to it, they made me do it. I had no choice. You don't understand. Have mercy on me, please!'

Massey lowered the sack over the man's head. 'Thankfully, your fate is not in my hands. I would rather not kill any man and I am neither your judge nor your executioner. I know who your masters are and what they are doing, by the way. Robert Wood, your friend who also swore falsely against my chaplain, told us everything before his accident in the pigsty. Very unfortunate, that. Not a nice way to die. What we don't know for certain is who you are. But we will find out, you can be sure of that.'

Their conversation was interrupted by the sound of hooves slowing to a halt towards the end of the pier. They heard boots crunch on the dirt as the riders dismounted and the thuds on the wooden planks that grew louder with their approach.

The silhouettes of two tall men came into view and Massey and the others were soon able to distinguish the broad form and rusty beard of Captain Talbott. Behind him followed a man they had seen earlier that day.

This time Captain Wild removed his hat when he addressed the young squire. 'I didn't expect to be back quite so soon,' he said with a wry smile. 'But our mutual friend, Captain Talbott, has fetched me back because he suspects you may be holding a man of great interest to me. Is this the fellow here?'

He turned from Massey to yank the sack from the head of the prisoner, who looked hard at the ground. The captain grabbed his chin and roughly pulled up his face so he could see it.

'Bring me a lamp,' he ordered.

A man at Massey's side walked over and held a lantern by the prisoner's face. Wild's face contorted in an expression of anger and disgust.

'You're right,' he said, nodding to Captain Talbott as he released his grip and stood up. 'This man's name is not George Massey as he has been pretending. He is Edmund Bracy, a murderer and a robber and he's known to have worked the highways in different parts of the country. He escaped me in our pursuit of Swift Nick Nevison. I've been searching for him for, what is it? About three years now. He's shown some nerve to come back here. It's a wonder how I didn't spot him in Chester this morning. I'm delighted that my fine friend, Captain Talbott, has been altogether more observant.'

Talbott smiled. 'I was actively searching for him,' he said. 'That's the difference.'

Wild looked at his fellow officer with affection, then sighed.

'What is happening to this great country of ours when the testimonies of highwaymen can send the innocent to the gallows?' he said, shaking his head.

'Hang him!'

The prisoner was dragged to his feet and the hood was roughly pulled over his head. He reared backwards, yelling, 'No, no, no!' in a muffled voice as he was tugged, pulled and pushed to the end of the pier.

A rope was already attached by one end to a landing post and tied into a noose at the other. The halter was lifted and pulled taut around the man's neck as he writhed and struggled.

The hood was lifted from the prisoner's head and he stood sobbing, shaking and sweating in an agony of fear as he stared into fifteen feet of blackness, just able to pick out the sandy bottom of the river bed at low tide by the glimmer of the lanterns.

'Any last requests, final words?' Captain Wild said to him. 'Do you want to apologise to these people for murdering their priest? Do you want to ask their forgiveness? Would you like to say to say your prayers?'

'Mercy, please, mercy!' the man begged tearfully, trying to force his body away from the drop. 'Let me go, damn you! Let me go!'

'May the Lord have mercy on your soul,' said Captain Wild.

The men holding the prisoner were fighting to restrain him but with a final powerful push they hurled him into the darkness.

There was a loud snap and then nothing but the dull thumping of the body swinging against the timber uprights of the pier.

After a moment a man lay down on the planks to look into the darkness below.

'Yes, that's it. I was right. It was the right length, all right. He's dead.'

Massey walked away with Captain Wild and Captain Talbott, leaving his entourage to bring up the highwayman's body and wrap it in a sheet. They left the scene on horseback in the direction of Puddington Hall.

Soon they were followed by a pair of horses pulling a cart and carrying a group of men positioned around a coffin.

The sounds of hooves and the rattle of cartwheels receded into the darkness, and stillness enveloped the riverside. The stars sparkled in the inky void above and a salty breeze blew in from the sea, guarding the secret of that night with a hush.

CPSIA information can be obtained
at www.ICGtesting.com
Printed in the USA
LVHW040838150723
752290LV00001B/64

9 780852 447000